Sometimes
wishes take a
touch of magic
to come true. . . .

Critics adore the "exquisite and enchanting" (*BookPage*) Edilean novels from "master storyteller" (*The Literary Times*) Jude Deveraux. . . . Uncover the romantic secrets of the idyllic Virginia town in these unforgettable *New York Times* bestsellers!

SCARLET NIGHTS

"Deveraux brings to life the sort of sweet and spunky heroines who attract the muscular men her fans expect and enjoy. . . . *Scarlet Nights* will hook readers and leave them with a smile."

—*Booklist*

"Readers familiar with the series will delight in immersing themselves back in the comfortable world of Edilean, and new readers should enjoy exploring it. . . . Deveraux's colorful cast and easy way with words shine."

—*Publishers Weekly*

"Deveraux is a master storyteller, and her books fairly shimmer with excitement and adventure, making her one of the most popular women's fiction writers today. *Scarlet Nights* is no exception. With strong characters, down-home charm, and an intriguing story, fans will enjoy catching up with the folks from Edilean."

—*Times Record News* (Wichita Falls, TX)

***Heartwishes* is also available from Simon & Schuster Audio and as an eBook**

DAYS OF GOLD

"Deveraux has a sure hand evoking plucky heroines, dastardly villains, and irresistible heroes, as well as a well-rounded supporting cast. . . . The romance sparks with enough voltage to keep readers turning pages."

—*Publishers Weekly*

LAVENDER MORNING

"Sweet and salty characters . . . entertaining . . . one of her most fun and pleasing tales."

—*Booklist*

"Quick dialogue, interesting settings, and plot twists."

—*Deseret Morning News* (Salt Lake City, UT)

And don't miss these bestsellers from Jude Deveraux, whose novels are "just plain fun to read . . . she keeps readers on the edge of their seats" (*The Advocate,* Baton Rouge, LA)

THE SCENT OF JASMINE

"Delightful. . . . Deveraux's enchanting heroine and engaging hero . . . steal the book. This is a tale to read for the simple joy of a well-crafted romance."

—*RT Book Reviews* (4 ½ stars)

SECRETS

"A sweet love story filled with twists and turns."

—*Booklist*

"The deceptions will keep readers trying to guess the next plot twist."

—*RT Book Reviews*

SOMEONE TO LOVE

"Fabulous. . . . Fast-paced. . . . Delightful paranormal romantic suspense."

—Harriet Klausner

Have you ever wanted to rewrite your past? Get swept away in the magic of

THE SUMMERHOUSE* and *RETURN TO SUMMERHOUSE

"Marvelously compelling. . . . Deeply satisfying."

—*Houston Chronicle*

"Entertaining summer reading."

—*The Port St. Lucie News* (FL)

"Deveraux is at the top of her game."

—*Booklist*

Savor "an intriguing paranormal tale"* in her wonderful trilogy

FOREVER . . .   FOREVER AND ALWAYS   ALWAYS

"Bewitching. . . . High-spirited. . . . Irresistibly eerie, yet decidedly a love story."

—Publishers Weekly (starred review)

"Engaging . . . a delightful otherworldly fantasy."

—Thebestreviews.com*

"Cannot be put down until the last word is read. . . . Truly amazing."

—*Romance Reviews Today*

"[A] modern fairy tale. . . . This is Deveraux at her most pleasurable."

—*Booklist*

Books by Jude Deveraux

The Velvet Promise
Highland Velvet
Velvet Song
Velvet Angel
Sweetbriar
Counterfeit Lady
Lost Lady
River Lady
Twin of Fire
Twin of Ice
The Temptress
The Raider
The Princess
The Awakening
The Maiden
The Taming
The Conquest
A Knight in Shining Armor
Holly
Wishes
Mountain Laurel
The Duchess
Eternity
Sweet Liar
The Invitation
Remembrance
The Heiress
Legend
An Angel for Emily
The Blessing
High Tide
Temptation
The Summerhouse
The Mulberry Tree
Forever . . .
Wild Orchids
Forever and Always
Always
First Impressions
Carolina Isle
Someone to Love
Secrets
Return to Summerhouse
Lavender Morning
Days of Gold
Scarlet Nights
The Scent of Jasmine
Moonlight in the Morning

Jude Deveraux

Heartwishes

a novel

Pocket Books
New York London Toronto Sydney New Delhi

Pocket Books
A Division of Simon & Schuster, Inc.
1230 Avenue of the Americas
New York, NY 10020

First Pocket Books paperback edition June 2012

POCKET and colophon are registered trademarks of Simon & Schuster, Inc.

For information about special discounts for bulk purchases, please contact Simon & Schuster Special Sales at 1-866-506-1949 or business@simonandschuster.com.

The Simon & Schuster Speakers Bureau can bring authors to your live event. For more information or to book an event contact the Simon & Schuster Speakers Bureau at 1-866-248-3049 or visit our website at www.simonspeakers.com.

Manufactured in the United States of America

10 9 8 7 6 5 4 3 2 1

ISBN 978-1-4391-0800-0
ISBN 978-1-4391-0801-7 (pbk)
ISBN 978-1-4391-4981-2 (ebook)

1

All Gemma knew for sure was that she wanted the job so much she would have murdered to get it.

Well, maybe not killed anyone, but certainly broken a few arms or legs.

She stood beside Mrs. Frazier and stared at the storage room full of dirty old boxes stacked neatly on new wooden shelves, and knew she'd never seen anything so beautiful in her life. "Original sources" screamed in her head. She was looking at containers full of documents that no one had touched in hundreds of years.

Mrs. Frazier, tall and majestic-looking, was gazing down her nose at Gemma and obviously waiting for her to say something. But how could Gemma put what she was feeling into words? How could she describe her lifetime fascination with history? Could she tell of the adventure of discovery that these documents represented to her? Or the excitement of the hunt to find new information, new—

"Perhaps it is all a bit overwhelming," Mrs. Frazier said as she flipped off the light switch, a sure sign that Gemma was to leave the precious boxes and their mysterious contents. Reluctantly, Gemma followed her into the cozy living room. Even the guesthouse that was to be used by whomever got the job was lovely. It had a large living room with a kitchen at one end, a big bedroom with a private bath, and the storage room they'd just seen. At the front of the house was an extraordinarily beautiful and spacious office with double French doors that opened out onto acres of lawn and flowers. Outside, just beyond a covered carport, was a three-car garage that was filled floor to ceiling with many more boxes full of uncataloged documents.

Gemma's mind was reeling with the enormity of the task the job entailed. When her adviser for her doctorate in history e-mailed her that he'd managed to get her an interview for a temporary job in the tiny town of Edilean, Virginia, Gemma had been pleased. But then he'd explained that their university was the alma mater of a woman who wanted to hire someone to go through her family's papers and write a history. Gemma had scoffed at the idea. What did that mean? Great-granny and Ellis Island? Too, too boring.

Later that day she'd stopped by his office to give him the courtesy of a personal reply. Gemma told him sorry, but now that her course work was done, she needed to work on her dissertation so she could finish her Ph.D.

"I think you should look at this." Her adviser handed her a letter printed on expensive, heavy vellum. It said that Mrs. Peregrine Frazier had purchased from her husband's family's estate in England several hundred boxes full of documents that dated back to the sixteenth century. She was offering a job to someone to catalog them and write a history from what was found.

Gemma looked across the desk at her adviser. "Sixteenth century" and "several hundred boxes" weren't exactly the normal genealogy. "Who else has seen these papers?"

"Rats, mice," her adviser said as he held up a fatly stuffed envelope. "It's all in here. The papers have been in the attic of a house in England since the place was built back around Elizabeth the First's time. The family—" He pulled a page from the envelope and glanced at it. "They were the earls of Rypton. They sold the house about the time of the American Revolution, but a generation later the family managed to buy it back. Just recently the old place was sold again, but this time the house went to a corporation that wanted the attics cleared, so they held an auction."

Gemma sat down. Actually, she half collapsed onto the chair in front of the man's desk. "So this Mrs. Frazier . . ."

"Went to England and bought every piece of paper that had been stored in the house over the centuries. It doesn't say exactly how much she paid for all of it, just that it was 'multithousands.' Seems there was a bidding war at the auction, but Mrs. Frazier came away with everything. I get the impression that she's a rather formidable woman. If she wants it, she gets it."

Gemma looked at the letter she was holding. "And no one knows what's in there?"

"No. The auction house hauled everything downstairs and divided it into lots. That they didn't open anything was part of what caused the bidding frenzy. For all anyone knows they could all be just household accounts and of little interest to anyone outside the family. How much beef the earl bought in 1742 would probably fascinate his descendants but no one else. Certainly not the Ph.D. committee." He paused. "But then something of a more universal interest could be in there," he added with a smile.

Gemma was trying to digest this information. "How long does this woman think it will take one person, with no staff, to go through these documents and piece together a family history?"

"She's offering two years to start, and that includes free housing on her family's estate, the use of a car, and twenty-five grand a year salary. If it isn't done in two years . . ." He shrugged. "I think the deal is that it'll take as long as it does. If I didn't have a wife and kids I'd try for the job myself."

Gemma was still trying to grasp the facts. If this information was legitimate, she might be able to write her dissertation from something she found in this massive amount of data. As it was, she hadn't even come up with a subject to write about, much less begun her research. She looked back at her adviser. "So what's the catch?"

"You're up against some stiff competition."

From his hesitation, Gemma knew it wasn't going to be good news. "Who?"

"Kirk Laurence and Isla Wilmont."

Gemma's face showed her surprise. The three of them were the same age and were all finishing their doctorates, but other than that, there was no resemblance between her and them. "Why would either one of them want a job like this? A little town in Virginia, living in somebody's guesthouse? Years of researching? That doesn't sound like either of them."

"I hear there are three grown sons. Unmarried. Rich."

Gemma groaned. "That takes care of Isla, but what about Kirk?"

"From what I understand, the trust fund his late father set up supports him as long as he's in school. All he has to do is charm Lady Frazier into hiring him, and he might be able to postpone graduation for years. I heard that if he can't get a job right after he finishes, he's expected to go into his family's business of making windows and doors." He looked at Gemma. "These papers could be a good chance for publication."

Gemma drew in her breath. Publication—the

kind past a dissertation—was what could make or break an academic's future career. Being published could mean that Kirk got out of having to go into the family business, and Isla might not be so desperate to marry someone who could support her.

When Gemma thought of the suave sophistication of Kirk and Isla, she could easily imagine their charming some small town woman. But even if Gemma didn't have a chance of winning over them, that wasn't going to keep her from trying. "How did this Mrs. Frazier get my name?"

"Seems that the president of the university is an old friend of hers. A couple of months ago he asked everyone in the history department to send him some recommendations of students for the job. All of us sent a few, and Mrs. Frazier narrowed it down to three people she wanted to interview, and you're one of them. By the way, I wrote a glowing reference saying that you'd do the best job that could be done."

"And I'm sure someone—or probably half a dozen others—wrote the same about Kirk and Isla."

"No doubt they did," he said. "The difference is that mine is true. You will go to the interview, won't you?"

"Of course. If nothing else, I'd like to see the stash." Gemma opened the door to his office, then turned back to look at him. "You realize, don't you, that if this Mrs. Frazier has an estate, that means country clubs with golf courses and dinners with three forks. Kirk and Isla are the kind of people she'll want living nearby, not Gemma Ranford who—"

"Who works harder in a week than those two butterflies do in a year."

"Thanks," Gemma said as she hoisted her heavy bag onto her shoulder.

He was glad she was going to try for the job. If anyone deserved a break, it was Gemma. He'd never had a student who worked harder than she did. "So where are you off to now?"

"Guess."

He grinned. "Punching the boys?"

"You got it. I have to do something to make sure they learn." As she left his office, she tucked the envelope into her satchel.

That night Gemma closed her bedroom door, got into bed, and started going through the packet of papers that Mrs. Frazier had prepared. Gemma read about the auction in England, about the town of Edilean—which was ten miles outside Williamsburg and William and Mary College—and thought about all of it. At eleven one of her two roommates returned amid a cacophony of giggles and stumbles over the furniture. She and her latest boyfriend went into her bedroom, and other sounds soon started.

Gemma pulled the covers over her head and used her book light to continue with the papers. There were photos of the Frazier estate. It was a large house on twenty-five acres, with two guesthouses set amid the trees. The Fraziers owned four huge car dealerships in Virginia, and there was a brochure from the one in

Richmond. *Biggest* was the word that was repeatedly used to describe the place.

But Gemma wasn't interested in the sales leaflet. What held her attention was the thought of going through the old documents and seeing what no one else had looked at in centuries.

There was a thud in her roommate's room, as though someone had fallen off the bed. "And the peace and quiet to give my full attention to it," Gemma said aloud.

As the sounds of intimacy grew louder, she put a pillow over her head. She couldn't afford an apartment of her own. The money she earned from tutoring what sometimes seemed to be most of the members of the athletic teams at the university went to her studies. That she'd made it so far on so little was a marvel even to her.

Now she was facing some serious study as she began to work on her dissertation—and she was worried about money. Deep research cost a lot. If she chose a subject that dealt with some aspect of history that happened far from school—and of course it would if she wanted fresh material—expenses would include travel, which meant food and lodging. Then there were books, supplies, even photocopies. For the last year she'd worried how she was going to pull it off. But finishing her Ph.D. would make the difference between obtaining a job teaching in a community college or at a top university. If she could get her dissertation from the Frazier documents, most, if not all, of these problems would be solved.

The noise across the hallway increased and Gemma held the pillow closer over her ears to drown out the sounds. "I'm going to try," she whispered. "I'll probably lose out to the butterflies, but I am going to give it my best shot."

And that's how she came to be standing in the guesthouse with the autocratic Mrs. Frazier. It was 11 A.M. on a beautiful spring morning, she'd driven in from the airport just a few minutes ago, and Mrs. Frazier had told her that Isla and Kirk were already there. Gemma realized that she should have anticipated that they'd arrive a day before the scheduled interview, as they were very competitive people. And by now Mrs. Frazier was probably in love with both of them, Gemma thought. After all, Kirk and Isla were known for being charming. "Those two are the lights of the history department," she'd heard a professor say at a faculty-student party. "Intelligent and well read. You couldn't ask for more," had been the reply. Gemma had heard all this because she'd been carrying a tray of drinks—yet another of her side jobs.

"My ride is here," Mrs. Frazier said as she looked out the living room window. Outside was one of those little utility vehicles with a truck bed in back. Driving it was a large, handsome young man. "Would you like to meet my son?" Mrs. Frazier asked.

Gemma knew that by all rules of courtesy she should go outside and meet the son, but she hated leaving the guesthouse and its treasure trove.

"Or would you like to stay here by yourself for a

while?" Mrs. Frazier asked in a soft voice, as though talking to a child.

"Here," Gemma managed to say.

"All right, then," Mrs. Frazier said as she went to the door. "Lunch is at one and it takes about ten minutes to walk to the house—or would you like for me to send someone to pick you up?"

"I'll walk," Gemma said, then watched as the older woman got into the little truck and left. Gemma let out a sigh of relief and nearly tripped over her own feet as she ran to the big office. From the smell of fresh paint, the room seemed to have been newly redone. Three walls were lined with beautiful cherry bookshelves, with cabinets along the bottom. In front of the French doors was a big old desk with brass fittings along the edges. Gemma wasn't an expert on furniture, but it was her guess that the desk was purchased at the same auction as the papers. The floor was carpeted in some modern, off-white fabric that was supposed to look like it was handwoven. On top of it was a huge, nearly worn-out old Oriental rug that looked as though people had been walking across it for centuries. The two pictures on the walls by the door were of men on horses, their hunting dogs looking eager for the chase to begin.

To Gemma's eyes, the room was heavenly. With the garden clearly visible through the glass doors and the shelves full of untouched documents, she wanted to stay there forever.

She turned about the room, looking at everything. On the shelves were wooden and cardboard boxes, baskets that were about to fall apart, a couple of metal tubs, and bundles of papers that were tied together with old ribbon. On the floor were two leather-bound trunks, a wooden bench with a hinged lid, and several small chests, one with nail studs all over it.

Gemma had no idea where to begin. Tentatively, with hands that were close to shaking, she pulled down what looked to be a hatbox, probably from the 1920s—and she dearly hoped it didn't contain a hat. Costume history was not her first love.

When she saw that letters were inside, Gemma drew in her breath. Letters and diaries had to be two of her favorite things in life. There was a pretty, comfortable-looking chair by the doors, but Gemma ignored it as she sat down on the rug and pulled out the first batch of letters. They were tied with dark grosgrain ribbon, and she slipped out the first letter and unfolded it.

Part of the letter was missing, but what was there was written in an angular, spidery hand that was difficult to read. It seemed that someone had gone to a great deal of trouble to save the last part of the letter.

> *Even though I'm an old woman now and have seen more than anyone should, especially that odious war that nearly divided our country, what I remember most vividly, and with the most heartache, is what happened to dear Julian and Winnie. I never believed*

that woman's tears when she said that Julian's death was an accident. Worse, I don't think Ewan believed her either. I will tell you a secret that I thought I'd carry to my grave. Remember the hysteria when the Harewhistle disappeared? I searched as much as anyone, but I knew it wouldn't be found because I took it with me when I went to England that long ago summer. I wanted its magic for selfish reasons but I ended up wishing on Winnie's behalf. I've never before told anyone, but I believe that the Stone gave them that extraordinarily beautiful child. Last week I wrote the story and put it where it will be safe. I hope that all the Fraziers read it and find out what their relative by marriage did to the Aldredge family. I hope that someday that woman's descendants lose that estate. They do not deserve it! I must go now. My old, aching joints don't let me write for long.

With love, Tamsen.

"Wow," Gemma said aloud. She'd already stumbled on a mystery and a romance. She glanced at her watch, told herself she had plenty of time before lunch, then stretched out on her stomach and began to read in earnest.

2

Colin Frazier was frowning. He had at least fifty things he needed to do today, but here he was, driving out to the guesthouse to pick up one of his mother's students. The other two were already in the main house, chatting so amiably to his mother that they sounded like long-lost relatives. The young woman, Isla, kept saying that everything was "exquisite," while the man had tried to buddy up to Colin's brother Lanny by talking about cars. Since Lanny had rebuilt his first transmission when he was eight, it was evident that the job seeker, Kirk, knew nothing about anything with wheels.

As for Colin's youngest brother Shamus, he stood to one side and moved a coin around on his fingers. Their parents had forbidden Shamus, who was the artist in the family, to draw anything for fear that he'd come up with some outrageous caricature of the visiting students and embarrass his parents—or actually, just their mother. Their father tended to laugh at whatever Shamus drew.

Everything had started about three years ago when Mrs. Frazier found out that the last earl of Rypton, her husband's very distant relative, had died without issue, so the title was being retired. What she wondered was if the title could be revived, which would mean that her husband could possibly be the earl and she the countess.

On the night she'd posed this question, the family was at home in the living room, and her three youngest sons had gone into riots of laughter. Shamus, still in high school, grabbed his sketchbook and made an unflattering caricature of their mother wearing a crown.

As they say, she was not amused.

Alea Frazier put her chin up and left the room.

"Now you've done it," her husband said. "I'll be in the doghouse for weeks. Lanny! Wipe that smirk off your face and start planning your apology." He glared at his youngest. "And you, young man, with your drawing . . ." He trailed off, as though the punishment he had in mind was too dire to speak of.

With a great sigh, Mr. Frazier heaved himself up out of his favorite chair to go in search of his wife. He paused in the doorway. "This is something that means a lot to your mother, so I want no more making fun of her. If she wants to be a lady, then she can damned well be one. Got it?"

After he left, it was a full two minutes before the three youngest boys were laughing again.

Lanny, the third eldest, turned to Colin, the oldest, because his big brother wasn't laughing. "Come on, lighten up. Don't you think this is hilarious?"

Colin raised an eyebrow. "What I want to know is what our dear mother plans to do in her quest to find out if Dad can be an earl."

Peregrine, Pere for short and the second eldest, said, "Think she'll make Dad buy her a castle?"

"With a moat?" Lanny asked.

Pere acted like he had a sword in his hand and attacked Lanny. "Will we brothers become sworn enemies and fight each other to become the next earl?"

Shamus was sketching his brothers' mock sword fight and didn't look up as he said, "Colin will get the title next. You two will have to kill him to get it."

At that, Pere and Lanny, their arms extended as they held imaginary swords, turned toward their brother, who was sitting at the end of the long couch. "That'll be easy," Lanny said and made a lunge.

In the next second, Colin was up. He grabbed Lanny about the waist and lifted him onto his shoulders.

At that moment Mr. Frazier reentered the room. "If you boys break anything, it'll come out of your allowance."

With a snort of laughter, Colin put his brother down. Their father had made them sound like children, but Colin had just turned twenty-seven, while Lanny and Pere were twenty-five and twenty-six.

"How's Mom?" Colin asked.

"All right." Mr. Frazier gave his eldest son a look that said this was only the beginning. When Mrs. Frazier took on a project, she became a force of nature, like a tornado that plowed across the earth, sucking up everything in its wake. And it looked like this earl of Rypton thing was going to be her next undertaking.

That was three years ago, but recently the old house in England that had belonged to the earls was put up for sale, and it took all Mr. Frazier's ability to talk his wife out of buying it. The compromise had been for her to purchase every scrap of paper—"our history" as she called it—that had been squirreled away in the house and have it shipped home to Virginia.

When she'd returned from her solitary trip to the auction—and before the bills arrived—the family thought she'd probably bought half a dozen or so boxes full of old papers. Instead, six FedEx trucks had arrived bearing professionally crated trunks, baskets, boxes, and even suitcases packed full of crumbling old documents.

Mr. Frazier wasn't happy when he'd had to move two vintage cars out of the guesthouse garage so it could be filled with what she'd bought. "Alea," Mr. Frazier had said with extreme patience as he looked at the collection, "who's going to go through all this . . . this . . . ?"

"Don't worry, dearest, I've taken care of that. I called Freddy, and he and I had a good long talk about how to go about this. He came up with a truly brilliant plan."

"Freddy?" Mr. Frazier asked, his jaw rigid. Frederick J. Townsend was the president of his wife's university alma mater—and her old boyfriend. The man she'd almost married. "And how is ol' Freddy?" Mr. Frazier asked, his teeth clenched.

"Excellent, as always. He's going to send me the résumés of some young people who are qualified for the job, probably Ph.D. students. I'll choose four or five of them to come here to be interviewed. Or do you think that's too many? Maybe I should cut it down to three. Yes, that's a good idea. Freddy promised that he'd send the very best the university has to offer. What do you think, dear?"

Mr. Frazier narrowed his eyes at his wife. He knew when he was being bamboozled. She was leaving out a great deal, such as the salary she'd probably already offered, and how long this person was going to be in their employ. And since she'd insisted on putting her hoard in the guesthouse garage, he had a suspicion about where this student was to live. "I think," he said slowly, "that you and I are going to sit down and you're going to tell me exactly what you're up to."

"Of course, dear," she said, smiling. "I'd love to tell you everything."

It was at dinner that night that the family was told of the plan to hire someone who would live in one of the guesthouses and spend two or more years reading and cataloging the material from England.

"Two years?" Pere asked in shock.

Lanny said, "Just make sure she's female. And pretty."

"I think the three girlfriends you have now are quite enough," Mr. Frazier said, but Lanny just grinned.

Mrs. Frazier turned to her eldest son. "Colin, what do you think?"

The family knew that Colin kept his opinions to himself. His mother often said that her eldest son had been born independent, that he went where he wanted to when he wanted to. His father said that Colin had been given the short end of the stick. By the time he was three, he'd had two younger brothers who flamboyantly craved attention. With his father working seventy hours a week and his mother dealing with two demanding children, Colin had learned to take care of himself—and to not bother anyone with his needs and wants.

"I think," Colin said slowly, "that the whole project will be good for you." Shamus, the last of his mother's five children, would leave for college next year, and their mother was going to be lonely. Only Colin lived in Edilean—and he spent so much time in town that he might as well be in another state. Someone living in the guesthouse and spewing out stories about the family's past would probably entertain his mother. Maybe there'd be moments when she'd forget how her children were scattered around the country.

But now, months later, Colin wished he'd been more involved in the whole process of letting someone stay on the family property for such a long time. He'd met two of the applicants for the job and didn't like either of them. The young man and woman were both tall and greyhound thin, their clothes sleek and expensive. The woman looked at Lanny with eyes that seemed to flash with a neon sign of a wedding cake, and Colin had seen the man pick up a plate and look at the manufacturer's name. So far, neither of them had so much as glanced at a book, and they'd certainly shown no interest in the dirty boxes in the guesthouse.

Colin could almost see the future. The hired one would freely wander about the place and come up with excuses of why he/she should join the family. And his mother's generous nature would allow it. He had visions of the man moving in with them and being there twenty years from now. His mother would say, "But my children left me, so why shouldn't I have Kirk to keep me company?"

All in all, Colin was beginning to see the whole project as a disaster.

As for the last job applicant, she hadn't even shown up for lunch. Lanny, extremely pleased with the first young woman, had volunteered to go look for her. To him, the more women around him, the better.

When asked about the third candidate, Mrs. Frazier had said, "Leave her where she is," in a way that made Colin groan. It looked as though his mother had already made up her mind about who she was going to hire and she didn't need to know anything more about the third one. But Colin's hope was that the other student was interested in something besides the family possessions.

"Mother," Colin said as they were going in to lunch, "I think the other woman should be here too and that you should talk to her."

"I've already found out everything I need to know about her. Let's just have a pleasant lunch, shall we? Kirk and Isla are such fun, aren't they?"

"Yeah, hilarious," Colin said as his mother swept past him. He caught up with her. "I just think—"

His mother turned on him. "If you're so interested in the other girl, then *you* can go get her. I left her in the guesthouse, and I assume she's still there." Mrs. Frazier went into the dining room.

Colin started after her but paused in the doorway. The dining room had been set with the best china, and their housekeeper, Rachel, was wearing a white uniform. She looked up, met Colin's eyes, and gave a shrug that said the getup was his mother's doing.

Colin's parents took their places at the ends of the table, and Mr. Frazier looked as though he'd rather be anywhere else in the world than there. Lanny was next to the lovely Miss Isla, with the handsome Kirk on his other side.

Across the table were three settings, one occupied by Shamus, the other two for Colin and the third candidate.

Mrs. Frazier motioned for her eldest son to take his seat.

Colin took a step forward, but he couldn't make himself sit down. "I . . . ," he said. "I'll . . ." He pointed over his shoulder, vaguely in the direction of the guesthouse, then escaped. He jumped in a utility truck and sped off.

By the time Colin reached the guesthouse, his frown was so deep his dark brows were nearly touching in the middle. He parked the little truck on the grass and walked the last steps to the guesthouse. Based on what he'd seen of the others, he thought it would be better to check on what the third student was up to. All least her car wasn't parked nearby and she wasn't filling the trunk with whatever she could carry. What had possessed his mother to leave a stranger alone in the little house? It was full of valuable antiques—all of which had come from England and arrived in a moving van weeks after the documents came.

Colin had his hand on the door handle of the library, ready to burst in, when he saw her. She was sitting on the old carpet, her back against the cabinets that had been installed only last week. Around her were six boxes of the documents his mother had bought.

Her face was turned away, but he could see that under her loose clothing she was small and trim, with shoulder-length dark blonde hair. There was a pen clipped to her sleeve, one in her hand, and three pens of different colors on the floor. By her knee was a thick notebook open to a page filled with writing.

As he watched, she bent forward, put what looked to be an old letter on the floor, and began to write in her notebook. When she made a note in the margin, she used a different color.

When she glanced up, he thought she'd seen him through the glass, but her eyes held a glazed look, and he realized she was seeing only what was inside her mind.

Her movement let him get a clearer view of her face. She was pretty, not beautiful like his friend Jean, or ethereal like his cousin Sara, but nice-looking. He thought that this young woman looked like . . . like she belonged in a library. She was the girl who went to church on Sunday and made pot roast on Friday.

What struck Colin most was that he had never in his life seen anyone look so . . . well, *happy.* If he'd ever before seen anyone doing exactly what he should, when he should, she was it. If Shamus were to draw her portrait, he'd label it *Contentment.*

Colin's frown went away. Now *this* is what he'd envisioned when his mother had first talked of hiring someone to research the family history.

Smiling, he turned the handle and opened the door. Now, if he just didn't scare her when she saw him . . .

The sound of the door opening startled Gemma out of her trance, and she looked up to see a very large man standing in the doorway. He was quite handsome, with his thick, dark eyebrows and his square jaw.

He had on a shirt that verged on being too tight; it clung to his muscles—and Gemma thought she probably knew every exercise he did. She'd had four years of working with athletes, so she knew what it took to get a body into the shape his was in.

He wore the same look she'd seen on the faces of "her" athletes. When first meeting someone they held back until they saw how their enormous size might affect that person. It was her guess that this man, with his thick brows and his big body, often intimidated people.

But not Gemma. The truth was that because of "her boys" he was familiar-looking to her, someone she was comfortable being near—which was a contrast to her encounter with Mrs. Frazier with her diamond earrings.

As Gemma stood up, she gave him a smile that came from her heart. "Hello. Did you come to get me for lunch?" She glanced at her watch. It was one-thirty. "Oh dear. I missed it, didn't I?"

"Completely," Colin said as he closed the door behind him. He nodded toward the open boxes on the floor. "Find anything interesting?"

"Love, tragedy, and something that people believed was magic," she said.

He sat down in the big chair by the door. "You found all that in such a short time?"

Turning her back to him, she held out her arms to the bookcases. When she did, her trousers tightened a bit, and Colin had a better look at her shape. She didn't get legs like that from sitting around all day.

"I'm not sure yet," she said, "but I think there might be real treasure buried in here." She looked back at him. "Are you one of Mrs. Frazier's sons?"

"I'm the oldest. Colin." He watched as she began to straighten the papers on the floor and put them back on the shelves. There was something quiet about her that he liked.

"I'm Gemma, and I guess I blew it with your mother, didn't I?" she asked softly as she slipped an old hatbox onto a shelf. "Missing lunch was very rude of me. Isla and Kirk would never—"

"They're too busy counting the silver to notice who's there or not," Colin said.

Turning, she looked at him in surprise.

"At least the boy is doing calculations," Colin said. "That girl is ready to tell my brother what size engagement ring she wants."

"You're rather perceptive, aren't you?"

"Nope. I'm just another big, dumb former football player."

She could see that behind his levity, he seemed to be asking her a question. "Big?" she said. "Are you kidding? I'm the official tutor for the football team, and two of my students make double-door refrigerators look svelte."

Colin grinned. "They should meet my little brother. He's still growing, and we're afraid he's going to resemble a Hummer."

"Will your family have to get him tags and a license?"

"No, but he does sometimes wear taillights."

They laughed together.

Colin was about to speak when his cell phone rang. He dug into his trousers pocket, pulled it out, glanced at the ID, then answered it. "You haven't finished lunch already, have you?" He paused. "Oh. Sure. Here? Now? No, uh, actually, I . . . I'm on my way into town and I'll eat there." He glanced at Gemma as he listened. "Sorry, Mom, I'll see you at dinner."

He clicked off his phone. "The whole lot of them are on their way here. I'm leaving. You want to go with me and get some lunch?"

"I'd love to, but I'm afraid I've already offended your mother, so I think I'll stay. Thanks for the offer, though." Gemma looked around the room to make sure she'd put everything back just as she'd found it. Turning, she looked at Colin, who was still sitting in the chair. "You'd better make your escape. I can hear them now."

"I think I'll wait a while," he said. "You really want this job, don't you?"

"You have *no* idea how much! None at all."

"Actually, I do. I wanted something once."

"Did you get it?"

"Yes," he said.

Gemma smiled at him, but she couldn't imagine what someone as rich as he was could want as much as she wanted this job. When she heard Isla's high-pitched laugh, she looked out the glass doors. Mrs. Frazier was walking between Isla and Kirk, just a few yards away now, and the three of them looked as though they were old friends. Obviously, Mrs. Frazier didn't seem to have the same opinions that her son did. Too bad *she* was the one doing the hiring.

Gemma took a step toward the door, but Colin reached it before she did and opened it to his mother.

"Colin," Mrs. Frazier said in surprise. "I thought you were going into town for lunch."

"I couldn't drag Gemma away from her research, so I thought I'd wait."

"Oh? Have you two become friends?"

"She's only interested in your boring old papers," he said as he opened the door wider for the other two.

"Hello again," Isla said brightly to Colin, sounding as though she'd known him for years. "Gemma, darling, you missed a truly exquisite lunch." Isla went to her and kissed her cheek.

Gemma's eyes widened. She didn't exactly travel in the same circles as Isla, and they'd certainly never exchanged kisses before.

"Gemma," Kirk said as he too kissed her cheek. "Isn't this place wonderful?"

"Yes," she answered.

"What you've done to this little house is marvelous," Isla said to Mrs. Frazier. "Please tell me you aren't your own interior designer."

"I purchased a few things that belonged to my husband's family," Mrs. Frazier said modestly.

"Mother, you bought everything that the first Frazier could possibly have touched," Colin said.

"Shamus," Gemma said, and everyone turned to look at her.

"Yes, my youngest son," Mrs. Frazier said. "I didn't realize you'd met him."

Kirk said, "Delightful young man. I'm a great admirer of his accomplishments."

"I think Gemma means the original Shamus," Colin said. "The one who helped found Edilean."

Again, everyone looked at her, and she nodded. She was so nervous she could hardly speak. Her deep desire for the job was making her tongue-tied.

"Where did you hear of him?" Mrs. Frazier asked.

Gemma took a deep breath. "The name was in the history of Edilean on the town Web site and in the genealogy of your family. I was wondering what happened to cause the break in the generation after him. I searched the Internet and found where the family house had been repurchased in the late eighteenth century by the son of the American settlers, Shamus and Prudence Frazier. But then the surname was changed back to Lancaster, and there was no more mention of 'Frazier.' Was the separation caused by the distance between America and England, or did something else cause the rift?"

When she stopped talking she saw the way Mrs. Frazier, Isla, and Kirk were staring at her. Behind them, Colin's eyes were sparkling, as though he was enjoying everything.

Gemma took a step back. "I'm sorry. I didn't mean to pry. I was just curious, is all."

"Yes, well," Mrs. Frazier said as she turned to Isla. "As for your question, I didn't use a decorator."

"But it looks like such a professional job. Do you mind if we see the living room again?" Isla gave Gemma a look that said she'd just lost the job.

"Of course." Mrs. Frazier left the room first, Isla close behind her.

"Put your foot in that one, didn't you?" Kirk said to Gemma, then left.

When they were alone in the room, Gemma looked at Colin. "Me and my big mouth! Why didn't I ask about the rug or the desk?"

"Because you couldn't care less about them."

"True, but I should have pretended to . . ." She paused. "I'm going in there and try to make your mother believe I'm not the world's rudest person." Gemma stopped in the doorway. "Quick! Tell me something she likes."

"Right now, my father's aristocratic relatives are her great passion."

"But I just—" Her eyes widened.

"Right. You asked about them and showed that you've already done quite a bit of research on your own."

Gemma stood there blinking at him. "But she's more interested in talking about decorating with Isla."

"I thought so too, but that was before I saw her face as she listened to you. My mother hates for anyone to know what she's up to. Let me borrow your notebook."

"But—"

"Trust me, please."

Gemma didn't understand what he had in mind, but she took it out of her big bag and handed it to him, then hurried into the living room with the others.

"This town sounds enchanting," Isla was saying, "and if I should be given the job I will enjoy becoming part of the community."

"I can't wait to dive into the research," Kirk said. "The excitement of discovery, the thrill of tracking down a story, the possibility of learning something that no one else knows . . ." He had a faraway look in his eyes that Gemma had never seen before, even though she'd been in classes with him for the last four years. They'd never been in a study group together, but then Gemma's workload prevented her from conforming to other people's schedules.

"I agree completely," Isla said. "It will be so interesting to start going through the documents. If I weren't enjoying the company of your family so much, I'd be in here now."

"And what about you?" Mrs. Frazier asked, looking at Gemma.

"She's already started," Colin said as he handed his mother Gemma's notebook.

Mrs. Frazier flipped through the pages. Only five of them had been filled with Gemma's small handwriting, but it could be seen that there was a lot of information in there. "Do you find that using different colors of ink helps you?"

"I sometimes use eight colors," Kirk said before Gemma could speak.

"I use color-coded dots," Isla said. "Oh, but it will be such *fun* to start going through everything."

"Is that how you feel too, Gemma?" Mrs. Frazier asked. "That it will be fun?"

"I think 'intense' would better describe it," Gemma said. "I would guess that most of the documents, probably eighty percent of them, are useless when trying to write a history because they're household accounts. If you want to find out the financial side of your husband's family, I'd suggest hiring a forensic accountant."

"I think Gemma means—" Kirk began.

Mrs. Frazier put up her hand. "So you're only interested in dealing with twenty percent of the papers?"

Gemma felt as though she'd yet again messed up, but when she glanced at Colin, he gave her an encouraging nod. "Yes," Gemma said firmly. "What I'd do first is go through every box and do a lot of sorting. What I couldn't use, I'd store, then I'd put the diaries and letters and personal papers in the library and start working from there."

Mrs. Frazier looked at Gemma for a moment, then turned to Isla. "And how would you begin?"

"The same way," she said quickly. "That's standard procedure."

Gemma shot Isla a look. There was no "standard procedure" for dealing with historical data. All researchers had their own way of working.

Mrs. Frazier turned to her son. "I think I'll take

a nap. Why don't I return to the house with Isla and Kirk, and you take Gemma out to lunch? You two must be starving. And while you're in town, why don't you show her your office?"

Turning, Mrs. Frazier handed Gemma her notebook, but she said nothing. She looked at Isla and Kirk. "Yesterday I had the heat in the pool turned up. Perhaps you two would like a swim."

In the next minute Colin and Gemma were alone in the guesthouse.

"Oh," Gemma said as she sat down on the couch. "I can't tell if your mother likes me or hates me." She looked up at Colin. "Is going with you a punishment or a reward?"

"I don't know. Right now, it could go either way. She's not too happy with me at the moment because last night I expressed some concerns about a stranger moving into the guesthouse. I liked the idea at first, but after I met Isla and Kirk . . . Well, let's just say that if my mother could have turned me over her knee, she would have." He looked at Gemma. "You want to go into town for lunch?"

"Yes, please," she said.

"Then follow me to the car and I'll make sure we're not seen. I don't want those two sucking up to *me*." He led her out of the guesthouse, then through the trees and along the edge of a landscaped lawn. As they passed the side of the big house, Gemma saw a very large young man, a teenager, standing behind a glass door and watching them. Finally, they arrived at the driveway in front of the house. There were six vehicles parked there, including Gemma's rental, making it look like a used-car lot.

Colin pulled keys out of his pocket.

"I guess that was your little brother I saw at the door."

"Probably," Colin said as he went toward a Jeep, the kind that looked like it was made to go up and down mountains. "That means we'll be ratted on."

"He's a tattletale?" Gemma asked.

"Worse. He's an artist."

She looked across the hood at him in question.

"Like writers tell everything that happens to them, my little brother draws everything. By tonight he'll have half a dozen pictures of you and me. He'll probably portray us as running away to escape Isla and Kirk."

The accuracy of that statement made Gemma smile as she got in the Jeep beside him. He backed up, skillfully and quickly maneuvering around three cars that were blocking him in.

When they were on the road, he said, "Sandwiches okay?"

"I like anything I don't have to cook."

"So much for my pot roast theory."

"What does that mean?"

"I had you pegged for someone who could make a super pot roast."

"I'm not sure what that says about your opinion

of me, but I can guarantee that I don't like being pigeonholed."

He glanced at her as he pulled onto the main road, his eyes asking if he'd offended her.

"Meat loaf," she said.

"What?"

"I can make a meat loaf that will make you cry."

"Would that be tears of joy or horror?"

Gemma smiled. "That's my secret." They were quiet for a moment as he drove them through the little town of Edilean. The streets branched out from a square with a huge oak tree in the center. She'd read on the town Web site that the tree was said to be a descendant of one planted from a seed brought from Scotland by the woman for whom the town was named.

As a historian, Gemma couldn't help marveling at the buildings around the town square. Some of them were modern, meaning that they'd been built since World War II, but most of them were older than that, certainly pre–Civil War. It looked as though Sherman hadn't applied his treachery to this Southern town.

She looked at Colin. "What's the office your mother mentioned? Do you have a job?"

He gave her a sharp look. "Are you asking if I support myself or do I live off my father's car business?"

Gemma instantly turned red. It was exactly what she'd meant. "I . . ."

"That's okay. It's an assumption everyone makes,

and two of my brothers do work for him. But I was recently officially elected Edilean's sheriff."

"Really?" Her eyes widened. "Do you have an office and a deputy and a case full of rifles, and what kinds of crime does this town have?"

Colin laughed. "Are you curious about everything or is it just me?"

"Everything, anything. So, do you?"

"I have all those things, and my jurisdiction extends to the wilderness area around Edilean, so I stay busy. After lunch, I'll show you my office."

Gemma hesitated. "Is your mother going to think I'm like Isla and after one of her sons?"

"She doesn't pry into our personal lives. So did you leave a boyfriend to come here?"

"Broke up with the last guy six months ago."

Colin had driven through the town and now turned down a narrow road. With trees overhanging above, like a canopy, it looked like they were heading into the wilderness. "What about the football players you tutor? No boyfriend there?" he asked.

"They think I'm their mother."

"Now why do I doubt that?"

"No, really, they call me Miss G, and they tell me their problems."

"Such as?"

"Looks like I'm not the only one who's curious."

"It's part of my job," he answered as he pulled into the parking lot of a grocery store. But it wasn't the usual glass-doored concoction. The building was long and low, with a roof that extended out over the front to form a porch. It looked like a retreat for rich hunters in the Adirondacks. If there hadn't been half a dozen people coming out with big metal carts, Gemma wouldn't have known it was a grocery.

Colin had turned off the engine and was sitting behind the steering wheel, looking at her as though he meant to stay there until she answered him.

Gemma shrugged. "Let's just say that I've had to learn a lot about birth control and the consequences of not using any. The boys' reading assignments are often pamphlets on the basics of being away from home for the first time. Sometimes I feel like a sex education teacher."

"If you have any really creative things to teach, let me know," Colin said seriously.

"So you can pass them on to your constituents?"

"Of course," Colin said. "As an elected official, they're all I care about, and I believe it's my duty to educate them." Smiling, he got out of the car, then waited until she was beside him. Together they went into the store.

The inside of the grocery was dim and cool, and to the right was a huge produce area that glistened with colors and seeming perfection. She followed Colin as he headed for the back of the store.

"Colin!" a woman said, and he halted. She was young and looked as though she hadn't had a lot of sleep lately—which was understandable. She was holding a two-year-old boy by the hand, and he was dancing about in the age-old pantomime of "bathroom quick!" On her hip was a six-month-old girl chewing on a bagel.

With a movement that seemed as though he'd done it many times, Colin took the little girl in his arms. With a smile of thanks, the mother lifted the boy and started running.

"And how are you, Miss Caitlyn?" Colin asked the little girl he was holding, and she grinned at him.

With a glance at Gemma, Colin kept walking toward the back, little Caitlyn secure and quite happy in his big arms.

As they walked, Gemma looked around the store. The items on the shelves were very high-end, and she thought the place was much too upscale for her to afford. She wondered where the local giant-size, cheap market was.

She followed Colin to a tall, glass-fronted case that was full of fresh-looking seafood. Yes, definitely out of her price range.

"Colin!" said a good-looking older woman from behind the counter. "You're just the man I wanted to see."

Before he could speak, a little boy, about four, came running up. He held up a toy truck in one hand and the wheels to it in the other. There were dried tears on his face, and he was looking up at Colin as though he were Superman. "Sheriff?" he whispered, a catch in his voice.

Colin started to reach for the truck but his arms were full with the baby.

Without a thought, Gemma took the little girl from him, and Colin squatted to eye level with the boy and snapped the wheels back into place. The child ran off just as his mother rounded the corner.

"*There* you are, Matthew. Do *not* run off like that again. Oh, Colin! Thank you."

"Any time," he said to the woman as she picked up the boy and left. The first woman came back and Gemma handed her daughter to her.

Through all this, the woman behind the counter had been watching. "Same as always, huh, Colin?" she said, smiling.

"Not much different. So what did you want to see me about, Ellie? You have a break-in?"

"You're funny. Can you make a delivery for me?"

"To our favorite little man?"

"Certainly my favorite, since he helped my daughter. Can you take a couple of boxes out to the farm?"

"Why isn't he coming in to get what he needs?"

"The club ladies are after him again."

Colin grinned. "Okay, pack it up. Anyway, I'm sure Gemma would like to see Merlin's Farm."

"Am I to take it that Gemma is your fellow babysitter? The young woman behind you?"

Colin turned to see Gemma inspecting the chickens that had just been taken off the rotisserie. "Gemma, this is Ellie Shaw, my . . . What are you?"

"Fourth cousin, removed once or twice," Ellie said to Gemma. "A town resident just did a genealogy for some of the families in Edilean, and we've at last found out how we're all related. I'd shake your hand, but—" She was wearing sterile gloves.

"It's nice to meet you," Gemma said. "Do you own this store?"

"What gave me away?" Ellie asked.

"Bossiness," Colin answered. When he heard a baby start to cry, he said quickly, "Could we get some sandwiches? To go?"

"Colin is our resident Pied Piper with the kids," Ellie said to Gemma, looking from one to the other in curiosity.

"Come on, give me a break," he said. "I'm trying to impress her that I'm the sheriff and that I deal with dastardly crimes."

"Impress her, are you?" Ellie asked.

Gemma thought she should clear the air. "I'm one of the applicants for a job that Mrs. Frazier is offering."

"Oh, right, cleaning out that mess she bought in England." Ellie looked at Colin. "So where are the other two who are trying for the job?"

"At home in the pool. Mom's taking a nap."

Ellie snorted. "Your mother never took a nap in her life."

"I know she hasn't," he said, smiling.

Ellie again looked from him to Gemma. "So what kind of sandwiches do you two want?"

"Roast beef," they said in unison.

"Side dish? I have coleslaw or potato salad."

"Coleslaw," they again said together.

"Coming up." When Ellie turned away, she was smiling.

"Like to look around?" Colin asked.

"So I can tell Isla about the place for when she lives here?"

"That's exactly what I had in mind." He was teasing, but whether or not she got the job was no joke to her and he saw it on her face. He lowered his voice. "I'll talk to Mom tonight, and I'll get Dad to talk to her too. And Shamus. Maybe the three of us can persuade her to choose the right person." He started to say more but broke off because a woman standing near the cereals started running toward him.

"Colin!" she said. "I went by your office today but Roy said you were away on family business. I am so glad to see you."

"Did it happen again, Tara?" Colin asked.

For the first time, Gemma saw his "sheriff face." In a second he went from teasing and laughing to very serious.

When the woman said, "Someone trampled my flowers again," Gemma had to restrain her smile. The news on TV was full of murders and other heinous crimes, but this woman was concerned about her tulips?

"Did Roy make casts of the footprints?"

"Yes. She came as soon as I called."

Gemma's eyes widened. Footprint casts? This sounded more serious than just flowers being knocked down.

"Colin, I don't know what to do," Tara said. "I have two little kids and with Jimmie away so much . . ."

Colin put his arm out to the woman and she laid her cheek against his chest as she tried not to cry. "Want to stay in our guesthouse?" he asked as he put his hand on her back. "The big one is taken, but you and the kids are welcome to use the second one."

She pulled away. "No, we'll be all right. That man you recommended is putting the cameras up, and Jimmie will be home tonight, so we'll be fine." Tara pulled a tissue out of her pocket and blew her nose as she looked at Gemma. "Is this a new girlfriend?"

"I'm one of the candidates for the job of cataloging the Frazier documents," Gemma said quickly, stepping a little farther away from Colin. She didn't want to be the cause of any gossip in the small town.

Judging from Tara's blank look, she had no idea what Gemma was referring to. "If Colin likes you, then you have my vote." She glanced at her basket. "I have to go before this thaws. Colin, thank you for . . . for everything."

"You have my cell number. If you hear or see anything, call me and I'll be there."

"Thanks," she said, then wheeled her cart away.

He turned to Gemma, looking as though nothing unusual had happened. "So this is the aisle where Ellie keeps the cereals. If you like Kellogg's Raisin Bran—the kind that real people eat—you have me to thank for its being here. I told Ellie that if she didn't start stocking Raisin Bran I was going to Williamsburg to—"

"What was that all about?" Gemma asked, cutting him off. "Please say you can tell me or I'll go crazy trying to figure it out."

Colin shrugged. "We don't know anything for sure. Someone keeps walking through Tara's flower beds in the middle of the night. Yesterday there was a light rain, so my deputy, Roy, could get some casts of the footprints. It's an old-fashioned technique, but then we're an old-fashioned town—and our budget is limited."

"Do you think it's malicious, meant to frighten her, or is it a robber . . . or worse?"

"No robberies, no outlet to her backyard, but it's scared the daylights out of Tara. She's having surveillance cameras installed."

"And you offered her a place to stay," Gemma said.

"Yeah, we mostly use the guesthouses for anyone who needs them. Ellie's waving at us. Our sandwiches are ready."

Gemma followed him to the back and waited as Ellie handed him a white bag.

"Did you talk to Tara?" Ellie asked.

"Yeah," Colin said. "Whoever's doing it doesn't seem to mean any harm, but I'm going to be cautious."

"You always are. Oh, by the way, Taylor took the boxes out to Merlin's Farm this morning, so you don't need to go. Did you meet our newest resident? Dr. Burgess?"

"Not yet," Colin said, "but I've heard of him." He turned to Gemma. "A retired professor of English history has moved here. He wants to be near Williamsburg, and he used to teach at Oxford."

"Sounds interesting. I'd like to meet him."

"I don't think he's in good health, poor man." She looked at Gemma. "If you two are planning to eat outside, you should know that there's a playgroup out there. Colin will be swamped."

"Thanks for warning us," he said, then moved aside for Gemma to go ahead of him toward the front. There was a big refrigerated cabinet full of fruit juice drinks near the registers. "Take your pick."

"Anything with raspberries," Gemma said as Colin held the door open. "What about you?"

"I'm a lemonade man."

"Pink or yellow?"

He gave her a look.

"Yeah, right. My boys won't touch anything pink either."

"So now I'm one of your boys?" He led them to the end register where the girl greeted him by name. Colin held up their food, she nodded, and they left. It looked like he had an account there.

"If I say that you are one of my kids, will it get me the job?" she asked as they got to the door.

"Why do you think I brought you to the most public place in Edilean?"

"I have no idea."

"By now at least three women have called someone in my family to say that you should be hired."

"Why would they do that? They don't know me from the other applicants."

"Ha! By now they not only know your name but probably your Social Security number."

Gemma laughed. "This town couldn't be worse than a college campus. We know who's researching what before the first book is opened."

He was standing by the front door and looking out. To the left, under the deep roof overhang, were several little tables, and they were full of young mothers with their children. One of them was the woman whose baby both Colin and Gemma had held. "That sounds like a scary place," he mumbled.

"And you look scared."

"Terrified. They know I can change diapers." Obviously, he wasn't talking about the academic life.

"Give me your car keys."

He looked at her. "What?"

"Give me your keys and I'll drive to the back and pick you up."

"My Jeep is a standard shift."

"Gee whiz. With a clutch and everything? However will I manage?" She batted her lashes at him in mock helplessness.

Colin gave her a one-sided grin and handed her his keys. "See you in a minute."

Gemma gave a nod, then sauntered out the front

door. She could feel the eyes of the mothers on her, but she didn't turn to look at them. When she reached Colin's car, she quickly got inside and started it. The man her mother had hired to teach her to drive had insisted that she learn on a standard shift, and now she was glad of it.

The moment she put the Jeep in reverse, she knew that something had been done to the engine to escalate its power. Colin might say that he wasn't involved with his family's car dealerships, but he owned a vehicle that was far from being standard issue.

Gemma had a moment of panic when she put the gearshift in first, let up on the clutch, and the car leaped ahead as though it were a cheetah taking off after prey. When she went around the corner of the grocery, even as slow as she was going, she was sure she was on only two wheels. She barely had the car under control when she saw Colin outside waiting for her. He was talking to two young men who were wearing aprons and unloading a pickup truck. She managed to bring the Jeep to a smooth stop, put it in park, then she slid to the passenger seat.

Colin got in beside her and put the food and drinks in the back. "Have any problems?"

"None at all," she said, then they looked at each other and laughed.

"Does this thing take jet fuel?" she asked.

"See that red button?" He pointed to the cigarette lighter. "That makes the wheels retract and I start flying."

"I can believe that. The brave sheriff jetting away to escape dirty diapers."

Chuckling, he drove out of the parking lot and turned a corner that took them back to the square. "If we sit anywhere in this town to eat, it'll be like it was at the grocery. In Edilean, I'm a fairly public person."

"I feel a 'but' coming on," she said.

"I have a secret. Like to see it?"

"Sure," she said, but there was caution in her voice. She didn't know him well enough to predict what kind of secrets he had.

"Last week I closed on a house, and no one in town knows I bought it, not even my family."

Gemma let out the breath she didn't know she'd been holding. "An old house?" There was hope in her voice.

"No, sorry. New by Edilean standards. Built about 1946 or 7, and fairly recently completely remodeled."

"Oh." Her voice showed her disappointment.

"It looks a bit like a Frank Lloyd Wright."

"Oh." Gemma perked up.

"My cousin Luke rebuilt the house. He lived there for a while, but then he married the woman who owns Edilean Manor, so he moved in with her. He and I worked out a deal in private, and now the house is mine."

"Edilean Manor," Gemma said, her eyes wide. "I saw photos of it on the Web site. Is it as good as it looks?"

"Better. I'll make sure you see it."

"Before I leave," Gemma said and frowned. In just a few hours the job had come to mean more than just the Frazier documents. She'd met people and was becoming involved in their problems. And maybe she and Colin were becoming friends. Or maybe more than friends. She was quite attracted to him, both physically and as a person. And she liked that he was so well respected by the people in town. Even the children liked him.

"*If* you leave," Colin corrected as he pulled into the driveway of a very pretty house.

To hide her smile at his tone, Gemma leaned forward to get a look at the house. It did indeed look a bit like a Frank Lloyd Wright design, with its deep overhanging roof and built-in flower boxes. The trim around the windows and door was of rich wood that glowed with warmth.

Colin pushed a remote attached to his sun visor, and the garage door opened. There was nothing inside, not so much as a garden hose. As the big door rolled shut behind them, he reached to the back and got the food. "Want to see the house?"

"Love to," she said as she got out and followed him.

There was a covered breezeway leading from the garage to the side door. It was made of wood of three colors, all of it sealed to preserve the natural shades.

Gemma ran her hand along the rail. "You say your cousin Luke did this? Or did he hire someone to do it?"

"He's the woodworker." Colin used his key to open the back door and they entered the kitchen. It was beautiful, with new cabinets painted pale yellow, and granite countertops of a deep gold. All the appliances were stainless steel.

The kitchen opened into a dining room that had more of the beautifully finished windows that looked out to the front.

"Wow!" Gemma said, and Colin smiled at her.

The living room was to the right, partially walled off from the kitchen-dining area, One whole side was a stone fireplace flanked by shelves for books and a big TV. There was a large Oriental rug on the floor, but it was the only thing in the room. In fact, there was no furniture anywhere.

"Mind sitting on the floor?" Colin asked.

"My favorite place."

"But only if you have a dozen books open around you and a notebook in your hand. And how many colors of pens do you use?"

"Seven—which is one fewer than Kirk says he uses. I'll have to ask him what number eight is."

They spread the food out on the paper wrappers on the carpet and began to eat.

"This is delicious," Gemma said.

"If Ellie makes it, you can bet it is."

Gemma looked around the beautiful room. There were glass doors along the back and they opened into a courtyard that had a garden beyond.

She looked back at him and again thought how

much she loved the look of him. In the last couple of years she'd spent so much time with athletes that she'd become attracted to larger men. Besides the boys that she'd tutored there'd been the coaches. One of the assistants and she had dated for months. But she'd broken it off when his lack of interest about anything but sports got to her.

She could feel that indescribable "something" that made her think that Colin was also attracted to her. However, she was very aware that he'd maneuvered the conversation so Gemma had admitted she didn't have a boyfriend, but Colin had said nothing about his own love life. If it hadn't been for her adviser telling her all three sons were unmarried, she wouldn't even know that. "How does your girlfriend like this house?"

"I told you that no one has seen it."

Which was a perfect nonanswer, Gemma thought, and she was damned if she was going to work to find out more about his personal life. "I like the house very much," she said at last. "You should be very happy here."

Colin moved to lean back against the wall, and took his time before speaking, as though he were contemplating what to say. "In the last year and a half three of my friends . . . well, actually four, got married, and it's made me think about my own future." He looked at her and smiled warmly. "I'm sure that's more than you wanted to know about me."

She wanted to say that she'd like to hear a lot more, but it was too soon for that.

They were quiet for a while, then Gemma asked him about his brothers.

"Real pests," he said, but there was so much love in his voice that it was almost embarrassing. He talked while they ate, telling her about his family, and she saw how close they were to one another.

He told her of his brothers Lanny and Pere, who worked in the family car business. He talked of how the development of Shamus's artistic abilities was of major concern to their family as they wanted the best possible art schooling for him. "Our mother interviews universities as though she's a general planning a battle. So far, none of them are good enough for her precious baby."

Lastly, he spoke of his sister, Ariel, who would soon be returning to Edilean to work as a doctor. Colin's chest seemed to swell in pride.

"I envy you," she said when he finished.

"What about your family?"

"I have a mother and a sister and they're exactly alike. They laugh over the same things, call each other every day. They're a pair."

"How do you fit in with them?"

"I don't," she said. "My father and I were best buddies, and after he died when I was twelve, I . . ." She shrugged. "Unhappy memories. The good news is that my sister married a rich man—he has his own plumbing company—and she sends me truly lovely gifts. All I have to do to repay her is babysit for whole weeks at a time."

Colin laughed. "So what kind of gifts does she send you?"

"A Kindle, some sports equipment, top-of-the-line laptop, and my BlackBerry. She said if I got this job she'd send me an iPad."

"It sounds like she cares about you," Colin said.

"It's mutual, but we aren't chummy. She has two children and wants a third. She and Mom are worried that I'll never get married."

"Whatever you do, don't let her talk to *my* mother. My poor sister got so tired of my mother's constant talk of having babies that last year Ariel swore she'd have her tubes tied."

"A drastic threat."

"My sister is the epitome of a 'drama queen.'"

"So who is your 'favorite little man' and isn't Merlin's Farm the place where those paintings were found last year?"

Colin's quick laugh nearly made him choke on his sandwich. "You really *listen,* don't you?"

"I read about the farm on the town Web site, and I like to find out things. Is it?"

"Yes," he said. "As you seem to know already, Merlin's Farm—"

"Built in 1674, wasn't it?"

Colin shook his head at her in wonder. "I have

a feeling you could tell me who the English king was then and what was going on in the world."

She could, but she wasn't interested in what she already knew. "The paintings caused a stir in the historical world, so of course I heard about them. They belong to the owner of Merlin's Farm . . . I don't remember her name."

"Sara Shaw, my cousin. She married the detective who found the paintings. They were hidden away in a secret room in the old house. You'll have to see it. The way the room was built behind the fireplace was really ingenious."

Gemma's eyes lit up, but she said nothing, just willing him to tell her more.

"Anyway," Colin continued, "Mike and Sara still live in Fort Lauderdale. They'll stay there until his retirement in a couple of years, then they'll move back here permanently."

"The paintings . . . ?" she prompted.

"Oh yeah. They were done in the 1700s by an ancestor of ours—"

"Charles Albert Yates," Gemma said.

"I'm sure you're right," Colin said. "Joce—the woman who owns Edilean Manor—thinks they were painted by a woman. She—"

"Wow!" Gemma said, her eyes wide. "A *woman* went down the San Juan River in 1799 and made paintings of the flora and fauna? What an extraordinary find!"

Colin laughed, but he was impressed with her memory and her knowledge. "You and Joce and Sara *have* to get to know one another." He finished his sandwich while looking at her, and he could see that she was thinking about the paintings and how a woman may have made them. He wasn't going to say so but he was *very* pleased that she'd not asked about the value of the paintings. The discovery of them had made international news and been reported by the BBC and in Paris. For a while the town had been inundated with tourists asking questions. With just a few exceptions, the *only* thing people had asked about was the money. How much were the paintings worth? Colin had grown so tired of the questions that he'd mumble, "Millions," then leave and let his deputy, Roy, handle them.

But Gemma didn't seem in the least interested in the financial side of the find—and he liked that very much.

She finished her sandwich. "And Sara is Ellie's daughter? And your 'favorite little man' who helped her?"

"You're going to be great at the research!" Colin said. "Yes, Sara is Ellie's daughter, and Mr. Lang is the caretaker of Merlin's Farm. He's in his mid-eighties now and we look out for him. When Mike and Sara are here, he moves into a house they remodeled for him." Colin wasn't going to go into telling Gemma about Mr. Lang's endless complaints about the tourists and having to live outside the old house, which he thought of as his.

Gemma wanted to ask what Ellie had meant about "club ladies" being after the old man, but she thought she'd asked enough questions.

She stood up. "Mind if I wander around the rest of the house and have a look?"

"Be my guest." He was very pleased that she liked the place so much.

She went down the hall and peeked into the three bedrooms and two baths. The master suite opened into the garden. She unlocked the door and stepped outside. She didn't know much about plants, but she'd put money on it that the trees weren't the usual ones you could purchase at the local shop. No, this place looked like a miniature botanical garden, like a place a person would pay to see.

As Gemma thought of all she'd seen of the town, of this man, his family and now of his house, she couldn't help a feeling of longing. Since her father had died, she hadn't felt she was truly at home anywhere. To belong somewhere and to someone was Gemma's deepest desire.

What would it be like to grow up in a town where people knew your name? she wondered. More than that, knew you as a person? In the grocery those people had known Colin well enough to drop a baby into his arms. Even the children knew that if Colin was handed a broken toy he would fix it. She heard his footsteps in the hallway.

"Are you okay?" he asked from behind her. "Nothing's wrong, is it?"

He had noticed the sad look in her eyes, and she quickly changed it. "No. Just the opposite. I was admiring the view. Your garden looks larger than the usual backyard."

"It's a couple of acres."

"Your cousin Luke couldn't have done the garden too?"

"Yes he did. And he's also Luke Adams."

Gemma's face looked blank.

"Luke Adams? Writes novels?" Colin asked.

"Sorry. I never read fiction. No time."

He grinned. "That makes for a change. Usually when Luke's pen name is mentioned, people nearly swoon."

"Swoon, do they?" she asked, smiling. "I think you've been reading the documents your mother bought."

"Actually, I did try to look at some of them. But then my phone would ring and I'd have to leave. Or sometimes I fell asleep. It's difficult for me to imagine someone wanting a job like the one you want. On the days I have to stay in the office, I get antsy." He pulled his buzzing cell phone out of his pocket and looked at it. "It's a text from Mom and she says Jean is there. I think we better go."

"Certainly!" Gemma said. "I can't afford to offend your mother again."

"I don't think you ever have."

"I wish I were as sure." When she got to the kitchen door, she turned to look at him. "I've had a lovely time today. I enjoyed meeting the people and especially seeing your house. Thank you."

"You're welcome," he said. "Want to drive back?"

"About as much as I want to jump onto the top of a speeding train."

"Come on, then," he said, "let's go and see if Kirk has made off with my mother's jewelry."

"Or if Isla has eloped with your brother."

"Shamus would never allow that."

Laughing, they left the house together.

3

GEMMA STRETCHED OUT on the bed in Colin's childhood room and looked around her. It was still the habitat of a teenage boy, but instead of posters of football players or other athletes, he'd hung pictures of men Gemma didn't recognize. But she had an idea they were law enforcement agents, real ones, not actors who played them on TV. Considering what she was seeing, she wondered why he hadn't become an FBI agent or joined the CIA. But then, she'd already seen the answer. He loved the little town of Edilean and the people in it.

After they'd left his newly purchased house, he'd driven them straight back to his family's home. Hours earlier, when Gemma arrived, Mrs. Frazier had greeted her at the front door and immediately led her back to the guesthouse and shown her the documents. Gemma hadn't been given time to get her suitcase out of the car, so she had no idea where she was staying in the big Frazier house.

Colin told her that he'd asked his mother to put her in his old room. "There's an outside staircase, so you can come and go as you please," he said. "And it's on the third floor, so you'll have privacy."

"Your own private stairs? You sound like you were a very busy young man," she said, teasing.

He didn't seem to see her words as a joke. "I was called out so often in the middle of the night that when I was in the tenth grade, my father had the stairs put up so I wouldn't wake the family."

She didn't understand what he meant. "You weren't acting as sheriff when you were in high school, were you?"

"No, but I tend to volunteer for things. And, besides, I've always been . . ." He hesitated.

"As big as a bulldozer?"

"More or less," he said, grinning. "When I was fourteen, I used to go out with the firefighters and hold the hose."

"Isn't that illegal for someone that young?"

"Yeah, but after I slipped out a window six times and ran into a burning building three times, everyone gave up trying to make me stay home. I think they gave me the hose to hold just to anchor me in place."

"I guess that makes sense. So your family put you on the top floor and built a staircase just for you?"

"That they did."

As they pulled into the driveway, he told her that Lanny had already carried her suitcase up and she could rest for a while. "Jean is cooking dinner tonight."

"Is she a friend of yours?"

"Of our whole family. She's a lawyer who works in Richmond and she likes to cook special meals."

"I look forward to meeting her."

Minutes later, he stopped at the bottom of a tall staircase that went up the entire side of the house. She could tell that he meant to escort her up, but she didn't want him to. She liked him so much, was so very attracted to him, and she didn't want to do anything embarrassing. Besides, it was better to keep a distance from the son of someone she hoped would employ her. "I can find my own way around," she said.

"I'll just show you—"

"No, really. I'd like some time to go over my notes."

"All right," he said, but he sounded disappointed. "Come down about six. We'll have drinks, then dinner."

"Sure," she said as she started up the stairs, but he kept standing there. She realized he was waiting to see her safely up the stairs. Only when she got to the door did he turn and walk away.

Now, as Gemma lay on the bed and looked about the room, she thought about what she'd seen and heard that day. It had been a lot. First there were the untouched documents that had made her want to murder someone just to ensure that she got the job. Then Colin had come to the guesthouse and she'd been with him ever since.

How different his life had been from hers, she thought. He'd always lived in one place. He'd probably gone to elementary school with people who were his friends now. And then there were his many relatives.

As for Gemma, since she'd entered the university seven years before, her life had been transient. It wasn't so because she moved, but at the school everyone around her had come and gone. Over the years, she'd had four close women friends. Each one had declared she was going for her Ph.D., but one by one, her friends had found men, married, then dropped out. Now all four of the women had children—and their correspondence had dwindled to an e-mail every three or four months.

As for the few men in Gemma's life, they too had moved away. One of them had begged her to go with him. But she'd told him she was determined to stay where she was, that she had a plan for her life and wasn't going to deviate from it. The truth was, she hadn't been in love with him and didn't want to go.

From the beginning, her goals had never changed. After she was awarded her doctorate, and after she had a job at a good school, she planned to start looking about for a permanent life, which meant a husband, a home, and a family of her own.

Married to a man like Colin, she thought. Her

first impression of him was that he was a cross between the Incredible Hulk and one of those cowboys from a black-and-white TV show from the 1960s. Women were dumping babies on him one moment and asking for his protection in the next. If the women hadn't been talking to him about serious matters, she would have thought he was the town babysitter—and ancient.

But he was far from old. He was young and good-looking and . . . her potential employer's son, Gemma reminded herself.

She got off the bed and wandered about the room, looking at Colin's possessions. There was a large trophy on the floor in the corner. OFFENSIVE LINEBACKER, CENTER it read. On the closet door were stapled some ribbons for other sports: swimming, hockey, even one for show jumping a horse.

Must have been a Frisian, she thought as she envisioned the medieval knights riding into battle on their huge, heavy horses. The historian in her knew that Colin would look good in armor.

On top of his chest of drawers was an open box, the kind that expensive jewelry came in. Inside, instead of something intrinsically valuable, was a cheap little metal star with the word SHERIFF across it. From the look of it, it had been played with and carried about for years. The edges were worn down to a smooth dullness.

The toy badge conjured images of a young Colin, probably big even as a toddler, as he proudly wore a sheriff's badge. Smiling, Gemma ran her hand around the star, then glanced at the clock. If she didn't want to be late, she'd better get showered and dressed for dinner.

Thirty minutes later, Gemma looked in the mirror and knew she'd done the best she could. She'd put on light makeup and dark trousers with a teal blue silk shirt. Her shoes were sensible heels and well worn, but polished. She reminded herself that she was trying for a job, not to become a member of the family.

She had her hand on the doorknob, ready to go into the inside of a house that she'd not seen, but she chickened out. Instead, she ran to the side door, stepped onto the little porch, and ran down the stairs to the ground. Now what? she wondered. Should she go to the front door and ring the bell?

"Oh, crap!" she heard a woman say. A few feet away was a screen door, and when Gemma looked inside she saw a large, modern kitchen. Standing in the center of it was a tall, beautiful woman, her lustrous dark hair pulled back into a soft chignon. She had on black silk trousers and an emerald green top that clung to her rather remarkable bosom. This wasn't what Gemma had imagined when Colin had said the woman coming to cook was a friend of "the whole family." If she was someone's girlfriend, Gemma certainly hoped she wasn't Colin's.

With a jolt, Gemma realized that for all of the woman's elegance and beauty, she was leaning over the island, holding her left hand up, and blood was trickling down her arm. She wasn't moving, just staring at the blood with glassy eyes.

Gemma threw back the door, ran inside, grabbed the woman's wrist, and pulled her to the sink. She turned on the cold water and pushed the woman's hand under it.

"Where's the first aid kit?" Gemma asked, but the woman didn't say anything. Gemma grabbed a dishtowel on the countertop and wrapped it around the cut finger. She turned off the water, then led the woman to sit down on a tall wooden stool, and went in search of bandages. She found a big box of first aid supplies in a white metal box hanging on the wall in the walk-in pantry.

With the box in hand, Gemma hurried back to the woman, who hadn't moved so much as an eyelid since she'd left her. Gemma was regretting having left her cell phone upstairs. If she had to call an ambulance, she'd need it. But then, she reminded herself that Colin was probably nearby, and he'd know what to do.

Gently, Gemma removed the cloth from the woman's hand. She needed to see how bad the injury was before she called for help. When she saw that the cut was shallow and not very big at all, she looked at the woman in disbelief, but she was still sitting in stony silence, her beautiful face drained of color.

Carefully, Gemma bandaged her finger. "I think you'll be okay now."

The woman said nothing.

"I'm Gemma. I'm one of the applicants for the job and—"

"The rolls!" the woman said as she jumped up, ran to the big stove, and threw open the oven door. She started to reach for the hot metal sheet, but since she was keeping her injured hand elevated and the other one was bare, she couldn't get them out.

"I'll do it," Gemma said as she picked up pot holders and removed the tray of bread.

"I'm a real wimp," the woman said as she sat back down on the stool. "When it comes to blood, especially my own, I'm a coward. I'm Jean Caldwell, and thanks a lot for this. If you hadn't come by I probably would have fainted, then dinner would have been ruined. That would have meant the Fraziers would have to order in pizza—which the men would have loved." Jean sighed. "Maybe you shouldn't have saved me."

Gemma smiled, but Jean's face was still too white. "Why don't you stay seated and let me help with this?" The top of the stove had a bubbling pot on each of the six burners.

"You can cook?"

"Not at all, but I'm excellent at following directions. It's what I've been doing since I was five."

"Oh, right, school. I remember thinking that I couldn't wait to get away from the professors and be free. Little did I know that bosses make teachers look like angels."

"I take it you've never had Dr. Fredrickson."

Jean smiled. "Colin said you were funny."

"Did he?" Gemma said and couldn't help feeling good at the compliment. His girlfriend wouldn't make such a remark, would she? "Do I need to do anything to any of this?"

"Turn off that left back burner, and stir that orange pot. Good. I hear Colin took you with him when he played hooky this afternoon."

Gemma didn't turn around. There was something so possessive in the way Jean said his name that Gemma's heart began to sink. "He . . ." she said tentatively.

"I don't blame either of you," Jean said. "I've met Isla and Kirk. She came in here and started giving me cooking instructions. I got rid of her by asking her to chop onions. Then that prissy little Kirk came in and stuck a spoon in my osso bucco. He said it needed more salt. Colin took him away before I slammed his face in the pot. Would you like some wine?"

Gemma worked to keep any expression off her face, but the euphoria she'd felt all day was leaving her.

Jean refilled her own glass from a bottle of red wine that was sitting open on the stone countertop. "I need this if I'm going to face those two at dinner." She pointed to a cabinet and Gemma opened it to see wineglasses. "Sorry to be such an invalid, but I've been in court all day. My feet are killing me. Then I had to drive the nearly seventy miles from Richmond, and when I got here I was introduced to that Isla. She seemed to think she and I were destined to be best friends."

Gemma nodded, glad Jean was speaking of something besides Colin. "I'm sure Isla believes she's won. She doesn't consider me a worthy opponent, so she doesn't bother with me, either here or at school."

"I can't see her in that mess Alea bought, so what is she really after?"

"I think she wants Lanny, but Colin says she's after Shamus." Gemma watched to see if Jean would show any emotion at Gemma's mention of Colin's name, but she didn't. Either they weren't a couple or Jean was *very* secure.

Jean laughed. "That sounds like something Colin would say. The other brother, Pere, isn't here. He's the pretty one. Isla would probably do a lap dance for him. Would you turn down the heat under that big skillet? Colin doesn't like his beef overcooked. Thanks."

"The problem . . ." Gemma said as she slowly sipped her wine. She was trying to adjust to what she was beginning to see as a fact: Colin and Jean were a couple. "Is that Mrs. Frazier likes Isla."

"I wouldn't be so sure of that." Jean lowered her voice. "You can never guess what the Fraziers are thinking."

"Even Colin?"

"He's the worst! The stories I could tell you!" Jean said. "He knows a lot of people, and he listens to them, takes care of them. But even people who consider Colin their best friend don't know what *his* problems are. He keeps them to himself."

"I'll have to remember that," Gemma said and

thought how he'd evaded her more personal questions. She was trying to recover from finding out that Colin was taken.

"Don't worry about it. All the Fraziers keep their secrets. Would you put those rolls in that basket and cover them? Thanks. You're a good sous chef. So where was I?"

"The clandestine nature of the Fraziers."

"Clandestine. What a perfect word to describe them. Anyway, the point is that just because Alea puts up with Isla's and Kirk's endless gushing doesn't mean she's going to give the job to one of them. I know Colin's already told her he thinks she should hire you, and I'm certainly going to vote for you."

It looked like Jean was considered a member of the family. "Shouldn't you get to know me a little first?"

Jean held up her hand with the bandaged finger. "I always vote for people who save my life."

"It was hardly that. Although there was a lot of blood and the body doesn't hold all that much. Who knows what could have happened?"

"I agree," Jean said as she raised her glass in a toast. "I think you and I are going to get along quite well. Although I wish you weren't quite so pretty."

"No one's ever said that to me before."

"Honey, with some highlights, a good cut and some decent eye makeup—" She broke off, looking at Gemma in speculation.

"What?"

"I was just thinking of someone in town who'd

be perfect for you, that's all." She got off the stool and went to the stove. She was half a foot taller than Gemma, and with her high heels she looked like she'd just stepped off a Paris runway. "You wouldn't mind grating some cheese for me, would you? I figure I have about ten minutes before a Frazier starts demanding food. They eat enormous quantities of it, preferably all beef. I told Colin—"

"What did you tell me?"

The two women turned to look at him. He'd showered and changed into black slacks and a white shirt that wasn't as snug as his other one had been. He looked very good, and Gemma couldn't suppress the flutter that came to her heart and body. She had a vision of standing on tiptoe and slipping her arms around his neck. She could imagine how good his body would feel against hers.

"I can't persuade you into a tie?" Jean said, going to him and putting her arms around his neck. She aimed to kiss his lips, but he turned his head away so her kiss fell onto his cheek.

Gemma turned away. Damn, damn, double damn! she thought. She was as bad as Isla in looking at a Frazier with wedding bells in her eyes.

"Is Gemma helping you cook or are you two hiding out in here?" Colin asked.

"Hiding," Gemma and Jean said in unison.

"Your mother couldn't possibly be thinking of hiring one of those two," Jean said as Colin moved away from her and went to the stove.

"I hope not. What is all this?" he asked when he was standing beside Gemma.

"I have no idea, but it smells divine," she said and took a step away from him. He smelled too good for her to be close to him.

"It does." He picked up a lid. "Got a spoon?"

"Here," Jean said from his other side as she handed him one.

"There you are!" Mrs. Frazier said from behind them. "Jean, dear, give me a glass of that wine. Better yet, Colin, pour me a shot of tequila."

Gemma stayed by the stove and watched as Colin and Jean hurried to do her bidding. She couldn't help thinking that they were a beautiful couple, her so tall and lovely, him so strong and masculine.

Mrs. Frazier dropped down onto the stool, threw back the shot Colin handed her, then chased it with half a glass of wine. "Now I feel better."

"What has set you off into binge drinking?" Colin asked, an eyebrow raised.

"I hardly think that this small amount constitutes a binge. In fact—" Mrs. Frazier broke off as she drained the rest of the wine and held out her glass for more.

"Where is everyone?" Mr. Frazier asked as he came into the kitchen. "Alea, are you getting drunk? Without *me*? Colin! Alcohol quick!"

He grabbed another glass and poured his father a shot. After the second one, Mr. Frazier put the glass down and collapsed onto a stool next to his wife.

"Alea, so help me, if you hire one of those two people I'll divorce you."

"If I were stupid enough to employ one of them, I'd let you," she said.

Gemma, standing apart from the others, drew in her breath.

"Then Gemma gets the job?" Colin asked. He was standing beside Jean, the tequila bottle in his hand.

"Of course." Mrs. Frazier looked around her son to Gemma. "I never had any doubt. When you saw those old documents I thought you were going to have an orgasm."

"Mother!" Colin said, while Jean laughed.

Mrs. Frazier kept her eyes on Gemma. "You can't imagine how much ridicule I've had to endure from my own family merely because I want to find out about our history. But right away I saw that you felt the same way I do. And Colin adores you!"

"Mother, I don't think—" Colin began.

"Tristan," Jean said loudly, and they all looked at her. "I was thinking that Gemma and Dr. Tris would make a wonderful couple."

"Good," Mr. Frazier said. "That boy needs a family."

Gemma stepped forward to put her hands on the cool countertop; she needed something to hold on to or her knees were going to give way. She had the job. She really and truly had the job. For the next two years—or more—she'd be living in the pretty little guesthouse and finding out the secrets buried in those old documents. And she was being set up for a date with a local.

Right now, her future looked so good she thought she might investigate employment at William and Mary College. Maybe she could get a teaching position there and stay in Edilean forever.

They were all looking at her expectantly, but she didn't want to tell them her thoughts. "What's this Tristan's doctorate in?" Gemma asked.

"Medicine," Jean answered. "If you'd let me keep bleeding, he'd be here now."

When the mention of Jean's injury made people start asking questions, Gemma stepped to the back. The four of them were gathered around the island, listening intently to Jean's story of how she'd cut herself, and how Gemma had come to her rescue. The screen door was nearby, so Gemma slipped outside.

She stopped near a tall bush that was covered with pink flowers and took a few deep breaths. This is it, she thought. This lovely place would be the site of her first full-time job.

"Overwhelmed?" Colin asked from behind her.

"No," Gemma said. "Not at all."

"My family isn't scaring you off?"

"Just the opposite. But . . ."

"But what?"

"All of you, Jean included, seem very close to each other. I promise I'll not intrude on you."

"You're no intrusion. Mother will want you at the house every night for dinner and—"

"Absolutely not!" Gemma said firmly. "I'm here to do a job, and that's what I'll do."

Colin gave her a teasing smile that she'd seen before. "The truth is that you want to read while you eat, don't you?"

"Oh yeah."

"All right. I'll tell Mother she can't adopt you. With our sister in California now, Mom doesn't have a girl to lavish gifts on. But don't be surprised if new shoes show up now and then."

"Jean says I need a hairdresser." She hoped that mentioning her would make Colin say something about their relationship, such as saying there wasn't one.

Colin frowned. "Jean sometimes oversteps herself. I think your hair is fine. We better go in. The other two will leave in the morning."

"I hope no one tells them they're not getting the job until after we eat. It won't be a pleasant dinner with Isla and Kirk being miserable, and Jean has done a lot of work."

"Compassion for your enemies," Colin said as he held open the screen door and Gemma slipped under his arm to go back into the kitchen. "I like that."

"Sorry, but it's actually self-protection. When you do tell them, I want to be locked inside your room at the top of the house."

"Hidden away with my old sheriff's badge?"

"Exactly. Is that what started you on your lifelong pursuit of being a sheriff?"

He smiled. "Mom loves to tell the story of how I wore that badge continuously from the time I got it for my second birthday until I was eight. She likes to elaborate on how she used to have to tape it on me while I was in the tub with my brothers. Someday when you two are alone, ask her about it."

"I will," Gemma said, and a little thrill ran through her at the thought that she was going to be there and could ask questions. "*That's* what you wanted. You said there was something you'd wanted as much as I wanted this job. You wanted to be the sheriff of Edilean."

His smile was so warm that she took a step toward him. "Yes," he said softly. "You're exactly right."

Neither of them saw that across the room, Jean was frowning at them.

4

GEMMA LAY IN bed, staring at the ceiling of Colin's room, and wondered if it was safe yet to go downstairs. Last night's dinner had been awkward, and at times truly unpleasant. She'd said very little, only complimenting Jean on her food, but otherwise remaining silent. She was afraid that if she spoke she'd somehow reveal that she'd been hired for the job.

She sat beside Colin, Jean on his other side, and across from them were Kirk and Isla, with Lanny in the middle. Mr. and Mrs. Frazier took the ends. Young Shamus had, somehow, managed to escape the ordeal.

Isla dominated the conversation as she told amusing stories of what went on at the university. She and Kirk had received their masters from other schools, so they hadn't been there nearly as long as Gemma.

Isla was a good storyteller, and everyone laughed at her portrayals of professors and students. It was only when she started on Gemma that things got embarrassing.

"Gemma is our resident student," Isla said. "She's been there longer than a lot of the professors."

"We call her Mother Goose," Kirk chimed in.

"Yes," Isla said as she took a bite. "Gemma is nearly always followed by a gaggle of football players. They trail after her all across campus."

"You should hear her!" Kirk said as he went into a falsetto. " 'Who is Mussolini and what is a fascist?' 'Who wrote the Declaration of Independence and if I hear "John Hancock" even as a joke that person will be benched.' 'Why was it impossible for the South to win the War Between the States? Remember what Rhett said?' "

Gemma was glad when no one but Isla laughed at his impersonation.

"What you did sounds quite laudable," Mrs. Frazier said to Gemma as she cut Kirk an icy look.

When he didn't seem to mind, Gemma guessed that he'd figured out that he wasn't going to get the job. But it looked as though he thought Isla had won.

As for Isla, all evening she could hardly take her eyes off Lanny. They kept exchanging quick looks, and twice Isla gave what could be called a giggle.

Both times, Gemma and Jean looked at each other across Colin. The second time, he said, "Am I in your way? Would you two like to be together?"

"No," Jean said, "I like the view." She gave Colin

a look that let him know that *he* was the view she liked.

Any doubts Gemma'd had about their being a couple were banished in that one look. Gemma kept her head down so no one could see her expression. She had the job, so she had no right to feel that she'd lost everything. But she did. It wasn't easy to wait out what seemed to be an interminable meal. By the time they got to dessert, she was ready to run from the room. Part of her wanted to tell Isla that she wasn't going to get the job, so she should stop making a fool of herself.

When the meal was finally over, Gemma was going to help clean up, but Mrs. Frazier dismissed the housekeeper and asked Isla and Kirk to "help." She then left them with the entire job.

Gemma knew that when Isla and Kirk finished the cleanup, they were going to be in a foul mood. She didn't want to be there. When she saw Shamus, an art kit under his arm, walk past the living room, she gave quick good nights to everyone and ran after him. He led her upstairs to Colin's room and left her there. She was glad to escape the tension downstairs, but she was far from sleepy. When she was finally alone, she began to think about what it meant that she was going to work there. She hadn't realized how much she'd been worrying about getting her dissertation done until the problem was solved.

She'd be living there two whole years, she thought as she undressed and put on her pajamas. And the more she learned about the job, the town, and the family, the happier she was with it all. The good time she'd had with Colin was just that. He'd be her friend, and that was going to have to be enough.

When she thought that tomorrow night she might be sleeping in the guesthouse, surrounded by all those original sources, she began to dance about the room. She'd have to fly home and pack up her belongings, then drive back to Virginia. All that would take at least a week, but as soon as it was done, she'd be able to start work.

She made herself stop twirling around and get into bed, but she couldn't sleep, so she got her beloved Kindle out of her suitcase and looked up Luke Adams. Maybe if she read a little fiction, it would put her to sleep. She found his first book, pushed the BUY button, and the novel appeared on her screen about thirty seconds later. She started reading—and didn't turn off the light until 3 A.M.

It was morning now, late for her, as she was usually at the gym by six or six-thirty every morning. She knew she should go downstairs, but if Isla and Kirk were still there and they'd been told they'd lost out to Gemma, they wouldn't be gracious about losing.

"Gemma Ranford," she said out loud, "you're a coward."

As she started to get out of bed, she glanced at her Kindle, with its black-and-white photo of Emily Dickinson, and she was tempted to slide the button and go back to reading. That this man, Luke Adams, wrote novels set in the eighteenth century fascinated her, and she really wanted to meet him.

She dressed quickly, then went down the outside stairs and into the kitchen. The housekeeper, Rachel, whom she'd met the day before, was there, but she wasn't wearing a uniform. She had on jeans and a T-shirt and she was young and pretty, with dark hair and eyes. She didn't look like anyone's idea of a housekeeper.

"The winner!" Rachel said as soon as she saw Gemma in the doorway.

"That I am," Gemma said as she sat down at the island. "Who's up?"

"Scared of Isla's wicked mouth, are you?" Rachel asked as she pulled a tray full of biscuits out of the oven.

"Terrified."

"You can rest easy because Mrs. F ran them both out this morning. It wasn't a pretty scene."

"Really?" Gemma's eyes were wide.

Rachel lowered her voice. "Seems Isla and Lanny did the naughty last night."

Gemma laughed. "I could see that Mrs. Frazier wouldn't like that."

"Lanny is a flirt. Did he come on to you?"

"Not at all."

"Oh, that's right. Mrs. F put you under Colin's protection, didn't she? About the only thing that makes Lanny back off is whenever his big brother lays claim to something."

"It was hardly that," Gemma said, but she was pleased to hear it. "Colin and I went into town for lunch because I was late. Could I have one of those biscuits?"

"Nope. I was told that if you came in here I was to send you into the dining room to eat with what's left of the Frazier family. Lanny's been sent back to Richmond in disgrace." Rachel grinned. "It'll probably be three or four whole days before his mother forgives him. And Shamus is with his school buddies."

"What about Colin and Jean?"

"Colin's at work, and she's gone. Jean just shows up, does something marvelous, jumps on Colin, then goes away to be a lawyer."

Gemma hid her disappointment at hearing that what she'd suspected was true, then she looked at Rachel in surprise. "You sound like you don't like Jean."

Rachel put a slab of ham in a skillet. "She's great. She gave me a Prada bag last Christmas. I expect a pair of Manolos for my birthday. She's always kind and considerate and she makes me laugh. I have nothing to say against her."

"But . . . ?"

Rachel turned around to face Gemma. "Colin seems to think Jean's going to move to itty-bitty Edilean, pump out three kids, and they'll live happily ever after."

Gemma thought of the house Colin had bought and what he'd said about his friends starting families. It looked like Rachel was right. "Isn't it fashionable for women today to give up their careers and become stay-at-home moms?"

Rachel snorted. "You've met Jean. Do you think Edilean is exciting enough for her?"

Gemma hadn't seen much of the cute little town, but it was true that she couldn't see Jean in her heels and her fabulously expensive clothes walking about. "Maybe she could be mayor," she said.

"And deal with lost dogs? I don't think so." Rachel pulled a buzzing cell phone out of her pocket and looked at the screen. "It's Mr. F. He's sitting at the table but there's no food. To him, this is a great catastrophe."

"He texted you from the dining room?"

Rachel was smiling. "That's right. He bought me a BlackBerry and pays the bills just so he can tell me where he is and where I'm to take his food. You'll learn that the Fraziers aren't like the rest of the world." The phone vibrated again, and she looked at it. "He's reminding me that I'm supposed to send you in."

Gemma got off the stool. "Now that Isla and Kirk are gone, I'd love to have breakfast with Mr. and Mrs. Frazier." Pausing, she looked back at Rachel, her face serious. "Is there anything I should know about these people? I'm going to be here quite a while."

"They're nice. A bit spoiled by too much money, maybe, but they're good people. Stay away from Lanny—unless you want to become a notch on his bedpost, that is—and let Shamus draw you. And when Pere comes home, don't fall for him. His parents don't know it, but his heart is already spoken for."

Gemma ran her hand along the cool countertop. "What about Colin?" When Rachel didn't answer, she looked at her.

Rachel wasn't smiling but her eyes were dancing. "Colin is the best of the lot. But you need to know that he is fantastically loyal and . . ."

"And what?"

"Jean owns him. Remember Shrek fighting the dragon to get to Princess Fiona?"

"Yes."

"That dragon is a delicate little butterfly compared to Jean. Unless you plan to fight to the death, stay away from Colin."

"Thanks," Gemma said and started toward the door. "What about some doctor? Tristan, was it?"

Rachel waved her hand in dismissal. "Dr. Tris is not to be had. The impossible dream. The mountain never climbed. If you even get a date with him, consider yourself lucky, but if you set your heart on him, it'll be broken."

Gemma raised her eyebrows. "What an extraordinary town this seems to be," she murmured as she went into the dining room.

Mr. Frazier was sitting at the head of the table, reading a newspaper. " 'Bout time," he said without looking up. "I'm starving."

"Sorry but it's just me," Gemma said as she sat down beside him. "No food. But Rachel was frying a piece of ham the size of a small pond."

Mr. Frazier put down his newspaper and grinned at her. "That sounds right. After last night I need sustenance. Did Rachel fill you in on all the gossip?"

"I take it Isla won't be invited back."

Mr. Frazier chuckled. "My wife believes that our sons are being seduced by every woman they speak to. Although I must say that Lanny is the only one who consistently says yes. If he ever—"

Gemma knew what he was going to say and cut him off. "I spend most of my days with very healthy young men. I can handle myself."

"Good!" he said, then looked up to see Rachel entering with a tray full of food. "I lost ten pounds waiting for you."

"You could stand to lose twenty," Rachel said, unperturbed. "Where's Mrs. F?"

"On the phone. She has half a dozen friends to call to tell about the job and Gemma and the latest of what some girl did to Lanny."

Rachel shook her head. "Nothing ever changes. You want raspberry or peach jam? No. Wait. You want both."

"Why not? We have Gemma's arrival to celebrate."

"Any excuse," Rachel said as she went back to the kitchen.

As soon as they were alone, Gemma and Mr. Frazier began filling their plates.

"What kind of car do you want?" Mr. Frazier asked.

"A Duesenberg," she said quickly.

"That's a doozy of an idea." His eyes were laughing as he let her know he knew the origin of the word.

"Gemma," Mrs. Frazier said as she entered the room and sat down at the opposite end of the table. Leaves had been removed so it was shorter than it had been last night. "I warn you not to make car jokes in this family or they'll never stop, and you'll not be able to come up with a reference that will stump them."

"That's a challenge to a historian." She looked at Mr. Frazier. "What about Duryea?"

"Duryea Motor Wagon Company," Mr. Frazier said. "Founded by Charles and Frank Duryea. They built the 'Ladies Phaeton' in 1893, and won the *Chicago Times-Herald* race two years later. But, alas, the brothers fought. Bad ending."

"I can see that I'll lose this one," Gemma said.

"Did you know that Shamus Frazier, the one who came here from Scotland about 1770, made the wagons for George Washington's troops at Valley Forge?"

Gemma's eyes opened so wide they were circles. "Really?"

"It's been passed down in my family that the man was passionate about wagons. Today we'd probably say that he had an obsessive-compulsive disorder and send him to therapy. But back then he just built the best wagons anybody had ever seen."

"Good enough to help win a war against a big enemy," Gemma said. "A hero."

Mr. Frazier looked at her with almost love in his eyes.

"For heaven's sake, Grinny," Mrs. Frazier said, "let the girl eat. You two have years to talk about history." Her words sounded displeased but her eyes glistened with happiness. "Right now we need to discuss practical matters. Gemma has to move to Edilean, so we have to figure out how to get her things here."

"I could lend you a pickup truck and you could drive there and back," Mr. Frazier said. "But I guess it depends on how much stuff you need to bring back."

"I thought I'd fly out tomorrow morning," Gemma said, "and rent a car to drive back. I don't have much to bring here."

"Not even books?"

They looked up to see Colin standing in the doorway. He smiled at Gemma as he took a seat across from her and helped himself to scrambled eggs.

"I do have a few books," she said, smiling back at him. He looked rested and happy. "But not as many as you'd think."

"You must want to say good-bye to people," Mrs. Frazier said, and they all looked at Gemma. "Last night Isla seemed to imply that there were a lot of young men in your life."

"Only my students," Gemma said. "And . . . This is embarrassing, but they were so sure I'd get the job that they gave me a party when I left." She looked down in memory. Her athletic students had surprised her, and it had been a joyous event. They'd given her gag gifts of tiny boxing gloves and a T-shirt with the bottom half cut away. They'd often teased her because when she trained with them she always wore large, concealing clothes. After an hour of hilarity, one of the biggest of the young men had hoisted her onto his shoulder and carried her back to her apartment. The others had followed so that she'd been surrounded by over a ton of young, muscular male flesh. It had been an exhilarating experience.

"That settles it," Mrs. Frazier said, "we'll have everything sent here and Gemma won't have to leave."

"I'm not sure . . ." Gemma began.

Mr. Frazier was looking at his wife as though he were confused about something.

"I think it's the perfect solution," Mrs. Frazier said as she got up and went to the sideboard, opened a drawer, and withdrew a couple of keys on a ring. She handed them to Gemma. "These are to the guesthouse and the garage. If you'll give me all the pertinent information I'll arrange for movers to pack and ship all that you've left behind."

"I couldn't possibly impose like that," Gemma said.

Mr. Frazier leaned toward her. "I can attest that my wife is brilliant at having things packed and shipped. England must be empty after all that she had sent home."

Gemma was torn between not wanting to cause anyone extra work or expense, and wanting so very much to stay. She looked at the keys in her hand. They were on a ring for Frazier Motors and she held them so tightly they bit into her hand. "Okay," she said at last, "but if I'm going to stay here, I need to buy some toiletries, and—"

"Colin will take you," Mrs. Frazier said quickly. "Whatever you need, wherever you want to go, he'll take you there."

Mr. Frazier looked at his wife in speculation, then turned to his son. "Take her into Williamsburg and get her a car."

"And she'll need office supplies," Mrs. Frazier said.

"Colored pens, for sure," Colin said, his eyes teasing.

"Yes, now go," Mrs. Frazier said. "I have a lot to do today and you two will just be in my way."

Colin looked across the table to Gemma. "It looks like we're unwanted."

Gemma smiled. She would love to spend another day with him!

The minute Colin and Gemma were out of the room, Peregrine Frazier turned to his wife. "Alea," he said slowly, "what are you up to?" When she didn't immediately answer, he ran his hand over his face. "It seems like lately I'm asking you that every other day."

Alea still didn't reply, just sat there looking at him with an expression he couldn't read.

"I gave in to you on those old papers, and now I'm paying the salary and living expenses of a student. I know that we can well afford that, but you're up to something with our eldest son and I want to know what it is."

Alea gave a sigh. "You and I have been married for over thirty years, so you must know what I want most in the world."

"To get someone in England to declare you a lady?" he asked, his voice a symphony of frustration. He hated it when his wife did this to him. It was as though she was saying that if he truly loved her, he'd intuit what she was thinking.

"If you believe that's what I deeply and truly want most in life, then you know nothing about me."

Peregrine resisted the urge to look at his watch, but he knew from experience that doing so would cause a fight. He just wanted to go to work, finish a couple of contracts, then play golf with his friend, Dr. Henry Shaw. But at the same time, he wanted to know what his wife was truly after because, sometimes, her schemes caused problems. Even though, with the exception of wanting to make herself into a countess, her plots had all been for him or their children, they hadn't always done what she meant for them to.

In high school, when their daughter, Ariel, cried because she didn't have many friends, Alea became the sponsor of the cheerleaders—which included purchasing the uniforms—but only if Ariel was put on the team. That had worked out well. When Lanny, at sixteen, was so shy he wouldn't even go to a dance, Alea arranged for him to spend a summer in Paris studying ballet. He'd been the only heterosexual male in the class. That had not worked out so well.

"Alea," he said patiently, "I really don't know—"

He cut himself off because he remembered something she'd said years before. When Colin was about four, she'd said, "I think he'll give us smart, beautiful grandchildren." It had been such an odd thing to say, considering the child's age, that it had stuck with him.

"Grandchildren," he whispered. When Alea smiled warmly at him, he knew he'd answered correctly, but he still didn't understand. "Are you saying that you don't care about being a countess?"

"Of course not! That my own family thinks that I'm such a shallow person that I'd want that—" She couldn't seem to find words to describe how bad that had made her feel.

Peregrine leaned back in his chair. "How long have you been working on this . . . this plan? Whatever it is?"

"Ever since Eleanor Shaw's first grandchild was born," she said quickly. As energy surged through Alea, she stood up. "Every woman in this town has grandchildren."

He knew what she meant. Not *every* woman, but nearly every woman who had grown children and was a descendant of the seven founding families did have grandchildren.

"Ellie Shaw has three grandchildren and her youngest daughter, Sara, is already pregnant. She's only been married a few months. Then there's Helen Connor. Twins! And her daughter-in-law named them after her grandparents!"

Alea was a tall woman, and she was top-heavy—a

physical trait that he'd always loved—but when she pulled herself up to her full height, she could be downright intimidating.

"All of them have grandbabies to spoil and adore," Alea continued. "Helen has only one child but *two* grandchildren—and more to come. What do I have? Five children and not even the hope of a grandchild."

"Ariel is probably going to marry that guy Frank Thiessen," Peregrine said meekly. He'd had no idea this was a problem to his wife. His belief was that these things would happen and it was best to let nature take its course.

Alea threw up her hands. "Our daughter hasn't finished her residency yet and when she does, do you think she's going to want to jump right into motherhood?"

"She might—"

Alea glared at him. "Don't you think I haven't talked to her about this? You think we haven't had a mother-daughter talk about her having children? The age of her eggs, the age of the man she wants to marry—this time, that is. Frank is what, the third man she's been seriously involved with?"

Peregrine kept his face straight but he vowed to call his daughter ASAP and tell her he loved her just as she was.

"And then there are our boys," Alea continued. "Lanny will *never* marry. He likes to . . . I don't want to think about what he does. Pere prefers to sit back and let women make fools of themselves because of his pretty face. He's not going to trade that pleasure in for some woman who expects him to help with the housework."

Peregrine felt as though entire lives had been going on in his house that he knew nothing about—and he was fascinated. "Shamus?" he asked.

"Have you seen him go out on a date? Even once?"

"No, I haven't," Peregrine said, but he also hadn't thought about it. He knew the cheerleaders sometimes used Shamus as the center for a pyramid, which meant that five pretty girls in short skirts climbed on him. But Peregrine had never heard Shamus say anything about the trick, certainly not in a lusty way.

"Which leaves Colin," Peregrine said. When his wife's face turned red with emotion, he knew he'd hit on the center of all her distress.

Alea sat down and lowered his voice. "That 'boy' is thirty years old."

"He has Jean."

Alea stared at him.

"You don't think he and Jean will get married?"

"Married, then divorced," she said.

Peregrine's mouth dropped open in shock. "I thought you liked Jean."

"I love her second only to my own daughter. I've enjoyed every minute I've spent with her. She makes me laugh. I love talking with her. She's a joy to go shopping with. But she's not right for Colin."

"Don't you think he should decide that for himself?" When she was silent, Peregrine stared at her.

Her eyes seemed to be trying to tell him something, but he didn't know what it was. How did all the things she'd just revealed relate to one another?

It hit him hard. "If you don't care about trying to become a countess . . . You hired Gemma for Colin, didn't you? This whole thing, buying all those old documents, remodeling the guesthouse, hiring a live-in researcher, it's all been for Colin, hasn't it?"

Alea looked at her husband as though he were extremely clever to have figured that out. "Our son takes his duties of being sheriff *very* seriously and he won't look at a woman under his jurisdiction. Did I ever tell you about the time I was waiting in the car for Colin and that Dolores Costas appeared at her door wearing a pink negligee?"

About fifty times, Peregrine thought but didn't say. He'd asked Colin about it, and he'd laughed. The woman was a single mother and her three-year-old had had a fever during the night, so she was in her pajamas and robe—which her daughter had thrown up on. Peregrine figured the truth was somewhere between the two stories, because many times he'd seen a woman make a play for Colin but be ignored. To Colin, all the people of Edilean were for him to watch over, and he would never consider making a pass at someone under his care.

Which is why Peregrine thought Jean suited Colin so well. His work in Edilean didn't have regular hours. He could be called on to do anything, from getting a doctor to a pregnant woman during a snowstorm, to finding lost people in the wilderness area, to tracking a rabid dog. A normal wife would be unhappy about how much time her husband was away, but Jean had a flourishing career. She was too busy to worry when the man in her life wasn't home by six.

"Do you know what Colin did?" Alea asked.

"I doubt if I have any idea."

"He bought Luke Connor's house."

"The one he remodeled?"

"Yes."

"That place is beautiful. What did Colin pay for it? Did he—?" Alea was looking at her husband hard. If their son had bought a house and was going to quit living in that awful apartment over his office, that meant he was getting ready to settle down, maybe to marry. Shouldn't Alea be happy about that? Oh. Right. Peregrine had never thought about it before, but he couldn't see Jean as anybody's mother. He certainly couldn't imagine her staying up all night with a sick child and the next morning answering the door wearing dirty pajamas. The truth was, he couldn't imagine Jean living in Edilean.

"So now do you understand?" Alea asked.

"Did you and your boyfriend Freddy plan all this?" He knew his wife hadn't seen the man who became president of their university in years, but it galled him that they kept in touch. Three times Frazier Motors had donated vehicles to the university to raise money. "If you don't want to do it for Freddy, then do it for me. Please?" his wife had pleaded.

Alea gave her husband a one-sided smile. "Freddy and I did go over the qualifications of each applicant rather carefully. I didn't want someone who was deeply attached to her family and would never consider moving to a small town. Wasn't that girl Isla a major disappointment?"

"What about Kirk?" he asked in wonder. "No, don't tell me. If three young women had shown up, Colin would have known in an instant what you were up to."

Alea smiled warmly at him.

"And Colin likes Gemma," Peregrine whispered.

"More than I ever hoped he would. When Freddy told me the girl tutored football players, I knew there was a real chance that something could happen between them."

"So what now?" Peregrine asked as he looked at his watch. He was going to forget about work and go directly to golf. He needed some exercise to clear his mind.

"I just want to put them together as often as possible."

Peregrine got out of his chair. This particular scheme of his wife's seemed harmless enough. It wouldn't be the first time Jean and Colin had broken up, and there'd be tears, but that could be handled by turning the whole thing over to his wife. Too bad about Jean though. He liked her, and he loved her cooking. "Well, dear," he said, "you can play matchmaker all you want, but be sure to keep me up-to-date." He paused. "What about Dr. Tris? Wasn't there talk about him? Maybe he and Gemma will like each other."

"Every woman in town has tried for that man. I can't imagine that our studious little Gemma will be able to win him. Even gorgeous Jean doesn't turn Dr. Tris's head."

In college, Peregrine had dated many women who were much prettier and certainly more glamorous than Alea, but he'd known she was the one for him the moment he saw her stride across the gym floor. It had been during a basketball match, and as he watched her, the ball had hit his head and bounced off. The whole school burst into laughter. Four months later, she was pregnant and two months afterward, they were married.

He kissed his wife's cheek. "I hope you're right, dear, and that you get what you want. Just don't do anything drastic, will you?"

"Explain the meaning of *drastic*."

Peregrine didn't want to think about what could happen. "How about if I grill some steaks tonight?"

"Lovely. I'll have Rachel get them today. Have a good time today, dearest. Tell Dr. Henry hello for me."

5

Gemma went upstairs to get her bag and when she got outside, Colin was standing by his Jeep, talking on his cell. He didn't look happy. When he saw Gemma, he gave a curt good-bye, clicked off the phone, and put it in his pocket.

She got into the car beside him, and he was silent as he maneuvered out of the driveway around the other vehicles. "Did something bad happen?" she asked.

"No, nothing. Everything is fine. Do you know what kind of car you want?"

"I told your dad a Duesenberg." When this elicited no response from him, she said, "How about if we do this later? When you're in a better mood?"

As they reached the highway, Colin stepped on the clutch, shoved the car into third, and she was thrown back against the seat. "No, I need the distraction. Do you know where I live?"

"In town somewhere?"

"I live in an apartment over my office. The downstairs used to be a shop that sold ladies' apparel, while upstairs was used for storage. There are only a few windows, and the place smells like mothballs."

Gemma was beginning to understand. "And you want to move into your new house."

"Exactly. But as you saw, I have no furniture. Jean said she'd go with me tomorrow to buy some. But she left a voice mail saying she has an important case early on Monday morning, and she can't get back until next week."

Gemma was thinking about what Rachel had told her. If Jean couldn't find time to spend a weekend, how was she going to live there? "I bet you didn't tell her you had a big surprise for her." Gemma thought Jean didn't seem to be the type who'd want someone else to choose her house for her, but that wasn't any of her business. What she wanted was for Colin to tell her about him and Jean.

But he didn't take the hint. "Do *you* know anything about furniture?" he asked.

"Not after about 1860, although I am familiar with the Bauhaus School. Mies van der Rohe never did anything for me, though. But then Rococo also leaves me cold, and no two styles could be more different, right?" Colin was looking at her. "Oh. You mean furniture today, don't you? What you can buy in a shop now. No, I know nothing about it."

"You and my father are going to get on well. He

lives in a world of past automobiles. He is extremely disappointed that none of his kids has inherited the family obsession."

"But you said that two of your brothers work for him."

"Work but don't love," Colin said.

Gemma couldn't imagine a parent being disappointed because he had a son who was a sheriff, a daughter who was about to become a doctor, and another son who lived for his art. "Maybe—" Gemma began, but the two-way radio in the console interrupted her.

"Colin!" said a man's voice. "You there?"

He picked up the microphone. "Yeah, Tom. What do you need?"

"How far away are you from the fork in K Creek?"

"Ten minutes," he said as he glanced at Gemma. "Hold on." He downshifted, then turned the car ninety degrees without so much as slowing down.

Gemma held on to the door and her seat, and felt as though she were on a ride at a fair—or a NASA training device.

Colin didn't so much as pause in talking on the radio. "I'm about eight minutes away now. What's up?"

"A four-year-old boy climbed a tree and he's sitting on a branch that's about to break. I've spent the last fifteen minutes trying to get him to jump to me, but he won't let go. Says I'm too old to catch him." They could hear the frustration in the man's voice. "The fire department is on the way with a ladder, but

I thought maybe if you were close, you could talk him down. Carl's here but . . ."

"Five minutes," Colin said and clicked off the microphone as he reached outside and put a red light on the roof and a siren went off. He glanced at Gemma. "I'm sorry, but I have to go fast."

She said nothing but her eyes widened. They were already doing sixty on the winding road. There were only a few feet visible in front of them. If a car—

She broke off her thoughts because a pickup with a boat attached was in front of them and Colin was heading straight into the back of it. He swerved to the left—and into the face of an oncoming car. Gemma tried to brace herself for the coming crash.

But then, as though it were like some Biblical drama, the truck beside them slammed on the brakes and jerked to the right, while the car expertly went to the left, its nose heading into the trees. In front of them, the way was clear, and Colin hadn't even slowed down.

As soon as they were past, Gemma turned to look behind them. Both the truck and the car had stopped, and a tall man from the truck was crossing the road to the car.

Gemma turned back around. They were doing seventy now.

"That was Luke, the author, in the truck," Colin said. "And it was Ramsey in the car. He's a lawyer."

"It was a pleasure meeting them," Gemma answered, still holding on.

Colin chuckled as he turned a sharp right onto land that had no hint of a roadway. "I didn't mean to scare you, but I knew they'd get out of the way. They're both relatives of mine."

She wanted to ask what he would have done if the road had been full of tourists, but she was too busy holding on to ask him anything. There were holes and little hillocks that made one wheel go down and another go up. Gemma was bouncing on the seat so hard her head scraped the ceiling.

"Shortcut," Colin yelled over the noise of the siren and what sounded like a metal tool box in the back bouncing up and down. "We're going across Merlin's Farm." He pointed to the right.

Half hidden under the trees was a small octagon-shaped building with a tall, pointed roof, like a witch's hat. There was a short door, and to the right of it was an open space in the wall, with a gate across it.

It didn't take a historian to see that the building was *very* old.

"That's . . ." Gemma began. "Is that . . . ?"

"Spring house. Water inside," Colin yelled back as he shifted gears. In the next second he went around a couple of big trees and a county sheriff car came into view. Colin skidded to a halt amid a dense cloud of dust and rocks.

Gemma stayed in the car, coughing, but Colin leaped out before the vehicle came to a full halt. When the car kept rolling, she saw that he'd left it to her to turn off the engine. She slid over the console, braked, and turned the motor off.

When she looked out the windshield, she saw Colin and two law enforcement officers in brown uniforms standing a few feet away from a big tree that had been struck by lightning. Half of the tree had fallen to the ground, creating what looked to be a ramp that led upward. It would be easy for a child to walk up it.

Above, sitting on a heavy branch that was bending toward the earth, was a little boy. He had blond hair and big blue eyes that were wide with fear. His mother was standing below and talking to him in a low voice, trying to keep him from moving and causing the branch to break further.

Gemma got out of the car and walked to stand near Colin, her eyes on the child.

"It's going to take them another ten minutes to get here," Tom, the county sheriff, was saying. He was in his late fifties, a tall, handsome man with gray hair. He turned his back to the boy's mother. "Carl tried getting out to him, but the branch cracked. Think you can catch the kid if he falls?"

"Sure," Colin said in a low voice so the mother wouldn't hear. "But that wood isn't going to hold much longer. I think we should get him down now." He walked toward the little boy and looked up. "Hey . . ."

"Sean," his mother said.

"Sean, my name is Colin, and I'm the town sheriff, and as you can see I'm pretty strong. What I want you to do is let go of the tree and let yourself fall. I'll catch you. It'll be like playing football. That okay with you?"

"No!" the boy said as he tightened his grip on the branch. It gave a resounding crack.

"He climbs everything," his mother said, her voice vibrating with barely controlled hysteria. "He gets on the kitchen countertops and into the upper cabinets. One morning I opened a door over the sink and he was sitting inside, smiling at me. He—"

Reaching out, Colin put his hand on her shoulder, and she quit talking. He turned back to the boy. "All right, Sean, I want you to be very still. Okay, buddy?" The child was only about six feet above his head, but he might as well have been ten stories away. And if Colin waited for the branch to break to catch the boy, both of them could be hurt.

"Cheerleading," Tom said from beside Gemma.

When she turned toward him, he was staring at her. "Colin's little brother does a cheerleader pyramid with five girls on him. The top one stands on his shoulders."

Gemma thought that was an odd thing for him to say. Local sports weren't exactly a pressing concern at the moment. When she realized what he was suggesting, her face lit up.

"Think you can do it?" Tom asked. "If the boy'll let you, that is. He's a heavy kid, and it'll take some muscle to hold him." He was looking her up and down in question.

Gemma had on her usual outfit of loose jeans and three layers of tops. Since she was used to working around virile young men, she'd learned to keep covered up. And she'd also learned to work out with them in the way that they did, which meant with weights.

Gemma unzipped her cotton jacket and removed it, revealing a pink cotton shirt under it. She unbuttoned it and took it off. Underneath she was wearing a fuchsia tank top that showed the lacy edges of her matching bra.

One thing about working out with men was that they loved upper body work. Deltoids and biceps seemed to be their main concern. Three years ago, when Gemma came up with the idea of teaching while exercising, she could barely lift a pair of two-pound dumbbells over her head. Now she worked with an Olympic bar, which was forty-five pounds.

When Gemma stood in front of Tom with a lot of skin showing, she knew her arms showed her workouts. Between boxing and thousands of reps for delts, her arms were firm and well shaped.

"Good girl," Tom said, smiling at her.

Behind them, his skinny young deputy—his name tag read CARL—was grinning. "You think you can climb up ol' Colin in those pants? Maybe you should take them off too."

Tom glanced at his deputy in reprimand, then

turned to Colin, who was still looking up at the boy. "Colin! This young lady—" He looked at her.

"Gemma."

"Gemma is going to do a Shamus and get the boy down."

"He's too heavy. She can't—" Colin began, but then he looked at her and his eyes widened. Gemma's body was fabulous! She was curvy and taut with muscle. Her large breasts were above a waist his hands could span. Words failed him. "Yeah, okay," he at last managed to say.

"Thought maybe you'd agree," Tom said.

When Gemma was standing in front of him, Colin looked at her in appreciation. "Those students of yours taught you a thing or two about working out, didn't they?"

Maybe it was because she didn't have on her usual layers of covering, or maybe it was the way Colin was looking at her, or maybe it was because she'd been without a boyfriend for months, but a strong feeling of desire ran through her. For Colin. For a man who was taken. Owned by a dragon.

"Hey, Colin," Carl said, "Jean know about you two?"

Colin gave the deputy a look to shut up, then he put his sheriff face back on and looked up at the boy. "If I lift Miss Gemma onto my shoulders, will you go to her?"

The boy looked down at Gemma in her skimpy top, her breasts well exposed, and almost smiled. "Yeah. She's pretty."

Colin looked back at her. "The kid's going to grow up to be another Lanny. Can you lift him?"

"I think so," Gemma said, but her heart was beating in her throat. When the tree branch cracked again and the mother put her hand to her mouth to keep from screaming, all Gemma could think was, What if I drop the child?

"Okay," Colin said, and his voice was that of a coach: calm, quiet, and reassuring. "I want you to step on my leg, and I'll help you onto my shoulders. I'll hold your ankles and balance you. When you're stable, reach out to him. Let him come to you, don't pull. Once you have him, hold on to him and I'll do the rest. Understand?"

"Yes," she said.

Unnoticed by anyone, Carl turned the video recorder on his cell on and stepped back to get a full view of the action.

Bending a bit, Colin extended his right leg so she could step onto his thigh. He held out his hands to help her. When she hesitated and he saw fear in her eyes, he knew he needed to give her courage. He didn't know her very well, but he'd seen that she had a competitive spirit. He said, "Come on, Ranford, those high school girls climb all over my baby brother. You gonna let those kids beat you?"

His tone—so like the trainers she'd worked with—took away most of her fear. She slipped out of her shoes, took his hands, and stepped up on his bent leg.

When she was steady, he put his hands on her legs and looked up at her. "I'm going to lift you up, and I want you to get onto my shoulders. Ready?"

Gemma nodded. She glanced up at the boy. He was watching them in fascination as he sat absolutely still.

Colin lifted Gemma as though he were overhead pressing her. But then she figured that for that exercise, at his size, he probably used a couple of eighty-pound dumbbells, which together weighed more than she did.

When Gemma was on his broad shoulders, she put her hands on the top of his head for balance. He held on to her ankles firmly and took a step back as she steadied herself.

Once she was standing, her head was nearly level with the boy's and just a foot away. She smiled at him. "Pretty cool, huh?" she said, trying to reassure him.

"Yeah. Can you get me down now?"

"Sure. I'm going to hold out my arms and you're going to come to me, right?"

The boy nodded.

Gemma reached out to the branch and Colin took a step closer, so she was very near the frightened child. She opened her arms. "Don't jump, just sort of fall toward me, okay?"

Again the boy nodded, and in the next second he fell onto Gemma. He was indeed heavy and he nearly made her fall backward, but she wrapped her arms around the child so hard that he almost couldn't breathe.

Colin didn't give her time to fight for balance. He released his hold on her ankles and took a step backward. For a split second, Gemma and the boy were standing on nothing, suspended in air, over six feet above the ground.

In the next second, Gemma, still holding tightly on to the boy, fell—and Colin caught them both in his big, muscular arms. As he held them, Gemma could feel his heart pounding against her cheek and the boy was holding on to her with a death grip.

Moments later, the child's mother pulled the boy away from her, and he let out a howl of relief as she took him away.

Colin didn't put Gemma down but kept holding her in his arms. "You okay?"

"Yes." She knew she should get down, but it felt good—and safe—to be so close to him. For a moment she let herself lean against him. It was as though only the two of them existed.

"Thanks," Tom said from behind them. "To both of you." In the distance they heard a siren. The fire engine was arriving.

"Look out!" Carl yelled.

Colin, still holding Gemma, leaped backward and knocked Tom down as the branch that had been holding the boy crashed to the ground.

When the noise and debris settled, Tom was on the bottom of the pile. "Colin," he said, "I love you like a son, but if you don't get the hell off of me my lungs are going to collapse."

"Sorry," Colin said as he rolled away and Gemma stood up.

Colin sat up, looking up at Gemma with pride. "You did well," he said. "You have a good sense of balance. And—"

"Holy crap!" Tom said because Gemma's face suddenly drained of color. Slowly, she turned on her heel and began to sink to the ground. She would have fallen if Tom hadn't caught her.

Colin was on his feet in seconds as he took Gemma from Tom. "Post-traumatic?"

"No," Tom said as he held out his hands. There was blood on them.

Reaching out with experienced hands, Tom pulled the bottom of Gemma's tank top up. The tree branch had cut her side. "No arteries cut, but it might be deep enough to need stitches."

"Call Tris," Colin said. "Tell him I'll be there in seven minutes." He ran with the unconscious Gemma in his arms to his Jeep.

Behind him, still holding his phone and still recording, was Carl. He only turned it off when Colin slammed the door of his Jeep and sped away.

6

Dr. Edward Burgess slowly opened his car door, put his cane on the pavement, and carefully swiveled around to get out. He winced in pain when he put his weight on his leg, and used both hands to heave himself out of the car. Across the road, his neighbor was sweeping her porch, and she paused to look at him in sympathy. She waved hello, and he raised his hand in a weak acknowledgment.

He leaned heavily on his cane as he locked his car, then, stooped over, he made his way up the sidewalk. He supported himself against the jamb as he unlocked his front door. When it was open, he turned to again wave at his neighbor. As he knew she would be, she was watching to make sure he got inside safely.

As soon as he was in the house, Dr. Burgess closed the door and leaned against it for a moment. He let out a sigh. "Nosy old bitch," he muttered as he tossed his cane toward the tall urn by the door. It went in with a resounding thunk.

Bending, he pulled up his pants leg and unbuckled the brace around his knee and tossed it at the cane. That done, he stood up, put his shoulders back, and flexed his neck. As he walked toward the cabinet against the wall, he unbuttoned his shirt, took off the belly pad that encircled his waist, and let it drop to the floor.

He took a couple of refreshing breaths, rubbed the skin over his hard, flat stomach, and opened the cabinet to pour himself a drink. He wasn't surprised to see that his ice bucket was full. He put a couple of cubes in a glass, poured it half full of thirty-year-old Scotch, then turned around and waited.

The hideous lounge chair that was part of the rented house's furniture was facing the wall—not the way he'd left it.

"Are you hiding?" he asked after he'd taken a sip.

The chair turned around, and his beautiful niece looked up at him. "What do you want so much that it's made you come to little Edilean?"

"Jean, darling," he said, "is that any way to greet your uncle?"

She tapped her upper lip. "Is that yours?"

He pulled off the thick gray mustache and set it on a shelf in the cabinet. "Have you eaten? I could make us some—"

"I know what you can cook. You taught me, remember? Why are you here?"

"I came to see you," he said. "How's your mother?"

"Doing as well as can be expected after all that you did to her."

"Jean, Jean, Jean," he said. "Why are you so hostile to me?"

"I don't know. Maybe it has to do with how you hacked Mom's bank codes and cleaned her out. Twice. Or maybe it was how my father went out with you one night and never returned. Take your pick."

He shrugged. "We've been over all this before and I thought it was in the past. As for your father, he had the reflexes of a tortoise. I never could figure out how he came to be my brother. I should have had a DNA test done."

Jean came out of the chair, angry. "I'm very good friends with the local sheriff. All I have to do is tell him about you and he'll run you out of town."

"Friends, maybe, but that's all there is," he said as she stalked toward the front door. "I just heard that for days now he's been inseparable from a pretty young woman who's living with his parents. In fact, an hour ago someone showed me the two of them on that . . . What's it called? YouTube. Disgusting invasion, that thing is. But I must say that I enjoyed the sight of her truly incredible body. And she appeared to be so very *young*."

Jean looked back at him, her jaw in a hard line. "Colin and I are in love."

"Really?" he asked, with a fake smile. Even with his dark hair dyed gray, he was a handsome man, and he'd kept his lean figure even as he neared fifty. He was her father's younger brother, adored and spoiled by their mother as he grew up, and always bailed out of trouble when he was an adult and learning the art of thievery.

Jean strode across the room to the door.

"Is it that trust fund he lives off of that you care about?" He put his hand over hers on the doorknob and his face softened. "Can't an uncle be jealous?" he asked. "I used to be the number one man in your life, but now I hear that my beloved niece is with a . . ." He smiled. "A sheriff. Of course I want to disparage him as much as I can."

Jean looked away for a moment. When he wanted to be, he was quite charming—and they had so much history together. She truly wanted to know what he was doing in Edilean. Was he again after her mother, or had he targeted someone else? She knew that anger wasn't going to find out anything. Besides, he was the one who'd taught her how to mask her feelings. Turning, she gave him a hint of a smile.

When he thought he saw her capitulate, he put his arm around her shoulders. They were both tall and thin, and he was only eleven years older than she was. Before she reached ten years old, she thought her uncle Adrian was the smartest, most clever man on earth. It had taken years for her to learn the truth about him. He was always after something, and every word he uttered was a lie.

"Come on," he said. "For old time's sake, let's

share a meal. I always did love to be in a kitchen with you."

She agreed, but only because she needed to know what he wanted. Throughout their cooking—which they did easily and without getting in each other's way—she talked to him. She tried to make it sound as though she was telling him about her life, but she was actually warning him. Just a few months before, when the search for the eighteenth-century paintings had been going on, Edilean had been full of FBI and Secret Service agents. "And a super-detective lives here now," she said at the end. She wasn't going to mention that Mike Newland spent most of the year in Fort Lauderdale.

"I know," he said, his deep blue eyes twinkling. "Jean, dearest, please relax. I came here only to see you."

"Why?" she asked as she put the risotto on the table.

"Is love too old-fashioned for me to say?"

Jean knew he was lying. When she was a child, he'd show up in her bedroom in the middle of the night. He never did anything as prosaic as ring a doorbell or knock. She'd be asleep, then wake up to see him standing there looking down at her. He'd put his finger to his lips for her to be quiet. She'd stand up and hug him and he'd shower her with gifts. There were pretty, smocked dresses from France, shoes of the softest Italian leather, dolls that were the envy of her friends. When she got older, there were earrings with real sapphires, and when she graduated from high school he'd given her a pearl necklace.

Her mother had been horrified the first time she found out that her brother-in-law had entered their house during the night. She demanded that an alarm system be installed.

"It won't matter," her husband, his older brother, said.

But she didn't believe him. She became a fanatic about keeping doors and windows locked and the alarm on. But one morning Jean came into the kitchen wearing a dress with a print of little bouquets of willow branches, their long, thin leaves in several shades of green, a pink ribbon tying them together. It had a Baby Dior label and Jean said Uncle Adrian had given it to her during the night. Her mother had been nearly hysterical, screaming that she wanted to put iron bars over every entrance.

Her husband put his hands on her shoulders and tried to calm her down. "Whatever you do, he'll see it as a challenge. You can put up cameras, bars, whatever you can think of, but if he wants to see his niece, he will."

"But she's a child! He wakes her up in the night and I don't like it."

"I *hate* it!" he said with passion. "I've hated it all my life. When I was a teenager and he was still in elementary school, he was always snooping in my room. I used to put my most private possessions inside a locked box, then put it in another box, then into a third one. Each one had its own lock. The next morning at breakfast, Adrian would spread the things out across the table for everyone to see."

She was calming down. "What if we asked him to please come to the front door during the day?"

"You don't think I have? He won't do it. Just let him see Jean and don't try to defeat him at his own game."

"But—" She couldn't think of any way to thwart the man.

It was after Jean's father died while she was in her first year in college that the real problems began. Her father, an accountant, had set up a trust for his only child's education, so her first three years at school were easy. Except for the grief of her father's passing, she enjoyed herself, and finances had been no problem.

But one day during the summer holidays, Jean came home to find her mother screaming. Every penny they had was gone. Jean's trust fund had been emptied, the insurance money was gone, two savings accounts had zero balances.

"I know he did it!" Mrs. Caldwell said when they returned from the bank.

"Who?" Jean asked.

"Your father's brother, that's who!"

"Uncle Adrian? I thought he was in jail," Jean said.

"He got out last week," Mrs. Caldwell said, "and I know he did it."

The next year had been horrible. The police could

find no way that Adrian could have taken the money. "It's just not possible," they said. Jean could tell that they thought her mother had taken her own money, probably as a tax evasion.

Jean helped her mother put a mortgage on the house that her father had worked so hard to leave debt free. Jean got student loans and a job so she could finish the last year of college. She had no more time for social events or dates. Worse was that she gave up her hope of law school. It cost too much.

During that awful year, she never saw or heard from her uncle Adrian. But her mother never ceased to complain about him. She'd had to give up her charity work and get a job washing hair at a nearby salon. They both knew that, eventually, they would have to sell their beloved home.

But it all ended almost a year after it began. Adrian showed up in Jean's bedroom one night, just as he'd always done.

She glared at him. In the last year he'd become the enemy, the one who'd caused their poverty. "Did you—?" she began, but as always, he put his finger to his lips. He loved secrets.

He handed her a little blue velvet box. Jean opened it to see a beautiful ring of diamonds and pink sapphires. When she looked up, her uncle was gone.

The next morning the bank called to tell Mrs. Caldwell that all her money had been redeposited—with a 12 percent increase.

It had taken a lot for Mrs. Caldwell's husband's

former partner to persuade the IRS that this wasn't new income, and that 40 percent of the money should not be paid in taxes, but he did it.

Mrs. Caldwell quit her job and Jean went to law school, but what had happened changed her mother. She became bitter and angry, and began to look for everyone's ulterior motive.

Jean never told her mother, but while she was in law school, she spent a lot of time with her uncle. She thought that the reason he'd put her and her mother through such hell was because he didn't see them as people. She thought that, maybe, if he came to actually *love* them he'd protect them, and he'd never hurt them again.

Over the years she was studying law, he taught her how to cook, to dress, even to dance. Unknown to her mother, several times he sent her plane tickets and she went to exotic locations where she met fabulously interesting people—and had quick affairs with several of them. Through her uncle she gained a sophistication few of the other students had. She did well in her studies, and her outside life was exciting.

The only flaw in their relationship was that her uncle never allowed her to mention what he'd done to their mother—or to Jean. To Adrian, what had happened was over and therefore she had no right to bring up the past.

After her graduation from law school, her uncle disappeared as quickly as he'd arrived, and she didn't see or hear from him for over two years.

But soon after Jean got a job at an excellent law firm in Richmond, Virginia, her mother called and said, "He did it again."

Jean knew exactly what her mother meant. This time, it was Jean who changed. The man she'd spent so many days and weekends with, who'd taught her so much, had thought so little of her that he'd yet again stolen from her mother.

It wasn't easy for Jean, but she supported her mother for eighteen months—and she never told of her association with Uncle Adrian.

By the time the money was returned to Mrs. Caldwell's bank account, she was too angry to recover. The trauma of her husband's death and the two long bouts with destitution had made her much older than her years. On Jean's last visit home, she had caught her mother burying gold coins in the backyard. "I need to hide them in case he does it again," she said.

Adrian's voice brought Jean back to the present. "Tell me everything about this man you love," he said as he took a bite of the risotto. She'd never seen him eat on anything but fine china and sterling silver, so now, seeing him with the cheap plates that came with the rented house was disconcerting.

"He's nice. He's kind," she said cautiously.

"So why hasn't he asked you to marry him?"

Jean narrowed her eyes. His lower status of living could be something he was using as a disguise or it could mean he was broke. When he needed money, he went for it anywhere. "Why do you want to know? If you think I know Colin's bank code and that you can wheedle it out of me, I don't and you can't."

"Bitterness never becomes a lady," Adrian said. "And at your age—" He broke off when he saw that he'd overstepped himself. "Dear Jean, I apologize for all I've done to you and your mother. Both times I was in a situation where I had no other source of income. I did my best to make it up to you, both financially and personally."

That remark hurt. Was he saying that all the time he'd spent with Jean while she was in law school was merely a repayment of a debt? Maybe that was true, because what they'd shared had clearly meant nothing to him. Later he'd still robbed her mother a second time.

When she looked at him, she realized that he knew exactly how he'd made her feel. She'd once heard someone say that when a person says something that hurts you, you better believe that it was intentional.

She stood up. "You're after something, and if you don't tell me what it is, I'm going to Colin right now and tell him everything."

He didn't get in the least upset, just smiled at her in a way that she used to find charming but now saw as devious. "Is it impossible for you to believe that I came here for the sole and only purpose of seeing you?"

"Yes, it is."

He smiled in what seemed to be approval. "Well, perhaps I wasn't telling the entire truth. I am a bit interested in what I read about this town."

"About Edilean? Oh yes, of course. You're after the paintings they found here last year. I should have known that all those millions would attract you. I'll tell you now that those paintings have nothing to do with *me*."

"I know," he said softly, "but reading those stories did remind me of something I'd lost."

"The Crown Jewels?" One time in Budapest a man had told her that the only thing Adrian had not stolen were the English Crown Jewels.

"Yes," he said, "and by that I mean my dear niece. Jean, you are the only person who means anything to me and I came to see you, to get to know you again. I apologize for the disguise but . . ."

"Your face is on too many wanted posters?"

He gave a smile that she well remembered; it used to make her feel that they were in a conspiracy together.

She sat back down at the table. Anger was only going to make him tell more lies.

"More bread, dear? I bought it at Armstrong's. It's a small town, but the grocery is excellent. And such an interesting woman runs it. She is a veritable fountain of information. A few groans of pain and she tells me everything about everyone."

Jean took a roll from the basket. "What do you want information about?"

"Nothing in particular. Just something to pass the time while you're in Richmond."

"Why don't you stay there instead of here?" She looked around the ugly interior of the little house.

"No one talks to one another in a city," he said. "Is that why you dislike little Edilean so much? You don't want people talking about you and what you do when you're not working?"

She started to protest, but he put his hand up.

"My dear niece, remember that I know you very well. You barely tolerate the rural nature of Richmond. How often do you go to New York and the pied-à-terre you keep there? Tell me, does that big, hulking boyfriend of yours know of that place?"

When Jean didn't answer, Adrian smiled. "I thought not. Did you know that your young man has some secrets of his own? He bought a house here in this little town. Has he shown it to you?"

"Not yet," she said.

"That's interesting. Did you know that he took that adorable little Gemma there on the day she arrived in town?"

Jean's involuntary intake of breath was his answer.

Again, he smiled. "Would you like to hear more of what I heard?"

Jean looked down at her plate for a moment, then back up at him. "I believe I would." She took a deep drink of the excellent wine. "Tell me everything you know."

7

Gemma awoke slowly and spent a few minutes remembering what had happened. She'd been on Colin's shoulders, then in his arms. Someone had yelled a warning, Colin had jumped to one side, then fallen, but making sure he didn't land on Gemma. She remembered getting up, but after that was a blank. Right now, her left side ached and her head felt a bit cloudy, but otherwise she was fine.

She was in a room that looked like a cross between a bedroom and a hospital unit. The bed had controls to raise and lower it, and near her was a big machine that kept up a rhythmical beep, but the rest of the furniture was homey and comfortable.

The most extraordinary thing was that curled up in a big blue chair, sound asleep, was an angelically pretty little girl, about eight years old. She was clutching a fat teddy bear that was dressed like a pirate, complete with a purple vest and gaudy jewelry.

The child stirred, and when the bear nearly fell, she opened her eyes. She had long dark hair and deep blue eyes and very long lashes. "Hello," she said.

"Hello," Gemma answered back and started to sit up. Under the thin blanket she was still wearing her jeans, but her shirt and bra had been replaced by a hospital gown.

"No one saw you," the girl said as she sat up straight in the chair and yawned.

"Saw me?" Gemma asked.

"With no clothes on. Uncle Tris made the men leave before he examined you. That's okay because he's a doctor."

"I've heard of him." She was trying to look at the big bandage over her ribs.

"My mother says that all the women in three counties know about her brother."

Gemma smiled as she managed to sit up. "You wouldn't know what happened to me, would you?"

"The whole world saw everything."

Gemma looked at the girl in question. What did that mean?

"When you climbed on Uncle Colin and got that boy down, Deputy Carl filmed it, and he put it on YouTube."

"That's not good," Gemma said as she swung around to get out of bed, but she was dizzy, so she lay back down.

"Uncle Tris gave you happy drugs." She lowered her voice. "He thinks I don't know what narcotics are, so that's what he calls them to me. He's afraid I'm going to grow up to be a drug dealer."

"I have to agree that that wouldn't be a good choice of careers."

The girl stood up, her bear held tightly to her. "This is Landy. Would you like to shake his hand?"

"Sure," Gemma said and held out her hand to grip the fuzzy paw. The bear wore a patch over its left eye. "Named for Orlando Bloom?" she asked.

The child's eyes widened. "Nobody knows that. Uncle Colin said you were smart and you are."

"What else did Colin say about me?"

"Just that he was worried that you were going to die. Uncle Tris said that if Uncle Colin didn't sit down and shut up he was going to give *him* some happy drugs."

Gemma smiled. "What's your name?"

"Nell Sandlin. My daddy is in Iraq."

"Oh," Gemma said and offered up a silent prayer for the man's safe return.

"When he comes home, Momma says we'll move back to Detroit—unless she can get Daddy to stay here in Edilean."

"What do you want to do?"

"I want my daddy to come home. We can live in an igloo, I don't care. Just so my daddy is with us."

Gemma would never tell the girl so, but she'd felt the same way when her father was taken away in an ambulance. But he'd never returned.

They heard voices outside the door.

"Uh oh," Nell said. "I promised I'd tell Uncle Tris when you woke up."

There was a clock on the table by the chair. It was ten minutes after four, which meant that Gemma had been out for hours. "Maybe you should tell Dr. Tris that I'd like to see him."

"Sure." Nell went to the door but paused with her hand on the knob. "Do you think you'll fall in love with my uncle?"

"I'll do my best not to," Gemma said, repressing a smile. "Unless you want me to."

Nell took a moment to consider this. "Momma says Uncle Tris is in love with an 'impossible dream' and that's why he doesn't fall for real women. But maybe *you* are that dream."

"I doubt that, but I'll consider it. I think—" She didn't finish because the door opened and an extraordinarily handsome man came in. He was wearing a doctor's white coat, a stethoscope hanging out of a pocket. He had black hair, blue eyes, and a jawline that could have been sculpted out of marble.

Gemma could see why there was talk of falling for the man, and she waited for her own temperature to rise—but it didn't.

Dr. Tris looked around the door at his niece. "I thought you and Landy were going to play nurse and tell me when my patient woke up." His voice was very pleasant.

"Landy fell asleep," Nell said. "And his necklace was blinking so . . ." She shrugged.

"I want you and Landy to go next door and tell Uncle Colin that Gemma woke up."

Nell's face was serious. "Should I tell him you found a brain tumor?"

"Out!" Tristan said as she ran past him, giggling. "And if you frighten Colin I'll sue you for malpractice," he called after her. Shaking his head as he shut the door, he turned to Gemma. "Sorry about that. My niece is much too knowledgeable for her own good. I blame it on TV. Or the Internet. I haven't decided which."

He paused at the foot of the bed and stared down at her. Gemma wasn't sure, but she thought he might be trying to ascertain if she was going to . . . well, probably start flirting with him.

But beautiful as he was, Gemma wasn't attracted to him. She couldn't explain it, but there was a faraway look in his eyes that almost made her feel as though he wasn't really there.

What the doctor saw seemed to relieve him and he let out his breath. "I'm Tristan Aldredge." He held out his hand to shake hers.

"Gemma Ranford."

He walked around the side of the bed. "I've heard about you from Colin. That was some feat you two pulled off this morning." He folded back the cover and lifted her gown to look at her bandaged side.

"What happened to me?"

"When the branch broke, it hit you and cut you along the rib cage. It wasn't too deep. The stitches I used will dissolve in a few days. You'll be sore for a while, so you shouldn't go dancing—or climbing on Colin—for a week or two."

"Did I pass out?"

"Yes, but I think you mostly had an overload of adrenaline. I hear you got a job you really wanted, then you were subjected to Colin's driving, then you climbed up and rescued a little boy. It's been a hectic couple of days. I suggest you rest for a day or two and you'll be fine."

"Has everything really been posted on YouTube?"

"Every second of it." Tristan smiled. "Tom has suspended Carl, but the rescue is on the Web. There's a second where you and the boy are standing in midair and some kid's already selling posters of it."

Gemma frowned. "It doesn't look bad, does it?"

"Bad?" He was checking her pulse.

"I mean I wouldn't want to cause any problems for Colin. Or with any of the Fraziers."

Still holding her wrist, Tris looked at her. "Afraid of losing your job?"

"Yes."

"The Fraziers would never fire you just because you—"

He broke off when the door flew back and Colin burst in—and Gemma's face dissolved into a smile. As pretty as Dr. Tris was, to her eyes, he looked small and insignificant next to Colin.

"How do you feel?" Colin asked. "Sore? In pain? Weak?"

"Hungry," Gemma said.

Colin grinned at her. "We can fix that." He looked at Tris. "When can we leave?"

"As soon as she's dressed."

When both men kept standing at the foot of the bed and staring at her, Gemma said, "Could I have some privacy please?"

"Sure," Tris said. "Mrs. Frazier sent some of your clothes over, and they're in the closet. Take your time."

She watched the two men leave, then slowly got out of bed.

Outside in the waiting room, Colin looked at Tristan. "You're sure she's okay? Nell said something about a brain tumor."

Tris cut his niece a look, and she muffled a giggle. "Gemma is fine. That was a scary thing she went through and that combined with the cut made her faint."

"Then Uncle Tris gave her narcotics," Nell said. "So Gemma slept for hours."

Colin shook his head at her. "You're already an Aldredge. What medical school are you going to?"

"None. I'm going to be a ballerina," Nell said as she got off the chair. "Could I have five dollars?" she asked her uncle.

"How about two?" he said, getting out his wallet. "And where are you planning to go?"

"You know Mr. Lang is picking me up." She looked at Colin. "He has puppies, and I'm going to get one."

They saw out the window that Brewster Lang's old truck had stopped in front of the office.

"Go!" Tris ordered. "Or he'll start blowing his horn."

Holding tight to her bear, Nell ran out the door.

"When did that start?" Colin asked.

"The last time Sara and Mike were home, Nell spent the afternoon at the farm with them, and she and Lang hit it off." Tris shrugged. "Yet another thing I don't understand about that child. I don't even get that weird bear. Anyway, Mike and Sara got in last night, and they invited Nell over to see the puppies. Lang picked her up."

Colin was barely listening. "You're sure Gemma's okay?"

Tris put his hand on Colin's big shoulder and looked him in the eyes. "She's fine. Very healthy. It looks like she works out some."

"Yeah, she does. And she's smart and curious and remembers things. She's a good sport and easy to be with, and—" He broke off.

Tris was behind the counter in the room where his secretary usually worked. She wasn't there today, as his office was closed. If the people of Edilean had any medical problems on Tris's days off, they had to go to Williamsburg—which was why Colin's sister, Ariel, was planning to work with him when she finished her residency. But Tris had come in at Colin's call.

"You seem to like Gemma," Tris said, his head down.

"Yeah, I do."

"So ask her out," Tris said.

"Gemma and I just met. And I need to finish some things first."

"I guess that means Jean. Too bad. Looks like that leaves me free to ask Gemma out."

"You mean on a date?"

"Yeah. Dinner and a movie. Hey! I know. Mike and Sara invited me to their barbecue. I'll ask Gemma if she'd like to go with me. I bet she'll love Merlin's Farm. She and Sara can talk about architecture until the sun comes up."

Colin was staring at him. "Gemma was injured. I don't know if she's ready to go—"

"I'm her doctor. Of course she can go."

"Go where?" Gemma asked from the doorway.

Tristan stepped forward. "I have been invited to a barbecue in a couple of weeks and I wondered if you'd like to go with me."

Gemma was pleased with the invitation. She needed to meet more people in Edilean besides the Fraziers. As it was, she'd already spent too much time with Colin.

"I'd love to go," she said, smiling at him.

8

GEMMA AND COLIN were in his Jeep and driving back to the Frazier house.

"Gemma," Colin began, "I'm really sorry that you were hurt. I shouldn't have involved you in my job."

"It was one of the most exciting moments of my life," she said.

"Yeah? Are you just being nice?"

"No, really. I spend most of my life dealing with books and papers, so being able to help rescue a child was great."

"What about your athletic students?" She was covered up again, but he remembered the shape of her. "Didn't they help you do more than just read?"

Gemma smiled in memory. "They changed my life in a big way." She glanced at Colin, and he gave a nod to encourage her to continue. "When I started tutoring, the boys kept falling asleep in my sessions and I was really annoyed. I worked hard to make the lessons interesting, but they were ignoring me. One day I touched one of the sleeping football players on the shoulder and he . . ." She shook her head. "He grabbed me about the waist, picked me up, and started running. He said he'd been dreaming and thought I was a football."

Colin didn't laugh. "You could have been hurt."

"If we'd been alone I might have been. But in the first month of tutoring one of the guys made a pass at me, so I never again had one boy at a time. On the day the guy grabbed me, there were four other boys there, and the others rescued me before anything bad happened. I'm still glad the kid wasn't a shot-putter and didn't try to throw me over a pole."

Colin was frowning. "Did you do something to prevent things like that from happening again?" His tone and formality were that of a law enforcement officer.

"Yes, I did. The truth is, it all scared me."

"Rightfully so."

"But when I told the guys I'd have to report the incident, they said it looked like I could teach, but I couldn't learn. I had no idea what they were talking about."

"The fatigue that comes from training for a sport," Colin said softly.

"You're right. One of the boys angrily said that if I did what they did, I wouldn't be able to stay awake to study either."

As Colin pulled into the driveway of his parents'

house, he was listening intently to her. "What did you do?"

"I couldn't resist a challenge like that one. I wanted to prove them wrong." She laughed. "And I was sure I'd succeed. I was young, healthy, and I kept in shape by rushing around the campus while carrying a heavy load of books. And I've never smoked and I rarely drink."

Colin was smiling. "How long did you last?"

"Three days. They had me doing cardio, weights, stretching, then I had to repeat it all again. And you know what? They were right. I was too tired to think, much less to learn anything. At the end of the week, I sat down with the original boys and had a serious talk with them. I patiently explained that while their job was athletic, mine was cerebral, so I couldn't continue with their very strenuous program."

"And how did that work out?" He was grinning.

Gemma laughed. "They listened to me without saying a single word, then they left and I didn't see them for four whole days. They didn't show up for their sessions. When they did return, they were different. There was no more joking and, worse, no one tried to learn anything. I was close to panic because if they failed, I'd lose my job—and it paid twice as much as any I'd had before. One night it hit me that I'd pretty much told the boys that I was smart while they were dumb. It was okay for them to be too tired to think, but I, Gemma Ranford, the Ph.D. candidate, *had* to have a clear mind."

"It was good that you could see that about yourself."

"Actually, the whole thing shook me up. It was a true epiphany. It's not comfortable to have to look at yourself without foggy glasses. The next morning I was at the gym at six A.M. and . . ." She shrugged. "Since then I've never asked my boys to give more than I give in return."

"What happened with their grades?"

Gemma grinned. "They skyrocketed so much that I was put in charge of the entire tutoring program. I started to require that anyone who works for me must work out with the boys. It's been so successful the university officially said that physical training was to be added to the requirement of being hired as a tutor for the athletes."

They were sitting in the car, he'd turned off the engine, and Gemma let out her breath. She'd never told anyone that story before. She'd tried to, but no one would listen. When the professors and her fellow graduate students had congratulated her on her ingenious program of working out with the athletes, Gemma always said it had been the boys' idea. But no one believed her. When she'd insisted, they'd turned away. Her colleagues and the professors didn't want to believe that the inhabitants of the athletic department could think. To them, thinking football players were too much like *Planet of the Apes* come alive.

Turning, she looked at Colin. His arm muscles

were bulging inside his shirt. He was an athlete who listened and understood. Brains and brawn together—her dream man.

"I think you did a good job," he said. "And I'm impressed that you could really look at yourself. Not many people can do that." He nodded his approval and smiled at her in a way that made Gemma's skin grow warm.

"What do you want to do now?" he asked. "Besides eat, that is?"

Gemma looked out the window at the front of the big Frazier house. It was an unusual structure. It seemed to have been built in sections over the years, and none of them quite matched. She looked back at Colin. "Would your family think it horribly rude of me if I moved into the guesthouse today? I'd really like to get started on the research. Remember what I was reading that first day?"

"Sure," he said. "You were sprawled on the floor with lots of colored pens."

"You and Kirk! What is it about my pens that so intrigues you men?"

"I think he was jealous; I was intrigued. You're an artistic scholar." Colin opened his car door. "You'll be happy to know that I anticipated what you were going to say. This afternoon while you were sleeping off Tris's drugs, I made some calls. Lanny sent you a car. It's a one-year-old Volvo with very low mileage. That sound okay?"

"Perfect."

"Mom had Shamus move your suitcase to the guesthouse, and Rachel packed your refrigerator."

"That sounds heavenly," Gemma said. She had her hand on the door handle. "Have you ever heard of something called a Harewhistle?"

"Not that I remember. Is that what you were reading about? Your 'love, tragedy, and magic'?"

"Yes," she said, impressed that he remembered what she'd said. "That word has stayed in my head. It keeps rattling around in there."

"Through everything? Isla and Kirk? Playing cheerleader with me? Through Tristan pouncing on you?"

"Unfortunately, it wasn't anything like a pounce," she said, but Colin was already outside. She watched him walk around the car. The truth was, Gemma wanted to stay in the guesthouse so she'd be farther away from Colin. She had never been so attracted to a man in her life!

There wasn't anything about him that she disliked. In fact, if she entered everything she'd ever wanted in a man into a computer, Colin Frazier would be what came out. Maybe it came from years of being around football players, but she really liked big men. She'd also grown to favor men who *did* things. Her colleagues, who spent their days reading and debating about things that had happened centuries ago, had come to bore her. But her students, more than a hundred of them over the years, only let her lecture so long, then they plunged into something physical—and she joined them. It had been a genuine challenge for her to teach something like iambic pentameter while she was slamming away at a hanging bag while wearing sixteen-ounce boxing gloves.

All in all, her tutoring and the subsequent workouts had changed how she looked at men. When she'd entered college, she'd imagined that someday she'd have an academic family. She'd be married to a college professor, with two intellectually oriented children. She'd have the same type of relationship with them that she'd had with her father. They'd constantly visit museums, and history books would be their main pleasure.

But the truth was that Gemma'd had more *fun* with the boys she taught than she'd ever before had in her life. And also, based on her months with one of the assistant coaches, she'd found that sex with an athlete was a great deal better than with a page-turner.

And now, this Colin Frazier seemed to be all that she liked in men in one beautiful package. He was smart, educated, resourceful, and an athlete. In the short time she'd been with him, the sight of his muscles under his shirt had come close to making her break into a sweat.

She remembered climbing on him this morning, standing on his broad shoulders, then later, being held in his arms. She didn't know when she'd ever felt such desire.

But Colin wasn't available. He belonged to Jean Caldwell.

Gemma wanted to think that she was above interfering with what seemed to be a very happy union, but she wondered what she'd do if Colin ever looked at her as something other than a friend.

"Probably make a fool of myself," she murmured.

"What was that?" Colin asked as he stood beside her.

"I was just thinking about Tristan and hoping that I don't make a fool of myself over him on our date. He's very nice-looking and a doctor too." She watched Colin's face closely. She didn't know what she was hoping for, a hint of jealousy, maybe? But there was none.

"He's a great guy," Colin said. "Hey! You should get him to tell you about his family. They've been doctors for generations, and he has a couple of scandals in his past that would probably interest you."

"Like what?" In front of them, at the end of the driveway, was a black utility vehicle, and Colin motioned for her to get in. "Until your side heals, you're to take it easy, understand?"

"Yes, Sheriff Frazier," she said, smiling.

"Good attitude." He held her hand as she stepped into the small truck. When Colin got in beside her, her side was pressed against his, and she felt her heart begin to flutter. What are you? she silently asked herself. Fourteen?

"Unmarried mothers," Colin said.

She had no idea what he was talking about and her face said so.

"You asked about Tris's family scandals. I don't know much about them except that a long time ago two Aldredge girls came home to Edilean pregnant but they weren't married."

"Sisters?"

"No. If I remember correctly, they were about fifty years apart."

"Single mothers are common in any family tree." She paused. "One of the people in the letter I read was named Winnie. I assume that's Winifred. Know anyone by that name?"

"No."

"How about a woman named Tamsen?"

"Not that I remember," Colin said. "You should talk to Luke's wife, Jocelyn. She's done a lot on the genealogy of people in Edilean."

"Luke the writer? The man who had sense enough to get out of your way?"

"Sorry about that," Colin said. "When there's an emergency—"

"You get there as quickly as you can so you can help people," Gemma finished for him.

"Yeah, I do." They had reached the guesthouse, and at the sight of it, Gemma gave a sigh.

"Looks like home to you?"

"More or less."

Colin unlocked the door. "It's a bit isolated back

here, so I want you to keep the doors locked. Okay?"

"Sure." She stepped inside the living room. Off the kitchen was a small, round table that was set up with service for two.

"I guess Rachel thought . . ." He didn't continue.

She didn't want him to leave, and from the way he was hesitating, maybe he wanted to stay. "Hungry? We can eat and I'll ask you about the Stone that grants wishes."

"A Stone? Wishes?" Colin looked at her in surprise. "You didn't mention wishes before, or a Stone."

"I guess not. Do you know anything about them?"

"Actually, I think I do. I may know what you read about, but I have to go get something. I'll be right back and—" He glanced at the table.

"I'll have everything ready."

"Great. I missed lunch too."

"Think Rachel made enough?"

Colin looked serious. "A salad is all I need," he said, then hurried out the door.

Smiling at his jest, she watched out the window as he tore across the property in the little truck. She wasn't sure, but she didn't think the manufacturer meant for the vehicle to go that fast. When he was out of sight, she went to the refrigerator and began pulling out glass containers filled with the delicious-looking food Rachel had prepared. Gemma hurriedly put dishes in the microwave and emptied bowls onto plates. By the time Colin returned, everything was ready.

He looked at the many dishes spread on the counter and grinned. "I guess Rachel knew a Frazier would be staying to eat."

As he picked up a plate, he handed her an old spiral notebook. On the battered cover was written in big block letters PRIVATE PROPERTY OF COLIN FRAZIER. SNEAKS WILL BE PUNISHED. THIS MEANS YOU LANNY. "I'm about to see all your secrets?"

Colin had his mouth full of deviled eggs and olives. "All of them in the year I was thirteen." He wiped his hands on a napkin and took the notebook from her. "My grandfather—Dad's father—used to tell us kids stories about our ancestors. I think half of them were a pack of lies, but I still wrote them down."

"What kind of lies?" Gemma was filling her own plate.

"According to my grandfather," Colin said, "it was our family, the Fraziers, who started this town, not the McTerns or the Harcourts. But only my sister, Ariel, believed him. We used to tease her that she wanted to be a princess so much that she'd believe anything."

"Sounds like she had a real fun childhood."

"Don't worry about Ariel. She can hold her own. Anyway, I used to write down some of the stories Gramps told us. Unfortunately, I decided that Mr. Wilson's geometry class was the best time for me to write. I still don't know how to use a protractor. Here it is. The Heartwishes Stone."

"Heartwishes?"

Colin handed the notebook to her, filled his plate, then sat down at the table.

Gemma sat across from him and read aloud.

Grandpa Frazier's story number 7
The Heartwishes Stone was given to a
Frazier man who saved his clan. He was a
big, strong man who moved a rock that had
sealed them in a cave. A witch gave him
the Stone to say thanks. She said that any
Frazier who made a wish from his heart
would get the wish if the Stone was nearby.
It works for lady Fraziers too.

"Think I'll win a Pulitzer?" Colin asked.

"Half of my football players can't write this well." She was rereading the little story and wondering if this was a subject for her dissertation. Family myth. It was a possibility.

"You look like a calculator started clicking in your mind."

She looked across the table at him. "I have an ulterior motive for wanting this job."

"Oh?" he asked as he buttered a slice of homemade bread.

She told him about her need of an original subject to write about for her dissertation.

"Finding something around here that's old but has never been written about shouldn't be too hard," he said. "Jean says Edilean is as weird as if a bunch of Martians had set up a town in the U.S."

"From what I've seen, I agree with her. Is there *any* crime here?" Gemma cut into a slice of cold roast beef.

"We had more than our share last fall, what with all those agents from the FBI and the Secret Service, plus several detectives from the Fort Lauderdale Police Department."

"Oh right," Gemma said, still looking at the notebook. "I'm looking forward to meeting this detective. Mike Shaw, is it?"

"Newland. I tend to forget Sara's new name," he said. "You want some more tea?"

"Sure," she said. "So tell me what happened."

"Nope. That's Mike and Sara's story. They can tell you when you go to the cookout." He stood up. "I've got to go to the office for a while. You want to go with—?" He broke off. "I guess I'm getting too used to you being with me." He picked up his plate and took it to the sink.

"I'll take care of this," she said. "You go on and see about saving people. Oh! I forgot to ask if there's Internet service in here."

"We had a router put in, so you have wireless. You look like you're dying to get rid of me."

"That's not true . . ." she began, but stopped. She didn't want him to leave but she couldn't say that. "Yes, you're right. I can't wait to dive into the books in the library. Tomorrow morning I'll tackle the storage room. The garage is last. What?"

He was looking at her in speculation. "How are you going to move boxes when you have stitches in your side?"

"Carefully."

"I'll come and help you. We'll weed out the money documents, all the boring stuff, from the others."

Gemma started to protest but stopped herself. "Okay," she said at last.

For a moment they looked at each other, then Colin said, "Sure you don't want me to help you clean up this mess?"

"I'm sure. I'm going to make myself a pot of tea and see what I can find out about your Heartwishes. Think it's like the Stone of Scone? Big enough to sit on?"

"I don't know. What exactly did your research say?"

"I don't remember it verbatim. I was a bit nervous when I read it, too worried about the job to concentrate. I mostly remember names. Winnie, Tamsen, Ewan, and poor Julian." She glanced at the table and the countertop with its food and dirty dishes, then back up at Colin.

He seemed to understand what she'd just thought. "You go find the letter and I'll clean up," he said.

"What about your office?"

"It was just paperwork, and Roy probably already

took care of it. She loves that stuff. Give her a computer and she's happy. That and a large sidearm."

Gemma laughed. "I like her already."

"I'll make some calls, clean up in here, and I'll meet you in the library," he said.

"You're sure?"

"Positive," he said.

Gemma waited until she was out of the room before she let herself smile—and then it was so wide she was afraid her skin would crack.

9

GEMMA LEANED BACK against the bookcase and looked at Colin. It was a sunny afternoon, and they were eating sandwiches she'd made from what had been put in the refrigerator. Colin had fixed them glasses of iced tea.

Surrounding both of them, as though they each were on an island, was a sea of letters, diaries, journals, deeds, legal papers. Anything anyone had thought was important at the time had been saved.

"This is ridiculous, you know that, don't you?" Gemma said.

"Which part?" he asked as he took a bite of his sandwich.

"This disorganization. I need to put these papers in chronological order."

"I thought you wanted to . . . What was it you said? 'Explore a family myth.'" He smiled. "Or maybe you want to find the Stone so you can make a wish."

She motioned her arm about the pretty library. "*This* is my Heartwish."

"So you'd be content to live in somebody's guesthouse and sort papers for the rest of your life?"

Gemma took a deep drink of her tea.

Colin waited, but she said nothing. "Come on, tell me what your life plan is."

"What about yours?"

"You've seen my life," he said. "I want to know about yours. What do you plan to do after you finish your dissertation?"

"Get a job, of course."

"Where?"

"Anywhere they'll have me."

When Colin frowned, Gemma knew why. She was purposely not answering his question. "Okay. I want the normal things every woman wants. Home, family, great job. Save the world. By the way, what is *your* deepest wish? You're a Frazier, so maybe this Stone will show up—if it wasn't sold at auction, that is—and you'll get your wish fulfilled."

Colin didn't meet her eyes. "I want what I have. I'm content."

Gemma remembered what Jean had said about the Fraziers keeping secrets, and she felt sure that Colin was evading the issue. But he had that right, didn't he? Gemma was a relative stranger to him, so he didn't have to tell her anything. When she got up, her side hurt and she winced.

"You okay?"

"Fine, but I need an early night." Yesterday after they'd eaten, they'd worked together for a couple of hours. Colin had called a woman named Jocelyn, the wife of the famous writer, and she'd attached the genealogy files she'd made to an e-mail. She told them how to download the software that would open them, and Colin supplied a credit card. Thirty minutes later, Gemma and Colin were looking at the family trees of what he called "the seven founding families of Edilean."

Gemma asked him what he knew about how the town started.

"No one knows the true story," he said, "but it's been passed down that it involved a wagonload of gold and a beautiful young woman named Edilean. She was a McTern or a Harcourt, we're not sure which. We don't know where the other families came from."

"Do you think they were friends of Edilean's? Did they come from Scotland together?"

"We're pretty sure the Fraziers came from Scotland, and so did the McDowells and the McTerns."

She glanced at the list she'd made of the names. "What about the Aldredges and the Connors? And the Welsches? Where did they all meet and why did they settle here?"

"No one knows for sure."

"I think the real question is why did they all *stay* here," Gemma said thoughtfully.

"Are you disparaging my beautiful little town?"

"No. It's just that Americans tend to move a lot.

Actually, I rather like what I've seen of this town so far."

"And you've seen little of it," he said.

"I'm looking forward to the barbecue."

"Barbecue?" Colin asked. "Oh, right. Your date with Tristan. I better warn you that—"

"Every woman falls in love with him?" Gemma asked. "Nell already told me." If she'd been hoping for a flicker of jealousy from Colin, she was disappointed.

They'd spent the morning in the garage while Colin took boxes off the shelves and showed the contents to Gemma. If there was nothing inside but household accounts, he put the box in the bed of the utility vehicle. When it was full, Colin drove it to another storage place on the estate and unloaded it. When he returned, they filled it again.

Through the whole process, he'd been adamant that Gemma was to lift nothing heavier than a packet of letters.

At noon they'd returned to the house for lunch.

Gemma was now looking down at him as he sat on the floor. "You don't have to spend the whole day with me. I'm sure your family would like some time with you."

"Actually, Mom told me to stay here with you. I think she's worried about your injury."

"That's nice of her." Gemma held out her hand for his plate and took them both to the kitchen. As she put them in the dishwasher, she took a few breaths. Part of her wished Colin would leave and let her work alone. But the larger part of her never wanted him to go away. Last evening and this morning they'd bounced ideas back and forth.

Well, actually, she'd talked and he'd listened. As they went through boxes and trunks and bags, making the first cursory inspections, they'd talked about Gemma's dissertation. He wanted to know what interested her. What era in history most intrigued her? Were there any historical mysteries she'd like to solve? Some myth she'd like to expose as false?

"You know, don't you, that the first rule of a dissertation is that no one other than your professors will read it?" she said.

"If you find out something about the eighteenth century, Luke will put it in one of his books and a million or so people will read about it," Colin said.

"If I did that, do you think he'd write me a recommendation and help me get a good job?"

"Definitely," Colin said. "Luke knows some people at William and Mary." He looked at her for a moment, and she knew he was asking her if that school suited her.

It almost seemed as if he were asking if she'd like to settle in Edilean permanently. Gemma felt blood rushing to her face and had to turn away. She really did need to get herself back under control!

At last, she said, "That school has an excellent reputation and I'd be proud to be associated with it."

Colin didn't say anything, but the way he smiled made her heart jump into her throat.

After lunch, they worked some more. Gemma was happy sitting on the library floor, but Colin persuaded her to move to the living room. He took the couch and she sat in the big club chair and they read in silence.

But as the hours went on, Gemma found that she couldn't concentrate. She kept looking at Colin, at his big body sprawled on the couch, one leg hanging down to the floor. There was a cold bottle of wine in the refrigerator, and she thought about suggesting that they open it. What happened afterward . . . Well, she'd leave that to fate.

At four, Colin stood up and stretched—and Gemma felt her heart start to pound.

"I need to go to the gym," he said. "This is too much sitting for me. I'd ask you to go with me, but with your side, you can't risk it."

Gemma thought that what she needed was sixty minutes on a treadmill, forty-five minutes with the gloves, then an icy shower.

"Listen," he said. "I want you in bed early tonight. You need time to heal. Promise?"

"Yes," she answered.

"If you need me, you have my cell number, and I put Mike's number on the desk in the library."

"Mike the detective," she said. "The one in Fort Lauderdale?"

"He's home now, and he'll know what to do in case of any problems," Colin said. "By the way, Mike set up a makeshift gym downtown in what used to be his wife's dress shop. It's very informal, only invited people go, and we don't have many women. But then, Mike scares them off."

"How does he do that?"

"I think I'll let Mike show you." He started toward the door, but hesitated. "You'll be all right here by yourself?"

"Perfectly fine."

"Okay," he said at last, then took a step toward her as though he meant to hug her or kiss her cheek good-bye.

Gemma knew she wouldn't be able to stand that. She took a step back and the moment passed.

When he was gone, she didn't know whether to be relieved or devastated. "He belongs to someone else," she told herself, then immediately went back to work.

Without Colin hovering over her and making sure she didn't strain herself, she started organizing. As far as she could tell, at some point in the life of the Frazier papers some industrious person had "cleaned up." Gemma had always found tidy people to be maddening. Their one and only goal seemed to be to have everything appear to be "neat." "Put away." "Out of sight." It didn't seem to matter that bills were mixed in with the kitchen utensils, that research supplies were thrown in with the shoes. Just so everything looked good!

For Gemma, she put like things together, and if she didn't have time to put something where it belonged, she left it out.

Unfortunately, whoever had stored away the Frazier papers had put them away by size. Small papers dated 1620 were in a box with small papers dated 1934. This lack of correct sequencing nearly drove Gemma crazy.

The first thing she did was take everything off the shelves in the library and storage room. A couple of times she reached too far and felt her stitches pull, but she learned to keep her elbow close to her ribs.

Once the shelves in both rooms were clean, she mentally categorized the space into decades. As she emptied the containers, she put dated papers into the proper areas. Once they were sorted, she would rebox them in archival storage containers that were acid free and wouldn't eat up the contents.

She didn't stop emptying and sorting until her stomach was growling. After a quick meal—and she silently thanked Rachel for her cooking—Gemma went back to work. When it grew dark, she turned on all the lights. She carried empty boxes from the house to the garage where there was now space since she and Colin had cleared out that area.

She fell into bed at 1 A.M., was up at six, and started work immediately. The days began to merge together as she went through everything and piled it high on shelves in the house. There were several boxes of account books in the garage that could be taken away to be stored elsewhere, but she had gone through everything inside the house.

When all of it was out, she went online to Gaylord

library supplies and compiled her wish list for storage boxes. Gemma was torn between going to the main house and disturbing Mrs. Frazier or e-mailing her. Electronic mail won out.

Mrs. Frazier replied instantly, saying that she'd reimburse Gemma for whatever she spent.

Gemma put in her credit card number, pushed the SEND button on the order, then leaned back in her chair and looked about the room. If Colin were there she'd open the wine in the refrigerator and they'd celebrate. But he wasn't there. In fact, she hadn't seen or heard from him in days now.

An hour later, he called. There was static on the line and a lot of noise wherever he was. She could hear men shouting.

"Gemma?" he said into the phone, and she knew he was shouting. "I'm sorry I haven't called you, but there's no cell service here."

"Where are you?" She had to shout the question three times before he heard her.

"At that ranger station," he shouted back. "Fire fighting. Whole family here. You okay?"

Fire? Gemma thought and many images of forest fires ran through her head. "Are *you* all right? Can I help?"

"I'm fine. No, stay there. I have to go. They need the phone. I'll be back when I can. Okay?"

"Yes," she said, then heard the phone click off. She stood where she was for a moment. So this is what it was like when you cared about a law enforcement man.

She went to the TV and turned it on. It took her a moment to find a channel with local news, but there the fire was, roaring across trees, destroying everything in its path.

She spent an hour watching, saw film of women at a table passing out food and drinks to firefighters and she saw Mrs. Frazier and Rachel. But she didn't see Colin.

She had to make herself return to work, but she left the TV on with muted sound. Whenever anything about the fire came on, she listened.

It took great effort on her part to give her mind back to her research.

As she looked at the massive amount of data around her, she tried to figure out where to begin. The logical way would be to start with the oldest documents and come forward. But Colin was right in that what truly interested her was his Heartwishes story. She hadn't realized it, but she'd been thinking of her dissertation while she worked. "The Origin of a Family Myth" was one title she'd thought of. "Myth and Reality in one Family" was another. "The Didacticism of a Myth." She must have come up with fifty titles, all of them centered around the Frazier Heartwishes.

She opened the refrigerator, saw that most of the food Rachel had prepared was gone, and knew she needed to go to the grocery. Besides, she wanted to hear what the locals knew about the fire.

She looked at her watch, saw that it was a little after four. Maybe if she drove into town—in the car she'd not yet used—she could stop by his office and ask his deputy what she knew. The keys were by the back door and the Volvo was in the carport. It was a pretty car with dark blue upholstery. It took her a few minutes to orient herself to the buttons on the car before she pulled out.

Every time she'd gone to the guesthouse she'd passed the main house, but now she saw that there was a narrow gravel drive out the back and she followed it. To the left was the Frazier house, but Gemma turned right and ended up on McDowell Avenue, which led her to downtown Edilean.

She parked under some trees across from the grassy little square, got out, locked the car, then stood and looked. Now what? she thought. She had no idea where Colin's office was.

"Hi, Gemma," said a voice behind her.

Turning, she saw one of the women she'd met in the grocery. In a stroller was the little girl she and Colin had held. Gemma went to the child. "How are you, Caitlyn?" she asked, and the girl smiled happily. Gemma tried to remember if she'd heard the mother's name.

"I hear you have a date with Dr. Tris."

"Sort of," Gemma said cautiously. She felt that the invitation from Tris was more about friendship than an actual date, but she didn't say that.

"Every unmarried woman in town has tried to get him to ask her out, so what did you do to entice him?"

Gemma wasn't sure how to answer that. "I don't know. I think maybe his niece got him to ask me."

The woman smiled. "I can believe that. He adores Nell." Little Caitlyn began to grow restless. "I have to go, but maybe we can have lunch sometimes."

"Yeah, sure," Gemma said as the woman waved good-bye.

Smiling, Gemma crossed the street to the square. She stood under the big oak tree and looked around.

Across the road, she saw stores, all of them obviously under some historic code for their façades, so their signs were barely visible. There was a drugstore and several unbelievably cute little boutiques that sold toys, children's clothing, outdoor gear, body products, a jewelry store called "Kim's," and a shop full of old maps and prints.

On the corner was a door and a window with DR. TRISTAN ALDREDGE written in dark green letters. Beside it was a tall, narrow brick building with SHERIFF written over the door. Gemma looked up and saw the small windows on the second floor. She smiled as she remembered Colin's description of his dark, smelly apartment.

She crossed the street to the office. An old-fashioned bell rang when she opened the door. Inside were two big oak desks, the kind a person saw in an old black-and-white western starring Henry Fonda.

On the far wall was a glass-doored case full of rifles, looking ready to be used if anyone tried to get the bad guy out of jail.

"You're Gemma," said a voice to her right.

She turned to see a tall woman, early thirties, with sleek black hair pulled into a bun at the nape of her neck. She wore a brown uniform that fit her athletic body perfectly. The heavy black belt around her small waist was filled with leather pockets, one of them containing a handgun.

"Oh," Gemma said, surprised that the woman knew who she was. "Did Colin—" She cut herself off. "YouTube."

"Right. Pretty heroic stunt for a civilian."

"It was Tom's idea, and Colin did all the work. I just grabbed the kid."

The young woman looked Gemma up and down. "Uh huh. If you want to work out together sometime, Mike's gym is at the end of the block. By the way, I'm Rolanda. Roy."

"I've heard about you. Colin says you're great on a computer."

"That's what he tells me, but it's really odd that when I can't figure out something, he knows how to do it. The truth is, he thinks that by flattering me I'll do anything that requires a person to sit in a chair for longer than fifteen minutes."

"Does it work?"

"Perfectly," Roy said, smiling. "He and I have an unspoken agreement. I let him dump the paperwork on me, and he lets me bring my son to the office when the sitter flakes out on me."

Gemma, ever curious, said, "Your husband . . ."

"Single mother. He wanted me *and* his old girlfriend. I said no."

"Imagine that."

The two women smiled at each other.

"What have you heard about the fire?" Gemma asked.

"It's under control. The family should be back today. Except Mr. Frazier might stay awhile. If any vehicle breaks down, he can fix it."

"Oh?" Gemma said and knew her expression was giving too much away. She had really missed Colin. "I'm just concerned, is all. Colin said there was no cell phone service there."

It was Roy's turn to look surprised. "He called you from the fire?"

"Just once. I haven't heard anything in a while."

Roy's smile broadened. "I heard you're going out with Dr. Tris."

"It's just to a barbecue," Gemma said, her mind on Colin. "How bad is the fire?"

"We've had worse." Roy was watching Gemma. "You're all Colin has talked about since he met you."

"Really?"

"Yeah." Roy was looking at Gemma in speculation. "He likes you."

Gemma willed the blood not to rush to her face and give her away. "We're becoming buddies."

"That's not what the town is saying."

Gemma didn't think she should reply to that statement. "I better go. I just wanted to introduce myself."

"Stop by any time. And if you have any problems about anything, give us a call."

"Okay." She had her hand on the doorknob but turned back. "What happened about Tara and her flower bed? She said someone was trampling it."

"Sleepwalking."

"What?"

Roy smiled. "Colin figured it out, but then he usually does. He's good at mysteries. He had her put up cameras to make sure. They showed Tara walking through her flowers, wearing her husband's shoes, and sound asleep. Dr. Tris gave her some pills to help her sleep and told Tara's husband to get a job that let him stay at home more." She paused. "I wouldn't usually tell anyone about a case, but this one is all over town anyway. Poor Tara says she wants to hide."

"I don't blame her." Gemma hesitated. "I need to ask you a question and I don't know how to say it."

Roy's face changed from smiling to serious. "If anyone is bothering you—"

"No, not that. Where's a grocery store that's, well, cheaper than the organic one?"

Roy's eyes lit up as she smiled. "Go there. You'll be pleasantly surprised by the final total. Colin didn't say so, but it's my guess that he took you there to show Ellie that you're now an honorary Frazier. She'll give you the family discount."

"Even though I'm a temporary resident?"

"If you're with Colin, that's enough for all of us."

"I'd think that privilege would be reserved for Jean."

Roy took a while to answer. "Doesn't she wear the most beautiful high heels you've ever seen? Two years ago she broke a heel off on our brick sidewalks and I haven't seen her in Edilean since."

Gemma could only blink at Roy as an understanding passed between them. She wasn't in favor of Colin and Jean being together. Smiling, Gemma said good-bye and left the office.

Instead of returning to the guesthouse, she decided to walk around the square at the shops. Each one was pretty and well kept. At the end of the block from Colin's office was a large building with locked doors and shades over the windows. Paint had been scraped off the glass doors but she could see that it used to read EDILEAN FASHIONS. This was probably the gym Colin had told her about. If her side wasn't so sore she would have knocked on the door, but she didn't.

After she'd circled the block, not going into any store, she got in her car and drove out McTern Road to Ellie's store. A couple of people waved hello, but no one stopped her. As before, Ellie was in the back behind the deli counter.

"I hear you're going to my daughter's barbecue with Tristan," Ellie said.

Gemma wanted to get away from that subject. "Is it true that Mike scares people in the gym?"

Ellie smiled. "If people sit around on the benches and talk too much, he can be *very* scary. So are you going with Tris?"

"Yes," Gemma said.

There were three other women waiting their turn, and all of them stared at Gemma as though to ask how she'd finagled that date.

Ellie's eyes twinkled. "Give everyone kisses from me, especially Tris and Colin."

At the mention of the second man, the women's mouths fell open. It seemed that Tris and Colin were the town's prize catches.

"Here you are," Ellie said as she handed Gemma a white package. "Lots of sliced turkey. Be sure and get some brown mustard. Colin likes it, but then you probably already know that."

Smiling, Gemma turned away, but Ellie's voice made her look back. "And Tris loves pickles. Better get at least four kinds. Now, ladies, what can I do for you?"

Gemma had to suppress her laughter as she went in search of mustard and pickles.

10

THE NEXT MORNING, Colin called again. The connection wasn't any better than the first time. "Mom and the others left," he said. "They'll check on you soon."

"What about you?" she shouted into the phone. "When do you get back?"

"I don't know. Days. I'm helping with the cleanup. Miss me?"

"Yes," she said.

There was what sounded like a crash and it was a minute before Colin got back on the line. "I have to go, but I wanted to tell you that no one's been hurt. I'll see you when I get back."

Gemma hung up and held the phone to her for a moment. That he'd called even when he was so very busy made her feel good.

By that afternoon, she was well into her research. As she dug deeper, she had to remind herself that she was doing a family history. She didn't have to be as precise as she usually would be. This was for fun, to please a family—or, more precisely, Mrs. Frazier.

The truth was, she was rationalizing. She didn't want to delve into medieval history but to stay in the nineteenth century. She wanted to know about the piece of letter she'd read. Who was Julian? Who was "that woman" who'd not cared about his death?

She'd been through Jocelyn's genealogy charts and had even exchanged a few e-mails with her, but they could find no one named Julian.

However, there were two Tamsens. One was an Aldredge, the other a Frazier. If the war mentioned in the letter was the Civil War, then the writer had to be Tamsen Frazier, as the Aldredge woman died before the war began. But the names made Gemma think there was a connection.

She e-mailed Jocelyn and asked what she knew about the Tamsens, but Joce said she'd only found dates. She didn't know if either woman had married or produced children. "The Aldredges tend toward fatherless children," Joce wrote. "We all tease Tris about that. And the Fraziers and Aldredges have been friends and have intermarried all the way back to the settling of the town."

"The friendship doesn't seem to have changed," Gemma wrote back.

"Nothing changes in this town," Joce responded. "I named my daughter Edilean."

A few more exchanges resulted in Joce saying that

she and her family would be at the barbecue. "Everyone in town wants to meet you. Even Roy praised what you did to save that little boy, and she thinks most women are victims waiting to happen. My best friends, Sara and Tess, will be there. They're both pregnant and have contests to see who can eat the most. So far, Tess is winning."

Smiling, Gemma wrote that she looked forward to meeting all of them, then went back to work. Mrs. Frazier came by the guesthouse, driving a red utility vehicle that had a crown painted in gold on the hood.

"My son Lanny's idea of a joke," she said, but she didn't seem to be displeased. She was fascinated by every word Gemma told her, especially about the Heartwishes. "Do you have to be a Frazier by blood? Must you be *born* into the family to get your wish?" she asked.

"I don't know," Gemma said, taken aback by the woman's vehemence. She started to say that the story of the Stone's magical powers was just a family myth, but she didn't. It looked as though Mrs. Frazier had a wish she wanted to come true. What the woman could possibly want that she didn't already have was beyond Gemma's imagination.

"Keep working, dear," Mrs. Frazier said as she handed Gemma a credit card. "It's the same one Rachel uses to buy for the household. Get whatever you need for the job."

"What's happened with the fire?" she asked before the woman ran off.

"Not too bad," Mrs. Frazier said. "A lot of damage, but no one's been hurt. Better yet, it's under control."

"Colin said he was helping with the cleanup."

Mrs. Frazier gave a little smile. "My son called you?"

"Just a couple of times," Gemma said and wished she'd not told that. The Frazier family loved Jean.

"That's lovely," Mrs. Frazier said as she climbed into her little truck. She was still smiling as she drove away.

Gemma didn't waste any time trying to understand the woman's enigmatic little smile but went back to work.

Mr. Frazier stopped by to give her a paycheck. When Gemma offered to tell him about her research, he looked as though he might fall asleep. She said, "Morgan," and he instantly came alive.

"Founded in 1909 by Henry Frederick Stanley Morgan in Malvern Link, Worcestershire. I bought two of them from his son Peter before he died a few years ago. I have an Aero SuperSport on order."

Gemma's eyes widened. "Don't those cost—"

"Ssssh!" he said. "You tell Alea and I'll make you drive it."

"Heard about how much I loved driving Colin's Jeep, did you?"

"What I heard is that you rode with him and didn't scream." He looked at her as though to say she'd done a good job. As he climbed into his little truck—black with red stripes on the hood—he said,

"Oh yeah, Lanny saw the tape of you climbing on Colin and he says he's in love with you."

"Isla will be heartbroken," Gemma replied, and Mr. Frazier laughed as he sped away.

Shamus visited twice. He was a quiet young man, saying hardly anything, but she had an idea that he saw a lot. On his first visit she started to tell him of the little she'd learned of his ancestors, but like his father, he didn't seem interested.

If there was one thing she knew about big, athletic boys it was that they were always hungry. She told him to sit on the couch while she made him a sandwich. He had his ever-present drawing case with him and he began to sketch while she loaded bread high with meat and whatever she could find in the refrigerator. She didn't have any potato chips so she sliced carrots. She set the plate and a quart of iced tea on the coffee table, then went back to work.

An hour later she looked up from where she was sitting on the floor, surrounded by books and papers, and Shamus had moved to the chair and was sketching. She went back to work, paying no attention to him. An hour or so later, he left, saying nothing, just raising his hand in farewell.

The next day he stopped by again. She opened the door to his knock but she'd been reading some letters and didn't want to stop. Shamus seemed to understand, as he motioned for her to sit back down. He went to the kitchen and minutes later he put a tray with a sandwich and tea down beside her. She smiled up at him as he sat down in the chair with his sandwich. The next time she looked up, he was drawing. She didn't know when he left. That evening there were two huge floor cushions outside her door and she felt sure Shamus had been the person who'd obtained them. Gratefully, she put one on the library floor and another one against the shelves.

As for the rest of the family, Lanny and Pere, she didn't see them. Rachel came by to pick up the bowls and to give her more "leftovers." Since most of the dishes hadn't been touched, Gemma knew Rachel had prepared them specially.

"Heartwishes, huh?" Rachel said without preamble.

"You've heard about it?"

"It's all Mrs. F can talk about. She's worried that it won't work for her, so she made Mr. F say three times, 'I wish for grandchildren.' Any day now I expect Lanny to tell us he's knocked up some girl."

"Hope it's not Isla," Gemma said, and they laughed.

As Rachel climbed into her UTV—this one in green camouflage—Gemma said, "I haven't heard from Colin in days. Nothing bad happened at the fire, did it?"

"We've not heard anything either," Rachel said. "But Colin flies a helicopter, so they keep him pretty busy. Are you missing him?"

"It's just that—" Breaking off, Gemma shook her head. "I just want to know that he's okay."

"How are you going to choose between Colin and Dr. Tris?"

"Tris is just a friend, that's all. I hardly know him. Colin's a friend too and I don't know him very well either, but—" When Rachel started grinning, Gemma decided to shut up.

"Friendship is great, isn't it?" Rachel said, then sped off toward the house.

Absolutely no one was helping her keep her distance from Colin!

❦

The next morning Gemma awoke at 4 A.M. and couldn't go back to sleep. For the last several years she'd started her day with an energetic workout, and now the lack of activity was making her restless. At five she gave up the struggle and got up, dressed, and went to the kitchen to make herself breakfast. It was still dark outside, so when she heard a tap on the glass door and saw what looked to be a man wearing a mask, she jumped. It took her a few moments to realize it was Colin. She went to the door, turned the latch, and opened it.

"I'm glad to see you did lock it," he said as he stepped inside.

He looked awful! The "mask" he was wearing was soot and smoke, so thick on him that she couldn't see his skin. "Come in and sit down. You look exhausted."

"No. I don't want to dirty your furniture. I dropped Pere off and I was going home, but I saw your light on and wondered if anything was wrong. What's that smell?"

"Oh!" she said as she hurried to the kitchen. "It's turkey bacon."

When she turned back to him, he had a look of hunger in his eyes. "How long has it been since you ate?"

"I don't know. Yesterday sometime." He put his hand on the door. "I need to get home and—"

"I cut up red peppers and onions, and I have cheese and eggs. I make a great omelet. And I bought some of Ellie's seven grain bread. It's a few days old but if I put enough butter on it you won't be able to tell."

She could see that he was giving in. When she motioned him toward the kitchen, he went to a stool by the bar, and sat down. She quickly poured him a glass of orange juice and he drained it in one gulp. Toast lavished with butter kept him busy while she whisked four eggs. She'd already chopped the peppers and onions and sauteed them in oil. She put them with the cheese on the omelet and put the plate in front of him.

He didn't say a word until all the food was gone.

"Better?" she asked when he looked up.

"Much," he said, then gave a huge yawn. When he tried to cover it, he smeared the dirt on his face.

"How long has it been since you slept?"

"I think it's three days now." He started to stand up. "Gemma, you're a real treasure. Thanks for this.

I've got to get home so I can get cleaned up. My skin is itching. And I need to sleep."

When he took a step and stumbled, she was afraid for him to drive. Gemma put her hand on his back and pushed him toward her bedroom. "Shower's on the right. Take your time."

"Clothes . . ." he said.

"I have a jersey so big you and Shamus together could wear it, and I have matching sweatpants. Go on! Once you're clean, I'll drive you to your place and you can sleep."

When he gave her a one-sided grin, his white teeth stood out against the dirt on his face. "Ten minutes," he said.

Gemma watched him leave the room, and when she heard the shower running, she couldn't stop the desire she felt. Colin, naked, and just a few feet away. She scrambled a couple of eggs for herself, ate, then cleaned up the kitchen. When she heard the water turned off, she realized she should have found the clothes beforehand and laid them out for him. Maybe while he was drying off, she could slip into her bedroom and get the clothes.

She glanced inside and saw that Colin was lying facedown across her bed, clean, a towel wrapped around his middle, and he was sound asleep.

She took a few steps toward the closet, but the sight of Colin's nearly nude body sprawled across her bed was not to be ignored.

It was dark in the bedroom, but a soft light from

the kitchen highlighted his deep muscle and made his skin appear golden. He was damp from his shower and she very much wanted to feel his warm skin.

For a moment she closed her eyes as she inhaled the fragrance of him. It was as though his sheer masculinity filled the room. She could smell it, feel it, taste it; it surrounded her.

When she opened her eyes, she saw that Colin was looking at her, his eyes only half open, shaded—and they were as full of desire as she felt.

He held out his hand to her, beseeching her to take it.

She couldn't resist as she touched his palm with her fingertips, then felt her hand enclosed by his much larger one.

When he turned onto his back, he pulled her toward him and her other hand fell onto his chest.

"I've wanted you since the first moment I saw you," he whispered.

"Me too," she said as he pulled her into his arms. When his lips touched hers, his kiss was everything she'd hoped it would be. Too often, she'd caught herself looking at his lips and wondering about them. When he moved his lips to her neck, she put her head back. She was wearing the loose-fitting clothes that she worked in, and they came off easily as Colin's big hands went under her shirt.

"Beautiful," he murmured as his mouth sought her breasts.

Seconds later she was nude and her arms were

open to him. When he moved on top of her, she gasped from the weight of him—the wonderful, heavy male weight of him. She clasped her legs about his waist and moved as he entered her.

There were a few quick, hard thrusts and then it was over.

"Thanks, babe," Colin said, and collapsed onto her. Instantly, she could feel his soft breathing on her neck. He was asleep.

Gemma lay still for a moment, decidedly unsatisfied, but Colin's skin against hers felt good.

After a while, she thought she should get up, but it wasn't easy getting him off of her. She pushed on his shoulder, but she may as well have been trying to move a boulder.

"Colin," she said softly, but he didn't respond. "Colin!" she said louder. He still didn't move.

She did her best to scoot out from under him and when she did, she felt a sharp pain in her side. "Great," she murmured. "Torn stitches."

Frustrated, she elbowed him in the ribs. With a grunt, he rolled off of her, but his right arm looped around her as though she were his teddy bear, and he pulled her close to him.

"Come on, Jean," he said. "Let me sleep." He turned his head away from her.

She stopped moving. "I am Gemma," she said clearly and rather loudly.

"Ah, Gemma," Colin said. "Smart and brave."

If she'd heard those words an hour ago, she would

have been pleased, but now they were both naked, they'd just had a quickie version of sex, and worst, he'd called her "Jean."

It took some effort, but she managed to disentangle herself from his arm and stand up. She stood beside the bed, looking down at him, and she felt disgusted with herself for allowing her desire to override her common sense. Gemma knew that she was the only single woman she knew who'd never had a one-night stand. One friend said it was the only way to go. "No complications. Get in, get it done, then leave," was what she preached.

But Gemma had never been like that. Maybe it was because she seemed to live in a world of history, but she believed that sex should mean something more than just the physicality of it.

Today, she'd broken her own code. She'd allowed plain old lust to make her forget herself.

She stopped thinking when she felt something warm run down her side. She couldn't see in the nearly dark room, but when she touched it, she felt her wet bandage. Damn! She'd reopened her wound.

As she went to the bathroom, all she knew for sure was that she had to leave the guesthouse immediately. She quickly pulled on her clothes, not paying much attention to what she put on, grabbed her bag and car keys, and went outside. Once she was in the car, she wasn't sure where she was going, but it seemed sensible to go to the doctor to have her side looked at.

When she got to Tris's office, it was still early

and there was no one on the streets. Now what? she thought. Did she sit in her car and wait for the town to open up?

When someone tapped on her window, she gave a little yelp. Leaning toward her was Tris's beautiful face, a hot coffee mug in his hand. She put the window down.

"Are you all right?" Tris asked.

"My side is bleeding."

"Come inside and I'll look at it." He opened the car door, and when she stumbled, he took her arm in his. Minutes later she was sitting on an exam table, her shirt pulled up, and he had removed her bandage.

"It's okay," he said. "This dampness isn't blood and you're healing well. It looks like the gauze got wet. Did you take a shower or get in a tub this morning?"

"I . . ." Gemma began and found herself fighting tears.

"Did something happen?" Tris asked. "Gemma?" He took a step back. "I'm going to call Colin."

"No!" she half shouted.

Tris paused. "Okay. No Colin. How about some whiskey?"

Gemma managed to give him a half smile. "Thanks, but no."

When she started to get off the table, he helped her, and he didn't let go of her hand. Tris led her to the big chair and had her sit down. He moved a chair to across from her. "Now tell me what's made you so angry at our illustrious sheriff."

"I . . ." She hesitated, but there was something earnest in Tris's beautiful face that made her confide in him. It took her only minutes to tell him everything. She told about her days spent with Colin, and how much she liked him. "He showed me the house he'd bought before anyone else knew about it. When he left to fight a fire, he called me from there. I was beginning to think there was something between us, but then he called me Jean. And everyone talks of them like they're about to get married but Colin never mentions her—except to say she's going to help him buy furniture." She put her hands over her face. "I don't know what's going on. And now *this*!"

She told him of her very brief sex with Colin.

To her consternation, Tristan grinned. "Good!" he said.

"Good?" She could feel anger rising in her. "You don't understand! Mrs. Frazier dismissed one of the job applicants because she slept with Lanny. If she hears what I did, she'll fire me and I've just begun the work, and—"

"I've known Alea Frazier all my life, and Lanny too, for that matter. Colin told me his mother hired you because you were interested in the research. Besides, if she let everyone Lanny had slept with make her decisions for her, half of the county would be eliminated." He took his cell out of his pocket. "I'll call Rachel and she'll get Colin out of your place, then you and I can go out to breakfast."

"I've already eaten."

"Then you can have some decadent, sugary thing. Or better yet, something chocolate."

Even the thought made her feel better. "You're a good girlfriend," she said, then was shocked. "I didn't mean—"

Tris put up his hand. "It's okay. My last woman friend said I was a 'latent homosexual' because I didn't want to marry her."

"Saved her pride."

"Didn't do much for mine," he said, then spoke into the phone. "Rachel? Hope I didn't wake you, but Gemma and I need your help." He went into the waiting room to finish the call.

Twenty minutes later Gemma was sitting in Ellie's grocery at a table across from Tristan. The store wasn't open yet, so Tris had led her through the back. Around them was a bustle of employees as they replenished goods and produce. Ellie had been too busy to attend to them, but it seemed that Tris being there so early was a regular occurrence, and he knew where to get what.

On a plate in front of Gemma was a pastry that had chocolate in and around it, and there was a mug of some thick goo that was nearly pure chocolate. After four big bites and two gulps, she felt a great deal better. "You're a good doctor," she murmured, her mouth full.

"I learned about chocolate and women in my first year of med school. It's never failed me."

He was eating an egg burrito that she had an idea

Ellie made just for him. Gemma couldn't help noticing that every female worker who walked by made sure Tris saw her. Gemma had received many up-and-down looks as though to ask what about her made her rate. "I don't think it takes chocolate to make you successful with women."

With a self-effacing look, Tris glanced down at his plate. "So tell me, Gemma, what kind of birth control are you using?"

She stopped chewing, paused, then started again and swallowed. "I, uh, ran out."

"And haven't bought more," Tris said.

Gemma started eating again. "The whole episode was too quick to produce anything."

"Spoken like a teenager," Tris said.

"It's okay," Gemma said. "I've done enough research with my boys to know about the right time of the month. This isn't it."

"All right," Tris said, then was silent for a moment. "Tell me about your research."

"Mostly, I've been trying to add to Joce's genealogy. She's a friend of—" She cut herself off. "I'm forgetting where I am. You must know Jocelyn."

"I helped deliver her twins."

"Then you know a great deal more about her than I ever want to," Gemma said, and Tris laughed. "I haven't done as much work as I'd like to."

"The Fraziers driving you crazy?"

She didn't think she needed to say more about her

and Colin. She'd said too much already. "The family does visit rather often."

"With or without their clothes?" Tris asked.

"It's too early to laugh about it," Gemma said, but she did smile.

"You want more chocolate?"

"No, that was enough. I better get back to work—if Rachel's had time to remove Colin, that is."

"Sure," Tris said, but he had his head down and he made no motion to move.

Gemma looked at him. "Is there something you want to tell me? Or ask me?"

"Heartwishes," he said. "Have you found out anything more about that?"

"No, and I've been searching. Did Colin tell you about it?"

"Yes." He looked at her. "Mind if I tell you a story?"

"I would love to hear anything that takes my mind off my own problems."

"Colin and I had breakfast the day he left for the fire and he told me about the Heartwishes Stone. We laughed about it. That night I told my sister and niece. I meant it as entertainment, but Nell believed every word I said, and she got quite upset. She said that she's part Frazier and the wish from her heart was that her father would come home and that they'd get to stay in Edilean. She had Addy and me stand up, and repeat her wish three times. She said she wanted to make sure the Heartwishes Stone *heard* us."

When he was silent, Gemma waited. He seemed to have more to say.

"Last night Addy got a call that her husband had been shot in Iraq and—"

"Oh!"

"No, it's okay. He's all right, or will be. He's been flown to a hospital in Miami. My parents live in Sarasota, and they drove down there immediately. Jake will be fine, but his injury is bad enough that he'll be discharged from the army. He'll be home for good in about a month."

"That's wonderful," Gemma said.

"There's more. Before Jake signed up, he was a top car mechanic, and he had a good job in Detroit. The owner of the garage where he worked said that when Jake returned, the job would be waiting for him." Tris looked at Gemma. "The morning after Nell made her wish, we heard that the place where Jake was supposed to go back to work blew up. It was at night and no one was hurt, but now Jake has no job to return to."

Gemma leaned back in her chair and looked at him. "What else?"

"On the same day we heard about the explosion in Detroit, Mr. Frazier's head mechanic at his service center just outside of Edilean gave notice that in four months he's moving to California to be near his wife's relatives. Mr. Frazier called me to say that Jake had the job if he wanted it. That was a few days ago, then last night the call about Jake's injury came in. It's as though Nell's wish came true, in less than a week, and all of it happened *after* she made her wish."

"You do know that it's all coincidence, don't you?" Gemma said.

"I'm sure it is, but then today . . ." He looked hard at her.

"You mean *me*?"

Tris nodded. "Yes. Rachel told me—"

Gemma drew in her breath. "That Mrs. Frazier made her husband wish for grandchildren."

"Right."

Gemma swallowed. "But wouldn't they come from Jean?"

"Colin won't tell me what's going on with her, but what if they did stay together?" There was anger in his voice. "Will she commute back and forth to Richmond?"

"I saw a law office here in town. Maybe she could—"

"Infiltrate MAW—the law firm of McDowell, Aldredge and Welsch? My cousin is one of the partners, and I can tell you that they'd never let an outsider in."

"But she'd be Colin's wife. She'd belong," Gemma said, even though the words stuck in her throat.

"It won't happen," Tris said firmly.

Gemma ran her finger over her plate to get the last bit of chocolate, and put it in her mouth. "How long have you disliked Jean?"

"Since she ran her hand up my thigh at a party."

"Did you tell Colin?"

"I tried to, but he wouldn't listen."

Gemma thought about what he'd told her. "Look, I'm sure this Heartwishes thing is just a family myth. If it were true, the Fraziers would have been granted wishes for centuries, but I can't see that they have. Or have they?"

Tris gave a bit of a grin. "No. If it had been up to Mrs. Frazier, her daughter would never have attended medical school. Her wish would have made Ariel stay in Edilean, get married, and she'd have six kids by now. And if Mr. Frazier had his way, all of his children would be crazy about cars and want to take over the family business."

"It's a good thing there is nothing that does grant wishes, isn't it?" Gemma said. "Everyone's wish would conflict with everyone else's."

"Not to mention people getting angry and wishing ill on others," Tris said.

Gemma looked at him. "And what about you?" she asked. "If Nell is part Frazier, so are you. If you did have a wish, what would it be?"

"I . . ." He leaned back in his chair and didn't seem inclined to say any more.

"I told you about my stupidity with Colin, so you can tell me your secrets."

"Yeah, but I'm a doctor. I'm used to people's secrets."

"And I'm an historian. I'm used to two-hundred-year-old secrets."

He smiled. "All right. I'm looking for *her*."

"Who?"

"The one they write all the songs and novels about. My sister says I'm too romantic, but I feel that I'll know her when I see her." He took a breath. "And I want her to like me for more than what I do or what I look like." He looked down at his plate for a moment, then back at Gemma. "Maybe the Heartwishes Stone works for my sister, but it's not working for *me*."

"It's not possible, of course, but I wonder what could have activated the Stone now after all these years."

"You. Maybe you opened something in those papers. Maybe the Stone is in there but you haven't seen it."

"Not possible," Gemma said. "I've been through all the boxes. There was only paper in them and a few sentimental things."

"Such as?"

"Ribbons, lockets full of strands of hair, the usual Victorian sentimentality."

Tris just stared at her.

"I really don't believe in magic," she said. "And I'd think that you, as a man of science, wouldn't either."

"I wouldn't usually, but in the time since Nell put on her little drama and made her wish, everything has turned upside down. I didn't get to bed last night, and I'm taking Nell and Addy to the airport today." He ran his hand over his face. "I went to the office early this morning to write some prescriptions for patients before I left. My head was full of Jake's return, then you showed up with your story about Colin, and . . ." He raised his eyebrows. "I think I need some sleep."

"I agree," Gemma said. She saw a customer wander by and knew the store had opened. "If you're like Colin, you better get out of here before people start asking you to look at their warts."

They stood up, gathered their trash, and put it in a bin.

Tris put his hand on her shoulder. "Thanks, Gemma. You needed to talk to me, but I ended up doing all the talking."

"I enjoyed it. I miss my friends from school." She rubbed her arm. "And I especially miss working out with the boys."

"Oh, right. That's what gave you the body the Internet is drooling over."

"Not quite," she said, laughing.

"You'll meet Mike at the barbecue. He's a major jock, so you two can . . . do whatever it is people do in a gym."

"I guess you were born with those pecs and you don't know what a forty-five-pound plate looks like." They were walking toward the back of the store.

"I stop in now and then and do a bit," he said as they reached the back truck ramp. "I'm beginning to see what Colin finds so fascinating about you."

"Is that why he called me Jean?"

Tris didn't laugh. "What are you going to do the next time you see him?"

"I'll act like it was nothing. No big deal—and it wasn't."

"I think that will be more difficult than you think," Tris said. "Listen, if you have any symptoms of, you know, tell me, will you?"

"I'll be crying on your doorstep." They had reached his car. "Today I'm going to start some serious research on this Heartwishes thing."

"Let me know about that too," he said as he got into the car.

"Every word." She pulled her BlackBerry out of her handbag. "Let me have your e-mail address and I'll tell you everything as I learn it."

Smiling, he told her—and he wrote her a prescription for birth control pills.

During the next week, Gemma had difficulty concentrating on her work. She'd read for an hour, make notes, and try to fit all that she was learning into what she knew. But at the end of the hour, she'd stare into space and think about Colin. She kept going over every second of their time together, every word they'd exchanged, and especially their brief moments in bed. She rationalized his calling her Jean. Gemma had asked Rachel, and she said Colin and Jean had been together since he graduated from college. So of course he'd make a mistake, since they'd been together such a long time, and besides, he'd been very tired that morning.

For the first day, she thought about nobly telling Colin that what had happened between them was "nothing" and that it wouldn't happen again. She prepared her speech with the precision of a commencement address.

But Colin didn't show up, so she couldn't tell him anything. Nor did he call or text her. Was he feeling guilty? she wondered. Was he agonizing over how to tell her that he was sorry for what he did? Was he preparing what he was going to say as carefully as Gemma was gathering her defense?

Day after day, she imagined a new scenario, that he had confessed to Jean about what he'd done, how he hadn't been faithful to her. Would they stay together? Break up?

Gemma worried constantly about her job, knowing that it could be taken from her. To lose the perfect job, and for what? To have a roll in the hay with a man who had a permanent girlfriend? It wasn't worth it!

On the other hand, if Colin did break up with Jean . . .

By the time Tris was to pick her up for the barbecue, she had run through so many emotions that she honestly didn't know how she was going to react when she saw Colin. Her hope was that he wouldn't be there and she wouldn't have to deal with him.

11

Tris picked Gemma up at eleven. The first thing she asked him was if Colin would be there. She hoped not, but in case he did show up, she had her speech ready to explain why she had fallen into bed with him.

"I don't think so," he said, "but if he does come, he might have Jean with him." He glanced at her as he drove. "Can we men look forward to a girl fight?"

"You wish! So how's your brother-in-law?"

"Better," Tris said, smiling. "My dad's a retired doctor and he said Jake's injuries look good. They're healing well and the prognosis is for a full recovery."

"What about Nell?"

"She's the happiest child on earth. Addy said they had to pull her away from Jake last night. And how about you and Mrs. F's wish?" He looked down at her flat stomach.

"I bet you still believe in the Easter Bunny. Is this Merlin's Farm as good as it says on the Web site?"

"You'll have to judge that for yourself. But talk to Sara. She knows a lot about the farm's history."

"How many people am I going to meet today?"

"A dozen or so humans, and maybe Mr. Lang. He's in a class all to himself."

"Sounds interesting," she said. "I'd like to hear about when the FBI agents were here."

"We were overrun by them. And the Secret Service. Ask Mike. He'll tell you all about it. On second thought, he probably won't tell you anything. He's a man who loves to keep secrets. Ask Sara."

Tris turned into a driveway and before them was what Gemma knew was a very old house. Only many years could cause walls and a roof to sag in that particular way. She'd often paid entrance fees to visit houses just like it. "Oooooh," she said, her eyes wide.

"You and Sara are going to be best friends," Tris said as he parked the car in front of the house and gave a quick burst of the horn.

The front door opened and a pretty young woman came out. "Tris, if you wake my babies, you're dead meat," she said.

"Put some whiskey in their formula and they'll go right back to sleep," he said as he went to his trunk and opened it.

"I'm going to tell the La Leche League you said that, then see if you're laughing," the woman said as she turned to Gemma. "I'm Joce and I think I found Julian."

"That's great," Gemma said. "Did you bring any data?"

"It's only a few sentences and it's all in my head." They started toward the house.

"Hey!" Tris called. "I have lots of stuff to carry in and I need help."

"After the horn and the whiskey crack, no woman is going to help you. Maybe I'll send Luke out," Joce said as she opened the door.

The next hour was a blur for Gemma. She met people she'd been hearing about since she arrived in Edilean, and it wasn't easy to keep names and faces together.

Tess was an extraordinarily beautiful young woman, hugely pregnant, and married to a tall, good-looking lawyer named Ramsey McDowell.

Sara Newland was pretty in a way that made Gemma think of Raphael Madonnas. Everyone else had on jeans, but Sara was wearing a top of white lace and a skirt of pale blue linen. She too was expecting a baby.

When Tris paused in the hallway, his arms full of bags of ice, Gemma leaned near his ear and said quietly, "It looks like these people didn't need any magic to make babies."

"They aren't Fraziers," he said.

When Gemma looked up, she saw Tess staring at

her. There was something about the woman that was a bit off-putting.

"I thought you were after Colin," Tess said, her tone that of a challenge.

Gemma straightened her shoulders. "Colin is my employer's son and he showed me around Edilean. That's all."

"Tess!" Sara said. "Be nice. Gemma, would you like to see the rest of the house?"

"I'd love to." Gratefully, she turned her back on Tess. As soon as they were out of earshot, Gemma said, "Please tell me the town isn't saying I'm going after Colin."

"I think they're hoping you are. He's our friend and protector, but personally, he leads a lonely existence. Jean's rarely around, and when they broke up a few years ago, we were all glad."

"But they're back together now?"

"Yeah, maybe. I'm not sure exactly what their status is," Sara said. "Whatever is going on, they haven't married, and there's not been an offer of an engagement ring. This is the kitchen. We had it completely redone."

Gemma wasn't interested in kitchens, new or otherwise. She was concerned about the local gossip and didn't want to be part of it. "I'm not after anyone," she said. "I'm here to do a job and that's all."

Sara led her to the stairs and they went up. "I think I should warn you that you're causing a bit of a stir around town. You've been seen with two bachelors, Colin and Tris. This is Mike's and my bedroom."

Gemma looked at a big four-poster bed that was obviously an antique, as was everything else in the room. The bed was draped with the same red and blue Indienne cloth that she'd seen at Mount Vernon. "Martha Washington style?"

"As best as I could manage," Sara said, smiling. "Out that window you can see the front garden."

Gemma looked out to see what had to be an acre of concisely laid-out rectangles and squares, all edged with boxwood. Each bordered shape contained flowers, often with an ornamental tree in the center. Red tulips would fill two boxes, while yellow tulips were in another one. In the distance Gemma could see an orchard in bloom. "It's gorgeous. And . . . and accurate," she said, giving the garden her highest compliment. It was an accurate layout of a formal eighteenth-century garden.

"Thank you," Sara said sincerely. "You wouldn't know it now, but all winter long we had backhoes in here and about fifty workmen. We put in over a hundred fruit trees and six hundred shrubs. I lost count of the bulbs and annuals."

"Don't get her started or she'll tell you the Latin name of every plant," came a deep, raspy voice from the doorway.

Turning, Gemma saw a man who was instantly familiar to her. He moved like some of the athletes she'd tutored. He had a confidence about him that came from knowing he could physically handle whatever came his way.

"Hello," Gemma said, grinning. "You must be Mike." She held out her hand for him to shake.

He didn't take it. Instead, he shot out his fist as though he meant to hit her in the head.

"Mike!" Sara said.

Years of training made Gemma react instinctively. After she ducked his fist, she turned sideways to him and her hands came up to protect her face.

Mike put out his left, Gemma dipped again, and she brought her right to his ribs. Of course he blocked her, as she knew he would.

Smiling, he reached out to shake her hand. "Nice to meet you, Gemma."

"A true pleasure," she said.

Behind them, Sara groaned. "I can see that you two are going to be friends."

Mike pulled a key from his pocket. It was on a ring with a pink flamingo on it. "Sara's idea," he said, "but the key is to my gym. You're welcome at any time."

"Thank you," she said. "My side was cut and I haven't been able to work out since I got here."

"How's the injury now?"

"Still red, but healed," she said.

"Think you can do some boxing?"

"Of course," she said. She knew that true athletes didn't complain. If she did, invariably, someone would say, "You want some cheese with that whine?"

"We all saw the way you stood on Colin's shoulders and got that kid." Mike's eyes were laughing. "At last year's fair I did the same thing with him, except that he held on to my ankles and danced around the ring."

"Like a trained bear," Gemma said.

"Exactly! Come on downstairs and I'll get you something to drink. Take any supplements?"

"Fish oil, Bio-E, Adren-All. The usual."

"Michael," Sara said, "should I start getting jealous of you two?"

Gemma stepped away from Mike. "Sorry, I—"

"Yes, definitely," Mike told his wife. "And the only way for you to win me back is to start going to the gym with me every morning."

Sara walked between them to leave the room. "In that case, I hope you two have a great time. You can visit your son on alternate weekends." She went down the stairs.

"She isn't angry, is she?" Gemma asked.

"Not at all." Mike put his hand on Gemma's shoulder, and she knew he was checking out her deltoid.

"Soft," she said.

"Absolute mush. Maybe this afternoon . . ."

"Gladly," she said, and smiling, they went downstairs.

In the kitchen, Mike gave Gemma a glass of juice. "No carbonation, no sugar."

"And no flavor," Tess said.

"Did you meet my baby sister?" Mike asked.

She looked from one to the other. It took a moment, but she could see the resemblance.

"Tris is looking for you," Tess said. "Are you two an item? Have you thrown out Colin already?"

Mike looked at his sister. "You'd better back off of her. She can take you down."

"I think I'll find Tris," Gemma said and left the room, drink in hand. When she went outside, she saw more garden, more lawn, more trees, and close by were several old buildings that she knew had once been part of a plantation. In the shade of a big tree was a huge stainless steel grill. Tris was standing by it, talking to a tall, handsome man who was holding a pair of tongs.

"Hey!" Tris called when he saw Gemma. "Come meet Luke."

"He's the author you've never heard of," said a voice to her right. She didn't need to look to know it was Colin, but she did turn. Like she had to breathe, she had to know how he felt about what had taken place between them.

It took only a glance to see that he didn't remember what had happened. He smiled at her as though she were his sister, fondly, even protectively, but certainly not with any adult, male-female interest.

Of all the things she'd imagined in the last week, that Colin wouldn't even *remember* what had happened had not been one of them. The red hot heat of the anger that surged through her was something new. She'd never before felt anything like it—but she was determined not to show it. She took a few breaths, then looked back at Luke. "Actually," she said as she turned so Colin was out of her line of vision, as she couldn't stand to look at him, "I read your first book." She went toward Luke, her hand extended. "I loved it. Your research was excellent."

"A couple of guys at the college look over my manuscripts. They're sticklers for perfection. If I get even a shoe buckle wrong, they let me know."

"Did you meet Mike?" Tris asked.

"He greeted me with a fist aimed at my head."

Luke looked concerned, but Tris laughed. "So what did you do?"

"Ducked, of course, then I came back at him with a left uppercut." She demonstrated.

Through this exchange, Colin had been left standing, as excluded as though he weren't there.

Gemma kept her back to him as she looked at the grill. "What's cooking?"

Luke was looking over Gemma's head at Colin, whose face showed his bewilderment at having her back turned to him. "Nothing yet," Luke said, "but Mike ordered the most organic of the organics from Ellie. Have you met her?"

Before Gemma could answer, Colin stepped forward. "I introduced her to Ellie."

Gemma still couldn't stand to look at him. "Tris and I had breakfast together at her store. I had some divine chocolate concoction."

Gemma's refusal to include Colin in the conversation was now so pronounced that Luke quit looking puzzled and showed his amusement. "So Gemma,"

Luke said, "Tris was telling me about some magic Frazier thing. What is it?"

"The Heartwishes Stone," Colin said as he again moved forward, but this time he stepped between Tris and Gemma. Given that Colin was so large, this meant that Luke had to take a step back.

Chuckling, Luke said he thought he was needed in the house.

The last thing Gemma wanted was to cause more gossip. "I think I'll go with you," she said, but she stopped when Tris said to Colin, "Have you found out anything more about this Stone everyone's been talking about?" That sparked her curiosity.

Luke went into the house, but Gemma stayed by the grill. She still had her back to Colin.

"Tris," he said, "would you mind if Gemma and I—" He broke off when Tris's cell rang.

"Sorry, but my profession says I have to answer this." He pushed a button and listened. "I'll be there as soon as I can." He looked at Colin. "Mr. Gibson had a heart attack. I have to go to the hospital."

"I'll drive you," Colin said.

"No thanks!" Tris said quickly. "He's under care now, so I can travel at less than warp speed." He looked at Gemma. "I'm really sorry, but I have to leave."

"I understand. Don't worry about me." When he seemed to want to say more, she put her hand on his arm. "Go! And thanks for all your help."

"You're very welcome." He bent forward to kiss her cheek, but then glanced at Colin, and on impulse he gave her a quick, sweet kiss on the mouth. "I swear I can still taste the chocolate," he said, then started running toward the front of the house and his car.

For a moment Gemma stood where she was. She was very aware of Colin standing close to her, but she didn't look at him. She thought of several things to say, but none of them came out. Instead, she just turned on her heel and started toward the house.

Colin placed all two hundred-plus pounds of himself in front of her, but she didn't look up at his face. "Gemma, I apologize for whatever I did to make you angry at me."

"I'm not angry. I think I should help in the kitchen." She tried to step around him, but he blocked her path.

"This is because I fell asleep in your bed, isn't it? Rachel sent Lanny to get me up. I was so dead asleep he said he thought he was going to have to fire a canon to wake me up."

Gemma listened with her head down. "Fine. I understand. You were tired."

"And you fed me that wonderful breakfast. It was great to eat a home-cooked meal."

She didn't reply, just stepped around him. "I really do need to go inside now."

"Sure," he said. "I didn't mean to keep you."

When Gemma got inside the house, she saw that Tess and Sara had been watching out the window.

Tess was smiling in an I-told-you-so way, but Sara went to Gemma and took her arm. "Whatever you're doing to Colin, I *love* it!" she said softly. "He needs to have his whole life shaken up."

Gemma didn't want to discuss her personal problems with someone she'd just met. In spite of what Tris had said, she still worried that if Mrs. Frazier found out what had happened, she'd lose her job.

"Sorry, but I have no intention of doing anything with any of the Frazier sons. Is Joce around?"

"Sure," Sara said as she let go of Gemma's arm. "She's upstairs with the babies."

"I shouldn't disturb her."

"I'm sure she'd like your help."

Gemma went up the stairs and found Joce snuggled in the big four-poster holding a baby with a bottle, about eight months old, another one squirming on the bed beside her.

"May I?" Gemma asked as she looked at the baby on the bed.

"He'd love it," Joce said. "He's David and this one is Edilean."

Gemma gently picked up the little boy and held him as he pulled at her hair, then tried to put her necklace in his mouth.

Joce nodded to the bed beside her and Gemma climbed up, the baby on her lap. "Too much for you downstairs?"

"Oh yes," Gemma said as she tickled little David and made him laugh. "That woman Tess . . ."

"She takes some getting used to, but I can tell you that if Mike likes you, she will."

"He gave me a key to his gym."

"Wow! What did you do to get one of those?"

"I've done a little boxing."

"That would do it," Joce said, smiling. "Want to hear what I found out about Julian?"

"Definitely."

"He was the grandson of Shamus and Prudence Frazier, who were—"

"One of the founding seven."

"You've been doing your research. Yes, they were part of the original group who first settled this town. Their eldest son, Ewan, went back to England, reclaimed the title of the earl of Rypton, and bought the Lancaster house back."

"Wasn't there a name change somewhere?"

"That's why I had so much trouble finding Julian. For some reason, the name Frazier was dropped and they reverted back to Lancaster. But then, my ancestors were named McTern in Scotland, but in America they were known as Harcourt. I have no idea why."

"People change their names for all sorts of reasons. What else?"

"Ewan Frazier married a woman named Julia McBride, and they had a baby, Julian. But she died in childbirth and the next year he married Rose Jones. By the dates, she was already pregnant when they married. She gave birth to Clive."

"So who was Winnie?"

"I have no idea, but I'll keep searching." When little Edilean finished her bottle, Joce put her on her shoulder to burp. "So what's going on with you and Colin? Luke said you weren't speaking to him."

Gemma didn't want to lie, but neither did she want to tell the truth. "Too much gossip was starting and I don't want to be labeled a home wrecker."

"Whose home would you be wrecking?"

"The one Colin plans for him and Jean."

"Luke's old house," Joce said. "He hated selling that place, but Colin wore him down. When Colin wants something, he goes after it and doesn't give up."

"That's what my college adviser said about Mrs. Frazier."

"Colin is worse," Joce said. "Would you mind looking after the babies for a minute while I make a trip to the bathroom?"

"Sure. Why don't you go downstairs and get something to drink and visit with your friends? I'll look after the babies. I can make raspberries on little bellies for an hour at a time."

Joce laughed as she got off the bed. "Where'd you learn to do that?"

"My sister has two daughters, and when I'm around, she and her husband take a second honeymoon. I think they're now on their sixth one."

"You are my new best friend."

"You're the third candidate proposed to me today."

"Oh?" Joce asked. "Who were the others?"

"Sara for history, Mike for sports, and now you for babysitting."

"You're leaving out Tess," Joce said without cracking a smile, but then her face softened. "When you get to know Tess, you'll like her. She's had a tough life, and she tends to be hostile to newcomers."

"I guess I'll always be a 'newcomer' because my job here is temporary."

"Are you kidding? Luke said that both Colin and Tris were about ready to go into one of Mike's horrible kickboxing bouts over you."

"Far, far from it," Gemma said, but she couldn't help being flattered. "Tris and I are becoming friends. He likes me because I don't have any raging lust for him."

"Raging lust? Interesting choice of words. Do you save that for Colin?"

"I give it all to my job—which I want to keep. Fooling around with my employer's son isn't something I plan to do."

"I'm glad you know your own mind. When I first came to Edilean I was a mess. The most important person in my life had recently died and left me an old house I didn't even know she owned."

Gemma looked down at the two babies on the bed. "You look like you found your way."

"Yes, but I had help." She paused at the doorway. "Gemma, if you have any problems, personal or work related, you can come to Sara or me. And you may not believe it, but Tess is also a good listener."

"Thanks," Gemma said. When she was alone with the babies, she set herself to making them laugh and was quite successful.

"Mind if I join this party?" Colin asked from the doorway.

Gemma took a breath before she looked up at him, and when she did, all she could remember was the two of them together and naked. But it was obvious that he remembered nothing. So much for Joce's words about two men being interested in her! She'd gone to bed with one of them and he'd completely forgotten the experience. She looked back at the babies.

Colin sat down on the side of the bed. Instantly, little Edilean put her arms up to him and he picked her up. Gemma remembered that Ellie had said he was a Pied Piper to the kids.

"How long are you going to keep ignoring me?" he asked.

"You and I were seen together so often that people started gossiping about us. I don't like that and I think it should be stopped."

"People in Edilean gossip about everything. Your breakfast with Tris, and the way you two leaned toward each other and whispered the whole time, has eclipsed whatever they thought about us."

"Tris is okay; you are not."

"Why . . . ? Oh. Because of Jean?"

"That's right," she said as she played patty-cake with David. "You're practically a married man."

"I'm not, really."

This conversation wasn't going the way she wanted it to. The homey setting, even the babies, was making her relax, and she couldn't allow that. She frowned at him. "Is this where you tell me that Jean doesn't understand you, and that you and I should go out to dinner to talk about it?"

Colin blinked at her a few times. "Is that what you think of me?"

"I don't think of you one way or another," she said. "But I'd appreciate it if you'd stop showing up at my house before dawn, then running around naked. If you want something on the side, find someone else."

Colin's face showed his shock at her words. "I . . ." He got off the bed, still holding the baby, and stood up. "Forgive me, Miss Ranford. I was presumptuous. I—"

"Is everything all right in here?" Luke asked from the doorway.

Colin put Luke's daughter in his arms. "Everything is fine. Great. Couldn't be better. Is there any beer downstairs?"

"Gallons of it," Luke said, looking from Colin to Gemma and back again.

"That'll be a start." He moved past Luke and went down the stairs.

"What was that about?"

Gemma was so angry her jaw was aching, but she didn't want to show that. "I'm not feeling well. Could someone drive me home—I mean to the Frazier estate?"

"Gemma," Luke said quietly, "I don't know what's going on between you and Colin, but I don't think you should leave. Stay and have a margarita or two, and chill out. Besides, there's nothing a man likes better than thinking a woman is home alone and crying over him."

She looked at him in disgust. "Is that true?"

"Not in my personal experience, but I heard it in a country-and-western song, so it has to be true."

Gemma couldn't help herself as she gave a little laugh.

"That's better," Luke said. "You want to help me carry the kids downstairs? Everyone wants to see them, and they're fiends for being the center of attention."

"Actually, I think I'd like that. Mike—"

"Wants to beat you up," Luke said.

"He can try. I'm pretty fast and he's getting old. What is he, about forty?"

Luke grinned. "Please, please let me hear you say that to Mike. I'll dedicate my next book to you if I get to hear that. And if you hit him . . ." He trailed off, as if he couldn't think of anything good enough to equal that sight.

"All I have to do is imagine Colin Frazier's face on Mike's and he may not live."

Luke's eyes widened. "Everybody loves Colin," he said quietly.

"Now you've met someone who doesn't," she said firmly.

Luke stood there looking at her for a moment, then seemed to recover. "Get Davie and let's go." He paused at the doorway. "You know, I was a little concerned that Tess might frighten you, but I'm not worried anymore."

Gemma scooped up the baby.

"Okay?" Luke asked.

"I'm armed and ready."

Smiling, he followed her down the stairs.

12

THEY WERE SEATED around Sara and Mike's dining table, and Gemma marveled at the beauty of it all. The table, with its yellow and green color scheme, looked like something out of a chic decorating magazine where the credits listed Brunschwig & Fils, Scully & Scully, and ABC Carpet.

"This is beautiful," Gemma said as she took a seat on the long side of the table. She thought she was seating herself beside Mike, but Colin took the chair next to her.

"This way, you won't have to look at me," he said so only she could hear.

"Thank you," Sara said to Gemma's compliment. Sara was at one end of the table and Mike at the other. Ramsey, Tess, Luke, and Joce took the other chairs, and they started passing bowls of food around. They were all friends and knew each other well, so Gemma ate and listened. They complimented Mike on the food and Sara on the decor of the house.

Gemma was acutely aware of Colin next to her, and when she had to pass a bowl to him, she avoided his eyes.

"How can I apologize and redeem my name?" he asked while Ramsey was telling a story about a fight at his law firm.

"I told him that if he sued and Don sued him back, then he sued again, that the only person who was going to win would be me," Ramsey said.

"And that scary thought made them settle out of court," Tess said, and they all laughed.

"There's no need to apologize," Gemma said to Colin under the cover of the laughter. "I just think it's better if we don't see each other."

"We're not seeing one another. We're—" He stopped when everyone grew silent. "Sorry, what was that?"

"We all want to know about the Heartwishes Stone. Have you found out any more about it?" Sara asked Gemma.

"No, nothing new." She told them of Tamsen's letter. "She said she'd written down the story and put it somewhere 'safe' but I don't know where that could be."

"With her lawyer?" Ramsey said, and everyone groaned. "No, I'm not kidding. There's always been a law firm in Edilean, so maybe she left something with them. There's a warehouse full of old documents. I don't think anyone knows what's in there."

"How do I—?" Gemma began, but Tess cut her off.

"You don't. I'll put one of the girls in the office on it and see what we can find." She looked at Colin. "Have you had any wishes that have come true?"

"I could make one now," he said in such a pathetic way that everyone had to stifle laughter.

"Okay, Gemma," Ramsey said, "you have to tell us what Colin did to make you so angry at him."

Gemma felt the blood rush to her face. "I, uh . . . I . . ."

"Let up on her," Luke said. "She's new here and she's not used to being asked to tell everything about her life."

"It's something *I* will *never* get used to," Mike said with such feeling that the others laughed.

"Speaking of which," Gemma said loudly, "I'd love to hear the inside view of finding the paintings and I want to see the secret room." As she'd hoped, everyone started at once, and within seconds they were retelling a long, complicated story that made no sense to her. There was something about a woman named Mitzi who was convicted of murder.

"Good save," Colin said under his breath to her. "Do you think you could spare me five minutes to talk about whatever I've done to you? I certainly didn't mean to be naked in your house."

Everyone had stopped talking and heard the last sentence.

Colin didn't even try to explain as he stood up. "Anyone want another beer?" He left the room to get more beer but came back with a baby in each arm. "They were getting bored."

"Colin, I do believe you're ready to be a father," Sara said. "Decided on the mother yet?"

Colin shook his head. "Today is not my day for women. Any of you men know the cause when a woman gets mad at you?"

"No idea," Mike said.

"None," Ramsey said.

"I just apologize and take the blame," Luke said.

"You poor things," Joce said. "Why don't you underappreciated dears go outside and enjoy yourselves while we controlling women clean up?"

"Sounds good to me," Ramsey said as he took a baby from Colin. Two minutes later all four men and the two babies were outside.

Gemma knew what was coming: an interrogation. She held her breath as she waited for the women to pounce on her with questions. They'd want to know what lovable, saintly Colin could possibly have done to make anyone angry.

But to Gemma's relief, the three women said nothing to her. Even Tess was quiet. They quickly started clearing the table in that way that showed they'd known each other a long time. Gemma took two bowls into the kitchen and Sara handed her a roll of plastic wrap. Gemma covered containers and Joce put them in the refrigerator.

"What would you wish for?" Sara asked Gemma as she put dirty plates in the dishwasher.

"You mean from the Heartwishes Stone?" The truth was that after hearing Tris's story she was almost afraid to say, but then she reminded herself that she wasn't a Frazier. "I guess it would be to get a good job at a great university. It feels like I've spent most of my life working toward that."

"Sara is disappointed that you aren't wishing for True Love. She's a serious romantic," Tess said.

"Did Mike court you with kickboxing?" Gemma asked Sara.

The three women looked at one another as though there was some great secret in Sara and Mike's courtship.

"Sorry. I didn't mean to pry," Gemma said.

"Don't mind them," Sara said. "They're just laughing at me. You guys ready to join the men?"

"Sure," Tess said. "Even being able to smell the beer cheers me up." She was rubbing her big stomach. "Gemma, you have any more boyfriends besides Tris and Colin?"

"You have a lover outside your husband?" Gemma shot back.

All the women laughed.

"She was the same way with me when we first met," Joce whispered as they went out the door. "She'll quit after a while."

"Actually, I'm beginning to like it," Gemma said.

Colin was waiting for her outside the door, and

as soon as they were alone, he said, "If you'd just tell me what I've done, maybe we could fix the problem."

Gemma didn't want to look in his eyes for fear that he'd see everything. "I told you that I don't want to do anything to jeopardize my job. I think it's better if you and I stay apart."

"Because of Jean," he said. "If you want to know the truth about her and me, why didn't you ask *me*?"

"Would you have answered me?" she asked.

He hesitated, as though considering his answer. "Yes. I believe I would have." For a moment, he stared at her, seeming not to know what else to say.

Gemma walked away to join the group sitting in the shade and took a chair near Mike. They stayed outside for an hour, sitting on big chairs and talking amicably. Gemma didn't drink for fear that she'd get too relaxed and blab about what happened between her and Colin. The babies were on a blanket and everyone took turns playing with them.

Gemma was quiet as she listened to them talk about people they'd known for years, had even grown up with. She liked what they were talking about. Luke wanted Mike to help him with a plot idea for a book. Sara was talking to Joce about one of the old buildings around them, while Tess and Rams—as he was called—talked with Colin about the man Tris had mentioned, Mr. Lang.

They know each other so well, Gemma thought. The group knew each other so thoroughly that they easily slid from one topic to another. This is it, she thought. This is what I'd like to have, to belong to. I'd like to be part of this easy camaraderie where I know people and we care about each other.

To Gemma, the only downside to the day was Colin. Whenever he spoke, she looked away.

"Gemma," Sara said, "we're leaving you out."

"No, it's nice. I spend so much time alone that it's great to hear other people talk."

Mike got up. "Gemma, could I see you inside for a moment?"

Gemma wanted to run around the house to the road and keep going. Was her ignoring of Colin going to get her a "talking to"? She followed Mike into the house and shut the door behind her. "Look, I'm sorry about Colin, but—"

"You thought I invited you in here about him?" Mike asked as he opened the lid of an old wooden trunk. "Colin can handle his own problems. Besides, I'm sure he deserves whatever you dish out to him." He pulled out a pair of boxing gloves. "I thought you might like to do something familiar."

"I would," she said, but glanced down at her jeans and flowered shirt. It would be difficult to move in them.

"I thought about that, so we got you a welcome gift." Mike handed her a paper bag. "Sara guessed at your size."

Inside the bag was a new workout outfit of shorts and T-shirt, even a sports bra, and in the bottom was a pair of soft shoes, the kind worn in a boxing ring.

"I can't accept these," Gemma began. "It's too much."

"It's nothing. I hear you think you can take me."

Gemma grinned. "Luke has a big mouth."

"Go on, get dressed."

She hurried to a powder room off the kitchen and put on the skimpy gym clothes. She wasn't used to working out dressed in so little, but she reminded herself that today she wasn't around a bunch of boys with rampant hormones and little impulse control.

When she was ready, she went through the house in search of Mike and saw him outside. He had on a pair of hand pads, and Luke was taking some half-hearted, bare-knuckle punches at them.

She started toward the door when she saw a flash of something in the sunlight. It was a bracelet and it was on Jean's arm. It looked like she had arrived, and she'd taken a chair close to Colin. If possible, Jean was better-looking than Gemma remembered. Not as beautiful as Tess, but then Jean was older. That thought startled her. She'd not realized it before, but Jean was older than Colin by at least six or seven years. If she'd had anything done to her face, it might be more.

Jean was laughing about something Rams was saying, and she reached out to pat Colin on the thigh. "Bet she wishes he were Tris," Gemma mumbled, then felt a surge of guilt run through her. Jean was the innocent party in all this. Gemma opened the door and went outside.

She was glad that the sight of her in the skimpy clothes brought the conversation to a halt. Her years of sweating were worth it if for just this moment! She kept her eyes on Mike and walked toward him.

When Mike lowered his pads, Luke stopped hitting and turned to look Gemma up and down. "If this is what boxing does to a body, sign me up for lessons." He took a breath. "I mean—" He turned to his wife. "I meant—"

"We all know what you meant," Joce said as her husband took the seat next to her. "Come on, Gemma, let's see you knock Mike out."

"I have five on my brother," Tess said.

"I put fifty on Gemma," Luke said.

Mike smiled at Gemma as he helped her on with the big gloves. Instantly, they were trainer and student, and that special bond of trust mixed with teaching flowed between them. A trainer might have no sympathy when a boxer complains about a hard hit, but if he's knocked out, it's the trainer who's the first on the scene.

"Just show me some punches," Mike said softly. "I want to see your form. You kick?"

"Yes."

"Good. I brought the side pad." He leaned his head near hers. "Show Colin what he's missing—and what he doesn't remember."

Startled, she looked at him.

"I'm a detective. I figured it out."

"Do they all know?"

Mike was lacing her glove about her wrist. "I doubt it. No one's said anything to me. Ready?"

At her nod, Mike picked up the heavy pads and slipped his hands inside.

"Two left jabs, right cross, left hook, dip, right, left, dip, repeat. Got it?"

She nodded again, and slowly, she punched at Mike's gloves. Correct form had been drilled into her. What most people didn't know was that the lower half of a woman's body could be as strong as a man's upper body. The average woman would never be able to beat a fit man on arm strength alone, but the trick was to throw the muscle of her lower body into her arm punches. It had taken months of repetition for Gemma to learn how to do this. Like a marionette on a string, when her arm shot out, her hip and leg went with it. If she made a punch correctly, she felt it in her glutes—where so many women held so much muscle.

"Good girl," Mike said when she'd finished the slow round, and she knew he was complimenting her on her technique.

"Squash the bug," she said, referring to the way a fighter twisted on his toes to put power behind his fist.

Mike stepped back from her. "So I hear you think you're faster than me," he said loudly.

She'd already seen enough to know that she wasn't, but it would be good to pretend she thought she was. "I sure am, old man," she said just as loudly.

Mike winked at her and put his hands up again. "Luke! Time us. Three minutes."

Gemma knew that three minutes of flat-out, no-holds-barred punching was hard. She hadn't worked out for weeks, but she was determined to do it.

Mike raised the pads, Luke yelled, "Go!" and there followed three minutes of a lightning fast drill. Gemma kept her eyes on Mike's face, keeping his hands in her peripheral vision. He'd decided that her technique was good enough that she could also take some random punches. He didn't tell her when he'd be coming at her head and she needed to duck to miss him. Sometimes he lifted a left hand pad, sometimes a right—and sometimes his hand shot out, aimed directly for her face. She had to drop straight down, then come up with a left uppercut. If she leaned forward, which was bad technique, he reminded her by clipping her on the chin with his mitt.

When Luke called time, sweat was running off Gemma's face. She made a swipe at it with her glove, but it didn't help.

Mike picked up the big leather pad that was leaning against the tree and said, "Colin?"

For the first time, Gemma looked at the others. They were all still seated and watching her with varied expressions on their faces. Sara looked as though she was worried Gemma would be hurt; Joce was frowning; and Tess was smiling in approval. As for Jean, she seemed to have no expression at all.

All the men were grinning—except for Colin. He

walked toward them and buckled the big pad over Mike's ribs.

"She hurt her side," Colin said. "I'm not sure this is good for her."

"I think it's exactly what she needs," Mike said.

Colin looked at Gemma. "If you don't want to do this—"

"You think I can't?" she said belligerently. "But then, even you said that I'm 'smart and brave.'"

Colin looked puzzled for a moment, then his face showed that he remembered. "Holy crap!" he said under his breath. "It wasn't a dream. It was you."

"You want to get back?" Mike said.

"Gemma," Colin said. "I'm so sorry. I didn't mean—"

Mike stepped between them. His hands wore the pads and his ribs were protected from her kicks. "Three minutes," he said to Luke. Gemma gave more punches to Mike's raised hands and when he turned to the left, she slammed her right shin into his side. The resounding smack echoed off the trees and made everyone gasp.

Colin had stepped back, closer to the tree, but he was directly behind Mike and she couldn't help but see him.

When Rams yelled, "Come on, Gemma, show him up," her kicks increased in speed and force. She knew Rams was referring to Mike, but in Gemma's mind she was hitting Colin. How dare he *forget* her? Like she didn't exist! But then he was a Frazier and rich, while she was—

Her punches were frantic, getting harder and harder. When Luke called time, she didn't hear but kept kicking and hitting.

She stopped when Mike threw his arms around her and pinned hers to her side.

"That's enough," he said into her ear in that special voice that trainers use. It was half dictator, half guardian angel.

She buried her face in his sweaty neck so no one could see her. "Did I make a fool of myself?"

"Far from it. Even my sister is looking at you in awe, and Sara wants to adopt you."

"Yeah?" Gemma asked as she pulled away from him.

The audience started clapping in appreciation of the show, and they came forward.

"You were great," Joce said.

Tess said, "Mike tried to teach me to do that but I wasn't any good at it."

"See you in the gym next week?" Luke asked Gemma, then he elbowed Rams. "Maybe if you show up, Gemma will go a few rounds with you."

"No thanks," Rams said and there was such sincerity in his voice that everyone laughed.

Gemma enjoyed the accolades, but when she looked past them, she saw Jean still seated and watching all of them. When Jean stood up, she looked like she wasn't sure what to say or do. As for Colin, he was still standing by the tree.

Sara pulled a clean towel from Mike's bag of

equipment and handed it to Gemma. "Who wants some watermelon?" Sara asked. "Luke, will you help me with it?"

In the next minute everyone had left, leaving Gemma standing alone with Colin. She still had on her gloves and she couldn't get them off by herself. She looked for Mike, but he was talking to Sara.

Colin took Gemma's hand and began untying the laces. "I'm sorry," he said softly. "Really, really sorry. If you want to bring charges against me, I'll understand."

"Charges? What for?" A lot of her anger was gone, worked out in sweat and exertion.

"Rape," he said, his face serious. "If I pulled you to me, you wouldn't have been able to get away. Even if I was asleep and dreaming, that's no excuse. Legally, it's still rape."

Gemma shook her head. "It wasn't forced. If it was, I was the one who did the . . . You know."

"Yeah?" he asked, his eyebrows raised. "If you . . . ? Then why are you angry at me?"

"Because you *forgot*!"

Colin looked like he wanted to laugh but didn't dare. "Only partially. My dreams have been haunted by you. Maybe we could—"

"Colin," Jean said as she walked close to him and slid her arm through his. "I think you should let Gemma clean up now, don't you?" She looked at Gemma. "You were really impressive and you look great in those shorts. Doesn't she, Colin?"

"Yes, she does." He looked like he was trying to

remember seeing her out of them. "Jean," he said, "I need to talk to Gemma. In private."

"Of course," she said as she backed away. "How about if I meet you at your apartment later?"

"Fine," he said. As Jean left to go to her car, Colin kept his eyes on Gemma. When they were alone, he said, "I'd like to talk with you."

"I need to shower and change, then maybe—"

"You'll find a way to avoid me," he said. "What if I offer to let you practice a few punches on *me*?"

She didn't smile. "Where do I sign up?"

"There's a little summerhouse in the back. We can talk there. Please." Colin looked over her head, and she knew he was letting Mike know they'd be back soon.

With a sigh, Gemma nodded.

Colin led her to a pretty little lattice structure, painted a deep blue-green. Around them were tall hedges and to the right was a huge tree with heavy branches that spread out above their heads.

"This is beautiful," she said. "It's like an enchanted garden where nothing bad could ever happen."

"Far from it," Colin said, his tone almost menacing.

"Does that mean that something bad did happen here?"

He didn't answer, but sat down on the mossy grass beneath the tree, and she took a seat a few feet from him. "I don't usually . . ." he began. "I mean, I've never . . ."

"Look," she said, "it was nothing. No big deal.

Women today jump in and out of bed with men all the time. You were my first—and only—one-night stand and it upset me, that's all. Let's leave it at that, okay?" She started to get up, but he caught her arm.

"I don't want it to end between us," he said.

"Jean," she said simply.

"Is your only objection to me Jean?"

"Is this a trick question?"

"I mean, do you like me otherwise? I'm concerned that you haven't seen me at my best. You've experienced the speed I need to drive at when I get an emergency call. And you ended up with stitches after I got you to help me. And I can't imagine that you'd want a repeat performance in bed after what happened the first time."

"You're right," she said solemnly. "I'd prefer it if when someone needed help that you'd feel no urgency, but take your time. And you should have let that little boy stay on that tree branch when it fell rather than risk a bystander getting a little cut."

Colin was grinning.

"As for our two and a half minutes in bed together—" she said.

"Ow! That hurt."

"Okay, three minutes."

Colin groaned, his hand to his heart. "You have wounded me. I'd sure like to try again," he said. "Try harder, so to speak."

Gemma ignored his innuendo. "What would happen if I show up, a stranger, then you dump

Jean—who is innocent in all this—and you and I start dating? I'm going to look like the worst kind of . . . well, slut. I don't like that. Not to mention that your mother will fire me from the best job I've ever had."

"My mother hired you because you love the research. It has nothing to do with your personal life."

"If you discard a woman your mother has a long history with, someone she adores, for a stranger, we'll find out what she really feels." Gemma took a breath. "And what if we break up? That's probable, as we hardly know each other. How do I continue working at your home afterward?"

"I know enough about you not to make you angry. Your punches—" Her look made him stop. "Okay, I see your point. I'll tell you the truth. First of all, there is no 'discarding' or 'dumping' involved in this. Jean and I aren't really a couple. I know it seems that we are, but we aren't. But, as you said, my family likes her, and because I refuse to date women in my jurisdiction, it's been easier to let people believe that Jean and I are together. Besides . . ." He grinned. "There hasn't been anyone else I wanted to spend time with. Do you think you and I could start seeing each other on a more than friendship basis?"

She took a moment to answer as what he said began to sink in. She wanted to yell "Yes!" but didn't. She had to keep sane about this. "I guess so . . . Eventually. But I think we should get to know one another a bit before we let the world—meaning Edilean and your family—see us as a couple." She stood up and looked at him. "If it's true about you and Jean—and no one seems to know this—maybe it would be better if first you told people that you've broken up with her. Certainly tell your parents. If they go ballistic . . ." She didn't finish her sentence.

"I know," Colin said. "They all love her, and I dread telling them that we aren't going to give my mother her Heartwish of marriage and children. But it has to be done. Then you and I will get to know each other. We'll become friends, and I'll keep my hands off that killer body of yours. Is that what you want to hear?"

"It's a start."

Gemma couldn't help how his words gave her hope. Whereas she couldn't bear being the Rebound Girl, someone who would get dumped later, it was wonderful to think that they really did have a chance together. That thought and the sight of him made her blood rush through her body. With him sitting and her standing, he was exactly the right height for her to step into his arms. She knew what his arms around her felt like, how her hands felt on him.

"You have to stop looking at me like that," he said under his breath, "or I won't be able to talk."

Gemma sat down, and looked back at the scenery.

"We Fraziers keep ourselves a bit separate from the rest of Edilean," he began. "We—"

"Why?"

"I don't know, but it's always been that way. My

grandfather used to say that the Fraziers are different from the others and always will be."

"How does that translate to now, to you and me? I mean, not that there is a you and me, but . . ." She wasn't sure what she was saying.

"I've never wanted people in Edilean to know me well. I think keeping a little distance makes them more comfortable about asking me for help."

"I can understand that," Gemma said. "Is that why you've let people think you and Jean are still together?"

"Jean . . ." He shrugged.

"She wants you back," Gemma said.

"She wanted us to try, but it hasn't worked. I told you that last fall there were weddings and babies made, and . . ."

"And you bought a house," she said, then lowered her voice as understanding came to her. "And you didn't show it to Jean because you knew she'd never live in it."

"Exactly," he said. "Gemma." He waited until she turned to look at him. "I *do* remember that night. I especially remember that I made a very poor showing of myself. I can do better."

She looked away.

"So will you go out on a date with me?"

She looked back at him. "A date?"

"Dinner and a movie."

"Or horseback riding? I saw your trophy. What do you ride? A Clydesdale?"

Colin didn't laugh but his eyes sparkled. "Budweiser uses my brothers and me as training for their horses. If they can pull us, then they can haul wagons full of beer." He reached out his hand to her, but she moved away.

"How is Jean going to take all this?"

"She knows it's coming. We haven't been . . . intimate in a long time. That's why—" He broke off. "I want to clear up one point."

"And what is that?"

"You weren't the one who came after me."

Gemma's face turned red. "I'll *never* live that down. You were sound asleep and I pounced on you. You didn't have a chance. Maybe you should bring charges against *me*."

When she saw his big hand held out to her, she took it, but she didn't meet his eyes.

"Gemma," he said softly, "I've liked you from the first moment I saw you." He took a breath. "I'd like to spend some time with you, lots of time, and see if there could be more between us. It won't be easy, but I promise that I'll keep my hands off of you until you say it's okay."

She was glad she had her face down and he couldn't see her expression. Not touching him wasn't going to be any easier for her. She pulled her hand from his. "You have to take care of things with Jean. I don't want people saying I broke up the two of you. And if she's going to be a dragon, I won't date you."

Colin snorted in laughter. "You've been talking

to Rachel. She calls Jean the Dragon Lady whenever she messes up her kitchen. Jean and I've known each other a long time, and between you and me, I think there's another man in her life."

She looked at him sharply. "Is that why you're going after me? To get her back? To make her jealous?"

"Don't you think that the fact that I'm not jealous of whoever Jean is seeing says everything?" He smiled at Gemma. "So would you like to start dating and see how we get along?"

"I would consider it," she said, then looked away so he wouldn't see the pleasure in her eyes. "On one condition."

"And that is?"

"That you quit being so damned secretive with me! I want to know about you, the *real* you. I'm tired of hearing how the Fraziers keep to themselves. I thought you were about to get married and no one seemed to know any different."

Colin nodded. "Reasonable requests. I apologize for everything. It's just that you're the first woman I've been interested in for a long time, and I make mistakes."

She liked what he was saying, but she was cautious. She stood up. "I think we should get back now."

Colin didn't move. "Watching your workout exhausted me. Help me up." He raised a limp hand up to her.

Smiling, Gemma took his hand and pulled—and

he drew her down so she was standing between his legs, her face level with his.

She didn't have time to draw in her breath before he put his lips on hers and kissed her. It was a gentle, sweet kiss, but it had all the passion in it that she'd felt since she'd met him. His strong arms encircled her and pulled her close to him; she could feel the heavy muscles of his chest against her breasts.

She opened her mouth under his and when she felt his tongue, she groaned. Her body grew weak in his arms as she became soft and pliable. Submissive. Do with me what you will, was her attitude.

Colin abruptly set her in front of him, at arm's length. "Real enough for you?" he asked in a husky voice. "Do you want me to tell you that I've desired you since I saw you reaching for a book on a top shelf?"

"Have you?"

He kissed her cheek. "I like your mind." He kissed her other cheek. "I like your body." He kissed her nose. "So far, Gemma Ranford, I haven't found anything that I don't like about you. Give me a little time, and I think I could feel something more than just 'like' for you."

"Me too," she whispered.

He again pushed her to arm's length. "That's it? No more words?"

"If I wanted more words in my life, I wouldn't want *you,* would I?" she said with as much haughtiness as she could muster.

Colin laughed. "So now I hear the truth. It's not my brain you like at all, is it?"

She ran her hand up his arm, over his bicep, up to his big, hard deltoid. "If all I wanted was a brain I'd have gone after Kirk."

Colin chuckled as he got up. "Let's—"

"I agree. Let's keep this quiet until you've told Jean. I really do like her and I don't want her hurt."

"Jean's tough, but I'll take care of it. Actually, I was going to say, 'Let's go see if Sara's brought out the desserts yet.' She makes these fabulous fruit things."

Gemma groaned. "I'm talking about affairs of the heart and you're only concerned about your belly."

"I rather like your belly too," he said. "When things get to that stage, will you wear those gloves for me?"

"Of course. Maybe we can spar."

"I was thinking more of you wearing *only* the gloves. Nothing else."

"Colin!" They heard a voice calling. "Are you out here somewhere?"

"It's Ramsey. I guess dessert is ready. You want to leave together or separately?"

"You go first," she said. "I'll be there in a few minutes." She stepped away from Colin. "Tell nothing to no one."

"If that's what you want, that's what I'll do," he said as he left the secluded area, and she could hear him talking with Ramsey.

Gemma wanted some time to herself to think

about what was happening in her life. She couldn't help remembering all that Tris had told her about his niece's wish and how it had come true. To Gemma, it almost seemed as though her wishes were also coming true. She had the job she'd wanted so much, and she was enjoying every minute of the time she spent buried in the old papers. And now a man she'd been attracted to from the moment she met him had asked her out.

The only problem was his former girlfriend. What Gemma wondered was whether or not Jean really felt that it was over between them.

And what about his family? Gemma thought. How were they going to react to their beloved Jean no longer being in the family?

Gemma put her hands over her face. All in all, she couldn't see this as turning out well. If she had any sense, she'd tell Colin to stay away from her.

But Gemma knew she wasn't going to do that. Being altruistic was good, but throwing away a man who seemed to be everything she'd ever wanted was just plain stupid.

She headed back toward the house.

13

Gemma," Sara said as she held out a plate of some strawberry dessert, "are you sticking with your Heartwish being to get a good job?"

Gemma's mind was so full of thoughts about her and Colin that she had no idea what Sara was talking about. "I need to shower and change."

"Don't do it on our account," Rams said.

"Yeah, keep the shorts," Luke said.

Gemma looked at Mike, and he shrugged. "Sure, why not?" Gemma said as she took the plate and went to sit on the grass under the shade tree. Colin was in a chair as far from her as he could get. She didn't look at him.

Joce spoke first. "We were talking about the Heartwishes Stone and thinking about what we'd use its magic for. Luke wants immortality."

"My goodness!" Gemma said. "You certainly know how to wish *big*."

"My wife left out the details," Luke said. "All writers want immortality. That's why we're so vain as to think someone would want to read our thoughts. But it would be nice to think that my grandchildren will like reading my books."

"I'm sure they will," Joce said, smiling at him.

"Wives' opinions don't count in this," Rams said. "What about you, Sara? What would you wish for?"

"There's nothing I don't have. I got the house I wanted, the man, and this." She rubbed her big belly.

"Ha!" Mike said.

They all looked at him.

"I was her third choice of man," Mike said, and everyone laughed.

"Is this a joke I'm missing?" Gemma asked.

"Come over some afternoon and help me feed and diaper, and I'll tell you all of it," Joce said. "But I'll tell you now that Mike was not her third choice."

"She wouldn't have been interested in me if she'd met me in an ordinary way," Mike said.

Tess gave her brother a hard look. "I would have arranged a meeting with Sara if you'd just bothered to visit once in a while."

"I would have if—"

"Order in the court!" Rams said loudly. "You two can argue later. Let's get back on the subject. Sara, my dear cousin, there must be something you want."

"Good health and safety for the people I love."

"Boo! Hiss!" Tess said. "You love everybody in

Edilean. If that wish were granted, we'd be a town with no illness, no accidents."

"Sounds great to me," Sara said.

"There is one thing you want," Mike said to his wife. "You told me just the other day."

Sara looked puzzled for a moment, then smiled. "That was a joke and don't you *dare* tell them what I said."

"Now you have to tell us," Luke said.

"Not me." Mike held up his hands in surrender. "I have to live with her. If she wants to confess, that's up to her."

Everyone looked at Sara.

"All right!" she said in exasperation. "I said . . ." She sighed. "It wasn't anything really. I just said that I envied Joce having twins. Tess, back me up here. Wouldn't you like to be carrying two babies, a boy *and* a girl?"

"Absolutely not!" Tess said. "One is all I'll be able to handle. The only mother I knew was our grandmother. Nobody could be worse than her. I'm afraid—" She stopped talking and took a drink of her iced tea.

Mike reached out his hand and took Tess's in his and held it. His eyes told her that he was with her.

"Tess, I'm sorry," Sara said. "I didn't mean to upset you."

"Before I gave birth I was really worried whether I'd love my babies," Joce said.

"And now she won't leave them for even minutes," Luke said.

"This is getting too deep for me," Colin said. "Any more of this strawberry stuff, Sara?"

"Sure, I'll get it."

"No you won't," Colin said as he got up and went to the little table. "Mike, what's your wish?"

"Easy," Mike said. "I want to take down a truly evil person."

"You and me both," Colin said as he sat back down.

"Excuse me if I'm being dense," Joce said to Mike, "but didn't you just do that last fall?"

"That was done by my wife," Mike said, smiling at Sara in pride. "And we had a lot of help. I'd like to end my career with fireworks."

Sara looked at Gemma. "My husband will soon retire from the Fort Lauderdale Police Department, and he's like a caged beast because I made him promise to take a desk job."

"Beast, am I?" Mike asked as he looked at Sara.

"You two can do that later," Rams said. "So who's left to make a wish? Colin?"

"What about you, Rams?" Colin asked.

"I got what I wanted when Tess said yes to me."

"That's nice," Gemma said.

"It's a cop-out," Luke said. "What is it? The lawyer in you can't reveal anything? You could wish for a backbone."

"You could wish for—" Rams began.

"Don't you two start!" Joce said. "I haven't had *my* wish yet."

They all looked at Joce. "I've decided to save my wish for when I really need it."

"I think I'll do that, too," Rams said.

"True Love!" Sara said. "One of us must wish for True Love."

Everyone looked from Gemma to Colin and back again, as they were the only unmarried people there.

"Colin is a Frazier," Gemma said, "so I'm not sure he should fool around with this."

"You believe in these wishes, don't you?" Joce asked, her eyes wide.

Gemma couldn't tell them what Tris had told her in confidence. "I'd just like to do some more research before—"

"I agree with Sara," Colin said as he stood up. "Why not wish for True Love? I've got a house now, so why not fill it?" He lifted his glass of lemonade and everyone picked up their glasses and held them aloft. "I wish that next year at this time we're all here together again, but that I will have my True Love with me."

"And she's expecting a baby," Sara added.

"Right," Colin said. "And that Sara has two babies—you better get to work, Mike—and Tess is the best mother in the world, that Mike has brought down a master of true evil, and—Who am I forgetting?"

"Luke!" Gemma said. "The writer."

"And Joce and me," Rams said.

Colin kept his glass lifted high. "Luke gets his books remembered forever, and Rams and Joce come up with something to wish for." He started to take a drink.

"What about Gemma?" Mike asked.

"The last person on earth I'd forget is Gemma," Colin said as he looked at her. "I hope you get everything you wish for in life."

Everyone turned toward Gemma and noted the way her face turned red.

"To answered wishes," Rams said and they all took deep drinks.

In Miami, sitting at her father's bedside in the hospital, Nell held up her bear. "See, Daddy, I told you."

"Told me what, sweetheart?"

"That Landy's necklace blinks."

"It sure does." He took the bear and held the necklace for a moment. It was a pretty thing, with a tiny, glistening rock inside a little cage made of gold. The necklace looked as though it could be valuable. "Where'd you get this?"

"It was in that box of junk jewelry I bought at the church rummage sale," her mother, Addy, said from the other side of the bed.

"Where'd it come from to get there?" he asked.

"I have no idea," Addy said. "Why are you interested?"

"No reason," he said. "It just doesn't look like junk and maybe somebody's looking for it."

Nell took the bear from her father. She didn't like what he was saying. She'd almost forgotten that daddies made rules that weren't to be broken.

"I don't think so," Addy said. "That necklace was stuck inside two flat pieces of lead, like somebody'd been using it for fishing. Nell and I had to use the vise on your workbench and two screwdrivers to get it open."

He chuckled. "Like mother, like daughter."

Nell clutched her bear and its necklace to her. "I like it."

"All right," he said, "you can keep it." He looked at his wife. "But later . . ." He left the rest of the sentence blank. She knew what he meant. When they got back to Edilean she'd find out where the necklace came from.

14

Colin left Merlin's Farm and his friends reluctantly. He'd wanted to drive Gemma home, but she'd declined his offer. He knew what she meant, that he was to clear things with Jean before Gemma would be alone with him.

He knew that Gemma was right, but that didn't keep him from dreading the confrontation with Jean. He parked behind the sheriff's office and started to get out, but instead, he sat in his car and looked up at his apartment windows. Gemma said she wanted him to tell her about his life, but he didn't want to do that. For so many years, he'd gone in the wrong direction, trying to be what he wasn't. His lifelong obsession with wanting to help people had, at times, made him almost forget himself.

Obligations to his family, to people he'd grown up with, to his hometown, and especially to a woman he'd once loved with his whole heart, had nearly overwhelmed him. These weren't things he wanted to tell a woman he thought he might have a future with.

As he looked up at the windows of the dreary apartment he hated, he envisioned what was coming. Jean loved drama and scenes—which was why she was so good in a courtroom—and he didn't know which way she was going to play this particular episode. Would it be tears, which would end up with Colin comforting her? Or would it be anger and her shouting at him and saying that he'd betrayed her?

Back when he was younger, her scenes had been something he needed. A rip-roaring good argument with Jean—who could give as good as she got—helped release some of his own rage at the way his life was going.

After one of their fights—and the following makeup sex—he'd be able to stand working at his father's car dealership for another six weeks or so. When the pressure inside him had built until he'd been ready to explode, he knew just how to push Jean's buttons to make her angry enough that they could have a fight.

But all that had ended long ago, Colin thought, as he leaned back against the seat of his Jeep. He had walked out just as she'd taken a job in D.C.

Closing his eyes, he let himself remember those first days with Jean.

When Colin was in his last year of school—University of Virginia—his father was begging him to join his car business.

"I'll give you anything you want," his dad said.

"Have a lawyer draw up a contract. You want fifty percent—eighty percent—whatever, you got it. You want me to retire and turn everything over to you and your brothers, I will."

The only thing Colin wanted, had ever wanted, was to be the sheriff of Edilean. The fact that the town didn't have a sheriff didn't bother him at all.

His father, in an attempt to "reason" with him—meaning to make his eldest son see things his way—said, "You need a job that pays you, one you can make money at. It's a matter of pride."

He'd added the last because he knew his son didn't need money. When Colin was sixteen, his father had complained about the software that kept track of all the cars his dealership sold. Peregrine Frazier had ranted and raved about it in detail, saying that the program was made for one dealership and about a hundred cars. "It gets confused when I put more than that in it," he said in derision.

At the time, Colin was a senior in high school and taking a computer course. The next morning he talked to his teacher about the problem, and together they wrote a new program.

Colin presented it to his father on the day he graduated.

"I'm supposed to give *you* a gift, boy," Mr. Frazier said, looking at the four CDs in puzzlement. "Is this music?"

"Stick it in a computer and see," Colin said.

When Mr. Frazier saw what the software could

do, he copyrighted it, paid a lot to have some IT guys smooth it out, then marketed it. Every penny in royalties that came in was split between Colin and his teacher. The money was enough that both of them never had to work again.

When Colin graduated from college he didn't want to sell cars, but he hated to see his father beg. Worse, he couldn't bear to tell him no. And too, there was the weight on him that his ancestors had always worked with anything with wheels. To not do so was letting down generations of Fraziers. So Colin had agreed to try it. He'd gone to work in the Richmond dealership and done his best to sell cars.

But he'd hated it. Selling was not something he liked and he was very, very bad at it. His sales were so low the other salespeople laughed at him.

It was Jean who changed everything.

Colin had been out of college for only a few weeks, was just twenty-one years old, and working for his dad. Jean came in to buy a car and she was so beautiful that all Colin could do was stare at her. His brother ended up making the sale.

Colin thought that was the end of the meeting, but she called him later and invited him out. They ended up in bed together, and two months later, they were living together in her apartment.

Like Colin's father, Jean encouraged him to stay in the car business, and for four years they were a couple. He was pulled into her life of candlelit dinners and nights out. He was fascinated by her law cases, and they often stayed up all night working on them. It was the closest Colin had come to real work in the world of law enforcement he so loved. Jean's world became his, but that was all right because being involved so deeply with her helped block out his unhappiness at his job. And besides, he was so young and inexperienced that everything about her was dazzling.

In college he'd been so involved in his studies—which consisted of anything that came close to pertaining to criminology—and sports that he didn't have time for much else. There'd been girls, but none of them held his attention for very long. He wanted a woman who was interesting, and who was more involved in life than in just wondering what she should wear.

Jean, six years older than he was, a lawyer and well traveled, had fulfilled that need in him, and for those years their life together had been good.

Colin didn't realize it, but he'd always assumed that someday they'd quit going out so often, quit flying to Napa for the weekend, and quit having their raucous fights. He thought they would become serious, and when they did, they'd move to Edilean. They'd live in a real house with a big backyard, not a terrace that looked out over a city. They'd have kids and attend church together.

Everything changed one evening when Jean came home and excitedly told him that she'd had a job offer in Washington, D.C.

"Of course I haven't accepted yet," she said.

Colin smiled. It was obvious that she'd wanted to

consult him before making such a big decision. But she didn't say that. In fact, she didn't ask him a single question.

"I want to see if I can get the same amount of money from Briggs. I'll play them against each other. I'll let them conduct an auction over me and the highest bidder wins. Oh! I have to call Mom about this. She'll be out of her mind with excitement." Jean patted his leg as she got off the couch, wineglass in hand, and went to call her mother.

Colin had sat there in silence, and it was as though his whole life suddenly became crystal clear to him. He was working at a job he hated and living where he didn't want to—all to please other people.

He knew that Jean was thinking of taking another job without consulting him because she was so sure he'd go with her that she needn't bother to ask him.

And why should she? Colin thought. He could go anywhere. He had no doubt that his father would love a reason to buy a car dealership in D.C. If Colin wanted to go to Italy, his dad would probably buy a showroom there.

When Jean returned to the room, she was even more elated—and was completely oblivious to the fact that Colin was saying nothing. They ordered in some Chinese food and she talked all through the meal. It was only when they'd finished that she slowed down.

"You're awfully quiet. Don't you have anything to say about this wonderful news?"

"I'm going back to Edilean."

"That's a great idea. Your parents will be thrilled that I'm getting such a promotion. I'll make partner in another three years."

She went right back into talking about *her* plans, and *her* life.

As Colin cleared away the meal, Jean got on her phone and started calling people to tell them her good news. When he finished, he went to the bedroom and got his suitcases out of the closet.

She didn't come into the bedroom for over an hour, and by then Colin was packed.

"Could I use your phone?" she asked. "The battery on mine gave out and I'm too excited to want to talk while plugged in. What are you doing?"

"I told you. I'm going home."

"Okay. I'll see you this weekend. I guess you'll need your cell?"

"Yeah, I'll need it," he said as he picked up his two suitcases and walked out the front door.

By the time Jean showed up in town with her fabulous news that she'd accepted the job and would be moving to D.C. in two weeks, Colin had rented an office in town. And he'd already had the showdown with his father.

Colin had politely listened to every argument his father came up with as to why he had to return to Richmond.

"We *need* you!" his father had pleaded.

Colin never came close to losing his temper or his resolve. He'd at last made up his mind, and he wasn't going to change it. "You don't need me, but the people of Edilean do," he told his father.

When Jean showed up in Edilean, she was angry. She burst into his newly acquired office and started in on him right away. "What the hell are you *doing*?" she shouted. "I've been left alone for two whole weeks, and I've had to make all the arrangements for our move by myself. Damn! But you can be so selfish!"

She looked around the place. Over the fifty or so years since the building was constructed, it had been many things. Its latest incarnation had been to sell sandwiches and sodas. Colin had donated all the fixtures to a retirement home, bought a couple of old desks, some chairs, and an old filing cabinet at an auction. He hadn't yet painted the three rooms.

"What is this place?" Jean asked, her upper lip curled in a sneer. "It's disgusting. And filthy."

"How about if I buy some mops and buckets, and you and I clean it?"

"I don't have time for your weird sense of humor right now. Are you packed?"

They hadn't seen each other or even talked on the phone for two whole weeks, and it looked like Jean thought Colin had been busy packing to go to her new job.

When he didn't move, she sat down on the old wooden chair across from his desk. "What is it *this* time?" she asked in the tone of someone who put up with a lot from him.

Colin marveled at how different he felt about her,

about life in general, now that he no longer had a job he hated. In just two weeks he'd achieved more soul-satisfying accomplishments than he had in years of working for his father.

"This is my office," Colin said with a calmness Jean had never heard before.

"I don't understand. How can you have an office here when we'll be living in D.C.? Do you plan to come down here on weekends?"

It had taken nearly three hours of talking—with tears from both of them—before Jean fully realized that he was breaking up with her.

In the end, she held on to her anger. Whereas she'd dumped a lot of men, she'd never had anyone say no to her. But tears, anger, none of it made Colin change from his decision. Even when Jean said she'd refuse the new job and keep the old one, he didn't relent.

Neither of them ever considered that she'd move to Edilean.

They parted with more animosity than Colin wanted, and it took him a long time to put her out of his mind. He missed her a lot, and often came close to calling her to tell her about something that had happened.

He did his best to bury himself in his work. He went to the county sheriff, Tom Wilderson, and talked to him at length. Since Edilean didn't have its own sheriff, the best the man could do was deputize Colin and keep him in a station in Edilean.

"But the county can't afford—" Tom began.

"I'll pay for it," Colin said. "All expenses are mine."

When Tom was able to close his mouth from shock, he agreed to Colin's proposal, as he liked the young man. But he also knew that Colin's family was rich, so Tom figured Colin would quit after a few months. Who wanted to settle domestic disputes instead of sitting by the pool?

Colin didn't quit, and over the years, Tom had found Colin's intelligence and calm demeanor invaluable. In the first year, there'd been an incident that Colin had handled well. Two brothers were fishing in the wilderness area around Edilean when they got in a fight, and one of them shot the other. In remorse and grief, the surviving brother had threatened to shoot a family that was having a picnic. Colin had talked the man out of the idea.

But as well as Colin's professional life had gone, the personal side had suffered.

For years after he split with Jean, they'd not seen each other. He'd dated a few women—none of them from Edilean—but it had never worked out. One woman hated his job as deputy sheriff in Edilean. He realized it was her own sense of prestige that concerned her, meaning that she'd wanted a doctor or lawyer. What had really horrified him was that after just four dates she was assuming they'd get married.

Another young woman was like that dreadful Isla, whom his mother had nearly hired. She'd been stunned when she'd seen the Frazier estate. Her greed for the place had made her dizzy. Colin dropped her the next day.

After years of these failed relationships, Jean had returned to his life.

About a year ago, he'd been in the county courthouse going through some old files when he'd looked up and seen Jean. He'd forgotten how beautiful she was and how put together she always appeared. Since he'd lived with her, he well knew the time and effort that went into her looks, but at the moment he saw her again, he forgot all that.

Minutes later, they were having lunch together, and she told him that she'd returned to her old law firm in Richmond. "I decided I'd rather be a big fish," she said. "In D.C. there were too many people like me."

An hour later they were in a hotel room.

His first impression of her was that she'd changed. She seemed less intense, less driven to win over everyone on her way to the top.

"I found out what's really important in life," she said as she sipped her glass of wine. "And you! It's like you've finally grown up."

Jean had the ability to make insults seem like compliments.

"I've been through a lot in the last years," he said.

"I hope *I* didn't cause you any pain when I broke up with you."

Colin didn't correct her. If her ego needed to think that, let her.

He still wasn't sure how it happened, but within weeks they were again going out together. Jean did her best to make him think she was now willing to compromise and make a life together. "I've missed you so very much," she said. "I didn't know I could miss anyone so much."

They went to bed a few more times, but it wasn't the same. Colin was no longer the unhappy young man he had been. And he was no longer dazzled by Jean or her job or even her beauty.

She'd been correct when she'd said that he'd at last grown up.

He'd known in his heart that he should break it off completely with Jean, but he couldn't do it. When she wasn't after something, she was fun and interesting. Her clients gave her tickets to plays and concerts, and he enjoyed them. And his family adored her. She and Lanny teased each other in a raunchy way, and Jean went shopping with Mrs. Frazier. The two women had decorated the guesthouse together. Jean bought art books for Shamus, and found out-of-print books on automotive history for Mr. Frazier.

Colin didn't want to take these things away from his family, but he'd had more than enough of being alone. Besides, there was no one else in his life.

For his own sanity, he cut out sex with Jean. She was willing, but he knew he didn't love her anymore, and he didn't want her to have the wrong idea about where their relationship was going.

About three months ago, Tom said he'd seen Jean

in Richmond with a man she'd introduced as her brother. "Good-looking young man named Elliot."

"About ten years younger than her?" Colin asked.

"Yeah, but then I guess you've met him."

Colin wanted to say "I *was* him," but he didn't. He knew Jean had no siblings, and that the only living relative she had was her mother. "An only child of only-child parents," she used to say.

Colin knew that if he'd been jealous of the young man she was introducing as her brother, it meant he still had feelings for her. The truth was, he was glad and that made him realize that it was time to finally break off their friendship. He dreaded the tears his mother was going to shed. She'd always been so sure Jean was going to be her daughter-in-law, but Colin couldn't help that. Part of him knew that as long as he had Jean as a companion, he would quit searching for someone to share his life with.

When he met Gemma, it was as though his prayers had been answered. If he were a superstitious man, he would have said the Heartwishes Stone was at work.

When he'd seen her sprawled on the floor, pens and papers all around her, she made him smile. When he spent time with her, he was nearly joyous at what he saw. She was quiet, so very much the opposite of Jean's up-and-down moods and her craving for excitement. Even Jean's cooking was done for drama. He well knew that she'd never scramble a couple of eggs. "How boring!" she used to say. "Call the deli."

But Gemma had made him an omelet and had cared enough that she'd told him to take a shower at her place. And she'd gone with him to the grocery, driven his car, which had been souped-up by Lanny, and she'd helped him rescue a child. Colin had seen the fear in her eyes that day, but that hadn't stopped her from climbing on him and grabbing the boy. Colin would never tell anyone, but he'd replayed that YouTube video at least fifty times.

As for what had happened the morning he showered in her house, it was true that at first he hadn't remembered their brief moment together. However, he knew his sleep had been restless that night and that he'd been having a dream about Gemma. When Lanny had woken him up in her house, Colin had fought against it.

"Whatever the hell you're dreaming about, I'd sure like to share it with you," Lanny said.

Colin, still not awake, almost hit his brother. To Colin's foggy mind, Lanny was saying he wanted a threesome with Gemma.

Later, when Colin saw her again, he was amazed at the joy that shot through him. When Gemma looked at him as though he were the lowest piece of slime on earth, he didn't know when he'd ever been so devastated—and bewildered. What in the world had happened to make her despise him?

He tried to get her to tell him, but she'd wanted nothing to do with him. Before he could find out, Jean showed up at the barbecue, uninvited, and he'd wanted to tell her to go away and never come back.

When Mike asked Colin to help with the big side pad, Colin was glad to get away from her. But his happiness soon left him when Gemma made her remark about being "smart and brave."

Everything hit Colin at once and he realized what he'd done—and he'd been truly horrified. He thought that in one of his dreams of lust he'd pulled Gemma into her own bed and . . . He didn't want to think what he'd done. She wouldn't have physically been able to get away.

Later, she would have worried that if she told, she'd lose her job, the one she so very much wanted.

He'd stood there by the tree, unable to move away, and watched Gemma frantically pound away with her kicks and punches. When Luke called time, she kept on going. That he, Colin, had been the cause of her hurt and anger made him feel ill. Mike had to hold her to get her to stop hitting.

Colin had nodded at Mike, letting him know that he wanted to be alone with Gemma. She didn't want to see or speak to him, but he had to let her know that no one had a right to attack a woman and get away with it. Even if it meant that Colin's career and his life as he knew it would be over, he was going to do right by her.

When she told him she hadn't been "forced," it was all he could do not to pick her up and kiss her. *She* had gone after *him*.

As soon as she said it, images began to come back to him.

When Jean came to him, he could hardly bear the sight of her. He knew that the way she'd slipped her arm around his was a show of ownership. How Colin regretted their friendship of the last year!

He got rid of Jean and took Gemma away so they could talk in private. It hadn't taken long to find out that Gemma's only real objection to him was Jean. Right then, he'd wanted to take the time to tell Gemma the full truth about him and Jean, but he'd only told her a bit of it. First, he needed to get everything straight between Jean and himself, then he could go to Gemma and tell her all of it.

15

WITH RELUCTANCE, COLIN got out of his car and made his way up the back stairs to his apartment. He knew Jean was waiting for him because her silver Mercedes was still in the parking lot.

The first thing he saw when he opened the door to his apartment was his suitcase on the floor. She came out of his bedroom carrying a tiny tube of toothpaste.

"There you are," she said cheerfully. "I waited to see you but you're so late that I was beginning to think I was going to have to drive home in the dark. Hope you don't mind if I borrow a piece of your luggage."

"Jean, I . . ." He trailed off, not knowing how to begin. She was going through the old cabinets against the wall.

"Colin, dear, have you been lashing yourself over this? But of course you have. Your deep desire to always do *good* must be tugging at you. So how was the rest of your little get-together with your Edilean friends? After you sent me away?"

"Fine," he said. It was obvious that even though she hadn't been in his apartment in months, she was searching for any items she'd left behind. "Let's sit down and talk, all right?"

"No," she said. "I think that everything has been said. I just wish—" She put up her hands. "No, I promised myself I wouldn't do this. It is as it is."

"Jean, please sit down and let's talk about this."

She glared at him. "There is nothing to talk about. You chose someone else. The end. That's all, folks!"

"You act like you and I were a solid couple and I dumped you."

"Again."

"What?"

"You dumped me *again*. For the second time. The first time was when I got a job in D.C. You were so jealous you walked out on me."

"Is that what you think I did?"

"I know that's what you did. You had a job you hated, while I loved mine. Then I got an even better job and you threw a jealous fit and left me. And you walked out on your dad too."

Colin drew in his breath, unable to answer her accusations.

"So now you met some young college student and you're leaving me. Again. I guess you think this one is going to put up with the way you ignore the women in your life."

Colin was recovering himself and there was a volcano of anger inside him. "I never ignored you. I lived *your* life," he said quietly.

"No you didn't." She stopped moving about the room and looked at him. "You *hid* in my life. You thought you were too good to be a car salesman, but you suffered through it and made everyone miserable, me included. I felt so sorry for you that I took you in and let you live my life."

"Is that how you see it?" Colin asked softly. "There was nothing in it for you? Nothing between us?"

"Sure," she said. "For a while. My regret—" She glared at him. "I regret that I gave you my best years. If I hadn't had to deal with *you,* I could be like those women today. *I* could have a couple of kids and be living in Georgetown now." Her voice was rising. "Do you know why I quit my job in D.C.?"

"Please tell me," he said, his voice cold.

"For you. You never realized that I left all that behind because of *you*. I missed you and wanted to be with you. I knew you didn't have anyone, so I came back."

His eyes grew colder. "The scuttlebutt around the courthouse was that you got fired. I heard that you were sleeping with one of the partners, and his wife threatened to divorce him if you weren't sent away."

For a moment, Jean's face seemed to swell with her rage, but then she smiled. "Misusing your badge to snoop, are you?"

"Jean," Colin said, "why do we have to part this

way? I told you when you came back that I didn't think it would work."

"And I said it would." She went to a cabinet and poured herself a drink.

"You're driving," he said.

"Don't worry. It's just club soda." She took a deep drink. "So what happens now? You get rid of me as soon as you can, then run back to your butch girlfriend?" She looked at him through her lashes. "You should have told me that's what you liked. I would have done a little dress up. You like whips and chains too?"

"Jean, I think you should leave. Better yet, I should go. You stay here and sleep. I don't want you driving when you're this angry."

"And where will you go? Back to Mommy? Or to your boxing boyfriend?"

He put his hand on the doorknob. He couldn't bear to hear any more of this. If she kept on, he'd be drawn into it, and he'd say things he would regret later.

"Oh, but that's right. You bought a house, didn't you? I spent months—years—trying to get you to buy a house with me, but you wouldn't. You've just met this . . . this hermaphrodite and you buy one for *her*?!"

Abruptly, all the anger left her, and she dropped down on the couch and began to cry.

Colin knew he could have left her rage and false accusations, but he couldn't leave her in tears. Reluctantly, he closed the door and went to sit beside her. Her sobs were shaking her shoulders, and when she leaned against him, he put his arm around her.

"Jean, I'm sorry," he said. "I'm sorry for all the hurt I've caused you. I didn't leave you because I was jealous of your job."

"Then why?" she asked. "I thought we were good together. I thought we had everything."

If he told the truth, he'd have to say that they'd had nothing *together,* that it had all been hers—or his father's. He left to pursue his own dreams, and that maybe he'd learned how to do that from her. Jean would never have taken a job she hated.

"Listen," he said softly and with sympathy in his voice, "why don't you stay here tonight?"

"You're going to your house? The one you bought for *her*?"

Colin dropped his arm from around her shoulder. "I bought a house here in Edilean before I ever met Gemma. Jean, I want to live here. In *this* town. What did you call the place? 'Incestuous,' wasn't it? You told me you wouldn't live in Edilean even if you were in a coffin. You must see that it could never work between us."

"Why didn't you tell me this years ago? Now I'm thirty-six and—"

He stood up. "If I'd known it, I would have told you. And please don't try to make me think that you're now so old and plain you can't get another man. From what I hear, you already have one. Or is he actually your brother?"

"Elliot is a guy I work with. I'm mentoring him."

"As I remember it, you're a *great* mentor to young men." For a moment, they almost exchanged smiles, and Colin knew it was time for him to leave. "Jean, I'm going to go now. I'd say I'd call you, but I don't think I should. For all your anger, you knew this was coming. My mistake was in leaving it too long. I'll . . ." He was at the door. "I'm sure I'll see you around the courthouses." He left the apartment, feeling part sad for what was gone from his life, and part elated at the mystery of the future that awaited him.

Inside the apartment, Jean stopped the tears and anger instantly.

"Bastard!" she said aloud, then went to the cabinet and poured herself a Scotch. One thing about Colin was that he had good taste in liquor—and he could afford the best.

She looked through the tiny, ugly kitchen to see what she could cook. Nothing. She hadn't eaten one of those revolting burgers at Colin's boring friends' house. She hated the things anyway. Besides, the sight of that girl in her tiny shorts and even tinier tank top slamming away at that hunk of a man, Mike Newland, made Jean lose what appetite she'd had.

Afterward, when Colin had dismissed Jean as though she weren't important, she'd been furious—but she didn't show it. In backwater Edilean, she knew to smile until her face ached.

When her glass was half empty, she called her uncle. "Have you eaten?" she asked as casually as she could, but she made sure there was a little hiccup in her voice.

"No. Jean, are you all right?"

"It's been a rough day."

"Come over and we'll talk about it."

Jean hung up, smiling.

16

Yawning, Gemma scrambled a couple of eggs and put two slices of whole wheat bread in the toaster. Last evening Ramsey and Tess had driven her home. Gemma hadn't wanted to ride with them, but Joce had nudged her forward. She'd felt instant camaraderie with nearly everyone she'd met in Edilean, but there'd been animosity between her and Tess.

Tess started talking the minute Rams pulled out of the driveway. "Okay," she said, "I think I came on too strong and made a bad first impression."

"You scared her to death," Rams said.

"Not really—" Gemma began.

"Mike likes you," Tess said.

"That means you could commit murder and Tess would testify in your defense," Rams said.

"Would you mind?" Tess said to her husband. "I'm trying to apologize." She looked back at Gemma but didn't seem to know what to say.

Gemma searched for a common ground between them. "It's all right. Maybe after the baby is born, we can work out together."

"If Mike had his way, Sara and I'd be in the gym now," Tess said.

"That's a good idea," Gemma said. "You could do light leg extensions and some arm work."

Tess shook her head. "You and Mike!"

Gemma was glad when Rams pulled into the Frazier driveway and let her off at the guesthouse. She thanked them, said good-bye, and unlocked her door. They only left when she was safely inside.

She was glad for the quiet after the long day. She picked up her canvas reading bag, put her cell phone and a box of letters dated 1775 in it, and went outside to read.

She was still searching for Winnie, still trying to find out more about the Heartwishes Stone. One thing she'd decided was that she would *not* make her dissertation about the Stone. Seeing the way the people of Edilean were so fascinated with the idea of being granted wishes, with everyone thinking what they'd wish for, made Gemma see the Stone as dangerous. What if the story of Nell's wish coming true got out? No amount of telling people that everything that happened was just a coincidence would stop what could become a stampede. People would descend on little Edilean in massive numbers—or on the Fraziers.

Gemma didn't like to imagine all the things that

could happen if the world heard about a Stone that could grant wishes.

To not make the Stone the basis of her dissertation wasn't an easy decision for her. A paper on an unusual subject that was backed up by facts could get her a very good grade—and that would help her get an excellent job.

But it wasn't worth it, she thought. A good grade, even a great job wasn't worth the risk. Besides, she'd rather get the job on her own merits, not because she'd started a riot.

She was in bed by ten. At midnight, she was awakened by her phone buzzing. It was a text message from Colin asking if she'd help him buy furniture for his new house. She knew what he meant, but she couldn't help texting,

> THE STORES ARE CLOSED NOW. GO TO BED.

He texted back.

> FUNNY. MEET ME AT FRESH MARKET AT 9 A.M. TOMORROW?

> WILL BE THERE.

she wrote back and turned off her phone.

This morning after she'd eaten, she took some time deciding what to wear. Was this to be considered their first date? she wondered. Were they going to one of those splendid furniture stores where everything cost a lot, or to one of those warehouses with no heating or cooling?

She had her hand on her only silk blouse when she thought that Mrs. Frazier and Jean would go to the classy place. Colin was a warehouse-type man. She put on jeans and a pink linen shirt.

When she got to the grocery—she'd used MapQuest to find it—she didn't see Colin. When he stepped out of a big black pickup truck, she smiled. "I guess the Fraziers change vehicles often."

"What?" Colin asked. "Oh, yeah, sure. You ready to go? I have drinks in the cab."

He got in the driver's side, leaving Gemma to get in by herself. She had to step up high to get in. There was a gym bag on the floor and his hair was wet. It looked like he'd worked out this morning. She wished he'd invited her, but from the bleak expression he was wearing, maybe he'd needed to be alone. It was obvious that something was bothering him.

Colin started the big truck and pulled onto the road. "It'll take over an hour to get to the store. Hope that's okay."

She said it was, but then they were silent. After about ten minutes, Gemma couldn't take it anymore. "Are you one of those men who wants a woman to beg him to tell her what's wrong?"

He glanced at her. "What does that mean?"

"You know, the man sighs loud enough to blow

magazines off the coffee table, she asks what's wrong, he says nothing is, and it goes from there. It can take hours to get him to tell her that he's angry about something his boss did."

"That's not me," Colin said. "At least not usually. But tell me, if a man's that much trouble, why does she bother trying to get him to tell her what's wrong?"

Gemma threw up her hands. "Survival! He won't leave her alone until she does drag it out of him, that's why! He won't let her read, watch TV, talk on the phone, nothing until he's told her whatever he's fretting about."

Colin raised an eyebrow. "Last boyfriend?"

"Last *two* boyfriends!"

"All right, I won't be number three. Jean and I had it out yesterday, and the things she said are still bothering me."

Gemma waited for him to continue, but he said nothing. "So you *are* one of those men who needs to be coaxed?"

"I'm trying to figure out where to begin."

"That's my problem too," she said. "I want to know about the Heartwishes Stone, but I think I need to go back to the beginning, to the first Frazier who came to the U.S."

"Was that a subtle way to tell me to start at the beginning?"

"I didn't think it was subtle."

Colin didn't smile as she'd hoped he would. Finally, he said, "The real, basic truth is that my relationship with Jean hasn't been the usual one, and I'm concerned that if I tell you, you'll think less of me."

"I believe that people are the sum of what they've been through in their lives. From what I've seen, you dedicate your life to helping others. If whatever you went through with Jean helped to lead you to that, then it couldn't be too bad."

He looked away from the road for a moment to glance at her. "I like that philosophy," he said and thought, And I like *you*. "Okay, here goes."

As he drove he began to talk, and he didn't have to tell her that he'd never told the story to anyone else before. Her impression from having seen him with his friends and the town residents was that people thought Colin Frazier didn't have any problems in life. He grew up comfortably well off, with no money difficulties. He'd been great at sports all through school, made good grades, and now he had a job he loved. What could be wrong?

But as Gemma listened, she heard a deeper story. Colin tried to be lighthearted when he said that his father had "talked him into" working for him, but Gemma had met Mr. Frazier, and her impression was that he could be a tyrant. From what Colin was telling her, Peregrine Frazier had bullied, badgered, and belittled his eldest son into taking a job he hated.

Colin told how bad he was at the job. His example of "bad" was when a single mother with three kids came in with a clunker with 140,000 miles on it. Colin set her up with a car for less than the dealership had paid for it. His father had deducted the discrepancy from Colin's paycheck. "My father believes in teaching lessons and being fair. He would have done the same thing to any of his other employees, so of course he'd do it to his son."

"Of course," Gemma said, but she didn't agree. Colin was there as a favor to his father, so shouldn't he have returned some favors?

Colin went on to tell of meeting Jean, and of being so in awe of her beauty and her general demeanor that he'd hardly said a word. "If she hadn't called me, I would never have seen her again."

From Colin's mood today, Gemma wondered if that would have been a bad thing.

When he said that he'd moved to Richmond to live in an apartment with Jean, there was sadness in his voice. But when he told of helping her with her cases, his voice came alive. "I learned a lot about the law, how it worked, and what could and couldn't be done, and I even did some footwork for the cases."

Gemma wanted to say "She used you as a free paralegal and a PI," but she didn't. She did say, "Roy said you were good at solving mysteries. Did you figure out any of Jean's?"

Colin gave a shrug of modesty. "A few. Now and then. Not many. I remember one where Jean was defending a man who said he was in another state when his wife was murdered, but his credit card receipts showed that he was near the scene of the crime. I posed as a truck driver and asked some questions at a place where the man's card had been used. I found out that it was his mistress who'd used the card. She knocked over a display so no one would pay attention to how she signed the receipt. It was a revenge killing because he'd told her he'd decided to go back to his wife."

"Looks like you were doing the work of a sheriff before you actually were one."

Colin gave his first smile of the day. "You're making me remember things I haven't thought of in years."

"So when did you break up with Jean? The first time, that is?"

"When the bad of my life outweighed the good. Dad and I were fighting because for six months I'd been almost giving cars away."

"Did he charge you for them?"

"Oh yeah," Colin said, "but I didn't care."

"Because Jean's salary was supporting the two of you?" Gemma didn't realize that she was frowning.

"No. She kept her salary. I paid for everything except her clothes. If I'd done that, I'd have been bankrupted." He obviously meant to make Gemma laugh, but she didn't.

"I'm confused," Gemma said. "Your father debited your paycheck, but you supported Jean? Oh, wait. I bet you have a trust fund set up by an ancestor."

Colin told her about the software program that was now being used by many of the car dealerships across the country.

She took a moment to digest that information.

"So I guess you can afford a house and furniture." He was looking at her to see how this new information would affect her, but she kept her face blank. "What happened with you and Jean?"

He went on to tell about the earlier breakup, how he'd just walked out. "It was cowardly of me," he said. "If I'd stayed and talked to her back then, maybe I could have kept her from thinking what she told me last night."

At last, Colin got to what Jean said that had so upset him.

Gemma listened to every word he told her and marveled at how Jean had twisted everything around so she was the victim of Colin. Gemma had to work to keep her anger down. She wanted to point out that it was no wonder Jean hated losing him. Where was she going to find another man to pay the rent, help solve cases, and keep her entertained at night?

Gemma thought the wise thing to do would be to keep her true opinions to herself.

"One minute she was complaining that I'm too good," Colin said, "and the next she was telling me that I'm the personification of evil."

"So if she knew what was going on, that you hated your job, and as she said, you were hiding in her life, then why was she trying to get you back? What does she *like* about you?"

"I look good in a tuxedo," he said.

Gemma didn't laugh at his attempt at a joke. "What else?"

Colin gave her a suggestive glance. "She always said I was good in the sack. I have a bit of endurance."

"Wow," Gemma said, her eyes wide. "Are you talking four minutes or five?"

Colin burst into laughter. "Gemma, you're going to unman me."

She smiled. "At least I made you laugh."

He took her hand and kissed the back of it. "Thanks," he said. "I know Jean was hurt and angry, but . . ."

"Her remarks still cut deep," Gemma said. "You know, of course, that her contradicting herself showed she was lying."

"You think so?"

"Definitely." She paused. "How are you going to deal with your parents? They like Jean a lot. When your dad finds out that she won't be cooking for him anymore, he's going to be very upset."

"I indoctrinated Dad to pain when I quit working at the dealership."

"You carry a lot of guilt, don't you?" Gemma said.

"You don't? You've never felt bad for disappointing someone?"

Gemma didn't say anything.

"Come on," he said. "I'm doing some soul baring here, so you can too."

"When my father died, my mother was devastated. She loved him completely and absolutely—and depended on him for everything. She wanted me to take over his household duties."

"Fix the car, that kind of thing?"

"More or less. She wanted me to pay the bills, remember when the insurance needed to be paid. When the kitchen drain broke, she wanted *me* to call the plumber. When I said I had too much homework to do all those things, she got angry. She said I wasn't much use as a daughter."

"How old were you?"

"Twelve."

"That's way too young for that," Colin said. "She should have been helping you."

"'Shoulds' don't always happen. In fact, in my life they never do. I couldn't handle what my mother wanted, so I retreated into books. I read constantly, studied, researched. Besides, I was missing my dad so much that it was like a disease spreading inside me. I had trouble thinking coherently."

"What did your mother do?"

"She turned to my younger sister, who lived up to all Mom's hopes and dreams. Together, they figured out how to run the household." Gemma looked at him. "See? I know a lot about guilt."

"You know what I think?" he said. "I think your mother is the one who should bear the guilt, not you. You and your sister should have been her first concern, and she had no right to dump adult responsibilities onto her kids, either of you."

"Thanks," Gemma said. "And I think every word Jean said about you was a lie. She just wanted you back so much that she said anything she could think of to make you feel like you couldn't leave her."

"Yeah," Colin said, smiling. He was silent for a moment, then said, "So what kind of furniture should we get?"

She looked him up and down, at the size of him. His muscles were still engorged from his workout.

Colin noted the way she was looking at him and his eyelids lowered in a seductive way.

"Strong," she said.

"Me?" he said. "I do all right. I once benched—"

"No. I mean we should get really *strong* furniture."

Again, Colin laughed. "You're not going to let me indulge my ego, are you? First you knock both sex and me down, and now you're saying I might break the furniture just by sitting on it."

"I guess you could prove me wrong on both counts," she said softly.

"I would love to do that," he said. "Genuinely and deeply love to."

She looked out the truck window to hide the warm glow that came to her face.

"Thanks," he said.

She looked at him.

"I really mean it, Gemma. Thank you for listening. I didn't sleep at all last night and I was at Mike's gym at five."

"By yourself?"

"Yes. Bad, huh?"

"Very bad. If a heavy bench press slips, it can kill you."

He was still holding her hand. "I guess you'll have to go with me next time."

"I'll be there at six-thirty tomorrow."

"I'll be waiting," he said as he pulled into a parking lot.

As Gemma had figured, the furniture store was an enormous warehouse that seemed to go on forever. She couldn't resist telling him her dilemma about what to wear.

"You guessed right," he said as he stepped down, then pulled a thick roll of blueprints from behind the seat.

Gemma got out of the truck and walked around to stand beside him. "How much furniture do you want to buy?"

He handed her a plastic pouch containing an architect's scale, mechanical pencils, and some triangles. "Know how to use those?"

"Only vaguely. You're not planning to furnish the whole house today, are you?"

"I am," he said. "I never want to spend another night in that apartment of mine and I'd like to get this over with. Besides, by now everyone in Edilean knows I bought the house, so why try to keep it a secret? You have any favorite colors?"

"Whatever color the book jacket is, that's what I like." She was feeling a bit like she wanted to say she'd wait in the truck. The only reason she'd ever seen the inside of a furniture store was because she'd gone with her friends before they got married. "Colin," she said tentatively, "I really don't know—"

He opened the glass door, and she saw what looked to be acres of furniture. Overhead ceiling fans whirred. To the right was a long row of antique shops; to the left were light fixtures.

"Come on, Ranford, buck up your courage," Colin said.

"I don't know where to start."

"I want a couch," Colin said firmly. "Something I can take naps on."

"I don't think your living room is big enough to hold that," she said without cracking a smile.

Colin put his hand to his heart. "Wounded again. Come on or I'll hide your gloves and you won't be able to box."

Gemma put her fists up beside her temples. "Then I'll take you on with bare knuckles."

"May I help you?" asked a woman behind them.

Embarrassed, Gemma dropped her fists.

"We want to furnish a whole house today," Colin said. "Free delivery, right?"

"Of course," the woman said, smiling. "Where do you want to start?"

"Couch," Colin and Gemma said in unison.

As the saleswoman started walking, they followed. "Leather or fabric? Rolled arms or straight? High back or low?"

"Fabric, rolled, high," Gemma said.

At the same time, Colin said, "Leather, straight, low."

"Ah, newlyweds," the woman said. "Well, come on, I've had a lot of experience at settling arguments."

Neither Colin or Gemma corrected her impression that they were newlyweds.

"Hungry?" Colin asked as he pulled one of two big sandwiches from a paper bag. On the way back from the warehouse, they'd stopped for them. He'd texted Luke from the restaurant, so when they got back, Luke and Rams were waiting. The three men carried in the king-size mattress and springs Colin and Gemma'd brought back in the truck.

"You and I could have carried them," Gemma said to Colin.

"Thanks, but no," he'd said.

Gemma trailed behind the men with bags full of sheets and towels. She pulled off tags and put them in the washer while the men set up the bed.

Luke and Rams left as soon as the bed was on the floor, so Colin and Gemma were now alone, standing at the counter in the kitchen.

"Ravenous," she said. She took her sandwich and a bottle of water and went to sit on the pretty rug in the living room.

When Colin appeared, he had a cold bottle of champagne and two glasses. "Rams left this and said it was from Tess. What did you do to make her like you so much that she sent champagne?"

"Rams said it's because Mike likes me."

"That would do it for Tess. She thinks quite highly of her brother." Colin bit into his sandwich. Chewing, he picked up his bottle of water. "To more days like this one," he said.

"Truthfully, I'd rather spend four hours in the gym," she said.

"Me too," he said, and they looked at each other and smiled.

Between them passed images of the day. There'd been a lot of laughter as they tried to envision how the furniture would look in the house—and they'd been equally bad at it. Their saleswoman, Mrs. Ellis, thirty years in the business, was used to couples like them, so she showed them how to measure and plan the arrangements in each room.

It took an hour or so for them to get the hang of what they were doing, but soon they'd adjusted and slid into a comfortable camaraderie. They were both good at compromises, and besides, as Gemma said, it was Colin's house. When Mrs. Ellis said that Gemma would be living there too, they hadn't corrected her. Instead, they'd looked away for a moment, then they went on as though nothing had been said.

The only time they halted was when they came to the third bedroom. The second had been easy, as they'd made it into a guest bedroom with twin beds.

"How about a baby's room?" Mrs. Ellis said.

Both Gemma and Colin had stood there, staring at her in silence.

"It does happen," she said, laughing. When they still said nothing, she said, "All right, we'll just leave that room empty for now."

Throughout the day, Gemma had been acutely aware of Colin's presence—and of the constant mention of their having a future together. When they started to buy a bedside table, Mrs. Ellis asked who slept on which side. Who liked to read in bed? Did they watch TV at night?

Gemma and Colin kept up the charade that they'd been a couple for a long time, might even have been recently married.

But every time the saleswoman mentioned something that hinted at their physical togetherness, Gemma and Colin had looked at each other. At first their glances had been shy, but as the day wore on, their eyes lingered. When Mrs. Ellis talked of a child's room, Colin had taken Gemma's hand in his and held it for a few moments.

Once, when they'd been leaning over the blueprints spread out on a dining table and when Mrs. Ellis had turned her back, Colin had kissed Gemma. It had been a quick kiss, as though he were a schoolboy doing something behind the teacher's back, and Gemma had laughed. After that, they'd held hands several times, and twice Colin had briefly put his arm around Gemma's shoulders.

Had anyone been looking, no one would have guessed they weren't a couple.

On the drive home, they'd gone back to just being

friends and talked about what had been bought and what they liked and didn't like.

Gemma was now remembering all the touches and glances, and from what she saw in Colin's eyes, he was also remembering them.

In the next second, they were in each other's arms and kissing.

"I've wanted you all day long," Colin said.

"Me too."

She didn't say that being so near him, leaning over blueprints spread on a table, feeling his breath on her cheeks, had at times made her close her eyes.

"We said—" Colin began and started to move away from her.

"Who cares about words?" Gemma said as Colin kissed her neck. She loved the size of him, the weight. When he slipped his shirt over his head and she was confronted with all his honey-colored skin, her breath caught in her throat.

"I don't have a condom here," he said, his voice sounding tragic.

"Tris put me on pills," she replied.

He kissed her deeply. "I want to do better this time," he whispered, then picked her up and carried her to the bedroom, where he carefully put her down on the mattress cover.

It was early evening and the light through the window shade cast a golden glow through the room.

"I want to see you," he whispered as he slowly began to remove her clothing. When her shirt was off he kissed her shoulders, her arms, and he put each of her fingers to his lips. Gemma lay there, her eyes closed, and enjoyed the sensation of this delicious man making love to her.

He pulled her up, his strong hands caressing her back, his lips on hers, his tongue seeking the inside of her mouth. Her bra strap came unfastened and his big hands caressed her breasts, making her moan with desire.

He removed her jeans next, slowly unfastening them, kissing her legs as he moved downward. When his hands caressed her through her panties, she clutched at him, wanting him *now*!

"Not yet, my sweet," he whispered as he unfastened his jeans and slid them off.

Gemma loved the feel of his skin on hers. His body was hard, with great, huge muscles. His stomach was divided into ridges, without any fat over his firm muscles. She ran her fingers over his abdomen, feeling her way down lower and lower.

When her hand reached the center of him, it was his turn to groan. She pushed him back on the bed and ran her hands all over him, looking at his nude form. He was a study of what a body should look like, a centerfold of all those professional football players on TV.

Gemma slipped off her underpants and straddled him. He helped her to sit down on him, and she thought she might faint when he entered her. She had desired him for so very long.

His strong hands around her waist helped to guide her. He caressed her behind, her thighs, down to her calves. "Beautiful," he whispered. "You are truly beautiful."

He flipped her over onto her back, and for long, luxurious moments, he made velvet strokes inside her.

Based on her previous experience, Gemma expected him to finish soon, for the pleasure to end quickly. But Colin didn't quit. Instead he withdrew and kissed her more. His hand went down between her legs where he pleasured her in a way that was new to her. He seemed to know spots in her body that she had no idea she possessed. His fingers knew what to press, what to rub, what to caress.

When she was to a peak that she'd never felt before, he entered her again. His gentle strokes had her clutching at his back; her strong legs were wrapped around his waist, holding him to her.

Again, when she was close to exploding, he withdrew.

"Okay?" he asked as he moved beside her.

"I may die," she managed to say.

"Good!" he said as he flipped her onto her stomach, put his big arm around her waist, and lifted her up. He entered her from behind, and Gemma put her hands on the wall to brace herself.

When his strokes became harder, she gasped out, "Yes! Yes!"

"I don't want to hurt you," he said, his voice gentle.

"Think I'm not strong enough to take it?" she said over her shoulder.

"Yeah?" he said. "Let me know when to stop."

He pounded into her with such force that she almost couldn't hold herself against the wall. She loved it!

When she felt herself ready to explode, she turned onto her back and she opened her arms to him.

"Ready?" he asked, smiling.

"Yes," she said and he entered her again, and this time he let himself—and her with him—reach the climax.

Shudders went through her, so strong they made her body convulse.

Minutes later, Colin rolled off of her, to lie beside her, his body sweaty. "Are you okay?" he asked.

"The best I've ever been in my life," she managed to say.

He picked up her hand and kissed the palm. "I'm not sure yet, but I think I am too."

She turned on her side to look at him. His dark hair was messed up, and there was a glow of sweat on him. She thought he'd never looked better. "It was exhausting, but I had a good time today."

"In spite of arguing about couches?"

"Maybe because of that." She was running her hand over his stomach. "You'll see that I'm right about the leather. It would have been bad for this house."

"Except for my chair."

"I can't believe you found a chair that has arms that flip back to hold a beer can."

"Or a mug of tea," he said. "And you think I don't know that the coffee table you picked out can be used as a desk?"

"You bought a desk," she said in defense.

"That's because *I* sit in a chair. You prop your delightful little derriere on a rug."

"Old habit," she said as he put his arm out and she lay her head on it. "Actually, I like everything you bought."

"*We* bought," he said. "I never would have thought of sticking the old stuff in with the new."

"I guess Sara's house was still in my head."

"Sara doesn't believe anything should be new. I think all of it will look good, and thanks to your expert measuring, it'll all fit."

"Mrs. Ellis helped with the placement."

"She was good at jamming in a lot everywhere, wasn't she?" Colin looked at Gemma. "So what are we going to do about filling the kitchen cabinets?"

"Don't look at me," Gemma said. "I don't know how to cook."

"I've seen that you make a great omelet, and you've bragged incessantly about your meat loaf."

"I mentioned it once! And then only in answer to your question. So who was it who made the pot roast you were lusting after? Jean?"

"Jealous already? Jean would never make anything

as mundane as a pot roast. If it didn't require some special pan sold only in Paris, Jean wanted nothing to do with it. Are we going to talk about her a lot?"

"Not unless you want to," Gemma said seriously.

He kissed her palm again. "Thanks, but I may have reached my limit. I don't know about you, but I'm hungry."

"For me or for food?"

"Food!" he said as he got off the bed and pulled on his trousers.

As she watched him walk out, his back muscles playing under his skin, she said loudly, "Looks like the honeymoon is over."

He looked around the doorjamb. "Feed me, then I'll show you that it's only just begun."

Gemma grabbed Colin's T-shirt off the floor and put it on as she ran past him to the living room.

Colin had taken only two bites when his cell buzzed and he pulled it out of his pocket. "It's Roy," he said as he looked at the text message. "I have to go. There's been a robbery in Edilean."

Gemma was up in an instant. "Need this?" she asked, indicating his T-shirt, which she was wearing.

"Yeah," he said as he put on his shoes and socks. When he looked up, Gemma had removed his shirt and was standing before him naked. When he'd seen her wearing her skimpy street clothes, she'd had a beautiful body, and he'd loved touching it in bed. But now, seeing her naked, she looked like a Vargas pinup.

Colin stood there looking at her, his eyes wide,

then he staggered back a step until he hit the wall. "Ooooooh," was all he could say.

Gemma, a bit embarrassed but extremely pleased by his reaction, said, "You have to go."

"I can't," Colin said. "My legs are numb. My brain has died."

"I'll—" Gemma took a step.

"Freeze!" he said. "You move and make a single thing bounce and I'll fall down dead right here."

Gemma was trying not to grin, but she couldn't help it. "All right, I'll stay still, but you have to go and save Edilean. Think it was someone stealing a pie off a windowsill?"

"I don't know," he said as he went to her, bent, and kissed her sweetly on the mouth. As he stepped away, he ran his hands down her sides. "Roy better have a damned good reason for calling me away," he said, looking as though he were about to cry. He left.

17

THE ROBBERY HAD taken place in one of the newer houses in Edilean. In Colin's opinion, too many houses had been jammed together on twenty acres that had once been farmland. The long-term residents had tried to stop the building when it began five years before, but they hadn't been successful. City people, charmed by the idea of living in "the quaint little town of Edilean, Virginia, a place untouched by time," as the ads said, had snatched up the houses before they were finished. Since then, a lot of people had moved out. Edilean, for all its proximity to larger cities, was too rural for them.

Colin knew more about the "newcomers" as they were called—and would be no matter how many years they stayed there—than the other original residents did, and he was somewhat familiar with this family. The wife was a stay-at-home mom with a young daughter and a three-year-old son. The husband worked in Portsmouth, something to do with the military. Colin's impression had always been that they seemed like a nice family.

"What happened to you?" Roy asked as soon as he got inside the house and she saw his messed hair and sleepy-eyed look. She'd already put yellow tape across the bedroom door and taken many photos throughout the house.

Colin gave her a look to be quiet.

"Oh, right," Roy said, "Jean." She was smirking at his general air of having just tumbled out of bed.

"We broke up," Colin said under his breath, and the way he said it told her he wasn't saying any more. "Tell me what happened here."

Roy filled him in on the details of a diamond ring that had been stolen. The owner had kept it inside a hidden compartment of her bedpost. Unfortunately, there were no photos of the ring. "From the way the bedroom was tossed about, it looks like the thief had a difficult time finding it. My guess is it was some local kids," Roy added. "Maybe on a dare. I think it was just dumb luck that they found the ring."

Colin stepped under the tape across the doorway and began to look around. While it was true that the room was in disarray, with pillows knocked off the bed, a corner of the rug rolled back, and a chair overturned, there was something about it all that didn't seem right. For one thing, putting the room back together would take only minutes. In a way, it looked as though the thief had moved things about as an afterthought.

He looked at the bedpost. The end had been screwed off, exposing a small hollowed-out area inside. Not much could have been hidden there, but a ring would fit easily. His first thought was of Mrs. Ellis at the furniture store. Only someone who knew furniture would know there was a hiding place there—or a customer who owned the same set.

He told Roy to find out who in the area had bought an identical bed and she made a note of it.

After Roy left the room, Colin walked about, looking at all of it. On top of the dresser were the usual perfume bottles and cosmetics, a few framed photos of the family. He didn't see anything in the closet that looked as though it hadn't been touched, nor did the bathroom seem to have been disturbed.

When Roy returned, she told him the bed had belonged to the woman's parents and that her father had made it. "It's one of a kind."

That news startled Colin. Only someone who knew the owner would know that there was a hiding place inside the post. It looked as though someone close to the family had done it.

Colin found the woman sitting in her kitchen, her hands shaking as she drank a cup of coffee. She told Colin that she was upset because the robbery had taken place in broad daylight.

"I was outside deadheading the roses, and the

kids were on their big play set. I came back in to make dinner, and it wasn't until after we'd eaten that I saw my bedroom had been ransacked," she said. "I don't want to think what could have happened if I or one of the kids had gone in and interrupted the thief." She took a drink of her coffee; her hand was shaking. "If only I'd kept my mouth shut!"

He listened while she told him that her aunt had died a few months before and left her a diamond ring. At the last playgroup at Armstrong's grocery that she'd taken her little boy to, she'd shown it off. "Anyone could have seen it. Half of the county goes to that grocery."

"Are we talking multiple diamonds, something that would need to be insured separately?"

"No, not really," she said. "The ring had a center diamond, then some smaller ones around it. I think the middle one was about half a carat, maybe a bit more."

"Do you know what it was worth?"

"I have no idea," she said, but looked down at her cup for a moment then back up. "Two or three thousand at the most, but I think I may have hinted that it was worth more."

She looked so guilty that Colin smiled warmly at her. "Bragging isn't a crime, and we all do it. I want to know about your bed. Who knew the ring was inside the post?"

"No one!" she said emphatically. "My father showed me that hiding place when I was a little girl.

My mother was very stingy and one time when I wanted something and she said no, he showed me where he hid a stash of money. It was our secret. When I got married, my parents were going to buy us new furniture, but I asked for the bed Dad had made. He knew why I wanted it."

"Did you tell your husband about the bedpost?"

"No, I did not. And I didn't tell my kids or my best friend. I never told anyone at all about that place. It was my own personal little safe."

"Do you have any siblings who your father might have told?"

"I have a brother who lives in Wisconsin. He and my father never got along, so I doubt if Dad told him. Do you think he flew back here to steal the ring?"

Colin wasn't sure if she was serious or being sarcastic. Whatever, he closed his notebook and looked at her. "Has anything else in the house been touched?"

"Not that I've seen. Roy went through every room. She said I'm a good housekeeper."

Colin gave her a small smile of reassurance and asked her to please not use the bedroom tonight. He didn't think it would turn up anything, but he wanted it dusted for fingerprints.

He and Roy left the house.

"What do you think?" she asked as soon as they were outside. "Kids daring each other?"

"No, I don't think so." He was looking up at the windows and frowning. He didn't want to say what he thought, but his instinct told him that this wasn't an ordinary robbery.

Inside the house, the woman's ten-year-old daughter looked at the little sprig of leaves her mother had left for her on her chest of drawers. She often left flowers, especially roses, but this was different. The leaves were long and thin, light colored and very pretty, and at the bottom her mother had tied a pink ribbon. She didn't know the branches were from a willow tree. Smiling, the child put the little bouquet under her pillow. Maybe she would dream of who had robbed their house and stolen her mother's pretty ring.

18

When Colin left the site of the robbery, his mind was so absorbed with it that he couldn't think clearly. His only real thought was to go home to Gemma and tell her what he'd seen and how puzzling it all was.

It wasn't as though there'd never before been a robbery in Edilean, but usually it was easy to see what had happened. The thief would break a pane in a glass door and let himself in. He usually took a TV, stereo, emptied a jewelry box, then ran out a different door.

But with this robbery, things were different. Colin didn't count it as significant that no one'd had to actually break in. Most of the people in Edilean left their doors unlocked, and they certainly did during the day when the owner was home.

What puzzled Colin was that this thief had so easily found the ring hidden inside a bedpost. The woman's jewelry box lid had been opened, but she'd told Roy that nothing had been so much as moved. To Colin, that meant the robber was accomplished enough to know by sight that none of the jewelry in the case was valuable.

And why had the furniture been overturned? he wondered. Did the thief think the police were going to believe he was searching under a chair?

Colin didn't think it was possible, but even though he was guessing, he'd say it was a professional job. But that made no sense. Why would a professional thief bother to go after a ring worth just a few grand?

As Colin pulled into his garage, he saw that the truck was still there. That meant Gemma was probably inside, and that thought made him smile. He opened the side door—and thought about telling her to keep it locked—and called out to her. When there was no answer, his smile faded. She was gone. Did she walk home or did someone give her a ride?

He called her cell but was sent to voice mail. He wandered about the empty house, saw that she'd made the bed with freshly washed sheets, and he stretched out on it. It was late and he knew he should shower and go to bed, but he didn't want to. Besides, he didn't want to wash Gemma off his skin.

He lay there, looking at the ceiling and thinking about her, especially about how she made him feel. That he'd talked to her about Jean, been honest with her and she'd not judged him, had been good. There were so many things he liked about Gemma, how calm she was, how . . . He grinned. How beautiful her body was.

He indulged himself in memory of their time together in bed. He liked the strength of her, the—

He broke off when his cell buzzed. It was his father.

"I hear you were out fighting crime today," Peregrine Frazier said. "What was it? Kids?"

Colin wasn't about to discuss a case with his father. His solution to every crime in Edilean was for Colin to turn it over to the Williamsburg police, and go back to selling cars.

"Dad," Colin said seriously. "I need to talk to you."

"Yeah? What's going on?"

"Is Mom there? Will she hear you?"

"No, I'm alone," his father said as he looked across the room at his wife. She moved to sit on the ottoman near him and put her head beside the phone.

"How upset do you think Mom will be to hear that I've broken up with Jean?"

"Well," Peregrine said slowly while waving at his wife to stop dancing about the room. "Your mother has always liked Jean. In fact, we all love her, but . . ."

"But what?"

"Neither your mother nor I could see her living in Edilean."

Alea Frazier was mouthing "Gemma! Gemma!" to her husband.

"Look, son, I wouldn't be too down about this. Breakups happen. I remember one time when I was in college, and I—"

Alea looked at him in threat.

Grinny cleared his throat. "I played golf with Henry Shaw today and he said you were at Sara and Mike's yesterday."

"No secret in that."

"He also told me that pretty little Gemma was so angry at you about something that she wouldn't speak to you."

Alea looked at her husband in horror, as that was news she hadn't heard. She made a grab for the phone, but her husband kept it out of her reach.

Grinny got out of his chair and turned his back on her. "What I mean to say, Colin, is that it isn't good to mistreat an employee so she gets angry at you. I think you should—"

"We made up," Colin said.

"Made up? What does that mean?"

"Dad, you aren't *that* old. Gemma and I made up," he said emphatically.

Grinny turned to his wife and gave a thumbs-up. "I'm glad to hear it. Henry said Gemma put on a sort of boxing exhibition. Did she?"

"Oh yeah," Colin said in a way that let his father know how good she'd looked.

"Sorry I missed *that,*" Grinny said, and Alea frowned at him. She pointed to her ring finger on her left hand. Grinny looked at her in disbelief, then turned away. "So you and Gemma are now on good terms?"

"We're friends," Colin said, "and that's all you're going to get out of me. Have you seen her in the last hour or so?"

"No," Grinny said. "She isn't with you?"

"Not at the moment. I thought she'd gone back to the guesthouse, but she's not answering her phone."

Grinny took a deep breath, as he always did before he started a speech. "You know, son, Gemma is a pretty young woman and she's fresh blood in this town, if you know what I mean. She's been seen out a lot with young Dr. Tris. If I were you, I'd make my feelings for her known sooner rather than later. I don't want you to hesitate and lose your chance."

"You mean I should hurry up and claim her as my own?" Colin said.

"That's exactly what I mean."

"Mom is there, isn't she? And she's nagging you to help her get one of her kids married."

"You're right on, boy. You hit that nail square on the head."

"Mom doesn't care who I marry, just that I do it, is that right?" Colin said.

"I think it's more the end result."

Colin groaned. "Not grandkids again. I wish Ariel'd come back so Mom could go after *her*."

"You're the oldest, so responsibility falls on your shoulders." Grinny was looking at his wife and she was nodding in approval at what he was saying.

"I'm doing my best, Dad. Would you check that Gemma got back safely?"

"Sure," Grinny said. He paused. "You think Jean will . . . I mean . . ."

"Come and cook for you?" Colin asked. "She probably would, but she might spike the punch with antifreeze."

"Too bad," Grinny said. "Too, too bad. You think Gemma can—"

"No, she can't cook. Good night, Dad."

"Good night, son."

As Colin got off the bed and went to the kitchen, he was shaking his head at his father's phone call and thinking about his mother listening. He knew there wasn't anything in the refrigerator, but he looked anyway.

The unopened bottle of champagne from Tess was there, and to his surprise, Gemma had filled the refrigerator with food. There was also a note from her. That she'd left it *inside* the refrigerator made him laugh. She was beginning to know him almost too well.

> *I had fun at the grocery. Tell you about it later. Sleep well. Gemma*

He pulled food out of the fridge, and minutes later, he was sitting at the counter and eating chicken, broccoli rabe, a big twice-baked potato, and drinking his favorite beer from the bottle.

When his phone buzzed, he grabbed it, hoping it was Gemma. Instead, it was a text from Sara.

> DID YOU HEAR WHAT GEMMA DID WITH MR. LANG TODAY?

Immediately, Colin called Sara. She answered on the first ring. "Tell me everything," he said.

"I want to, but Mike says I can't. He says it's up to Gemma to tell you. Think it'll get you two back together?"

"Don't play dumb with me! I'm sure Luke *and* Rams told you that Gemma and I bought a lot of furniture today. We *are* back together. Lang didn't play one of his tricks on Gemma, did he?"

"Calm down," Sara said. "Mr. Lang is now so in love with Gemma that I thought Mike was going to have to give him a pill to calm him down."

"In love with her? What happened?"

"I wasn't there, but—Uh oh. I've been caught. It's impossible to snoop when your husband is a detective. Wait a minute." As he listened, Colin could hear Mike's low voice in the background. "My husband says he expects you at his gym tomorrow at six-thirty A.M. He said Gemma said she'd tell you everything then. I'm hanging up now to keep from saying another word. We have to leave tomorrow, so call me and tell me what's up with that robbery. Good night."

Colin called Gemma's cell again, but still only got

voice mail. He left a message saying he'd heard that he'd been thrown over for Mr. Lang. Thirty minutes later, Colin had showered but there was still nothing from Gemma.

Finally, his father texted him that Gemma was okay and sleeping—and she didn't like being waked up. Colin went to bed and drifted into sleep, smiling.

19

After Colin left to investigate the robbery, Gemma took a shower and put clean sheets on the bed. She couldn't decide whether she wanted to stay there and wait for him or make her way home.

She wandered about the house, looking at the woodwork and thinking about the furniture they'd bought. She couldn't help wondering if she'd get to use that furniture. Would she ever live in a house that she liked as much as this one?

She thought about all Colin had told her about Jean and she knew she should feel some sympathy for him. The things Jean had said were hurtful. But then, Gemma was also sure she should feel sorry for Jean.

But she didn't feel any of what she should. Instead, she was glad of everything that had happened, happy that Colin had broken up with Jean and that he now . . . What? Belonged to Gemma?

It was a ridiculous thought. No one owned anyone else. She'd certainly never before felt that she possessed another person. No, Gemma had always been independent, the master of her own fate, the owner of little except what she carried in her mind.

She sat down on a kitchen stool. The truth was that since her father died, she'd "belonged" to no one.

Suddenly, she remembered that she'd thought that her "deepest wish" was to belong somewhere. And isn't that what was happening in Edilean? Since the day she'd arrived, she'd been falling into the clutches of the town. It wasn't just that she'd been meeting people. It was as though she'd been given a key to the very inside of the place.

In the short time she'd been in Edilean she'd seen that there were two sides to the town. There were the "newcomers" as she'd heard them called, and then there were the Fraziers and the McDowells, the Connors, the descendants of the seven founding families.

It was this older group that Gemma was being pulled into. It couldn't be just because she was staying at the Fraziers. It had to be more than that. What if she'd wanted to stay separate from the family? Or join some of the young women she'd seen in Ellie's store?

In a way, it was almost as though she'd had no choice in the matter. Almost as if someone had . . . She didn't want to acknowledge what was going through her mind.

It was as if her wish to belong had come from her heart and had been heard. By what? The Heartwishes Stone?

As she went to the refrigerator, she laughed at the idea. When she saw that the only thing in the fridge was a bottle of champagne, she closed the door and took a set of keys off the wall. The least she could do was get Colin some groceries. She looked at the big truck in the garage and hoped it hadn't been Frazier-ized and made into some lurching power beast.

When she backed out the vehicle, she was pleased to find that the truck was standard issue. As she drove, she told herself that the idea that *she* would be granted a Heartwish was ridiculous.

But then she remembered what Colin had written in his journal.

It works for lady Fraziers too.

What if the Stone granted wishes to women who were *going* to be a Frazier? she thought. But how could it know that? But then, she thought, if a rock could grant wishes—which it couldn't—and it read those wishes from a person's heart—absurd idea!—then of course it could know a person's future.

Still thinking of all this, Gemma went about the grocery filling her cart. She knew little of what Colin liked to eat, except for, as Jean said, beef, but she could guess. She got one of Ellie's fat chickens fresh off the rotisserie and put it in the basket.

By the time she got to the back of the store, her cart was nearly full, and all she needed was lunch meat. No one was behind the big glass counter. Instead, standing across from it, his back against the shelves between two aisles, was the oddest-looking man Gemma had ever seen. He was about five foot two, with a big, round head, no discernible neck, and a stout little body. When he turned to look at her, she had to work to keep from gasping. His huge eyes and small mouth made him look like a cross between a gnome and Gollum. His skin was pink and fairly tight, with few wrinkles. He could be forty years old or a hundred and ten; Gemma couldn't tell which.

Instantly, she knew who he was: the infamous Mr. Lang. And for some reason that she couldn't define, she liked him. Plain ol' *liked* him. She wanted to sit down with him and talk, get to know him.

But she didn't have to know him to see that right now he was very upset. For as solid as he was, he moved quickly, flitting back and forth from one side to the other, looking down one aisle then another.

Gemma didn't wait for introductions. "What's wrong?" she asked as she moved close to him. It was almost as though she wanted to protect him.

"They'll see me," he said in a deep, guttural voice that sounded as though it was rarely used.

She didn't waste time asking who. She looked down the aisle on the left and saw three women dressed as though they'd just come from church. They were in what appeared to be a very serious discussion about a jar of jam. The next aisle contained two women, dressed the same, but studying the label on a can of soup. There was no way Mr. Lang could race past either aisle and not be seen.

Gemma looked back at the little man. He was now lifting one foot after another, looking more desperate for escape with each second.

Gemma's mind raced. Was there some way she could use her body to conceal him and get him out of the store? If it were winter she could have thrown a coat over him, but she had nothing, saw nothing she could use.

With every second, her protective instinct grew stronger. She *had* to safeguard him! If she'd had a sword she would have stood in front of him and brandished it.

When she turned back, she saw a young store clerk walking past carrying a huge, empty box that had contained paper towels.

Gemma didn't give herself time to think but ran the few steps to the young man and grabbed the box. Mr. Lang seemed to have read her mind as he moved to the front of the big glass case. Gemma lifted the box over him and he obligingly sank down and the box rim went flat to the floor.

Seconds later, the five women came to the end of the aisles and they stopped at the sight of the big container in front of the glass case.

"It's not like Ellie to be so messy," one woman said.

"I think the overall service here has gone down in the last years," a second woman said.

"Do you think Ellie's in financial trouble?"

"For heaven's sake!" the tallest woman said. "Some clerk left a box behind. It isn't Ellie's fault. Let's just move the thing."

Gemma stepped around the box to put herself in front of the women. "I think it covers up something that spilled. You'd better not get your shoes near it," she said quickly.

"I hope it's not toxic," a woman said.

Gemma feared she was single-handedly destroying Ellie's reputation. "Actually, I think it's a broken bottle of maple syrup."

"I bet that Hausinger boy did it," a woman in a pink dress said. "I just saw him with his mother. That child is never disciplined."

"Where is someone to help us?" one of the women asked. "I need some sliced ham." She pounded on the bell on top of the case.

Gemma stepped between the women and the counter. Now all she had to do was keep the store workers from lifting the box and taking it away.

When Ellie came out of the back, Gemma wasn't sure how to tell her to play along. The women all started talking at once, very upset about the big box in front of the glass case. Gemma used the noise to slip to the back of the women and began waving her arms and vigorously shaking her head at Ellie. She pointed at the box and mouthed, "No!"

When one of the women looked back at Gemma, she dropped her hands.

Ellie doesn't miss a beat. "What can I get for you ladies today? The red snapper just came in." She had to listen to the women's complaints about the aisle being blocked, all of it presented in a way that was meant to sound constructive, even caring, but wasn't. When Ellie encouraged them to give their orders, one of the women looked at Gemma as though wondering who she was and said she was there first.

Gemma put her hand on top of the box, leaning on it in a proprietary way, and said that she hadn't made up her mind yet.

Ellie filled the orders of the women and dispatched them in record time. When one of them dawdled over the price, Ellie said she'd forgotten that for today only it was on sale at half price.

The second the women turned to leave, Ellie ran to the front of the counter. She told a clerk to follow the women to make sure they didn't double back, then she looked at Gemma. "What have you trapped? Please tell me it's not a rat."

Gemma couldn't help grinning mischievously as the two women lifted the big box straight up. Sitting on the floor, his legs crossed and looking perfectly content, was Mr. Lang.

"That's recycling at its finest," Ellie said, making Gemma laugh.

With the agility of a much younger person, Mr. Lang stood up and stared at Gemma for a moment. He started to leave, but then he turned back and said, "Thank you." He disappeared down an aisle.

"I'm not sure I've ever heard him say those words before," Ellie said as she nodded to a clerk to take the box away.

"You mind telling me what that was all about?" Gemma asked.

"Was Lang afraid the women would see him?"

"He acted like they had rifles and he was their prey."

Ellie chuckled. "If anyone did that it would be me. I'd go after him for overcharging me for his produce. Anyway, Lang knows about people in Edilean back to the 1930s, and he's become much sought after to answer people's questions about their ancestors."

"He's a genealogist?"

"Ha! Lang is a snoop, has been all his life. He likes to listen in on people and spy on them."

"That's not nice," Gemma said.

"Lang never tries to be 'nice.'"

"So who are the women?"

"They are members of the Edilean Ladies League and they want him to speak at their next meeting."

"But isn't that an honor? Or is he afraid of public speaking?"

"He's afraid of being seen. He likes to remain anonymous. If he could be invisible, he would be. Being recognized keeps him from being able to do his spying. He used to be somewhat feared in this town and he loved that, but now he's almost a celebrity." Ellie smiled. "Last fall when my daughter caught a couple of criminals, she inadvertently made Lang into a respectable person. It's been a joy to see his misery."

"That sounds ominous," Gemma said, but she couldn't help smiling at Ellie's gleeful tone.

Ellie waved her hand. "There's a lot of backstory to that man. Now, what can I get you?"

"Do you know what kind of lunch meat Colin likes?"

"I most certainly do," Ellie said, smiling as she went behind the counter. By the time she'd sliced the meat and packaged it, she was grinning broadly. "So you've conquered Colin and old man Lang too?" Her eyes were twinkling. "Welcome to Edilean, Gemma," she said. "But then, from the moment I saw you, I knew you belonged here."

"Thanks," Gemma said. Ellie had just said what Gemma had been thinking.

She drove back to Colin's house and put the groceries away. Her mind was fully on what had happened at the grocery. If Mr. Lang had spent his life snooping, he might be able to help Gemma piece together the mystery of Julian and Winnie and Tamsen.

After she'd put everything away, she still hadn't heard from Colin. Since in her experience he didn't let her know when he'd be returning, she decided to leave and walk back to the Frazier estate. It was about four miles, and it was getting dark, but she needed the time to think.

When she got back to what she now thought of as home, she said aloud, "I want to find out what Tamsen wrote about you . . . I mean the Stone." She felt ridiculous at saying such a thing out loud, but she couldn't help it, or maybe it was that she wanted to test the whole Heartwishes thing.

Twenty minutes later, young Shamus turned over in his sleep and knocked his favorite art kit off his bedside table. He'd found the thin wooden box in the stash his mother sent back from England. He'd taken the old papers out of it and left them in the guest-house. It was a pretty box, just the right size for his sketch pad, and Rachel had made him a cloth holder for his pencils. On the front was an intaglio carving of a tree. Lanny said it looked like the old oak tree that grew in the center of Edilean square. But their dad said the case was so old that the tree on it was long dead.

Shamus had liked the box very much and it had rarely been out of his sight since his mother said he could keep it.

In the morning he was not going to like that the fall had damaged the corner of the box. A piece of the wood had broken away, exposing the tip of some very old papers hidden inside.

20

THE NEXT MORNING, at 6:30 A.M., Gemma was outside Mike's gym. It wasn't yet full light and no one was about; she liked the quiet. She wondered if Colin would remember their appointment, but he opened the door to her. He was wearing a black tank top that showed his muscles and he looked very good. She felt such a spark of electricity shoot through her that she thought about grabbing his hand and heading back to her car.

He read her expression correctly. "Me too," he whispered, then stepped back and she saw Mike.

He looked from one to the other. "You two here to work out or you want to be alone?"

"To work, Master!" Gemma said loudly.

"She's got your number," Colin said to Mike.

Mike didn't smile. If there was one thing in his life he was serious about, it was his workouts.

For a few seconds, Gemma wasn't sure what to

do. Years before, she'd learned that it was a bad idea to go to the gym with a boyfriend. The first thing he wanted to do was establish that he knew more than Gemma, so he started telling her what to do and how to do it. One guy, a fellow history major she'd been on a date with the night before, handed her a couple of two-pound dumbbells and showed her how to do a bicep curl. "If that's too heavy for you, let me know and I'll get you something lighter."

Without a word, Gemma picked up a couple of twenty-five-pound dumbbells and started curling them. He left the gym immediately, and later he avoided her in the classroom.

Mike solved her dilemma. "You're used to working out with a trainer, aren't you?" he said.

"Yes," she answered. "We worked out in a group, and I miss the boys I used to train with."

Colin seemed to understand, and he stepped back. That he wasn't trying to play alpha male and take over made her like him more.

Gemma went with Mike, first for some cardio, then weights, and finally they got to the boxing. Through this, Colin had been working out by himself, but she'd been watching him.

He was phenomenally strong! He bench-pressed what it would take three average-size men to lift. He did dead lifts that would have dislocated the shoulders of most men.

When Mike saw her looking, he said quietly, "He's lifting light today. When he gets in here with his brothers and they start competing with each other . . . I've seen pros that were weaker than those guys."

"I could stand to see that," Gemma said as she got off the weight bench.

Mike told Colin he should take over the boxing with Gemma.

"Mike," Colin said, "you know that all I can do is pick up weight and put it down."

"Come on, Frazier," Mike said, "are you afraid of her?"

"Scared to death," Colin answered, his eyes on Gemma.

Mike put the big leather hand pads on Colin, then held Gemma's gloves while she pushed her hands in their gel wraps inside. "Now, you two have each other, so I'm going to do my own workout."

Gemma and Colin looked at each other for a moment, then he raised the pads. "Give me what you got," he said.

She hesitated. If it was true that he'd never trained in boxing, he wouldn't know how to deflect her punches, and besides, she didn't want to hurt him. He was strong, but everyone's skin bruised. Her first hits were light but strong enough to make the sound of leather slapping against leather that all boxers so loved.

Stepping back, Colin looked at her in disgust. "That's it? What about kicking? Did you forget how to do that?" He lowered his voice. "You're going to be nice to a man who forgot all about you after a quickie?" He winked at her.

She knew he was trying to goad her into hitting him—and it worked. "Put the side pad on," she said seriously.

"Too much trouble." He smiled in a taunting way. "How could little you hurt me?"

She didn't think about what she did, but twirled to put a spinning back kick hard into his stomach. She faked a front kick to distract him, then did a spinning backhand to his jaw, putting her whole body behind the punch. She'd never done the moves on a person before, just on a bag, but when she'd seen it done in a ring, the recipient *always* went down.

Colin staggered backward, bent forward, his hands on his knees, and tried to keep breathing.

Mike, who had watched the whole thing, began to laugh. "You better not ever make her angry."

"I can see that," Colin said as he stood up and flexed his jaw.

"I'm—" Gemma began.

"If you say you're sorry I'll take your pens away from you," Colin said.

She didn't smile. "I've never done that to a person before, and . . ." She took a step back as Colin was coming toward her. She'd never survive one of *his* punches!

When he reached her, he looked down at her in what could be called a menacing way, then he suddenly picked her up and lifted her up in an overhead press. In seconds, she was squealing in laughter as he twirled her around.

Just at that moment, Luke and Ramsey came in the front door.

When Rams saw Gemma high above Colin's head, he turned back to the door. "I'm outta here."

Luke grabbed his cousin's arm. "I thought you wanted to box with Gemma."

Colin set Gemma to the floor. "Come on, guys, let's put you two to work."

It was another hour before Gemma and Colin left the gym, and she felt good.

"Are you okay?" he asked when they got to her car.

"The question is whether you are." Reaching up, she touched his jaw, which was already showing a bruise. "Think kisses would make it feel better?" she asked softly, looking up at him. If it weren't daylight and in the middle of town, she would have pulled him into the backseat of her car and had her way with him. The look in her eyes made him take a step forward, but she put her hand on his chest. "I think we should go home."

He stepped back. "You're right. We need to shower and change. See you at church at ten?"

"Church?" she asked.

He was smiling. "Yeah, church. You are going with me, aren't you?"

"I thought we were going to keep us a secret."

"No need for that. Last night I told Mom and Dad that I'd broken up with Jean. And I said you and I were now a couple."

Gemma glanced skyward for a second. "They're going to hate me."

"Far from it," Colin said. "Actually, now that I think about it, they seemed almost glad."

"*Glad* that you broke up with a woman they love and ran off with someone they barely know?" When Colin didn't say anything, just kept staring at her, she said, "What is it?"

"My mother."

"What about her?"

Colin came out of his trance. "I was just thinking about how my mother is a force of nature. And when she wants something, she goes after it."

"And what she wants is—" Gemma took a step back and put her hands up. "Rachel said your mother wants grandchildren." Her eyes widened. "From *me*? I'm still trying to figure out what you like for lunch! I'm not ready for anything else. We need to—"

He kissed her on the mouth. "I know. Talk, get to know each other, that sort of thing. So you know where the church is? No, wait. I'll pick you up and we can go together."

"That's a lot of trouble," she began. "I'm—"

"I agree. It is a great bother," he said quickly. "If you were living at my house, it would be much easier on both of us." With another quick kiss, he turned away.

"It's too early to even think of that!" she called after him.

He turned around, walking backward down the center of the street, his arms outstretched. "What more could you want, Gemma? What man have you ever met who comes with a whole town attached to him?"

"Yeah, that's the problem," she called back. "I'd be moving in with all of Edilean."

"Sounds like heaven to me," he said as he got into his Jeep.

"And maybe to me too," Gemma said quietly as she opened her car door. She grinned all the way back to the guesthouse.

"Why didn't you tell me that we were expected to have dinner at your parents' house?" Gemma said to Colin. They were in his Jeep and heading toward the Frazier estate.

"I didn't know," he said. "But my sister and her boyfriend flew in from California last night. It was totally unexpected. I'd like to see them and for you to meet them. I think you'll like Frank. He's Mike's best friend. They're both policemen about to retire and they both love all that kicking and boxing stuff that you do. How'd you like church?"

"It was nice," she said, thinking of what he'd just told her and what she'd seen this morning. "The people seemed . . ."

"Seemed what?" he asked.

"I'm sure I'm wrong about this, but they seemed almost relieved that I wasn't Jean."

Colin laughed. "People in Edilean don't hide their feelings very well."

"So you agree that they don't want you to be with a tall, gorgeous lawyer?"

Colin groaned. "I'm not touching that one! I think you're beautiful just as you are. As for Jean, she's a difficult person to know, and she's not one to attend the local Scottish Fair. Speaking of which, you better put in your order with Sara now for your dress. What medieval person do you want to be?"

"A tall, gorgeous one. Think Sara can do it?"

Colin pulled into the driveway, turned off the engine, and looked at her. "What's really bothering you?"

"I'm afraid of facing your mother. Will your whole family be there?"

Colin glanced at the half a dozen cars around them. "Yes. Everyone wants to see Ariel and Frank. Even Pere is here, and you haven't met him." He took her hand in his. "Gemma, if you want to go somewhere else, we can. But the truth is that I'm beginning to think that everyone is glad that I broke up with Jean."

"Maybe your friends, but I saw how friendly Jean and your family were with one another, and—"

He kissed her hands, front and back. "If anyone is the slightest bit less than welcoming to you, we'll leave, all right? We'll go to my new house and eat cold chicken off each other's naked bodies, and I'll drink champagne out of your bedroom slipper. Sound good?"

"I like that idea. How about if we do that instead of this?"

"I'm thinking that way too," he said as he reached out his arms to pull her to him.

But a sharp tap on his window made him turn. A man with a beautiful face and the big Frazier body was outside.

Colin put the window down.

"Everyone is here and we're hungry, but Mom won't let us eat until you two are inside. Is this the famous Gemma I keep hearing about?"

"Gemma, meet my brother Peregrine, Pere for short."

He reached through the window, across Colin, to shake her hand. "I saw you on YouTube and I hear you're good at boxing. I'm a wrestler myself. If you want to learn how, I'd be happy to give you lessons. *Lots* of lessons."

"Arm out before I break it," Colin said good-naturedly.

Grinning, Pere did as he was told and opened the door. "Come on, I need to get back to Richmond, and Lanny's got a new girl."

"Lanny always has a new girl," Colin said as he got out, then went around to open Gemma's door. He held her hand as the three of them walked toward the house.

Pere paused at the front door and looked at Gemma. "I hope you're ready for this. Nobody knows why, but Mom's like she's been wired to a jet engine."

Gemma took a step back.

Colin pulled her forward. "I'll be there. Any problems, let me know."

Pere was grinning broadly. "So, Gemma, what's *your* mother like? What'll she think of ol' Col here?"

"My mother worships my father's memory and compares all men to him. She'll think Colin is too big, that his job is too dangerous, and she'll probably lecture him on gun control."

"Is that right?" Colin asked, looking worried.

"Every word of it."

"I'd like to see that meeting," Pere said, smiling as he opened the door.

Gemma's first impression was of cheerful chaos. Mrs. Frazier was ordering her family about, and everyone seemed to be talking, laughing, and arguing at once. It was a very loud group of people.

A tall, red-haired, beautiful young woman was standing to one corner, close to a man who was just barely as tall as she was, and it looked like his nose had been broken several times. He had to be Frank. She could tell that under his clothes his body was as toned as Mike's. Gemma gave him a quick smile of recognition of athlete to athlete before Mrs. Frazier took her arm, pulled her forward, and began introducing her to people.

The pretty young woman was Colin's doctor-sister Ariel, and the man was Frank Thiessen.

"Mike's told me about you," Frank said as he shook her hand. "Maybe we can work out together sometime."

"I'd love that," Gemma said. It was a high honor for athletes like Mike and Frank to ask her to join them. She wanted to stay and talk to him, but Mrs. Frazier pulled her away.

Next came Lanny's new girlfriend, Carol, who seemed even more overwhelmed than Gemma did. Pere's tall girlfriend was called Eloisa and looked vaguely familiar. Rachel had said that Pere's heart was "spoken for," but somehow, this bored-looking young woman didn't seem to fit that bill.

"She's a model," Rachel said as she came by with a tray full of hors d'oeuvres.

"Need any help?" Gemma whispered. "Please?"

"Sure," Rachel said as she went back to the kitchen, Gemma close behind her. "Welcome to Frazierland," she said as soon as the door closed. "Can you get the bread out of the oven?"

Gemma took a pot holder, opened the oven, and pulled out the sheet of hot rolls. It reminded her of the time Jean had been in the kitchen. "I bet they're regretting that Jean isn't here to cook some fabulous dish. I mean, not that what you cook isn't—"

"I know what you mean. Stir that red pot, will you? Has Jean given you any problems?"

"No," Gemma said. "I've heard nothing from her. Have you heard anything from the family?"

"Nothing, and that's interesting. I figured they'd

have a lot to say. And I was sure Jean would have raised a big stink. She really loves drama."

"What about in town?" Gemma asked. "What are people there saying about the breakup?"

"I haven't heard any gossip at all. Everyone is talking about Colin buying Luke's house and spending time with you."

Gemma groaned. "Everything is happening too fast!" She wanted to change the subject to something other than herself. "So is the model the one who stole Pere's heart?"

Rachel dropped a stainless bowl on the tile floor and it clattered loudly.

Gemma was staring at her because Rachel's face had turned bright red. It looked like the person who wanted Pere's heart was Rachel. "You—" she began.

"If you say a word, I'll poison your dinner," Rachel said. "I shouldn't have said anything."

"I don't mean to sound like a first grader, but does Pere know you . . . like him?"

"Pere doesn't know I exist. You saw the kind of woman he likes."

"I can understand that," Gemma said. "On the other hand, when I met Jean I thought she was the kind of woman Colin liked. But now . . ." She shrugged.

For a moment Rachel paused, a pot lid in her hand. "The Fraziers are from generations of money. As upper class as you can get in the U.S. They don't fall for the hired help."

"You could join the rest of Edilean and make a Heartwish for him," Gemma said, trying to lighten the mood.

"You think I haven't? I've been thinking of nothing else since I heard that story."

"You think the whole town knows about the Stone?" Gemma asked in horror.

"No. Only the seven families. If outsiders heard of it, this house would be picketed. The only reason I know of it is because I overheard Mrs. Frazier bellyaching about her nonexistent grandbabies."

"Don't remind me. I've become a fanatic about taking my pills." Except for the first time, she thought but didn't say.

"Can you mash potatoes with a hand mixer?" Rachel asked.

"Sure. Just point me to it." Minutes later, Gemma had on an apron and was whirring away at a huge pot full of cooked potatoes.

When Rachel went out, Mr. Frazier came in. He took a stool across the counter from her and helped himself to Rachel's tray of olives and cheeses.

"There's something I've been wanting to ask you," Gemma said as she turned off the mixer.

"What's that?" There was caution in his voice, as though he dreaded what she was about to say.

"Do you think they really sent a repairman for a broken axle, or did the Rolls-Royce people just make up that story?"

Mr. Frazier laughed. "I've always wondered that too. What do you think?"

"My dad said the story was true. How many Rollses do you own?"

"One Rolls, one Bentley," he said.

The kitchen door opened, and Pere came in. "I thought I'd find you in here," he said to his father. He looked at Gemma. "So you *can* cook."

"I can push the button on the mixer and use it on potatoes Rachel cooked."

"Better than I can do," Pere said. "What about you, Dad?"

"Much better. I thought mashed potatoes came out of a box."

"Actually, they come out of a transmission case," Gemma said solemnly.

"No, it's a crankshaft," Pere said.

"Fueled by the pistons," Mr. Frazier said.

The door opened and young Shamus came in, art case in hand.

"Too noisy for you?" Gemma asked.

"Ariel," was his reply as he sat down beside his father and brother.

Gemma ran a big spoon around the mashed potatoes. It looked like a giant lollipop. She handed it to Shamus.

"Hey!" Pere and Mr. Frazier said in unison.

Gemma opened drawers until she found more spoons, then gave the two men each his own helping.

She saw the gray duct tape on the corner of Shamus's wooden box. "What happened?"

"Broke," he said as he licked his spoon.

"My son the wordsmith," Mr. Frazier said, also licking.

"Wow!" Lanny said from the doorway as he looked at his father and two brothers sitting at the island with their big lollipops of mashed potatoes.

Gemma got another spoon, filled it, and handed it to him as he took the last remaining stool.

"So what are we talking about?" Lanny asked.

"I don't know," Pere said.

"Ask Shamus," Mr. Frazier said. "He's leading the conversation."

The door opened again, but this time it banged against the wall.

"Uh oh," Mr. Frazier said as he quickly cleaned his spoon. "I know that sound."

It was Mrs. Frazier, and she was drawn up to her full height. "Out! The lot of you! And you too, Gemma. No more hiding in the kitchen."

Gemma removed her apron and ran after the departing men. But Mrs. Frazier caught Gemma's arm, then kissed her cheek. "Welcome, Gemma," she said softly. "And thank you."

"It was nothing. I just gave them some potatoes."

"No, thank you for Colin. I haven't seen my eldest son smile so much since . . . Since he got out of college."

"I'm sorry about Jean. I know how much all of you like her."

"Jean is champagne. You can't live on wine, no matter how fine it is." Mrs. Frazier smiled. "But the Irish proved that you *can* pretty much live on potatoes. Now go!"

"Yes, ma'am," Gemma said, and smiled back, her nervousness greatly alleviated—even though she wasn't sure about the potatoes and wine analogy.

When all eleven of them were seated in the dining room, the table laden with enormous bowls and trays of food, Gemma soon found out that she was the center of attention. All the Fraziers, except for Shamus and Colin, bombarded her with questions about her research, where she'd grown up, what she wanted to do in the future.

She tried to answer everyone, but there were just too many queries. Mainly, she didn't want to talk about herself. If she did, she feared they'd ask about her and Colin, and it was too soon for that.

After several minutes of interrogation, she stopped them with a story of the first Shamus Frazier, the one who came from Scotland to America in the 1760s.

"His wife, the countess," Gemma said, "wrote a letter telling of a carriage her husband made for the beautiful Edilean Harcourt." She had their attention now and they ate in silence as they listened to her. "It was a yellow carriage with black seats, and Mrs. Harcourt called it her bumblebee."

When there was a quick intake of breath and everyone looked at Mr. Frazier, Gemma did too.

He gave no explanation for the attention turning to him. "Go on," he said. "What else did the letter say?"

"Prudence—that's Shamus's aristocratic wife—said the carriage was made to cheer Edilean up because the last of her children had married and moved out of their house."

"I understand that!" Mrs. Frazier said as she looked at her five grown children. "Go on, Gemma."

"Mrs. Frazier—the first one, that is—said that Shamus put a plaque under the seat, but he doubted if anyone would ever see it."

To Gemma's consternation, both Lanny and Shamus stood up.

"Shamus," Mr. Frazier said, and the young man grabbed a couple of rolls and left the room.

Gemma looked across the table at Colin, her eyes asking him what was going on.

He smiled. "Dad has a lot of the old wagons and carriages stored in warehouses in the back. One of the prettiest is yellow with black seats. My little brother went to see if he could find the plaque."

"You didn't think to tell me that you have eighteenth-century carriages stashed away? I could have searched them for information," Gemma said before she thought, then remembered where she was. She glanced at the others. "I'm sorry. I didn't mean—"

All of the Fraziers started laughing, and Lanny slapped Colin on the back. "Our brother likes to keep secrets."

"Better than blabbing everything to everyone," Colin answered and everyone started talking again.

Next to Gemma was Frank, but she hadn't been able to say a word to him.

Ariel, on the other side of him, leaned forward. "Gemma, would you like for me to take the attention off of you?"

"Could you please?" Gemma watched as Ariel reached inside her trouser's pocket and withdrew a diamond ring. Under the cover of the dining table, she slipped it on her left ring finger. "That should do it," Gemma said softly. She couldn't resist kissing Frank's cheek in congratulations—a gesture that brought everyone to a halt.

"Colin, it looks like you have some competition," Pere said.

Colin looked at Gemma, and this time he was the one wanting information.

Ariel broke the silence by reaching her left hand far across the table to her mother at the end. "Mom, will you hand me the carrots, please?"

No one paid any attention to her—but Mrs. Frazier did. She reacted with a little scream, grabbed her daughter's hand, and pulled so hard Ariel nearly landed in a bowl of collard greens.

"What in the world, Alea?" Mr. Frazier asked.

By that time, Mrs. Frazier had pulled her daughter

out of her chair and was hugging her, kissing her face, and crying copiously and loudly.

Everyone else was still seated, but they were staring at Ariel and her mother in wonder. Ariel clarified the matter by holding up her left hand and flashing her new ring.

Mr. Frazier, obviously well pleased, looked at Frank. "Think you can stand to be one of us?"

"I might survive it," Frank said. "I know now isn't the right time, but I'd like to talk to you about buying that old building you own, the one at the end of McTern road. Mike and I think it would be a good place to open our gym."

"It's yours," Mr. Frazier said. "And there'll be no talk of payment."

"I can't—" Frank began.

"Yes, he can," Ariel said loudly as she pulled away from her mother. "Anyone want to see my ring?"

All the women said yes and even Pere's model girlfriend seemed to come alive.

"Dad," Ariel said, "I want the biggest, most expensive wedding this town has even seen. And I want Sara Shaw to be my matron of honor."

"If you told her before I knew—" Mrs. Frazier began, but Ariel cut her off.

She put her arm around her mother's shoulders. "You were the first to know."

"You don't *have* to get married, do you?" Mrs. Frazier asked. There was so much hope in her voice that everyone started laughing again.

"No, Mom, I'm not pregnant," Ariel said. "I told you that I need to finish my residency first. Once we get back to Edilean and I start my practice, Frank and I will think about kids."

When Mrs. Frazier looked at Frank, he put up his hands in surrender. "I'm on your side. You think I wanted Mike to beat me in the kids department?"

Ariel looked at her brother. "Colin, help me out here."

He looked across the table at Gemma. "Sorry, but I'm on Mom's side too. I like the idea of settling down."

Gemma looked down at her plate as the two other girlfriends looked at her in curiosity.

Rachel saved her by opening the door to the kitchen with a loud bang. "I have six pies in the kitchen and whoever helps me clear up gets a piece." She left the room.

Everyone except Ariel and her mother started clearing the table.

Colin, his big arms full of dishes, got behind Gemma. "Sorry if I embarrassed you."

"You can make it up to me by showing me the carriages."

"I would love to." He leaned down so his lips were near her ear. "How about if we steal a pie and go see the wagons?" He lowered his voice even more. "Ever make love inside an eighteenth-century bumblebee?"

"Have you?" she shot back.

"No," he answered. "But I've imagined it in detail."

"I like fulfilling fantasies," she whispered as they entered the kitchen.

Rachel said quietly to Gemma, "His favorite is in the oven. After Ariel's news, no one will notice if you left."

"You're my new BFF," Gemma said as she went to the stove.

As she opened the oven, Gemma wondered what kind of pie Colin liked best. "Blackberry cobbler," she whispered when she saw it.

Colin leaned over her shoulder. "Ready?"

Just as Rachel had said, everyone was huddled around Ariel and Frank, so they didn't notice when Colin and Gemma slipped out the back door. She followed him to the nearest utility truck, four of which were lined up on the lawn. "Take your pick," he said.

She chose a plain green one.

"Coward," Colin said as he nodded toward the others, each of which had been personalized.

They didn't make it to the carriage barn. They stopped at Gemma's house to get spoons for the pie, took one look at each other, and headed to the bedroom. Clothes came off as they ran.

Since early morning in the gym they'd been wanting each other. There had been hours of silent foreplay as they touched fingertips, whispered to one another. By the time they finally escaped the company of others, they were at fever pitch with longing.

Gemma, naked, fell onto the bed, Colin on top of her, his mouth seeking hers as he entered her.

She gloried in his big body, at the way his skin felt under her hands. She loved the strength of him, how his thighs felt between hers.

It was an hour later that they rolled apart, both sweaty and sated.

"Just so you'll know," Gemma managed to say, "that was *my* favorite dessert."

"But you haven't tasted Rachel's blackberry cobbler," he said as he got up and went to the kitchen.

Gemma put a pillow under her head and thoroughly enjoyed watching him walk in and out of the room naked. He returned with the cobbler and a big kitchen spoon and sat down beside her.

He took a bite, chewed, swallowed. "Fabulous." Bending, he kissed Gemma, his lips firm against hers. When she reached out her arms for him, he pulled away.

"No, no, not yet. I'm still comparing." He took another bite of cobbler. "Good. Yes, very good. I can see merits in both of them. I can't quite decide between the two of you."

"Oh yeah?" she said as she took the full spoon from him. She started toward her mouth as though she were going to eat it, but she didn't make it. Instead, she let the warm, thick, sweet pie drop down onto her bare breast. "Uh oh," she said. "How will I ever get that off?"

Colin set the dish of cobbler on the bedside table, then turned to her. "It would be a real shame to let that go to waste."

"Wouldn't it?" Gemma said.

In the next second they were entangled again, a mass of arms and legs, mouths and necks.

Thirty minutes later, Colin rolled away. "You win," he managed to say.

"I didn't hear you."

"You taste the best. Better than all the cobblers ever made." He pulled her to him, snuggling her like a child's toy. "I think—" he murmured, but said no more.

Gemma lifted on her elbow and saw that he was asleep. She'd never been a person who could nap, so she quietly got out of bed and went to the shower. She'd never been so happy in her life.

21

BY THE END of the week, Gemma felt that she was becoming the kind of woman she used to detest. Over the years, she'd had to sit by and watch good friends transform from *I* into *we*. And no matter how many times it happened, it always startled her—especially the abruptness of it. She and her friends all dated and they loved to get together afterward to talk about how good or how awful the date had been.

But what always happened was that one day a friend would start saying *we*. It started out innocently enough. Gemma would ask her friend if she'd like to go somewhere on Saturday and her friend would say, "I'll have to check what we're doing this weekend."

The first time it happened, Gemma hadn't noticed, and she'd been unprepared for the *we* that soon escalated into *our*, as in "our" classes, "our" books and lastly, "our" time.

Before Gemma knew it had even begun, her

friend had left the group and she rarely ever saw her alone again. There was no more of their being just the girls. Her friend had become an *us* and to be with her meant that she brought with her a male who was pretty much always bored and yearning to be somewhere else.

The first time one of her friends showed up wearing an engagement ring, Gemma had naively said, "Promise that we'll always be friends."

By the time her third friend flashed a diamond ring, Gemma wanted to say, "Let's hit it with a hammer and see if it's real."

But now, she at last understood. She and Colin had spent every minute possible of the last week together.

When the furniture arrived, she and Colin directed the placing of it. It had been fun to argue about whether the blue rug went in "their" bedroom or the guestroom. Colin said the bedside table on "his" side of "their" bed was too small, so they'd switched it with one meant for the guest bedroom.

When one of the delivery men had trouble lifting Colin's big leather chair, Gemma sighed loudly and said, "It's too bad Lanny and Pere aren't here to help carry it in."

As Colin walked past her, he picked her up by the waist, carried her outside, set her in the chair, then carried them both inside.

The delivery man looked at Gemma's wide eyes and said to Colin, "I see what you're gettin' tonight."

And of course he was right.

That night they'd finally opened the champagne from Tess and they drank to *their* house and *their* furniture.

The next morning Colin had driven Gemma back to the guesthouse and for a moment he'd sat behind the wheel, not moving. "You like this place a lot, don't you?"

"Do you mean your parents' estate or the guesthouse?"

"Either. Both," he said.

"I love the guesthouse library. It's the most beautiful place I've ever worked."

He didn't say any more, just walked her inside, kissed her good-bye, and went to work.

Gemma spent the day reading the old Frazier documents and making notes. She was beginning to piece together a more complete story of the first Frazier who came to America. She was intrigued by him and wondered how he got an earl's daughter to fall in love with him. Maybe Shamus was so handsome—no, she thought. He was a Frazier, so it was probably his strength that won the lady.

Gemma entertained herself with a story of great passion, of a beautiful countess trapped under a yellow carriage, and along comes a man of extraordinary strength who lifts the vehicle and frees her. Of course she fell in love with him.

"Not scientific," she said aloud. "And certainly not dissertation material."

By four she found herself looking at her watch and wondering when Colin would show up.

At five he sent her a text.

> ELLIE GAVE ME SOMETHING TO COOK FOR DINNER. CAN YOU COME OVER AND PLAY? HOW ABOUT A SLEEPOVER?

Gemma threw clean clothes into a duffel, and put her computer and notes into another bag. She was at Colin's house, "their" house, fifteen minutes after he texted.

They made love as though they hadn't seen each other in months, with a desperate urgency she'd never thought was possible.

They showered together, then looked to see what Colin had bought at the grocery. They managed to cook a whole meal together, eating half of it as they cooked. They finally sat down at *their* table, in *their* dining room, and looked out at *their* garden.

When they finished dessert, the last of Rachel's blackberry cobbler, Colin looked across the table and said, "Have you ever felt as though you were exactly where you should be and doing exactly what you should be doing?"

"Yes," she said, and her heart was beating in her throat. She didn't feel she needed to say that here and now was where she was supposed to be.

After dinner, they talked. They still knew so few

facts about each other, and both of them had many things they'd never told anyone.

Colin told how he'd been made a full sheriff only recently. A special election needed to be held before the job could be filled, and he hadn't wanted to go through it. "The thought of sticking posters up around town touting me for sheriff wasn't something I could imagine myself doing," he said.

"So who ran your campaign?"

Colin looked down at his beer for a moment. "My mother hired some woman from . . ." He waved his hand.

"New York?"

"Of course."

Together they laughed about the whole thing.

They were in bed by ten and at the gym the next morning at six-thirty. This time, they were the only ones there. Mike and Sara had gone back to Fort Lauderdale, and Luke texted that he and Joce had been up all night with the babies. No one else showed up. After their workout, Colin bolted the front door and they made love on a couple of weight benches, then showered together.

After a week together, they'd fallen into a routine, with both of them spending their days separate and at their respective jobs. In the evening, Colin would text the single word Home and Gemma would leave the guesthouse and drive to *their* house.

A second robbery that was very much like the first one interrupted their peace. Again, it happened during the day, while the owner was home. This time a small wall safe had been opened and an antique brooch taken.

That night Gemma saw a different Colin than the one she'd been seeing. When he was silent, his brow furrowed, she knew she needed to get him to talk.

It wasn't easy. After she'd failed at several attempts at conversation, she said, "I guess you *are* the kind of man I have to beg."

He gave a little smile, then got up and went out to his car. He brought back a thick folder of photos that Roy had taken at the two crime scenes.

"Both times," Colin said, "the burglar walked in the front door, unseen by anyone of the house or any of the neighbors. And both times something that was hidden was stolen."

Gemma looked at the pictures. Both houses had trees around them that made it easier to get in without being seen. But then what? How was a hidden compartment in a bedpost found? Who knew how to crack a safe?

Colin spread all the documents out on the big coffee table Gemma had chosen. She sat on a pillow on the floor while he took the couch. Together, they spent hours reading the statements and going over the photos.

Gemma was startled to read that the little wall safe had contained $25,000 in cash as well as documents and the brooch. "But the thief left the money?" she asked.

"Didn't touch it." He pulled a paper from the bottom of the pile. "This is an insurance photo of what was taken."

It was a big, and very ugly, brooch with little garnets and dirty-looking aquamarines.

"I can't see that it would bring a lot of money when they tried to sell it," Gemma said. "It's certainly not fashionable. Unless it was owned by someone famous, maybe."

"No, it wasn't, and it was appraised at only two thousand two hundred dollars."

"That makes no sense," Gemma said. "Why would someone risk jail for a robbery of a pin they would sell for much less than the cash that was just sitting there?"

"You come up with an answer, let me know," Colin said as he stood up and yawned. "I don't know about you, but I'm bushed."

Smiling, she went to the bedroom with him and they made love. But afterward, Colin fell asleep and Gemma, ever curious, went back to the living room to look at the photos from the robberies.

She reread the questions Colin had asked the victims and their replies. There didn't appear to be anything linking the two families. They didn't know each other, never went to the same functions.

But on the back of one paper Colin had written *They both have ten-year-old daughters.* Below it he'd written, *School? Church? Clubs? Rival cliques at school? Did the girls steal on a dare?*

Gemma got her purse, found the little magnifying glass she kept in the zipped compartment, and began looking at the photos Roy had taken of the girls' rooms. It was 3 A.M. when she circled the two little branches of willow, their stems tied with pink bows.

Her impulse was to wake Colin and show him, but then she thought he'd probably seen the little bouquets. She crawled into bed beside him, put her back against his big one, and fell asleep instantly.

She was awakened by what sounded like the roar of a bull, and before she could open her eyes, Colin was pulling her out of bed. He lifted her by her shoulders and planted a hard kiss on her lips.

"I didn't see that and neither did Roy," he said as he began to dress. "Gemma, you are great, wonderful. I have to go to the office, and I'll need to talk to these girls before they go to school. If these branches were left by the thief, I'll look at all the files to see if someone matches that MO. Mike has contacts in the Feds, and so does Frank. Maybe I can tap into their files."

She was very pleased that she'd made him so happy.

When he was dressed, he kissed her again. "I don't know how long this will take. If I have to go somewhere to find out anything . . ." He looked at her as if to ask if that was all right with her.

"Go! Do your work. I'm going to get someone to show me those old carriages."

"Get Dad. He never has enough people to listen to him about his old wagons."

He kissed her again, then was gone.

22

COLIN CALLED HER at 10 A.M. and said he was going to D.C. to check out a lead. He said the robberies might have been committed by someone the FBI had been hunting for years.

"I'll miss you," he said.

"Me too." She was smiling as she hung up.

Gemma took Colin's advice and asked Mr. Frazier to show her the carriages, and they ended up spending the whole day together. As he talked knowledgeably about, as she'd been told, "anything with wheels," she began to understand his disappointment that none of his children shared the Frazier passion. What would happen to all that the family had so carefully stored over the centuries if there was no one to carry it into the next generation?

As for the pretty little yellow carriage, Shamus had already removed the seat and photographed the plaque. It read:

A GIFT TO
EDILEAN TALBOT MCTERN HARCOURT
FROM SHAMUS FRAZIER
1802

"A man who uses as few words as my Shamus," Mr. Frazier said.

"And both of them are artists," Gemma answered.

"And my Shamus gets straight As in school." Mr. Frazier's voice was full of pride as he took her to a second warehouse.

By evening, she was ready to snuggle with Colin and tell him all that she'd seen and heard and what she'd thought about it all. But he didn't return. At about eight, he texted her that he was still in D.C. I'LL BE BACK AS SOON AS I CAN, he added.

At 1 A.M. her phone woke her. Colin told her that his brother Pere had been in a car wreck.

"Was he badly hurt?" Gemma asked, sitting up and wide awake.

"Not bad," Colin said. "Tris is with him, and they promised to keep me informed. I was going to come back, but Dad said not to."

"Should I go to the hospital?"

"No," Colin said. "The place will be packed with people. But, Gemma, would you find out the truth? If it's serious they might not tell me."

"I'll find out," she promised. "I'll call Tris and ask him."

"Thank you," he said. "Now go to bed."

"It's lonely without you here hogging all the space."

"It's lonely here without you in every way," he answered and they hung up.

Gemma tried to sleep, but she was worried about Pere. The next morning, she got up early. She knew it was no use going to the gym. There were some people who could work out alone, but she wasn't one of them. If she was by herself, ten minutes after she got to a gym, she began thinking of something she'd read, or needed to read, and left. She wouldn't even be aware of what she was doing. She'd just find herself at her car, her keys in her hand, and minutes later, she'd be back at work.

She managed to doze a bit, but when she finally awoke it was still early, and she wondered if Tris was at Ellie's having his egg burrito before the store opened. Fifteen minutes later, she was at the back loading dock. One of the men waved at her and she went inside. As she'd hoped, Tris was sitting at the table and drinking coffee, an empty plate in front of him. He'd just finished eating.

"Gemma!" he said. "What a wonderful surprise." He guessed why she was frowning. "Pere is fine. Just a broken leg. He swerved to miss some critter crossing the road and hit a tree. And yes, he was probably going too fast."

Gemma let out her breath and sat down. "Colin

was afraid Pere was seriously hurt and no one was telling him." She got out her phone, excused herself to Tris, and quickly texted Colin that Pere was okay. When she finished, Ellie asked if she wanted anything to eat.

"Whatever is the least amount of trouble," Gemma answered. She looked back at Tris as a thought came to her. "Is Pere in a cast?"

"From crotch to ankle. It's going to take him a while to recover from this."

Gemma was looking at the tabletop, and when Ellie put an egg sandwich and a big mug of tea in front of her, she spent a lot of time saying thanks.

Tris had been watching her. "You have something in mind, don't you?"

"Not really," Gemma lied. "Have you met Pere's latest girlfriend?"

"I wouldn't call her 'latest.' They've been together for over a year," Tris said. "Who have you been talking to?"

"No one," she said, lying again, but she couldn't tell him what Rachel had told her in confidence. "It's just that she didn't strike me as someone to settle down and raise a family. How about you? What did you think of her?"

"I don't think a single thought has ever gone through my mind when I'm around Eloisa. When I look at her it's all physical."

"My point exactly." She took a bite and chewed slowly while Tris tried to figure out what she was up to. "Do you know the interior layout of the Frazier house?"

"I spent a lot of time there when I was a kid. Why?"

"I was just thinking about that little room off the kitchen. I saw a bathroom with a shower next to it, and isn't there a big couch in that room?"

"You mean the old porch. Mrs. Frazier did the same thing my mother did. After Colin was born, she had the porch enclosed so she could watch the children while she was in the kitchen—not that Alea ever did any cooking, but she does love to supervise. Mr. Frazier called the room a jail because she put a gate across the doorway and locked the kids inside."

Gemma was patiently waiting for him to finish. "I want you to suggest to the Fraziers that Pere should stay in that room while he recuperates."

"Why? He could stay at his place in Richmond. He'll be fine there."

"Don't you think that Pere will need constant tending and that he'd be better off at home?"

"Did Alea put you up to this?"

"No. I was just thinking about Pere, that's all."

Tris wasn't understanding. "That's good of you, but Rachel is the one who'd get stuck with taking care of him, and she already has too much to do. But maybe you're right that he'd be better off in Edilean. He could stay upstairs and I know just the nurse for him. She—"

"No!" Gemma said, then lowered her voice. "I mean, it's not fair to anyone to have to run up and down stairs all day. But maybe someone could help with the cleaning so Rachel can spend as much time as needed with Pere."

At last Tris understood what she was telling him. "Oh, yeah. I see. I think that would be a great idea. Pere will need entertaining, won't he?"

"And a nurse won't do that."

"Are you kidding? The nurse I have in mind plays chess and juggles, and she's beautiful. She could—"

Gemma was glaring at him.

"Right. Nurses don't entertain their patients. Maybe it's better to get someone Pere already knows and feels comfortable with."

"Think you can get Mrs. Frazier to agree? She might want to put him upstairs and hire that juggling nurse."

"If I were to hint to Alea Frazier that more than just recovery might come out of this, she will sew her son's feet to the floor of that room. I must say that Rachel has done a good job of keeping this a secret. How long has it been going on?" Before Gemma could answer, Tris said quietly, "Uh oh. The store has opened and we've been found out. Here comes old Dr. Burgess. I'll have to ask him to sit down. Damnation but I need to talk to you. I may have found the Heartwishes Stone."

"You what?!" Gemma said much too loudly as someone grabbed the back of her chair and she almost tipped over. Tris was up in a second, one hand steadying Gemma, the other taking the arm of a bent old man. When Gemma's chair stopped wobbling, Tris helped the man to sit down between them.

"Dr. Burgess," Tris said, "I really want you to let me examine you."

"I've had too many doctors poking and prodding at me," he said in a smooth voice, looking more at Gemma than at Tris. "I can no longer bear the sight of a needle."

Gemma tried to be pleasant as Tris introduced them, but she was quite annoyed. Why had Tris let her go on and on about Pere when he had something so important to tell her? She desperately wanted to hear what he had to say.

Dr. Burgess was chattering on about how he was so very hungry and wanted one of Ellie's pastries and her coffee. When he fumbled about as he started to get up to go to the counter, Tris told him to sit, that he'd get the food for him.

"What a dear boy you are," Dr. Burgess said as Tris left.

The second he was alone with Gemma, the old man moved his chair a bit closer to hers, and she had to give him her attention. Whereas she'd liked odd-looking Mr. Lang from the moment she first saw him, she didn't like this man, who had moved much too close to her.

"It's you I wanted to talk to," he said, smiling at Gemma in a way that would have been appropriate from a much younger man but that she found a bit creepy from this old man. "I don't know if you've been told that I'm also an historian. I would love to hear about your research. I want to know what you've been finding out. From the gossip around town, it's truly fascinating. And also," he said with a sly look, "I hear that congratulations are in order for your engagement to our local sheriff."

"You've heard wrong," she said. "There is no engagement. Colin Frazier and I have only been dating."

He put his age-spotted hand on her arm. "But you are living with him, aren't you?"

She pulled away from him and picked up her bag.

"Oh dear, I've offended you," he said. "I do apologize. I thought it was normal today for young couples in love to live together. Maybe I'm wrong."

Tris returned with coffee and a plate of pastries. "Gemma, you aren't leaving already, are you?"

"Gemma—may I call you that?—was just about to tell me all about her research."

"She's good at her job," Tris said, looking from one to the other as he sat down.

She wanted to stay with Tris and hear about the Heartwishes Stone, but more than that, she wanted to get away from this old man. In spite of his protestations of hunger, he hadn't touched the pastries. She glanced at the big belly that protruded under his old cotton shirt. The cuffs were frayed, the collar discolored around the neck. If he was hungry for something, it wasn't for cream puffs.

It hit Gemma all at once what was bothering her about the man. He was an ailing historian who, by the poverty of his clothing, hadn't been very successful in his career. The man was an academic, which meant that he desperately wanted to be published. She had no doubt that he'd heard rumors about the Heartwishes Stone and he planned to find out all he could from her, add to it, then get published. She had a vision of newspaper articles, magazines, tabloids, TV, the Internet, all of them splashed with stories of the Heartwishes Stone. Minutes after the stories appeared, Edilean would be inundated with . . .

She didn't want to think of what would come into the peaceful little town: everything from rampant greed to the truly needy. All the horrible things she envisioned were the reason she'd decided never to write about the Stone in anything that would possibly be published. She'd even thought of talking to Mrs. Frazier and explaining why the document Gemma wrote for the family's private use shouldn't include the story of the Heartwishes Stone. It was one thing to write of an old legend, but things that were happening *now* seemed to be going back to that Stone.

She had to shake her head to clear it.

"Are you all right?" Dr. Burgess asked, his hand yet again on her arm.

Gemma didn't want to be near the man any longer. She stood up and looked at Tris. "I'd like to talk about Pere some more. Could I come by your office?"

"I'm booked solid today. I'll be so glad when Ariel gets here and can help out. How about dinner tonight?"

"Great," Gemma said. "I'll come by your office at six."

"Perfect." He smiled at her. "And don't worry about Pere. I'll take care of everything."

"Nice to have met you, Dr. Burgess," she said quickly, then kissed Tris's cheek and left.

As soon as she got to her car, she texted Tris to tell Burgess nothing about her or the Stone.

I DON'T TRUST THAT MAN.

He wrote back,

THANKS FOR THE TIP

An hour later she was in the guesthouse, but even the beauty of the library couldn't make her keep her mind on her work. She kept thinking about what Tris had said, that he may have found the Heartwishes Stone.

At twelve-thirty, she got a text from Joce.

DID YOU HEAR SARA'S NEWS?

She typed back that she hadn't heard anything about Sara.

Joce wrote back:

CALL ME OR COME OVER AND I'LL
GIVE YOU LUNCH AND TELL ALL.

It was the break Gemma needed. She practically ran to her car and was at Joce's beautiful old house five minutes later. The door was ajar, so she pushed it open. She very much wanted a tour of the house, but from the cacophony it seemed that both babies were crying.

Joce looked exhausted and frantic. "They're dirty at both ends," she said.

Gemma didn't reply, just took a baby and stripped him/her—it turned out to be a him—and plunked him down in a sink full of warm water. Like magic, he got quiet.

Joce looked at her in awe.

"My sister taught me how to do this."

For the next few hours, she and Joce worked like a team, with washing babies, feeding them, then washing again, and redressing. Joce never stopped telling Gemma thanks. When the babies were ready to go down for their second nap, it was three hours later.

"Why don't you lie down and take a nap yourself?" Gemma said to Joce. "I'll listen for the babies and look after the house."

"I couldn't allow that," Joce said. "You've done too much already."

Gemma had to practically push her up the stairs, with Joce saying thanks at every step.

While they slept, Gemma toured the house on her own and got the laundry done, cleaned up the kitchen, and put the living room back in order. When everyone was still asleep, she checked the fridge and found ingredients to make a meat loaf. She smiled as she worked, remembering Colin teasing her about her meat loaf, which she'd never made for him.

At a little after five Joce came downstairs with two smiling babies in her arms. Gemma took one.

"I can't thank you enough for this," Joce said as she looked in the oven window. "Sometimes I get so overwhelmed I can't think. If it weren't for friends like you I don't know how I'd manage. I don't know how Sara is going to cope. She knows so few people outside of Edilean."

"Are you saying she had her baby?"

"Good heavens! You came over to hear the news and I forgot to tell you. Last night Sara had an emergency C-section and delivered twins."

Gemma quit bouncing the baby and stared at Joce. "Twins? Didn't she have a sonogram so she knew how many kids she was having? Or did she just not tell anyone?"

"She didn't know. The second baby was positioned behind the front one in such a way that no one saw it on the sonograms."

Gemma was having trouble collecting her thoughts. "At the barbecue, Sara wished for . . ."

"I know. She wished for twins."

Gemma sat down at the kitchen table, the baby held firmly to her. "Boy or girl?"

"Two boys. Mike said he's already ordered martial arts gear for them."

"How is he?"

"Excited. Bewildered. Scared out of his mind."

"I wish—" Gemma began, then swallowed. "I mean, I hope that they come back here and live."

"Me too, but Mike has a couple more years to go before he can retire. Now that his friend Frank is going to be living here, he really wants to be here too." Joce looked at Gemma. "You don't think there really is anything to this Heartwishes Stone, do you?"

"No, of course not," Gemma said, but she didn't sound convincing. She glanced at the wall clock. It was five forty-five. "I have to go. I have a date with Tris at six."

"Date? But Colin—?"

"Not that kind of date," Gemma said. "A date to gain information." She put the baby in her high chair and kissed her.

"Let me know what you find out," Joce called as Gemma ran to the front door. "And I'll never be able to thank you enough for today. I feel like a new woman."

In his office, Tris greeted Gemma warmly, his hands on her shoulders as he kissed her cheek. He was wearing his white doctor's coat and looked very professional.

Four women were there, all of them looking at her in speculation—and as though they were ready to fight to protect Tristan.

He led her back to his office and closed the door behind her.

"Are they your harem?"

"Pretty much," he said as he took off his white coat. "At least they think they are. And besides, they think you're stepping out on Colin."

"Or are they angry that I'm going out with *you*?"

Tris chuckled. "Would you like to go to my house for dinner? I have a refrigerator full of food."

"I'd love to," she said.

As they left his office, she couldn't help being glad when Tris told the women who worked for him that if he was needed, he'd be at home. "With Gemma," he added.

When they were outside, she said, "This is going to be all over town." Somehow, that didn't bother her. "Should I follow you in my car?"

"Sure," he said as he got out his keys.

As Gemma followed Tristan in her car, she couldn't help but be curious about where he lived. They went down a road she'd never seen before that seemed to go into the nature preserve that surrounded Edilean. They left the paved road and turned onto gravel, but when she still didn't see a house, she began to wonder if he lived in a tent on vacant land. There was another turn, then they came to cattle bars, and he drove over them.

To her left, through the thickly wooded area around them, she saw a sparkling blue lake with ducks swimming about. Ahead of her was the house. It wasn't large, but it was lovely. Better yet, it was in an idyllic setting, with the lake directly in front of it.

She stopped behind Tris and got out of her car. It was wonderfully quiet, with only the sound of birds and the wind in the trees. "This is gorgeous," she said. "Have you lived here long?"

"All my life, and my dad grew up here too. It's called the Aldredge House and part of it is old. Not old by Edilean standards, no eighteenth century, but it was built in the 1840s."

"For that time period, shouldn't it be a modified Colonial?"

"I think it was, but generations of Aldredges changed it."

She walked toward the lake to look up at the house. It was two stories, with windows all along the front, and she saw a chimney above the roofline. She could imagine sitting by a fire on snowy days. On the far left was a low-roofed room that seemed to be all glass. "Is that a conservatory?"

"Yes," Tris said. "My ancestor who built the house was a master gardener."

"What about you?"

"I've been known to frequent a nursery now and then. Come inside and I'll show you the rest of it. You have to tell me what's old and what's new."

"Ah! A challenge," she said as she followed him in a side door. They went into a large hallway, with a tile floor and an oak staircase at the end.

"Old," she said, then nodded toward the door to the right, silently asking if she could open it. It was a large family room, with bookcases and a big TV, very cozy. It took only a glance to see that the room was newer than the hall and she told him so.

Across the hall she opened a door to a long room that was wide on the right but narrowed at the other end where she saw the kitchen with its dark cherry cabinets. "This is old and I don't think it's always been one room. So how'd I do?"

"Perfect," he said. "My mother had the walls torn out on this side. Right after Addy was born, Mom told my dad that she wasn't going to be stuck alone in the kitchen, and that if he wanted dinner on the table he damn well better let her see what her kids were up to. Two days later, the walls were down."

"I think I like your mother."

"Me too," Tris said. "Can I make you a drink?"

"Can't. I'm driving, but if you have it, I'll take a tonic water with lots of lime juice."

"Coming up."

"Mind if I . . . ?" She nodded toward the door to the conservatory, and he waved his hand for her to go. It was a beautiful room that looked like a Victorian garden. And as she'd gathered from his self-effacing tone, Tris was also good at gardening. Plants—mostly orchids—were everywhere, hanging from the ceiling, in floor pots, all in a lush display that made her want to sit in one of the wicker chairs and read. What she liked best was that Tris didn't confine the larger plants but had them growing out of the ground that surrounded the beautiful hand-painted tile on the floor.

Tris handed her an icy drink. "This is the only room that no one has touched. My dad said it was the favorite room of my great, great, etc. grandmother who built the house, and that she spent most of her time here." He leaned forward to remove a dead leaf from an oncidium orchid. "She was one of the women who had a baby with no husband."

"In normal circumstances, that wouldn't be interesting, but since it's been remembered for so long, I think there's a story there. I'd love to hear more about her. What was her name?"

"Louisa. I don't know much about her, but Joce said she called my grandfather and talked to him about our family. He said that Louisa Aldredge's child's birth certificate said her brother and his wife were the parents."

"I'm sure that's what was considered the proper thing to do at that time," Gemma said. "So . . . Sometime in the 1830s or 40s Louisa Aldredge had a baby out of wedlock, had to give him up, so she built herself a house in the wilderness, and lived here all alone with her plants."

"You are as romantic as Sara," Tris said, grinning. "I'll have you know that when my dad remodeled these rooms, he found surgical instruments dating back to about the time the house was built. And there were also some toy trucks from about that time. My guess is that Louisa built so far out of town so her clients wouldn't be seen going to a female doctor. And I think she lived here with her son."

"Sounds like you know quite a bit about her."

Tris shrugged. "Aldredges, male and female, tend toward medicine, so it wasn't a big leap to figure it out. Now, to more important matters."

"The Heartwishes Stone?" Gemma said quickly.

"I was thinking more in the lines of food. I have a housekeeper who comes in twice a week and brings me things she cooks at home. She likes to experiment, so I never know what's waiting for me."

"Let me guess," Gemma said. "She's young and pretty and unmarried."

"Have you met her?" Tris asked, his eyebrows raised, and they laughed together.

She couldn't help her amusement at the way Tris pretended not to know that women fell over themselves over him. She'd seen grown women halt in the street when they saw him, and Tris would smile at them in a shy way, as though he had no idea why they were gaping at him.

He opened the refrigerator door and began pulling out bowls that were covered with plastic wrap, and handed them to her. There were several vegetable salads, cold meat and chicken, and little cubes of cheese.

As they unwrapped the food and put the bowls on the table, they talked. Neither of them suggested heating the meal. Gemma wanted to ask Tris about the Heartwishes Stone, but she also wanted to let him tell her in his own time.

"So what's with you and Dr. Burgess that you don't trust him?" Tris asked as soon as they sat down at the table.

"Nothing I can put my finger on, but I think maybe he might want to find out what he can about my research so he can publish it."

"You think the Fraziers' family history will entice some editor to put it in print?"

"You know very well what he's after," Gemma said.

"Oh, that." Grinning, Tris looked at his plate. "I think you're right. He's been grilling everyone in town about anything he can find out about the Stone. This morning Ellie said that if he tried to pry more information out of her, she was going to set his skinny butt on the slicing machine."

Gemma laughed. "He does have skinny legs, doesn't he?"

"Ellie said he was complaining that everyone in town is so secretive."

"And by that he means The Seven."

It was Tris's turn to laugh. "So that's what we've become, is it? Wasn't there a movie about us?"

"You mean *The Magnificent Seven,* and it had nothing to do with the lot of you."

"Maybe it will once you write about us," Tris said. "This morning after you left, Dr. Burgess asked me about the robbery case Colin is working on, but I said, quite honestly, that I didn't know anything."

"I hope the robbery will become the latest gossip around town and overshadow the Stone."

"I heard that there were a couple of break-ins and that kids probably did it," Tris said.

Gemma looked down at her glass. "I don't know much more than you do."

"Did you hear about Sara?" Tris asked.

"Yeah. Nice, huh?" Gemma was quiet for a moment, then said, "All right, enough chitchat. You said you think you found the Heartwishes Stone. I want to see it—if that's possible, that is—and I want to hear every word of the story."

"Nell found it," Tris said as he went to the side of the room and swung out a framed photo on a hinge to expose a little wall safe. He quickly turned the combination, took out what looked to be a lady's silver compact, and handed it to Gemma.

It was surprisingly heavy. As she examined it, she saw that it was pretty but scarred in the front, as though someone had pried it open. Based on her knowledge of history, the little case looked to be late Victorian or Edwardian. It wasn't remarkable in the least, but rather plain.

"My sister and Nell took a couple of screwdrivers and a chisel to open it."

"I understand curiosity," Gemma said as she lifted the lid. The inside was filled with lead. She looked up at Tris.

"Go on, take the top layer off," he said.

Gemma was able to get her thumbnail under the lead and peel it upward, the lead bending as she lifted. Inside was a pretty little necklace. There was a little gold cage holding a tiny chip of some kind of stone. Gemma held it up to the light. "Uncut diamond?"

"Yes. I had my cousin Kim look at it, and it is a diamond, but it's not worth trying to cut it into a shape."

Gemma kept holding it aloft and looking at it. It was pretty but oh so simple—and so much smaller than she'd imagined. And she'd seen it before. "This was on Landy."

"What an excellent memory you have," Tris said. "I can see why you're good at research."

"How did you get Nell to give this to you? You didn't . . . ?"

"Steal it? I should be so clever. I had to trade her two Helen Kish's and one Heidi Plusczok for it."

"And they are?"

"Doll designers. I swear that child is going to be a negotiations lawyer. And thank heaven for eBay or I never would have been able to get them."

Gemma kept looking at the necklace. "Where? When? How?"

"I'd like to say it was my powers of deduction, but it was just a hunch. And I still don't know for sure if that's what the letter you found was talking about. Anyway, the day you were hurt, Nell said that Landy's necklace was blinking."

"I remember her saying that, but I paid no attention to it," Gemma said.

"Me neither. Nell lives in a world of her own. But I guess my brain registered it. Remember when I had to leave the barbecue for Mr. Gibson's heart attack?"

"Of course," Gemma said. That had been the day she was so angry at Colin—and it seemed like a lifetime ago.

"By the way, it was an anxiety attack, and he's fine now. I was quite annoyed at being called away, and I was planning to go back to the party. I called my sister at the hospital in Miami to see how her husband was. He's fine, but Nell wanted to talk to me. She took the phone and went in the hall and started in on an incoherent story about her father taking Landy's necklace away from her and I *had* to save it."

"Why would he take his daughter's necklace from her?" Gemma asked.

"My brother-in-law thought it came from the church jumble sale. He thought it might be valuable and someone could be missing it."

"Nice guy."

"He is," Tris said. "But the truth was that Nell had lied to her mother about where the necklace came from."

"Ahhhh," Gemma said. "And the plot thickens."

"Right. My devious little niece stole the necklace from me."

"Okay, so now I'm confused. Wouldn't you have noticed that you owned a necklace encased in lead and silver?"

"I would have if I'd ever seen it. Nell told me over the phone that she just happened to find the necklace behind the man."

Gemma smiled. "I guess you know what that means."

"Oh yes. Every child who has ever lived in this house since it was built has been fascinated by 'the man.'" He motioned for her to follow him as he walked toward the fireplace. On the far end of the big mantel, a four-inch square of wood had been inserted. On it was carved the profile of a handsome young man. He wore the stiff collar of the early nineteenth century, and his hair curled about his neck. His cheekbones were high, his chin firm. He looked almost exactly like Tristan.

"An ancestor of yours, I take it," Gemma said.

"I assume so. I always thought he looked like my father, but my mother said he looks like all the Tristans. The name goes back a long way in my family. Anyway, no one knows who he is for sure, and as kids all of us wondered about him. One of our favorite rainy day things to do was to make up stories about him. Colin used to say he was a man who fought for justice in secret."

"That sounds like him," Gemma said, smiling. "It's my guess he was the father of Louisa's son."

"That's what I think too, but that wasn't something the adults were going to tell the children, was it? Whoever he is, no one today knows for certain why he was chosen to be immortalized in the end of a fireplace. My mother wanted to take the tile out and frame it. She was always afraid it might catch fire, but Dad wouldn't let her." Tris looked at Gemma. "It's a good thing she didn't." Reaching out, he touched the bottom left corner of the square, then the top right, then he pushed in the middle. The little square sprang open to reveal a hole inside the mantel.

"Nell figured out the code to open that?"

"All by herself," Tris said.

"I am proud to know her." Gemma leaned forward to look inside the hole. "It looks as though it was made especially to hold the necklace in its box."

"That's what I think too." He pushed it closed, then stepped back and motioned for Gemma to try it.

She got it on the second try. "Truly amazing that the child figured that out."

"And told no one!" Tris added. "She knew that if she did, someone would take the box away from her."

"Then she lied her way into getting her mother to help her open it," Gemma said in admiration. "And it was very clever of her to hide it in plain sight around the neck of her teddy bear. It was as though she was daring any adult to see what she'd done."

"That's my dear little niece," Tris said. He went back to the dining area and they began to clear the table. "So, anyway, Nell was on the phone to me and practically hysterical because her father was going to take the necklace away from her. Of course all the problems were caused by the lie she'd told, but she didn't want to own up to that little detail."

"Interesting that she was telling *you* the truth of what she'd done and not her parents."

Tris gave a little laugh. "Why do you think she loves to stay with me? I let her get away with murder.

You should have heard Addy when she found out that I let Nell ride in Mr. Lang's truck with him."

"He's not—?"

"No, no," Tris said. "No deviant sexual behavior, but the man is eighty-five years old and he's still driving."

"In that case, I agree with Nell's mother," Gemma said.

"Yeah, me too," Tris said. "It won't happen again, but the problem is that I let Nell wrap me around her fingers, and she knows it. She knew that I'd be more interested in her story than in trying to teach her not to steal. I leave that up to her parents."

He paused as he put the bowls Gemma had covered in the refrigerator. "When Nell told me where she'd found the box and what was inside it, I remembered that it was blinking the day I met you, then later . . ."

Gemma nodded. "Right after that, Nell got her wish for her father to come home and live in Edilean."

"Exactly," Tris said. "So if it was blinking again on the day of the barbecue, then—"

"Someone was making a wish. I guess you found out about our little game that afternoon."

"I called Sara, and she went over everybody's wishes."

"And since then, Sara unexpectedly had twins," Gemma said softly as she thought about what had been said that afternoon. "At least no one wished for something bad."

"I think your mind works like mine," Tris said. "If the world found out that there's a possibility that something like this existed . . ."

"No Frazier would be safe," Gemma said. "I could see Shamus being kidnapped on his way home from school and some crooks demanding that he wish so and so would win the lottery."

"Or they'd demand weird things like being able to stop time."

"Good one," Gemma said. "How about spirit transfer? Or wish for the power to be able to take over the world."

"When I heard of Sara's babies, all I could think of is the bad that could come from this. I wish it weren't already all over town."

"Me too," Gemma said. "Colin says . . ." She broke off.

Tris gave her a little smile. "Got it bad for him, don't you?"

Gemma smiled modestly. "We get along well, and he's easy to be around."

"That's not what other women have said."

"You mean Jean?"

"No," Tris said. "The other women Colin dated when the two of them weren't together. They wanted his full attention, and when they didn't get it, they weren't, shall we say, pleasant."

"But Colin does give a woman his attention," Gemma said. "We talk about everything."

"That you get Colin to talk at all is something no other woman has achieved."

Gemma was smiling as Tris went to the picture on the wall and opened the safe, ready to put the silver box back in it.

"Wait!" Gemma said. "I think there's something you should know about wall safes. Is it okay if I tell you the truth about the robberies?"

"Sure. Colin and I talk about his cases all the time."

She told him how the robber had opened the safe in one house. When she finished, Tris said, "It sounds like someone is looking for something small that's well hidden." He nodded at the necklace.

"But who could know what the Heartwishes Stone is? Know that it's small enough to fit into a little safe? I've done a lot of research and I didn't find out what it looks like. I mean, until now, that is. *If* that's the Stone, which we're not sure of."

"So where do I hide this thing if not inside a safe?" Tris asked. "Maybe I should put it back where Nell found it."

"The thief found a brooch inside a bedpost, so I doubt if that picture will hinder him. Why don't you give it to me? I'll have Shamus sketch it and I'll photograph it. At least that way, whatever happens, we'll have a record of it."

"Where will you keep it?"

"In its lead case, and I think I'll put the compact

in with my other makeup so it won't look like anything special."

"Gemma, that's quite clever," Tris said and smiled at her warmly. "Are you *sure* you're set on Colin? No other man has a chance?"

He was a truly beautiful man, but she wasn't interested. "I think perhaps I'm absolutely sure." She looked at her watch. "It's after nine. I better go. The gym comes early tomorrow."

He walked with her out to her car. It was a beautiful night. "I'm glad you've come to Edilean. You're a good addition," he said as he kissed her cheek. His eyes sparkled. "And if you ever find out what a lowlife Colin Frazier actually is, you know where I live." He opened the car door for her.

"I'll be sure and tell him that you said—" Gemma broke off because she was suddenly overcome with a wave of nausea that she couldn't suppress. She bent over and threw up her dinner on the ground.

Instantly, Tristan changed from being a teasing friend into a doctor. He put his arm around her shoulders and led her back into the house.

"Stomach flu," Gemma said, her voice rather loud as she tried to drown out her thoughts of what could be the cause of her being sick. "Or maybe I ate something bad. It's probably food poisoning or a twenty-four-hour bug. I'll be fine in a few minutes. I bet you have a lot of patients right now with whatever I've caught. It rained on Thursday and I got wet. I bet that's what this is."

Tris didn't say anything as he led her to a powder room just off the hallway. He disappeared for a moment and returned with a little plastic cup. "Urine sample," he said.

"Sure. To check for food poisoning, right?"

"To find out what caused you to throw up. See that room?" He pointed to a door she'd not noticed before. "I'll be in there." He closed the bathroom door.

As Gemma did what he'd told her to, she tried hard not to think. Of course it was some stomach virus. They were always going around, weren't they?

By the time she finished and left the powder room, she was shaking. Tris, wearing his white coat, was standing in the doorway of the room he'd pointed out to her. It had been set up as an exam room.

"It's smart to have this in your house," she said, and she knew her voice sounded nervous. "Do you get many patients out here?"

"Some. Gemma, I want you to sit down there and take some deep breaths. Use what you learned in training and calm yourself down."

"Sure," she said as she watched him pick up the cup and leave the room.

She knew he was gone only minutes, but it seemed like hours. She looked about the little room and tried to use her historian's brain to make a story out of what she saw. The exam table looked old, and she wondered if Tris's father had bought it back in the 1950s. Against the wall was a tall metal cabinet with glass doors and it also looked old.

She told herself to get up and go look at it, but her legs didn't seem to work. And her curiosity failed to elicit any response from her.

When Tris opened the door, Gemma was sitting just where he'd left her, and she looked up at him.

"How are you feeling?" he asked in what she figured was the voice he used with his patients.

"Food poisoning?" she whispered.

"Gemma . . ." he began, and she saw the answer on his face.

She put her hands over her face. "I'm not ready for this," she whispered. "I have a job. I hardly know Colin."

Tris put his hand on her shoulder. "How about some tea and toast? I'd offer crackers, but I don't have any." When Gemma didn't move, he bent and helped her up. "Come back to the living room and we'll talk."

Minutes later, they were sitting on his couch and Gemma was trying to eat the toast Tris had made for her, but whatever went down wanted to come back up. He'd removed his white coat and was once again her friend.

"A baby?" Gemma said. "You're sure?"

"Absolutely. Tomorrow I'm going to give you some prenatal vitamins, and I'll get you an ob-gyn. Under the circumstances I don't think I should . . ."

"Yeah," she said. "That could get in the way of friendship." She looked at him, and what she was feeling was in her eyes. "What do I do? How do I tell Colin?"

Tris put his hand on hers. "Gemma, if you don't want this, I can arrange an abortion. No one but you and me need ever know that this happened."

She jerked her hand from his. "I never want to hear anything like that again!"

"Good," he said, and for the first time, he grinned. He took her hand again. "Gemma, everything will be fine. I've known Colin all my life, and he'll do whatever you want."

"You mean make an honest woman out of me?" she said and there was disgust in her voice. "I've always wanted a man to feel like he *had* to marry me."

"If Colin weren't madly in love with you, he would never marry you, but he would take care of you financially."

"He is not in love with me!"

"You think not?" Tris got up to get her more tea. "I've never in my life seen Colin act obsessed as he does around you. Even when we were kids, he was always the steady one. When one of us would come up with some harebrained scheme, the others would agree to go along with it, but not Colin. He never cared if everyone was against him but always had his own values."

"He took a job from his father that he hated."

"Colin has a very, very strong sense of family."

"Jean . . ."

"That was purely physical and Colin was dazzled by her," Tris said as he filled a mug with hot water.

Gemma looked glum. "If Jean is dazzling, what am I? The bland, boring consolation prize?"

"You are love," Tris said as he put milk in her tea and took it to her.

"But we've known each other a very short time."

"You're right," Tris said as he sat down beside her. "It's a known fact that in order to fall in love, you have to know a man two-point-six-eight years."

Gemma couldn't laugh. "What am I going to do? This isn't what I planned for my life. I wanted to wait until my dissertation was finished, until after I had a good job. *Then* I was going to look for a man to spend my life with." She looked at him. "But Mrs. Frazier wanted grandchildren so she wished for them."

"You don't think unprotected sex had anything to do with it?" Tris asked.

Gemma groaned. "I'd rather think this was caused by magic than by my own stupidity."

Tris laughed. "Okay, it's getting late. I'm going to drive you home. Tomorrow I'll get your car to you and I'll bring you some vitamins. Let me know as soon as you tell Colin, and I'll get Rachel to help with your diet. You need to eat well."

When he helped her to stand up, she looked at him. "A baby?"

"That's right. A big, happy Frazier baby. Wonder what he'll wish for when he grows up?"

"Don't remind me." She started toward the door, Tris close beside her. "I guess we know why the wishes were activated. Your niece pulled the lead away from the Stone and the genie escaped."

"Guess so," Tris said. "Have you thought of any baby names yet?"

"You're enjoying this, aren't you?"

"Yes," he said. "Colin is my friend as well as my cousin, and I was dreading the day he'd come to me and say that he and Jean were going to get married. I always wondered if I'd be able to pretend that I was happy for him. But now he's had the good sense to . . ."

"I know," Gemma said. "You don't have to say it." They were at Tris's car and he helped her into the passenger seat. "You won't tell anyone about this, will you?"

"I would never reveal the secrets of a patient or a friend. Until you personally tell me it's okay, I won't say a word. Buckle up. You have two people to worry about now."

23

GEMMA THOUGHT SHE wouldn't sleep much after Tris left her at the guesthouse, but she did. In fact, she fell across the bed and was asleep in an instant. When she awoke early the next morning, the first thing she thought of was that when she'd first arrived in Edilean she'd so much wanted to belong to the place. Had that been a wish from her heart? Had Nell's blinking necklace "heard" her? Had it known that she was destined to be a Frazier by marriage? Colin's grandfather said the wishes included "ladies." So maybe the Stone did include wives. In that case, she thought she should call Ariel in California and tell her to take a pregnancy test.

Gemma lay in bed and ran her hand over her flat stomach. She couldn't imagine it growing with a child. But according to Dr. Tris, that was just what was about to happen.

She put her hands behind her head and looked at the ceiling. So now what happened? she wondered. Of course the first thing was to tell Colin.

On the other hand, what if he did what Tris had hinted at and asked her to marry him out of a sense of duty? What kind of marriage would that be if he spent his life feeling that he'd been forced—or tricked—into marriage?

Gemma got up and as she showered, the idea that she was expecting a baby seemed like a fantasy. She didn't feel in the least ill, and wasn't there supposed to be morning sickness? She put her hand on her stomach. "Are you so determined to be different that you're going to make me ill in the evenings?"

She got out of the shower, dressed, ate a solid, good-for-you breakfast, and started to work. She was writing about what she'd found out about the first Shamus Frazier, and as she wrote, she nearly forgot her life-changing news. In the quiet of the library, she could put aside her concerns about her future.

At one point, she couldn't resist looking at what was possibly the Heartwishes Stone. It was such a small thing, a little oval cage, no bigger than the tip of her little finger, and inside was the tiny rock that glistened when she held it up to the sunlight. Could this little object really and truly grant wishes?

Even though she told herself it was wrong, she clasped it in the palm of her hand and said, "I wish that my baby lives a long and happy life." She opened her hand to see if the Stone was changing color as it had when Nell had it around the neck of her teddy bear, but the necklace was the same.

"This is ridiculous," she said as she put it back in its lead case, and closed the top of the compact. As she'd told Tris, she put it in the little basket that was near the bathroom sink and held her other cosmetics. It was hidden in plain sight.

That afternoon young Shamus showed up at her door. She didn't get up to open it, just motioned for him to come in. He went directly to the kitchen and made a couple of sandwiches for them, then sat down to draw.

They had developed a routine where they said little to each other, and she knew that Shamus liked the silence that usually surrounded her. She'd seen that the inside of the Frazier house was more turbulent, more active, than she liked, so maybe it was the same for him.

"I'm going to have a quiet child," she said, then glanced up at Shamus. She hadn't meant to say it out loud, but he didn't seem to have heard. He just kept sketching on his big pad.

Later, she nodded toward his wooden art box on the table. Gray duct tape was all along the bottom, and it was very ugly. "Why don't you leave that here and I'll see if I can fix it?"

He nodded once but didn't look up. Whatever he was drawing today was certainly absorbing.

She went back to trying to put her copious notes

into a readable form. Twice she found herself looking at the names of the family she was writing about. The Fraziers seemed to love to stick to the old names, but she couldn't bear to saddle her child with "Peregrine." And what about the girls? Would Alea want her to name the child Prudence? Gemma reassured herself by remembering that Mrs. Frazier had named her daughter Ariel.

As Gemma was musing over this, Shamus left, raising his hand in farewell, and closing the door after him. She saw that he'd left his art case behind, and peeping out from under it was a piece of paper. Since Shamus rarely let anyone see his drawings, Gemma was overcome with curiosity. Getting up, she went to the coffee table. When she picked the drawing up, what she saw so jolted her that she sat down heavily on the couch.

Shamus had drawn Gemma sitting under a big tree like the one at Merlin's Farm, and she was reading. She looked absolutely absorbed in her book, oblivious to her surroundings. It would have been a completely accurate portrait except that there were three little boys, each one the spitting image of Colin, near her. One was swinging by his hands from a low tree branch. The second one was wearing a sheriff's badge and cowboy boots, and looking like he was about to arrest the boy in the tree. The third one, wearing a diaper that looked decidedly soggy, had constructed an obstacle course of rocks and twigs, and was running four tiny cars over it.

Gemma could only stare at the picture in open-mouthed astonishment. But then, she leaned back on the couch and couldn't help laughing, as the drawing looked very true to life. She could envision herself in just such a position, absorbed in her reading as her children occupied themselves.

"Whatever made him draw this?" she whispered, and remembered her comment about having a "quiet child." It seemed that he had combined that with Mrs. Frazier's very vocal desires for grandchildren, and Mr. Frazier's frequent statements about wanting a child to inherit the ancestors' passion for wheels. Add to it that Gemma kept her hand protectively on her stomach most of the time and that she went to the bathroom every few minutes, and it looked like Shamus had figured out her secret. In a single picture, he had put his parents' Heartwishes with what Gemma had accidently told.

Gemma carefully stored the drawing in a portfolio and went back to work, but every half hour or so, she'd look up, smile, and shake her head in wonder.

At six, she received a text message from Colin and her heart leaped. So this is what it's like to be in love, she thought, then told herself she was being silly. It was too soon for that. But then, wouldn't it be better if she were in love with the father of her child?

COULD YOU MEET ME ASAP AT MER-
LIN'S FARM BY THE SUMMERHOUSE?

MIKE AND SARA AREN'T HERE. IT'S JUST US.

Gemma could feel her heart beginning to race and her mind filled with all sorts of possibilities. Did "just us" mean that he wanted a tryst, a secret assignation? Merlin's Farm, with its atmosphere of spirits long gone, was about as romantic as it could get. There they'd have privacy. They'd be away from his family, and the people who would talk about them.

She hurriedly put on some makeup and ran to her car. On the short drive there she imagined lying in his arms and telling him about finding the Heartwishes Stone. And later, as they lay under the stars, she'd tell him about the baby. And then what? she wondered. She hoped he'd be overcome with joy, that he'd lift her in his arms, twirl her around, and they'd talk about their future life together. *Happiness* is what she wanted and needed.

As Gemma pulled into Merlin's Farm and drove toward the barn, she laughed at herself. For all her protestations of wanting a career and independence, when it came down to it, she wanted to be Cinderella and have a big, strong man rescue her.

She saw Colin's Jeep parked near the secluded area that held the little lattice summerhouse, and she pulled in beside it. The moment she saw Colin she knew he hadn't invited her there for a tryst. He looked worried, as though he had something truly awful to tell her.

"Hi," he said as soon as she got out of the car. He put his hands on her shoulders and gave her a perfunctory kiss.

"What's wrong?" she asked.

"Jean," he answered.

Gemma had to work to keep from rolling her eyes. He had invited her to this beautiful, romantic place, but it looked like she was going to have to discuss his ex-girlfriend.

"What about her?" Gemma asked, trying her best to be an adult. She congratulated herself on not shouting, "What does Dragon Lady want now?" She sat down on the grass and looked up at him; Colin stayed standing, looking too nervous to sit down.

Colin told her about searching old files and finding out that many years ago a young thief had left behind a willow branch tied with a pink silk ribbon.

"So he's restarted his career?" she asked. "Do you have photos of this man?"

"Yes, but there's more. He went on to commit some major robberies all over the world. Banks, the Romanian consulate, a couple of penthouses in Hong Kong. He's scaled buildings using suction cups. He can open any safe made."

"I guess a screwed-on bedpost was easy for him."

"Very easy." Colin was looking at her as though he had something important to tell her, but he didn't seem to want to say it outright.

"Why would a professional thief come to Edilean?"

"He's Jean's uncle."

Gemma refrained from saying curse words and tried to keep her face calm. She wasn't going to give in to her anger at her baby news being overridden by Jean's criminal relative. "I take it you weren't told about the uncle."

"Not a word. Jean said she was an only child of only children."

"I can see why she didn't tell a man who loved law enforcement that she had a notorious thief for an uncle. Maybe she didn't know him."

"Ha! He was under surveillance while she was in law school, and he spent a lot of time with her. According to the files I read and the pictures I saw of the two of them, they were inseparable for years. She traveled with him. I knew she'd been places all over the world, but I just found out that she went with her uncle, a man who—" He couldn't seem to find the right words to describe Jean's concealment of this part of her life.

Gemma knew she should offer him sympathy because his former girlfriend had lied to him, but she couldn't do it. If he was really over her—as he said he was—would it still make him this angry to find out that she'd hidden things from him? But she kept her thoughts to herself. "So now you need to find her uncle."

"Yeah, I do."

"What does Jean say about all his?" She held her breath, hoping that he'd say he hadn't spoken to her, that he was letting his deputy, Roy, ask the questions.

"Jean says she hasn't seen him in years, but I think she's lying." Colin stopped pacing to look down at Gemma. "That's what I want to talk to you about. I don't believe all of this is a coincidence."

"All of what?"

Colin waved his hand. "You, me, Jean, her uncle, the robberies. I think there's a reason it's all happening at once."

"What's your theory?" she asked, genuinely interested.

"I think Jean told her uncle that she and I broke up. Knowing her as I do, she probably told him it was all my fault. I'm beginning to think the robberies in our little town are an attempt at revenge."

"But if he knows Jean, maybe he can figure out the truth about you two. And there might be another reason he's here." She told him of how Tristan had found what he believed to be the Heartwishes Stone. "I still don't know how everyone in town found out about it. Did you tell anyone?"

"I didn't have to. That legend is known by a lot of people. It wouldn't be a leap for anyone to go from you looking at the old papers to wishes being fulfilled. I guess Tris told you about his brother-in-law."

"Yes," Gemma said, "but I didn't know he told others."

"Jake was suddenly brought home from a war and got a job here in Edilean, all in a couple of weeks. People notice that sort of thing."

"And Sara's twins," Gemma said. "It seems to me that a Stone that grants wishes would be enough to attract an international thief."

"I'm afraid so," he said. "All this makes what I have to say even more difficult."

His tone made the hairs on Gemma's neck stand up. "What do you want to tell me?"

"If Jean's uncle is committing these crimes in retaliation for my having broken up with his niece, or he wants what you're researching, I'm concerned about *you*. If he's anything like Jean, I think he'll go after whatever he wants without worrying about the repercussions."

She was trying to conceal her disappointment about how far away from what she'd thought this meeting was going to be to the reality of it. "Since you're the one who caused Jean pain, maybe her uncle wants to show you up to the whole town. Possibly make you an object of ridicule."

"To humiliate me?" Colin said. "That's possible. But now I'm concerned that he wants this Stone and may think that *you* have it."

She could tell where he was headed. He wanted the two of them to stay apart for a while. But Gemma didn't want to do that. "Do you think Jean could have instigated the robberies?" Gemma asked. "Maybe Jean asked her uncle to do something that would embarrass you."

"I don't think so," he said, but he wouldn't meet her eyes.

To Gemma, it looked like he wasn't going to tell her all of what he was thinking. "So what now?" she asked.

He was looking at her intensely. "Is something wrong? Have I done something to upset you?"

"No. You haven't done anything," she said and knew she was lying just as much as he was. "I'm just concerned for your safety, that's all. What do you plan to do now?"

"I'm going to question Jean some more. I've got to use anything I know about her to get her to tell me the truth. I need to find out what's going on and why. So far, the robberies have been petty, but I worry that they're a prelude to something larger. In one job, four innocent people were killed during his escape."

Gemma was quiet for a moment as her visions of talking with him about having their baby were replaced by scenes of him with Jean. She brought herself back to the present. "You want us to stay apart and make the town believe we've broken up, don't you?"

"I think that's the best for now." He gave her a crooked grin. "I thought about picking a fight with you, one that was so bad that you'd throw me out, but I decided not to risk it. I was afraid you'd not forgive me, then where would I be?"

"The same place you were a few weeks ago," Gemma said. She glanced at her watch. She could feel the beginning of nausea rising in her. If she didn't leave soon, she'd be throwing up, and that was not the way she wanted him to find out about the child they'd created. "I need to get back to work." She got up and started toward her car, but he caught her arm.

"You're angry at me." He seemed to be astonished at the idea.

"I understand about your work and what you need to do." She thought about what he'd just said. "How would you have picked a fight with me?"

"Forget I said that," he said. "Why don't we go somewhere out of town and have dinner and talk about all this?"

Gemma had a grim vision of herself throwing up at the table. "I'll take a rain check. I really do need to go."

"Work!" he said. "I could pick a fight with you about how much you work."

It was her turn to be astonished. "But I thought you liked hearing about all I was finding out about your family. Didn't you?"

"I did. I do," he said. "Although the part about Tris has been hard to take."

"Tris? What does he have to do with the robberies?"

"Nothing that I know of."

"Then why did you bring him up?"

"It's just that I was surprised when he said that you'd told him about my case. He knew many details I'd not even told my deputy. Maybe I should have made you cross your heart not to tell. And of course there's the two of you and that damned Stone! It would have been easy to pick a fight."

Colin was smiling, but Gemma took his words seriously. She'd never before been accused of betraying anyone's trust. "But I thought—" She could feel her face growing red. "You're right. I shouldn't have told about your case. I was in the wrong. I apologize." The nausea was growing stronger and she took a step toward her car.

"Gemma, I'm the one to apologize. It was okay to tell Tris. I do. It's just that—"

When he cut off, she turned to look at him. "It's just that what?"

"Nothing. Forget about it." He stepped beside her. "I'll see you in a few days."

"I want to know what you were going to say."

He looked away from her. "Nothing. I don't listen to gossip."

"What gossip?"

Colin ran his hand over his face. "It's just déjà vu, that's all. You spent an entire day with Tris, but I understand. Jean was always out with other men too. I pretended to be above it, but it did hurt."

"Déjà vu? Hurt? Other men? What in the world are you talking about?"

"You and Tris, that's what!" he said, as though it were a given.

"What about Tristan?"

"Gemma, I don't want to fight. I asked you to come here so I could tell you the truth, not to argue. You and I have to stay apart for a while because I need time to get all the information out of Jean that

I can. And I'm concerned that you may be in danger of some sort of revenge. Plus, there's your knowledge of that Stone."

"Of course," Gemma said. "I understand completely. You're telling this month's girlfriend that you need to spend time with last month's girlfriend. And, by the way, while you're with her, I'm to stay away from other men. The only question is whether you and I are on for next month. Or do you have someone else picked out?"

"Gemma! By everything that's holy you're being unfair! Do you have any idea what I have to put up with because you spend so much time with Tris? His house is very isolated, and half a dozen people told me you were out there with him at night. And he drove you home. Were you too drunk to drive?"

She wasn't about to tell him the real reason for not driving. "If this is what you think of me, it's a good idea that we stop seeing each other. I'm sure your family will be pleased to see you back with your beautiful lawyer girlfriend. And since you seem to forgive her for everything rotten she does to you, I'm sure you two will be very happy together. Now, if you don't mind, I'd like to go back to work."

"I don't mind at all," Colin said. "I hope you and Tris will be very happy."

"Good! Because it looks like you and Jean are a perfect match after all."

"Maybe we are," Colin said.

Gemma couldn't take any more. She got into her

car, slammed the door, and drove off in a flurry of gravel.

Just as angry, Colin drove to his office. He was determined to go back to work. The sooner he got the crimes figured out and arrests made, the faster he could get back with Gemma. If she wanted to, that is.

An hour later, he hadn't done anything. He kept going over their argument and trying to understand it.

After a fight with Jean, Colin had always felt better. They said horrible things, accusing each other of infidelity, laziness, stupidity, whatever they could come up with. They covered every subject, from her leaving the kitchen a mess to Colin's constant moroseness, to Jean's inability to see anything except her own wants and needs.

After hours of spewing venom, they would run out of energy—and out of bad things to blame on the other. They'd take a breath, look at each other, and one of them would say something trivial. Colin would say something like, "You hog the bathroom."

Jean would retaliate with, "And you'd rather watch sports on TV than go dancing."

"And you'd rather—" Colin would begin, but he'd not finish because in the next minute they'd be in each other's arms. The sex that followed would be as heated as their argument had been.

But Gemma was different. He'd asked her to meet him at Merlin's Farm because he didn't want to start their phony—and temporary—breakup in either of their houses, places where they'd made love. He knew that he'd missed her so much over the last days that all he'd want to do was climb into bed and hold her. He thought that the neutral ground of the summerhouse would be better.

It had never occurred to him that there'd be a fight. He would have said that he and Gemma had nothing to argue about. From the beginning they'd been a perfect match, easy and comfortable with each other.

While it was true that she'd been angry at him for forgetting their time in bed together, they'd solved that, hadn't they? And he'd made it up to her.

He thought he'd ignored the fact that over the last few weeks people in Edilean had delighted in telling him that Gemma had been seen with Dr. Tris again and again. None of his real friends, the people Colin had grown up with, had said anything, but the newcomers had told him. Everywhere he went, someone told him of Gemma and Tris.

"Their heads were together over chocolate," one man said. "Now there's a man who knows how to win a girl's heart."

At the grocery, Colin was meant to overhear a nurse say that Tris was staying at home that night alone—with Gemma. "I'm not sure," the nurse said loudly, "but I think it's the beginning of a real love affair."

"Nobody deserves it more than Dr. Tris," the other woman answered even louder. "It's about time he settled down and had a family."

Colin almost stepped in and told them that she belonged to him, not Tris, but his lifelong habit of keeping his personal life to himself overruled him.

It was Mr. Lang who told him that Tris drove Gemma home after what Lang called a "date."

"It wasn't a date," Colin snapped at the old man. "And what were you doing out there anyway?"

Mr. Lang shrugged and looked around Colin's office. He gave out less information about himself than any Frazier did. He looked back at Colin. "If you like her, you better work to keep her."

"Let's leave my life out of this. You see or hear anything about the robberies?"

"No," Mr. Lang said, and Colin knew the old man was not going to say anything more.

Colin had hated the idea of telling Gemma that they shouldn't see each other for a while, but his only concern was for her safety. And he wasn't going to tell her that her suspicions about Jean were at the center of his thoughts. He could easily believe that Jean would come up with some scheme for revenge. He'd seen her do some nasty things to people in her office when they did something like try to steal a case from her. And she'd been *very* angry that day in his apartment when he finalized their breakup.

But Jean aside, Colin didn't understand why Gemma didn't see that he was thinking only of her. From the way she'd talked, you'd think she thought Colin *wanted* to spend time with Jean. It was almost as though Gemma thought Colin was glad this was happening so he could get back with Jean.

And then there was all that had come up about his friend Tris. If anyone had asked, Colin would have said that he wasn't in the least bit jealous, so he was shocked by what had come out of his mouth. It was as though every word anyone had said about Gemma and Tris was screaming in his head.

Colin was sure it was all untrue. Wasn't it? In the next second, he had his cell phone out and was calling Tris.

"Is there anything between you and Gemma?" Colin blurted out as soon as Tris answered. Even to himself he sounded belligerent and ready to start a fight.

"What's this about?" Tris asked.

"I want an answer to my question."

Tris hesitated. "Is this rhetorical or do you want an honest answer?"

Colin was silent.

"Okay, I'll tell you the truth," Tris said. "There's nothing between Gemma and me except friendship, but that's not for lack of trying on my part."

What he was saying didn't give Colin any peace. "Why did you drive Gemma home? Did you get her drunk?"

"You know, if you and I weren't friends I'd deck you for that one. I have to go. Don't talk to me again until you're human."

"And you stay away from Gemma!"

"Colin, I mean this, if you two break up, I'm going after her." Tris hung up.

24

GEMMA BURIED HERSELF in work for an entire week. Twice she drove to a grocery in Williamsburg. She didn't want to face Ellie and all the questions about where Colin was. Or worse, have to endure looks of pity because she'd been dumped by a man the town loved.

During the week, she read constantly and made copious notes about the Fraziers' ancestors. The family made their usual visits and were always pleasant and thoughtful. Shamus spent hours sitting with her, and she found that when he wanted to talk, he did. He brought a four-inch stack of college brochures and showed them to her and asked her opinion of where he should go to school.

Gemma had three friends who taught at some of the schools, so she called and asked questions. They were able to eliminate four of the schools as unsuitable for Shamus.

When he left, he kissed her on the cheek and said, "Welcome to the family."

When she'd been hired, she'd never expected to become part of the family. She hadn't thought about it much, but she'd assumed that she'd meet some people in town, maybe even a man, and that would be her social life. Involvement with the Frazier family had not been part of her imaginings. But she'd been drawn in by them and now she couldn't imagine life without them.

Since she had no training partner, she didn't work out once, and she was sure her muscles were turning to Jell-O.

Joce e-mailed her to yet again say thanks for giving her a day of peace. Curious, Gemma wrote back and asked if she'd told anyone about the day they'd spent together. Joce wrote back,

> ARE YOU KIDDING? I TOLD EVERYONE IN TOWN WHAT A KIND AND GENEROUS PERSON YOU ARE.

Gemma looked at the screen and grimaced. "Everyone" meant that by now Colin knew she'd spent the day with Joce, changing diapers and scrubbing the kitchen sink, and not with Tris as he'd accused her. But he'd not apologized.

For two days Gemma carried her phone with her everywhere she went and imagined telling Colin she might forgive him if he swore to never again be jealous. But he didn't call.

At 7 P.M. every evening, she threw up. For a solid hour, she fought nausea, and she learned to just lie down and be quiet until it subsided.

It was nearly a week after Colin had made his accusations that Gemma woke up and said, "Enough!" She'd had all she could take of being miserable. She knew that what she needed to do was to take charge of her own life. She wasn't going to waste any more of her time waiting for some man to rescue her.

She went to the desk in the library and began to make a list of what she needed to do. The most important thing was that she *was* pregnant. Like it or not, together with the father or not, that was the way it was, and she needed to make plans.

She knew that what Tris had said about the Frazier family helping her financially was right. She would never consider living off of them, but help would be appreciated.

A big part of her wanted to run from Edilean and never look back, but she wasn't naive enough to think that she could raise a child absolutely alone. She thought about going to her mother, but she'd be embarrassed by her daughter being an unwed mother. No child deserved that.

No, it was better to stay in Edilean, where her child would have adoring grandparents, and where Gemma had met people who were becoming her friends.

The first thing Gemma needed was a real job, one that paid more than twenty-five grand a year. To get that, she needed to write her dissertation and get her Ph.D.

It took her less than an hour to compose a letter to her adviser. She listed six topics as possible subject matter for her dissertation, and asked for approval for one of them so she could get started.

Her best proposal was to write about women in medicine in the 1840s in rural Virginia. Tris had told her that his family had an enormous number of family documents that she was welcome to see. Historically, the Aldredges had been mostly doctors, and Gemma had found some really interesting information about them in the Frazier papers. The first doctor in their family was a Matthew Aldredge, and he sewed his own scalp back together. She thought that would be a dramatic beginning to her paper.

After she sent that letter off, she wrote four more to professors, asking if they knew anyone at William and Mary College who she could talk to about a possible teaching position there.

The only thing she didn't know how to solve was Colin. She feared that when she saw him again she might come apart, but she vowed that she wouldn't. They'd had a brief affair, it was over now, and she needed to—she hated the phrase, but it was appropriate—move on with her life.

By the weekend, she felt better. She got up early and drove into Williamsburg to find a gym. Using the key Mike had given her to his gym and risking running into Colin was more than she could take. She spent thirty minutes on a bike, forty-five with light weights, then put on her gloves and hit a bag for twenty minutes. She was a little worried about kicking, considering what was growing inside her, so she skipped that.

She showered at the gym, put on clean clothes, and for the first time in days felt good.

The next task she set for herself was to face Edilean and its pity. She wasn't ready to see Ellie and have to answer questions, so she parked downtown and went to the square. She'd seen a shop there that had held no interest for her, but it did now.

It was an elegant little boutique called Yesterday and it was on the other side of the square from Colin's office. When Gemma opened the door, an old-fashioned bell jangled. All the fixtures in the store, the wall shelves and the big glass case at the end, were old, taken from buildings of an earlier era. The mahogany woodwork was suitable because it held the prettiest, most old-fashioned baby clothes Gemma had ever seen. They were of the softest cotton, with what looked to be hand embroidery on them.

Behind the counter was a tall, delicately pretty woman, probably in her forties. Smiling, she came to the front. "You're a friend of Mrs. Newland, aren't you?"

Gemma had to think about who that was. "Sara," she said. "Yes, I am a friend of hers." Just the thought made Gemma stand up straighter. To belong, she thought. That's what she'd wanted and what she was getting.

"Dear Sara," the woman said. "She's one of my best customers. In fact, she called and ordered a matching outfit for each one of the many sets she'd already bought. I'm Olivia Wingate and how may I help you?"

Gemma almost blurted out that she was going to have a baby, but she couldn't allow herself that pleasure. Instead, she gave the first lie she could think of. "My sister is expecting her third child and I'd like to get her something different than the usual clothes."

"You have come to the right place. How much do you know about heirloom sewing?"

"Nothing whatever."

"Would you like to just choose an outfit, or do you want to learn about how it was made?"

"*Learn* is my favorite word in any language," Gemma said and put her handbag on the glass counter. "I'm all ears."

An hour later she left the shop with three breathtakingly beautiful baby outfits, each one wrapped in tissue paper, and carefully slipped inside a lavender-colored bag with YESTERDAY printed in blue. Her mind was full of new words, such as entredeux, wing-needle, pintucking, and bullion roses, but most of all, the idea that she really and truly *was* going to have a baby was finally sinking in.

For the first time, she thought of the prospect not as a burden and of work that had to be done, but as a joy. She very much liked her nieces, and she'd enjoyed playing with Joce's children and they were beginning to know her. And Gemma looked forward to seeing Sara's new babies.

At the thought of Sara's newborns, Gemma realized she should get Sara a gift, and she knew just what she wanted. She'd seen two blue shorts sets, perfect for little boys. Mike would probably like a couple of T-shirts with the Ringside logo on them, but there were too many female hormones raging inside Gemma to consider that.

As she turned back toward the shop, she came face-to-face with Colin. Her first reaction was to smile. She'd missed him very much and she so wanted to share her news about the baby.

In the next second, his accusations rang in her head, and her smile faded.

"Gemma . . ." he said, reaching out his hand to her.

She stepped back and made herself smile. "How are you?" she asked as brightly as she could manage. "Beautiful day, isn't it?"

"Gemma, could we go somewhere and talk about things?"

If he'd said this to her a few days before, she would have said yes, but not now. "I have so many errands to run and I need to get back to the guesthouse. We'll have to talk some other time." She turned toward her car.

"Did you hear what happened to Mike?" he asked.

She didn't want to look back, but she couldn't

stop herself. Me and my curiosity! she thought. "What about him?"

The seriousness left Colin and he smiled at her. "I only tell gossip over food."

"I'm not hungry," Gemma said and took a step to the curb.

"If you didn't hear about Mike, then I guess Joce didn't tell you about Luke. Oh! But that's right, only a few of us know. It looks like your Heartwishes Stone is working."

"Damn!" she said aloud as she looked back at him. Curiosity was an addiction, like a drug. She *had* to know what he was talking about. "Where?" she asked, her teeth clamped together.

She hated his knowing little smile as he led her to a sandwich and smoothie shop around the corner.

"What can I get for you, sheriff?" asked the pretty young woman behind the counter.

"The usual, Jillian, and Gemma will have whatever you can make with lots of raspberries in it."

"I'll take the mango drink," she said. "I've given up raspberries. Forever," she added.

He led her to the back of the shop. As with many stores in Edilean, this one was quite narrow but extended back for the full block. There were no other customers, so they were alone as they sat down in a small booth.

"How have you been?" Colin asked.

"Great," she said. "And you?"

"Missing you," he said softly as he reached out to

take her hand, but she moved it away. "Gemma, there are things I can't tell you, but I—"

"In that case, I have work to do," she said as she started out of the booth.

The young woman came with their drinks, blocking Gemma's exit. "Is everything all right?" she asked.

Gemma knew that whatever she said in front of the girl would soon be all over Edilean. "Everything is just fine." She sat back down.

The girl put the drinks on the table and left.

"All right," Colin said with a sigh. "Let's leave things as they are. There was another robbery."

"Oh?" she said and wanted to ask questions, but didn't. She gave her attention to her drink.

Colin lowered his voice. "We've kept this one from the town, but it's the same MO. There was a ten-year-old girl living there, and a sprig of willow tied with a pink silk ribbon was left behind." He paused. "Gemma, I can't thank you enough for spotting that in the photos. It was because of you that I knew what to look for in this new robbery."

She kept looking at her drink and didn't meet his eyes. "Tell me about Luke and Mike."

"Oh yeah," Colin said. "I guess you heard about Sara having twins, just what she wished for."

"Of course. Joce told me and so did Tris."

As she said the name, she watched him, and saw the hurt in his eyes. It looked as though he really did believe there was something between her and Dr. Tris.

Yeah, she thought. Prenatal vitamins. "I was just in that little shop Yesterday, buying baby clothes for my sister, and I realized I'd forgotten about Sara. Think she'd like some little blue rompers for her boys?"

"She'd love them," Colin said, "and it's nice of you to think of her. She—"

"And then there's Joce. It's a little late, but I thought I might get her babies something. In fact . . ." She reached into her shopping bag and withdrew one of the outfits she'd bought and spread it out on top of the tissue paper on the table. She'd been told it was a day gown, suitable for a boy or girl, made of Swiss batiste, and trimmed with tiny, hand-embroidered honeybees.

"Isn't it pretty?" Gemma said.

Colin touched the hem of it. "Very nice. Mrs. Wingate has lots of these things. She lives out near Tris and—" The mention of the name made Colin stop talking—and she realized that no matter how unhappy she was, he was worse. Maybe that should have cheered her up, but it didn't.

Gemma put the gown back in the paper and into the bag, then took a deep drink of her smoothie. "I really need to go. I'm setting up interviews at some universities and I need to find out about them. As soon as I get approval on my subject matter, I'm going to be working on my dissertation in the evenings."

Colin watched her gather her bags. "Wait! I haven't told you about Luke and Mike."

"That's all right. I'll get Joce to tell me, or I'll call Sara. Anyway, I need to get Sara's Florida address so I can send her my gift."

"They're moving back here."

"How wonderful!" Gemma said as she stood up. "It was so nice talking to you." With a smile, she left and hurried around the corner to enter the heirloom sewing shop.

"Did you forget something?" Mrs. Wingate asked as soon as Gemma was inside.

To Gemma's absolute horror, she burst into tears.

"Oh, my goodness," Mrs. Wingate said as she hurried forward and helped Gemma to a chair. She took her bags from her and gave her a tissue from a box on the counter.

"I don't usually cry," Gemma said, "but lately I haven't been able to stop."

"Excessive hormones will do that," Mrs. Wingate said.

"I don't have—" Gemma began but glanced at the woman. "How did you know?"

"I opened this shop right after my husband passed away, and you can't imagine all that I've seen. So many young women come in here pretending to be looking for a gift for a relative, but they've really just found out about the baby they're carrying, and they want someone to talk to."

"What do you do with them?"

"First, I listen, then I send them to an Aldredge. Is young Tristan . . . ?"

"The father?" Gemma asked. "No."

"Ahhh," Mrs. Wingate said. "Have you told our sheriff yet?"

"Hell will freeze over before I—" Gemma took a breath. "I mean, no I haven't. We had an argument and he . . ." She shrugged.

"I understand," Mrs. Wingate said, "and you can rest assured that I'll tell no one. Although, dear, you do know that you can't hide the coming event for too long."

"Especially since twins seem to infest this town."

Mrs. Wingate smiled. "They do, don't they? In fact, just this morning one of the women who sews for me finished some outfits for twin boys. I have a feeling that dear Sara's good fortune will send several people to my shop to purchase gifts for her."

Gemma gave a sniff and smiled back. "It was good business of you to think of that."

"I have to think ahead. I'm trying to survive in a world of mass production. Now, come with me and I'll show you some different items."

"Do you have a restroom?"

"I have to have one when so many *enceinte* ladies like yourself visit me. Right through there."

Gemma smiled at the use of the French word. Her grandmother thought *pregnant* was a vulgar word and that no one with a respectable upbringing would use it.

When Gemma returned, Mrs. Wingate had spread some of the prettiest clothes she'd ever seen across the counter, and she got another lesson, this one in storybook smocking. When Gemma said that Mike would like some martial arts guys on his son's play suits, Mrs. Wingate opened a laptop, logged on, and Gemma chose some photos that Mrs. Wingate said were suitable.

"I'll have two outfits ready by the end of the week," she said. "Why don't you come back then and we'll talk about . . . everything?"

When Gemma left the shop she felt much better, so good in fact that she'd added a fourth outfit for the baby she was going to have. Mrs. Wingate was certainly an excellent saleswoman!

As soon as Gemma got to her computer, she e-mailed Joce and asked what was going on with Mike and Luke. Joce wrote back,

> SORRY I DIDN'T TELL YOU, BUT IT'S BEEN CHAOS AROUND HERE. LUKE HAD AN OFFER OF A MOVIE DEAL. BRAD PITT WANTS TO PLAY THOMAS CANON. AND I CAN'T BELIEVE NO ONE TOLD YOU ABOUT MIKE. HE WAS IN A RESTAURANT IN FORT LAUDERDALE AND RECOGNIZED SOME GUY WHO WAS WANTED FOR THE MURDER OF FOUR YOUNG WOMEN. MIKE BROUGHT HIM IN AND THEY FOUND ANOTHER WOMAN TIED UP

IN THE CREEP'S HOUSE. MIKE SAVED HER LIFE! AS A REWARD, HE'S BEING ALLOWED TO TAKE EARLY RETIREMENT WITH A FULL PENSION. HE AND SARA AND THE BOYS WILL BE MOVING BACK HERE PERMANENTLY AT THE END OF THE SUMMER.

Gemma slumped back against the chair. It seemed that yet more of the wishes had been given. If Luke's movie was a hit, it could give him the immortality he'd asked for. And Mike had brought a "truly evil" person to justice—just as he'd wanted to do. She e-mailed Tris about everything, from her 7 P.M. morning sickness to all the wishes that were being granted.

That night as she was getting ready for bed, she glanced at the silver compact in her makeup basket. She opened it and looked at the pretty little necklace. On impulse, she said, "I don't think you're magic but if you are, would you please make Colin come back into my life?"

When the necklace did nothing—not that she had actually expected it to—she closed the case and went to bed.

25

"TELL HER."

The words were so loud that Colin jolted awake. He'd fallen asleep in the big leather chair he'd bought with Gemma, and when the words were shouted, his feet came down, which made the chair spring forward. He was almost catapulted across the room.

He'd been so hard asleep that at first he didn't know where he was. Papers had fallen off his lap and were now an inch deep on the floor. He looked around the room almost as though he expected to see someone there, but he knew he must have been dreaming.

"Tell who what?" he murmured as he got out of the chair. It was raining hard outside, but the words in his head drowned out all other sounds. "Tell her. Tell her. Tell her." Over and over.

A crack of thunder immediately followed by a

flash of lightning almost made him reach for his gun at his belt. Last night he hadn't bothered to undress. He'd had a sandwich and a beer, then settled down in the chair to yet again go over the files about Adrian Caldwell, aka John Caulfied, aka . . . The list was endless, but whatever name the man used, he was Jean's criminal uncle.

In the last few days he'd talked to her often about the case. It hadn't been easy, but he saw to it that they never mentioned anything personal, just kept to the facts about her uncle. Colin had gone to her apartment in Richmond, and twice she'd come to his office in Edilean.

As Jean told him of her relationship with her notorious uncle, Colin had been shocked that he'd known nothing about the man. Colin had lived with Jean for years and would have said that he knew everything about her, but in the last few days he'd realized that he knew next to nothing about her.

Jean told him of her childhood and how her uncle used to sneak into her bedroom in spite of an alarm system and the iron bars her mother had put on the windows. "When I asked how he got in, he laughed and said that if we could get out, he could get in," Jean said.

She told of the two times her uncle had cleaned out her mother's bank accounts. "Mom didn't recover from the last time," Jean said bitterly. "And now, no matter how many safeguards the bank puts on her money, she still worries." She looked at Colin. "Didn't you ever wonder why I have my assets in four banks and why I deal with three brokers?"

Colin was too embarrassed to say that he didn't know that she did. But then, he'd been the one to pay the bills. Some male code of honor had kept him from inquiring into Jean's finances.

She told him how she and her uncle had made up while she was in law school. "I thought that if he knew more about my mother and me, if he saw us as people, it would keep him from stealing from us."

"But it didn't work," Colin said.

"No. Not at all. I think it made him feel that we owed him for *not* doing bad to us." She told how her mother had nearly had a mental breakdown after the second time. "When I met you I was still supporting Mom, and paying off her debts. I was doing all I could to make her feel safe. I don't know how we would have survived if you hadn't helped with my bills."

With every word she spoke, Colin was more shocked at how little he'd actually known about Jean. She'd kept her secrets to herself, never telling him about her past life or her current one.

But then all he'd thought about back then was how much he hated his job of trying to sell cars. He hadn't been aware of what Jean was going through. No wonder she was always ready to have a fight with him and relieve the tension she was under.

And Colin had never seen that she was hiding horrific things, that she was under major stress, and that she always lived in fear of it happening again.

But now he was trying to make up for his past oversights. He listened carefully and watched her face and body movements, and what he saw now was that she was holding something back. With every question she answered, he had a feeling that she was hiding something. He didn't think she was outright lying, but she was certainly being evasive.

It was his guess that Jean knew where her uncle was and had been in contact with him recently. And the more Jean talked, the more her secrecy made him fear for Gemma. During the last week, Jean had made several remarks about Colin's new girlfriend, even saying that he'd dumped her for a "younger model." The words, and her tone, had made the hairs on Colin's neck stand on edge. All he could think was that he had been right to protect Gemma at all costs.

But knowing he was right hadn't helped when he'd seen Gemma in Edilean. She'd been so cool to him, smiling, showing him baby clothes. He'd missed her so very much, but she didn't seem to have given their separation a thought.

Of course he'd found out that Gemma hadn't spent a whole day with Tris. Colin knew he should have called her to apologize for accusing her of that, but an apology would have defeated the whole purpose of the separation. Right now it was better that he and Gemma were apart—and that Jean thought they wouldn't get back together.

As for Gemma, the less she knew, the better.

But last night things had changed. Colin had been going through the paperwork of the case, and rereading transcripts of his recorded interviews with Jean. Yet again he was marveling that he'd lived with her but had known so little of the truth of her life. With a jolt he realized that he was doing the same thing to Gemma that Jean had done to him.

Since he'd been a child, Colin had had the Frazier creed that their family was different, separate from the other people, drilled into his head. His father had never spoken of it, but Colin's paternal grandfather had talked of little else.

"We're not like them; we're not the same as them," his grandfather used to say, meaning the people of Edilean.

"Why?" Colin would ask.

His grandfather had no real answer. "It's always been that way and always will be," the old man said. "Just remember to keep family business to yourself."

Last night Colin had wondered if things could have been different between Jean and him if he hadn't obeyed his grandfather so completely. What would have happened if he'd sat down with her and told the truth about how much he hated his job? How much he wanted to move back to Edilean and figure out a way to become the sheriff?

"We would have broken up years before," he said aloud. Uncle or no, Jean deeply and truly hated the little town.

"Everyone there knows what I'm doing," she used

to say. "You have that creepy little man, Brewster Lang, skulking about. You remember that day when I forgot to lock my car? When I came out of the store, he had opened the door and was looking inside my car!"

"He didn't know who you were," Colin had said, defending the man who'd helped him on so many cases. Mr. Lang could spend an hour in town and hear more than all the gossips combined would know. Better yet, his information would be based on fact. That Colin had long ago decided not to delve too deeply into Lang's methods of finding out things was something Colin didn't want to look at too closely.

Last year, Lang had helped him find out the truth about the man Sara was planning to marry. Colin's plan had been to present her with facts and do all he could to prevent the marriage. But Mike, who became her husband, stepped in before Colin had all the data he needed.

Another roar of thunder then lightning that made the lights flicker brought Colin back to the present. He glanced at the wall clock and saw that it was just after 2 A.M. The words "tell her" were still echoing in his head.

He needed to go to bed and in the morning he'd go to Gemma and tell her the truth about . . . about . . . "I'll tell her how I feel about her," he said as he turned toward his bedroom. *Our* bedroom, he couldn't help thinking.

He hadn't reached the doorway when his cell

phone and his landline went off simultaneously—and Colin's heart nearly stopped. Only an emergency from home would set both phones ringing at this hour.

He answered them both at once, one at each ear. "What's happened?"

His mother was on his cell, his father on the landline.

"Shamus didn't come home last night," his mother said, her voice nearly in tears. "Rachel called me." His mother was in California with her daughter, Ariel.

"Your little brother stayed out all night and told nobody where he was going," his father said. He was at the company apartment in Richmond, where he always stayed when a dealership was conducting a big sale. "I hope that boy is with a girl."

"Is that your father I hear?" Mrs. Frazier asked.

"Yeah, Mom, he's on the other phone."

"Peregrine!" Mrs. Frazier shouted. "You went off and left our son *alone*!"

Colin put the two phones together.

"It's not like he needs a babysitter," Mr. Frazier said. "Nobody's gonna pick him up and put him in the trunk of a car. He barely fits in the back of a three-quarter-ton pickup."

"Always making jokes, aren't you?" Mrs. Frazier said. "My youngest son is lost because you ran off and left him to fend for himself. He's probably starving."

"Rachel will—"

"Don't you start on that again! Rachel and Pere

are falling in love. Everyone but you saw it. I came here to California just to give them some privacy."

"Ha! You went there to nag poor Ariel into getting pregnant."

"I did no such—"

Colin put his cell down on the coffee table and laid the handset to the landline on top so they could yell at each other. He took a shower, put on clean jeans and a shirt, and when he returned, his parents were still arguing.

"If you'd leave that girl alone, maybe she'd find time to get pregnant," Mr. Frazier was saying. "Frank wants kids, so that's half of the battle."

"Since when does what a man want have anything to do with babies? I'm the one who had to carry your children. Did you forget that Colin weighed ten pounds and two ounces when he was born?"

Colin rolled his eyes. He'd been told that once a week during his childhood. He picked up the phones. "I have to go look for my itty-bitty, helpless baby brother and I need my cell. Go to bed, both of you." He clicked both phones off at the same time and put his mobile in the leather pouch on his belt, right beside his gun.

He went out to the garage, got in his Jeep, and opened the big overhead door. When he saw the storm outside, he was glad he had his new house. In the last years at his apartment, he'd had to park on the street. At his parents' house, his dad saw every garage as a place to store his cars, either the antiques or the ones he'd paid so much for that he wouldn't allow anyone to drive them. The cars the family used—which were changed for new models every year—sat in the driveway in the rain, sun, and snow.

"At least Gemma has a carport," he said aloud, and he liked thinking of her warm and snug in her bed.

He had an idea where Shamus was. Colin didn't think any of his family knew how much time the boy spent at Gemma's place. Shamus would walk there, not driving a utility vehicle, which he said was like putting up a neon sign telling where he was.

One afternoon Colin had seen Shamus give a single tap on Gemma's door, then open it. Obviously, his visits were so familiar that he didn't need to wait for her to let him in. Two hours later, Colin had parked nearby, meaning to go in to see Gemma, but he stopped a few feet outside and looked in. Shamus was on the couch, his big body bent over a drawing pad, his feet on the coffee table beside an empty plate and glass.

Gemma was sprawled on big cushions on the floor with neat stacks of papers around her, her beloved colored pens in a row by her ankle.

It was then that Colin realized that he loved her, and that maybe he had since he'd first seen her. He suspected that at first his attraction to her had to do with her fitting an image of how he'd always seen his future. But whatever the reason, from the first moment, he'd wanted to be with her. Never in his life had he felt more comfortable with anyone than he did with Gemma. He never felt in competition with her, as he had with Jean. With Gemma, he'd never felt anything but a deep sense of belonging, of being where he was supposed to be when it was time—and that feeling went all the way down into his very bones.

As he drove, the wipers on as fast as they'd go, Colin knew that he'd made a mistake with Gemma in not trusting her and in letting his jealousy show. Colin wondered if on some unconscious level he'd always known that Jean was concealing part of herself from him and that's why he'd done the same to her. Maybe he'd realized that to show vulnerability to someone as aggressive as Jean would be like a gladiator admitting fear.

But Gemma was different. Gemma was *real.*

Colin pulled into the drive, and when he saw her Volvo under the carport, he gave a sigh of relief. He knew that for the second time in his life he was going to have to bare his soul to another human being. The first time had been when he'd told Gemma what Jean had said to him on that horrible day in his apartment. He'd survived that time of revelation. And now he knew that if he wanted Gemma—and he did—then he was going to have to "tell her" everything, including the truth about how he felt about her. What was it Mr. Lang had said? "If you like her, you better work to keep her." The old man was right.

When Colin knocked on her door and Gemma

didn't answer, it was as though his heart jumped into his throat. Had his ruse failed and Jean's uncle taken her? Or was she with Tris? Had Colin's stupidity driven her to another man?

He had to work to calm himself down. When he turned the door lever and it opened, fear began to go through him. He hoped she was asleep in her bed and hadn't heard his knock over the storm. But if she was, he was going to remind her that he'd specifically told her that she had to keep her door locked at all times.

But her bed was empty. It had been slept in, but there was no one in it now. He looked about the place with a lawman's eye, but he saw no signs of struggle. Her pajamas had been tossed on the unmade bed, so it looked as though she'd dressed before she went out. But her car was here, and he'd never seen Gemma drive a utility vehicle, even though Lanny had said he'd made one available to her, so where was she?

"She's with Shamus," Colin said aloud as he went outside and got in his car. He drove over the winding gravel paths that ran through the Frazier land until he came to the big warehouse at the back in record time. The rain was coming down so hard that he couldn't see but a few feet in front of him, but he knew the way. The long, low building was at the very back of his father's property, and next to it were the acres of state-owned land of the wilderness preserve. The warehouse stored some of their family's oldest artifacts, including the yellow carriage that Colin thought should be in a museum. But when any of his sons said that, Peregrine Frazier said that the family kept what was theirs.

When Colin pulled up to the front door, he saw a light seeping out from under it. There were no windows in the building, and there were several security devices. Shamus knew all the codes—none of which would hinder Jean's uncle, Colin thought.

He parked up against the porch so he wouldn't have to fight the rain. When he saw that it was unlocked and the alarm was turned off, just to be on the safe side, he withdrew his firearm from the holster, held it at arm's length and went inside, quietly closing the door behind him.

26

SHAMUS," GEMMA SAID, her voice heavy with sleep. "Why don't you do this tomorrow?"

He was sitting in the back of a big Conestoga wagon and sketching the little yellow carriage, which was a few feet away. "I couldn't sleep," he said, without looking up. "But you should go to bed."

"I can't leave you here alone. Your family is worried about you." She was sitting behind him in the wagon bed on a big piece of canvas.

"They're mad at Colin, not me."

"I know," Gemma said. "So am I. But the good news is that he's absolutely miserable." A noise made her look to the left to see Colin standing there and putting his gun back in the holster. "Speak of the devil . . . So, sheriff, what brings you out on this lovely morning?"

"My little brother. You're causing a fury."

Shamus glared at his brother. "Why have you been with Jean these last days?"

Colin glanced at Gemma. It looked like she hadn't told anyone about Jean's uncle. But then she wouldn't after he'd bawled her out for telling Tris too much.

Colin hoisted himself up onto the end of the wagon, beside Shamus, but a few feet from Gemma. The rain outside made it loud in the warehouse, and in spite of all the many overhead lights, the forms of the old wagons and carriages, all made by past Fraziers, created a ghostly air in the big, hollow building. Shamus loved it; Colin never had. He took a breath as he prepared to tell his brother the truth. "All the years I knew Jean, she was lying to me. She said she had no aunts, uncles, or cousins."

"That proves she's not from Edilean," Gemma said.

Shamus snorted.

"Her loss," Colin said. "Jean's late father has a brother who is an internationally notorious thief. He breaks into places like the U.S. Consulate in Romania and takes things."

"Like what?" Gemma had heard all this before, but her curiosity was taking over.

"Whatever anyone pays him to get. The man has no conscience, no morals. I got Jean to tell me the truth about her life, and the bastard's cleaned out her mother's accounts twice. He's either filthy rich or destitute."

"Did Jean tell you where he is?" Gemma asked.

"She says she hasn't seen him in years."

"You haven't found out that she lies all the time?" Shamus asked. He had his back to both of them and was still sketching.

"Yeah, I know that now," Colin said. "She certainly didn't tell me about her uncle."

"What does she lie about?" Gemma asked Shamus.

"She's not faithful to Colin," the young man said. "Never has been." There was anger in his voice.

"I know," Colin said softly to his brother. "I've found out more than I ever wanted to." When he looked at Gemma, there was longing in his eyes.

Turning, Shamus glanced at Gemma in question and she knew what he was asking. She shook her head. No, she hadn't told Colin about the baby and didn't want to do it now. "So you're saying that Jean kept secrets from you?" she asked with as much innocence as she could muster.

"Yeah," Colin said. "Just as I did to you."

Shamus gave a little guffaw of laughter. "Gemma's smarter than you are."

Colin grinned. "That wouldn't be too difficult." Thunder rolled around outside. "I really hate to break up this party, but I think we should all go home to bed. And you, little brother, are going to call our parents and tell them you're okay."

Shamus didn't move. "You made Gemma cry."

"I know," Colin said, "and I regret it. I thought

it would be better if Jean's uncle heard that I'd broken up with Gemma. I was afraid . . . am still afraid that . . ." For a moment he looked at her and his eyes held hers. All that he felt—and feared—was there for her to see. "I won't do it again," he said, and there was promise in his voice.

Shamus flipped his drawing pad closed and got off the wagon.

Colin followed, and they stood at the end, both of them lifting their arms up to Gemma to help her down. She went to Shamus and he swung her down to stand beside him on the side away from Colin.

"How long will it be before you forgive me?" Colin asked.

"I have no idea," Gemma said. "Tris and I will talk about it."

When Colin groaned, Shamus grinned. "She should never let you off the hook," he said.

Colin took a breath. "I'll work hard to make that statement untrue," he said, looking at Gemma, then he lifted his head. "Little brother, I'm taking you home and after I make sure you call Mom and Dad and tell them you're sorry for worrying them, I'm taking Gemma to my house and I'm going to start begging. Pleading. Whatever I have to do to get her to forgive me."

Shamus nodded. "You should listen to her. She has a lot to tell you."

"And I want to hear every word," Colin said.

Gemma didn't dare look at Shamus for fear that

her face would give away her secret. Whereas Colin was talking about one thing, she was sure Shamus was referring to the baby. As Gemma kept her eyes on Colin, she knew she wasn't going to easily get over her hurt. The things he'd said about her and Tris still rang in her head. There needed to be some big changes between them.

As for Gemma, she was going to have to give up some of her own independence. They needed to become a team, not two individuals who came together when their paths happened to cross.

Shamus and Colin were watching her, waiting for her reply.

Her eyes were on Colin's. "I think we need to do a great deal of talking."

"I agree," he said, and they left the warehouse.

27

Colin was waiting for Gemma when she pulled into the carport of the guesthouse. As soon as they were inside, he turned to her.

"I made mistakes," he said. "I should have explained about Jean from the beginning. And I should have told her about you the day after I met you. I shouldn't have been jealous of you and Tristan. I shouldn't—"

He broke off because Gemma reached up and put her fingertips over his lips. "If it's going to work between us, I need to know what's going on. I need to know where I stand. I can't take spending a glorious day with you then the next knowing you're with Jean. I really need to know what I am to you."

Colin put his hand on the side of her face. "I love you," he said softly. "It's taken me a while to realize it, but I love you."

The pain of Colin's accusations was too fresh for

Gemma to say the words back to him. Maybe it was because of her love of research, but she needed to hear facts. "I want to know what you've been doing. The town knows you've been with Jean, and I'm tired of the looks of pity."

"Fair enough," he said and they sat down on the couch together. Colin began the long story of everything he'd found out on his trip to D.C. and what he'd managed to get from Jean.

"I still don't know what the man is after," Colin said, "and Jean says she doesn't know."

The sun came up and they were still talking.

"You won't leave me out again?" Gemma asked.

"Never," Colin said as he kissed her.

They made love, sweetly and gently, and Colin told her how the thought of losing her had nearly driven him insane. "I've never felt this way before," he said. "All I can think of is that I want to talk to you, be with you. I've spent my life alone. Even when I'm with my family and through all the years I was with Jean, I felt that I was alone. But when I'm with you . . ."

"I know," she whispered, her head on his bare chest. "I feel the same way. I love you, Colin. I think I have since I saw you standing in the doorway. I don't know what I would have done if your mother hadn't given me the job."

"I would have gone after you."

She raised her head to look at him. "And leave your beloved Edilean? Ha!"

He stroked her hair and looked her in the eyes.

"If you don't find a job here or you don't like this town, I'll go anywhere in the world you want to live."

She put her head down, smiling. This is what she'd wanted. She needed him to love *her* before she told him of their child she was carrying. She didn't want to go through life wondering if he was with her because he'd felt honor bound to stay with her.

"I need to tell you something," she said as she ran her hand over his bare chest.

He kissed her fingertips. "Anything."

"I—" She broke off because his cell phone rang, but Colin didn't reach for it. "Shouldn't you answer that? It might be important."

"I'd rather hear what you have to say."

"It'll hold," she said as the phone kept ringing.

Colin bent over the side of the bed and rummaged in his trousers to retrieve his cell phone. "It's Roy." He clicked the button to hear her, listened, and said he'd be right there.

"It's one of the newcomers. Their fifteen-year-old daughter isn't in her bed."

"Go!" Gemma said, pulling the sheet around her as she sat up. "Right now. Go find the child."

"You and I . . ."

"Can wait," she said as she reached out and put her hand on his shoulder.

He kissed the palm. "Do you know that I love you?" he asked softly.

"I think I realized it when I saw how unhappy you were in that sandwich shop."

He was still holding her hand. "And you?"

"Yes," she said simply. "I do love you."

"Me too," he said as he bent to kiss her.

But Gemma pulled away. "We still need to talk about Tris and every other man in my life, in the future and the present. I don't like jealousy."

"It's a new emotion to me. Never felt it before," he said.

"Not even with Jean?"

"Most certainly not," Colin said. He started to kiss her, but his phone went off again, this time with a ring that sounded like blaring trumpets.

Gemma drew back from him.

He looked at his phone. "It's Roy again and she's already there. I better go." He pulled her to him. "Gemma, I love you. You're what I've wanted in a woman for as long as I can remember. Will you think I'm crazy if I say that I feel that I've been waiting for you?"

"No," she whispered, so very glad to yet again be in his arms. "I know exactly what you mean."

"I think I needed Jean to . . . to occupy myself until you showed up." He kissed her forehead. "I wished for True Love and I found it." Again his phone went off, this time with car horns blowing. "It's Dad."

"You must go," she said. "We can talk more later."

He kissed her with all the longing he felt. "I love you. Don't forget that."

"I won't," she said, then he got into his Jeep and left.

Gemma watched him drive away, then locked the door behind her. When she was in school, she'd often stayed up all night to study. But now that she was pregnant, she seemed to need twelve hours a night. Earlier, she'd only just fallen asleep when Mrs. Frazier rang her to ask if she knew where Shamus was. Gemma had checked to make sure the boy wasn't sleeping on her couch, then told Mrs. Frazier that she didn't know where he was.

Gemma had tried to go back to sleep, but between the noise of the storm and worry, she couldn't. After about an hour she gave up, got dressed, and used one of the little trucks that always seemed to be nearby and drove to the big warehouse at the back of the property. She hadn't been surprised to see young Shamus inside, drawing the carriages his ancestors had made.

It was just minutes later that Colin showed up. So now it was hours later, and all she could think about was sleep. Ah, pregnancy, she thought as she fell across her bed and was asleep instantly.

When she awoke it was 6 P.M. She'd slept the entire day away! Groggily, she got up and picked up her phone. She had four e-mails and six text messages. Her adviser had approved her topic of women in medicine in Virginia in 1840, and a professor knew some people at William and Mary.

"Good," Gemma said, smiling as she went into the kitchen. She wanted to eat everything that was in it.

Four of the texts were from Colin. The missing teenager had been found with her boyfriend, and her parents were grounding her for the next twenty years. He wrote that he would be there in half an hour, but then he said that someone had spray painted the back of Ellie's grocery and he had to see to it. SEE YOU WHEN I CAN, he'd finished.

The last message was from Tristan and had been sent an hour ago. I NEED TO SEE YOU ASAP.

As Gemma ate her second piece of toast, she frowned. Colin's jealousy was absurd, but she didn't see any reason to fan it into flame, so she didn't immediately get in her car.

IS IT IMPORTANT? she texted back.

VERY came the reply. I NEED YOU AT MY HOUSE RIGHT AWAY.

That didn't sound like Tris, she thought. Maybe it was Colin's fear, or maybe it was that Gemma now had a life growing inside her, but she was cautious.

YOU KNOW WHAT HAPPENS AT SEVEN, DON'T YOU? she texted back.

While she waited for an answer, she noticed Shamus's art box on the coffee table where it had been for days. She picked it up and pulled the tape off the end of it to examine the damage. The corner was broken, but the piece was there, and as she fiddled with it, she noticed paper inside. More of his secret drawings, she thought, and wondered who the boy had portrayed with pinpoint accuracy.

When her phone buzzed, she put the box down.

I'LL HOLD YOUR HEAD AGAIN was the text. PLEASE COME NOW!

There was no denying that that request was from Tristan, and where better to be than with him when "morning" sickness hit?

She called Colin, but it went to voice mail, so she texted him that she was going to Tris's house to do some research. PLEASE MEET ME THERE, she wrote.

She grabbed a cold hard-boiled egg from the refrigerator and a bottle of fruit juice and went to her car.

As Gemma neared Tris's driveway, she didn't pull in. She didn't like Colin's jealousy, but she also didn't want to cause him any embarrassment, and for right now, for all she knew, half of Edilean was watching. She drove past until she saw another gravel road and turned down that. To her right she could see the top of what looked to be a large white house, and she remembered Colin saying that Mrs. Wingate lived near Tris.

Gemma pulled her car off the road into a large clearing in the woods. Bushes hid the entrance so her vehicle wouldn't be seen by anyone driving past.

If her sense of direction was right—and it usually was—then Tris's house was directly in front of her. She sent another text to Colin to let him know where she was, but the message didn't go through. The trees were blocking the signal.

It was because she was in the woods and not on the road that she saw Jean's silver Mercedes hidden under the trees. The second she saw it, she knew she should leave. She should run, not walk, back to her car and get out of there.

But she knew that the text message had been from Tris. Only he knew about her 7 P.M. nausea, and he needed her.

Quietly, she went to Jean's car. It was empty, but the fact that it was hidden furthered her belief that something was wrong. It had always been her guess that whatever was going on had to do with the Heartwishes Stone. If Jean's uncle was an international thief, wouldn't he want to steal something that was believed to be magic?

Gemma tried to send another text to Colin and an e-mail to Joce. She wrote,

> PLEASE SEND HELP TO TRIS'S HOUSE.
> SEND POLICE WITH GUNS.

If there was nothing wrong, she'd look like a fool, but better that than anything bad happening to Tris.

She went through the woods quickly, stopping where she could see Tris's house. It had been designed to look out the front at the lake, so the back of it had few windows. On the right was the big conservatory, and she could see the orchids inside. On the left were three tiny windows for a powder room and the laundry. Smack in the middle were two glass doors that led to the big room that had been added on to the house.

If Gemma walked straight up to it, she'd be seen.

It took her a few minutes, but she went to the side of the doors and plastered herself against the wall. After a few moments she quickly bent to look inside.

What she saw made her breath catch. There were two people in the room, Jean and an older man, who Gemma assumed was the uncle. What was astonishing was that the man was seated in a straight-backed wooden chair in the middle of the room and his hands were tied behind his back. Jean was a few feet away, her back to the man as she was typing out a message on her phone. There was a gun on the table beside her.

Gemma leaned back against the wall. She recognized the man. He was that awful so-called professor who'd been so offensive that day in Ellie's store. His disguise was half on, half off his face, but it was easy to see that he wasn't as old and certainly not crippled as he'd presented himself when she'd met him.

Gemma wasn't sure what she should do. She glanced at her phone and saw that none of her messages had gone through. It looked like Tris needed some new routers for his Internet service—or the wires had been cut.

She took a deep breath and looked back through the glass door. Jean was leaving the room, probably to find a better connection for her phone. Was she trying to contact Colin? She took the gun with her.

Gemma knew that the smartest thing for her to do was to go back to her car and leave. Let Colin handle this, she thought.

She gave one last look through the door before she

left, but she stopped cold. Since the man's back was to her, so were his hands. He was frantically working to loosen the tape Jean had used on him, and it looked like he was a few minutes away from being free.

Maybe Jean was involved in the robberies and maybe there was animosity between the two women, but Gemma knew she *had* to warn her.

Around the corner was a window that led into Tris's exam room. She ran to it, hoping that it wouldn't be locked. It wasn't. She pushed the window up, swung her leg over, and went inside. To the right was the sitting room and at the end was the kitchen.

When Gemma got to the doorway, she saw Jean standing at Tris's kitchen island, a cup on the way to her lips. Unseen by Jean, her uncle was behind her. He was holding aloft the belt to his trousers and he was about to wrap it around his niece's neck.

Gemma didn't give herself time to think about what she was doing. She silently ran the few feet, and yelled, "Hey Professor!"

When he turned, she did to him exactly what she'd done to Colin in the gym. She twirled around to put a spinning back kick into his stomach. When he bent in pain, she did another spin and hit him in the jaw with a punch that had all her strength behind it. Whereas Colin could take all she'd given him, the uncle couldn't. He went down, his head hitting the corner of the stone countertop. As he slid down, he left a stream of blood along the cabinets. By the time he hit the floor, he was unconscious.

Jean was standing there, the cup still halfway to her mouth, her eyes wide.

"Where is Tris?" Gemma asked.

With her hand shaking, Jean set the cup down as she stared at her uncle's unconscious form. The belt was still wrapped around one of his wrists. "Tris is in Miami, visiting his sister."

"No, he's not. He sent me a text about something only he and I know."

"He"—she nodded to her uncle—"was watching you and Tris, following you. If he wrote something private, it's because he saw the two of you together. Did it happen outside where he was able to see you?"

Gemma was sickened that the man had been skulking about in the dark that night, but she wasn't convinced that Tris was safe. "Tris wouldn't have boarded a plane without his phone."

"Maybe he came back and that's what threw my uncle's plans off. That I was able to sneak up on him is not something anyone else has been able to do."

"So where is Tristan?" Gemma demanded as she picked up the gun off the counter.

"I don't know where Tris is," Jean said as she sank down to the floor. "He was going to kill me," she said, looking at her uncle.

Gemma's main concern was Tris, but at the same time she didn't dare leave Jean and her uncle unguarded. She reached into her pocket for her phone. Her texts had finally gone through. With joy, she saw that there were two texts to her, one from Roy saying that Colin was on his way, and another one from Joce saying the police were coming.

Jean started talking. "He heard about the paintings that had been found in Edilean, and he knew I had a connection here. He was broke, so he came here to see what he could find out, if there was something worth stealing here. If he found nothing here he probably meant to get money from me. He's good at getting into bank accounts and emptying them. I just wanted him *gone*."

"Would he have killed you?" Gemma asked. She was nervous and wanted to look for Tristan, but she couldn't turn her back on those two.

Jean's voice was quiet. "You know that little trick with his hands that Colin does?"

Gemma wasn't sure what she meant, but then realized that Jean was talking about sex. The thought of sharing the man she loved with another woman made her hand tighten on the gun she held at her side.

"That's all right," Jean said. "You don't have to tell me. I taught Colin to do that. You know who taught me?" She looked at her uncle on the floor. "Him. When I was ten years old."

Gemma gasped.

"Colin doesn't know it, but before I changed it, my middle name was Willow. Uncle Adrian liked to rob houses with ten-year-olds in the family, and he'd leave behind a sprig of willow wrapped in a pink ribbon. He thought of it as a joke."

"Yet you spent time with him while you were in law school."

"Yeah," Jean said with a sneer. "I thought I was protecting Mom and me. And I thought he didn't know how much I hated him."

"Why did he start robbing here in Edilean?" Gemma asked. "He must have known that there's nothing here to meet his standards."

"Well . . ." Jean said.

When she didn't look at Gemma, she understood. "*You* committed the robberies here, didn't you?"

"Yes," Jean said. "I think maybe he was going to leave town, but then he heard of that damned Heartwishes Stone, so he stayed and began to watch you and Tris. He was convinced that you two had found the Stone and that's what you were being so secretive about. I thought that if I did some robberies using his old MO, it might draw the Feds here and that they might scare him into leaving. But he knew what I was doing and why—and he was amused. They were so very amateurish, the kind of thing he did when he was a teenager."

Gemma was disgusted by this whole story. "I guess he had a buyer."

"Several," Jean said. "If my uncle had sold that Stone, no one in the world named Frazier would have been safe."

They heard gravel flying outside as a car skidded to a halt. "That's Colin," Gemma said.

Jean looked at her, her eyes pleading. "Look, I know the robberies were wrong, but I didn't know what else to do. I was losing everything. On that first night at the dinner I cooked, I saw how much Colin wanted you. And I guessed that his mother had planned it all. She can be a conniving snake."

Gemma started to protest, but she knew that Jean was at last telling the truth.

"Please," Jean said. "I'm putting my life is in your hands. If you tell Colin what I did . . ."

Gemma looked at the man on the floor. He was beginning to stir. No one had been hurt in the break-ins. "Will evidence be found against him at the robbery sites?"

"On the last one, I left hair and a fingerprint." Gravel was crunching; Colin was running toward them.

This was a decision Gemma couldn't make quickly. She needed to think about it. "How did you find the ring in the bedpost?"

Jean gave a derogatory little snort. "The bed was homemade. The post was screwed on crooked. He taught me to first look for the obvious."

Colin threw open the door. His arm was around Tris, whose face was drained of color, and he was holding onto his left arm, which looked like it was broken.

Gemma wanted to hug both men and cry in relief, but at that moment a strong wave of nausea went through her, and she put her hand over her mouth.

Tris, in spite of the obvious pain he was in,

grinned at her. "It must be seven." He stepped away from Colin, who was looking at Gemma in fear.

"Are you all right?" he asked as he grabbed her by the shoulders.

Gemma's answer was to throw up on his shoes.

Colin erupted in anger. "I'll kill you for hurting her," he bellowed as he leaped toward Jean's uncle, who was pulling himself upright.

"Colin, no!" Tris yelled. "It's your kid who's making her sick."

Colin had the man by the front of his shirt, his fist drawn back to hit him, but when Tris's words reached his mind, he dropped the man to the floor.

"Gemma?" he asked, looking at her.

She was fighting more nausea.

"Get her to the sink," Tris yelled. "It's your turn to hold her head."

Outside was the sound of sirens. The police had arrived.

"That you felt you had to keep this secret from me . . ." Colin said as he held Gemma to him. Behind them, the police and Roy were handcuffing Jean's uncle Adrian. "I can never apologize to you enough."

"It's all right now," Gemma said.

He ran his hand along her cheek. "No, it's not. I thought you and Tris—"

"I know." She knew she should admit to her jealousy of Jean, but now was not the time. It felt too good to be held by him, to be reassured.

"I won't be jealous again," Colin said. "And I promise that I'll spend my life making it up to you."

"I'd like that," she said as he kissed her.

"I love you, Gemma. I will love you forever."

"And I love you," she said, then laughed when he insisted on carrying her to the car.

28

"OKAY?" COLIN ASKED Gemma for the thousandth time. It was the morning after Jean's uncle had been arrested, and Gemma was on the couch in the guesthouse, a quilt over her legs.

All she could do was smile at the way Mr. and Mrs. Frazier and even Shamus were hovering over her. Mrs. Frazier had wanted Gemma put to bed in their best guest suite, but Colin had said their house—his and Gemma's—was better for her.

"I'm not ill, I'm just pregnant," Gemma had said.

Those words had made Mrs. Frazier burst into tears—again.

In the end, they'd compromised. Gemma was to spend the next three days in the Frazier house, looked after by Mrs. Frazier, then she'd move into Colin's house for good.

"You're sure you're all right?" Colin asked as he looked down at her with a mixture of pride and wonder.

"Yes," Gemma said. "Please go and take care of the case. And find out about Tristan. I want to know how he is and what happened to him."

Roy stepped into the room, her phone in her hand. "I can answer that. Dr. Tris was halfway to the airport when he realized he didn't have his phone, so he went back to get it. He surprised Jean's uncle as he was searching Tris's house."

Gemma looked at Colin, and he took her hand as he nodded. She was right; Adrian had been looking for the Heartwishes Stone.

"Tris said the man escaped out a window and Tris went after him," Roy said.

"He should have stayed where he was and called me," Colin said.

Roy continued. "Tris knows that, but he was afraid the man would go to Mrs. Wingate's house, so that's why he chased him. The creep hid in the bushes and hit Tris with something. We don't know what it was, but we think it was a golf club. Dr. Tris said he thought the man was aiming at his head but Tris heard him and turned. The blow hit his left arm."

"How bad is it?" Gemma asked.

"Broken but not too badly. He'll be in a cast for a few weeks. His parents flew in from Sarasota, and his dad will take over Tris's practice for a while."

"What about Jean?" Mrs. Frazier asked. "How is she dealing with all this?"

Gemma couldn't help holding her breath. Had they found out that it was Jean who committed the robberies in Edilean? Gemma looked up at Colin. She knew that he'd spent the night questioning Jean, but there hadn't been a chance for him to tell her what he'd found out.

Colin spoke first. "She heard that Tris was going out of town, so she thought maybe her uncle would try to search the house. Seems the man had been spying on Tris for a while. He was hiding in the bushes when Gemma first threw up."

Colin looked at her, his hand squeezing hers in a renewal of his promises. Never again would she have to keep secrets from him.

He looked back at the others. "When Jean got there, she didn't see Tristan. By that time, he was unconscious and halfway down a hill and the uncle was back in the house. Jean didn't know that her uncle had already texted Gemma on Tris's phone to go there. Jean had a gun and she caught him off guard. She used surgical tape to tie him up."

Colin paused. "Jean tried to call me, but Tris's Internet service had been knocked out by the storm. If Gemma had shown up, thinking Tris needed her, the man probably would have made her give him the Stone, then killed her."

He had to take a few breaths before going on. "But Gemma very wisely didn't pull into the driveway but came around the side. By that time, Jean had arrived and taped her uncle to a chair. Unfortunately, the man was good at escaping any bondage. If Gemma hadn't attacked—which she shouldn't have done, by the way—he would have murdered his niece."

"All for a Stone that grants wishes," Mrs. Frazier said in disgust.

Everyone in the room looked at her. Now that her deepest wish had been granted, she could afford to be disdainful.

"Where is the thing, anyway?" Mr. Frazier asked. "I'd like to see it."

Gemma started to speak, but Colin interrupted her.

"That's between Gemma and Tristan," Colin said. "I've not seen it and don't plan to see it. I know it was hidden in Tristan's house for many years, so ownership of it goes to him. And when I talk to him I think he'll agree to give the guardianship of it to Gemma. If she wants to stay in Edilean, that is."

Mr. Frazier put his hand on his son's shoulder, and looked at the others in the room. "What do you say that we give these lovebirds some time alone?" He didn't wait for an answer but herded everyone out of the guesthouse.

When they were alone, Gemma threw the quilt off her legs and stood up. "I don't know about you, but I'm starving."

She turned toward the kitchen but Colin didn't follow her. When she looked back, he was on one knee and he had what was unmistakably a ring box in his hand.

Slowly, she walked back to him.

"Will you marry me?" he asked as he held out the little blue velvet box. She opened it to see a ring that had to be a family heirloom, three diamonds in a slightly worn basket setting.

"I thought you might like something old better than new," he said softly.

"I love it," she said as she took the box, then held it out to him.

He removed the ring, tossed the box on the couch, and slipped the ring on her finger. It fit perfectly. "Your mother told me your size."

"My mother?" She was astonished.

"I thought I should make myself known to her, so I called and asked her permission."

Gemma sat down on the couch. "Did you tell her about—" She glanced down at her stomach.

"When I called her, I didn't know about that."

She was sitting, he was still on one knee. "When did you do this?"

"Right after we met in the sandwich shop. As you told my brother, I was miserable." His eyes brightened. "You bought the baby clothes for our child, didn't you?"

"Yes." She held his face in her hands and kissed him. "I want to hear more, but your child is making me so hungry your ears are beginning to look appetizing." She stood up.

"Gemma?" he said, his voice sounding urgent. "You haven't answered my question."

"What question?"

He raised his eyebrows, then glanced at his awkward position.

"Oh!" she said, laughing. "You poor baby. Your knees must be killing you. Yes, I'll marry you. Yes and yes and yes."

"Great," Colin said. "Now help me up."

She put her arms out to him, but he didn't need help. He pulled her down to the couch. Slowly and with all the emotions they felt in their hearts, they touched and held each other. Their kisses were different, for their doubts and fears were gone, and all they could see was the future.

Unseen by human eyes, the Heartwishes Stone blinked. It had given two more wishes. Gemma belonged to a place and people, and Colin had found True Love.

Epilogue

GEMMA DIDN'T GET around to repairing Shamus's art box for weeks. By that time Jean's uncle had been extradited to Romania, where he was to go through the first of several trials. Quite a few countries wanted to question him.

Gemma told Colin the truth about the Edilean robberies and she pleaded on Jean's behalf. Gemma said that Jean had endured enough because of her uncle and she didn't deserve prison and disbarment. Colin had agreed with her, but he said the law was the law.

In the end, the FBI solved the dilemma. They arrived two days after the arrest of Adrian Caldwell, and they pushed Colin aside as though he were a country bumpkin, too dumb to know what he had. Gemma smiled as she watched Colin stand back and let the federal agents tell him, with their superior attitude, that only someone of Caldwell's caliber could have pulled off burglaries like the ones that had happened in Edilean.

"No wonder, sheriff, that you couldn't figure out who done it," they said, smirks on their city faces. "Nobody local could do something like this. Too bad you missed the hair and fingerprint the first time around. They tie into some big jobs, and they'll put Caldwell behind bars for the rest of his life."

Colin just smiled at them in good nature and invited them to do all their Christmas shopping in Edilean. They clapped him on the back and said they would.

Only Gemma saw Colin talking to Jean in such a ferocious way that she felt sorry for the woman. But later, Jean looked over Colin's big shoulder and mouthed "thank you" to Gemma.

After all the excitement, it was a while before everyone's lives settled down again. When Mrs. Frazier started asking Gemma what color she wanted for her bridesmaids, she and Colin eloped. They had a simple, private ceremony and moved into his house all in one weekend. They were two very happy people.

It was during the move that Gemma saw Shamus's art box and sat down to fix it. He had been Gemma's only attendant at the wedding, and she owed him for holding her bouquet while she and Colin exchanged rings. She'd assumed the papers were Shamus's drawings, but when she started to pull them out and saw the brittleness and the yellow that only age could create, her heart nearly stopped.

Slowly, carefully, she pulled the papers out of the bottom of the box. The first thing she saw was a name and a date. Tamsen Frazier Byan 1895.

Gemma collapsed into a chair and began to read.

12 February 1895

My story begins when my honorary aunt and uncle, Cay and Alex McDowell, were going to spend the summer of 1834 in England buying horses. They were planning to rent a house, but my mother wrote my father's oldest brother, Ewan, who was the earl of Rypton, and suddenly, all doors were opened and invitations were extended. I wish I could say it was done out of family loyalty, but it wasn't. Uncle Ewan's greedy, base born—but rich—wife hated us Americans so much she refused to use the Frazier name. But she knew that Aunt Cay's daughter had recently married Grayson Armitage, heir to one of the richest fortunes in America, and that's why Aunt Cay was invited to stay with them.

At home in Edilean, the invitation caused a flurry of activity. Since Uncle Alex would be traveling all over the British Isles to find the horses he so loved, Aunt Cay would be alone. The truth was, that was fine with her, for she loved her art almost as much as she cared for her family. If she had pen and paper and something to look at, she was happy.

But I, twenty-four years old and recently jilted, thought I was the most unhappy person on earth, so I set about to persuade her that I had to go with her. I shamelessly used the fact that Ewan was my uncle. That he was an earl and that his wife had refused to allow his working-class, American relatives into her house made no matter to me. All that was in my mind was to show the world—i.e., Edilean, Virginia—that I had better things to do than care that the man I'd been sure I was going to marry had chosen another to be his bride.

I can't remember how I came to invite a companion to go with me. I think it was Cay's doing. Perhaps she feared being saddled with a melancholy young woman who might need to be entertained, so she encouraged me to take a friend.

Whatever the cause, it was four of us who set off that spring of 1834. It was Cay and Alex, long married but as much in love as ever—when I saw them holding hands, I burst into tears—and Winnie and me.

Louisa Winifred Aldredge was my cousin and we had grown up together. Her father and brother were the town doctors—the third and fourth generation of Aldredge doctors in Edilean—and Winnie knew a great deal about medicine. She'd assisted her father since she was a girl. How she used to disgust us, her friends, when she'd come to our delicate tea parties with blood on her petticoat. Some of the girls would nearly faint with her vivid descriptions of surgeries and even amputations.

What we all liked about Winnie was that she was so very practical. Whenever we girls did something we shouldn't have—usually because we were dared by one of those outrageous Welsch girls—it was Winnie who calmed us down and helped us figure out what was the right thing to do.

I chose Winnie from among my many friends to go to England because she didn't feel sorry for me at having been discarded by a man I truly loved. Winnie was just matter-of-fact about the humiliation I'd been subjected to. She said, "Robert Allandale is no better than what comes out of the back end of a horse." She said it only once, didn't dwell on it, didn't elaborate, but that was enough. I knew how she felt and she wasn't going to change her mind. Winifred Aldredge was as solid as I was—in those days—flighty.

By the time we set sail for England, I had recovered enough that I could wave good-bye to our friends who came to see us off. Weeks later, when we reached Southampton, my head was full of the fact that my uncle had two sons who were of marriageable age. The oldest one, Julian, was to become an earl. Wouldn't returning with him on my arm make Robert Allandale green with envy!

I think I need to confess that it was I who stole the Heartwishes Stone. Even though I was only eight when he died, I was the child who knew the most about my grandfather Shamus of when he lived in Scotland. On cold winter evenings I would sit on his lap as he told me his old stories. My favorites were about the Heartwishes Stone. He told me how a witch had made it out of gratitude for a young, strong Frazier who had saved the lives of several people. Grandpa Shamus said that the Stone gave each person in the family a wish that would come true if it came from his or her heart.

He told me how his father, Ursted, had wasted his wish. When Ursted was a young man, all he'd wanted, what he'd craved, was to marry the beautiful Mary McTern, daughter of the laird of the clan. Ursted thought that such a marriage would give him power in the clan, and would make others see him as important. He was sick of his family being considered as little more than pack mules. "Haul this, Frazier," people would say. "Move this rock." With his lust for respectability in his mind, Ursted took the Stone out of its lead case and made his wish.

It must have come from his heart because the next day he found Mary McTern out alone and he took her by force. I don't like to think what that poor girl went through. All the Fraziers are large and unnaturally strong. Mary knew that to tell her father what had been done to her would cause a war within the clan, so she kept the secret to herself. When she missed her monthly time, she went to her father and told him that she was in love with Ursted Frazier and wanted to marry him. The entire clan was horrified. Sweet, beautiful, educated Mary to give her life to the loud, ignorant, violent-tempered Ursted Frazier? It was said that the wailing of her mother could be heard a mile away.

But Mary knew that the truth would cause people's deaths, so at sixteen, she married the twenty-two-year-old Ursted Frazier. Afterward, when the man was still laughed at, still considered to have no wisdom, he took his anger out on his wife. She hid her bruises as best she could and told her parents she was happy with her lot. She was a good breeder and produced eight big, healthy sons. When they were old enough, Ursted took his anger out on them as well as on his wife.

One by one, their mother told her four oldest sons about the Stone and they made wishes from their hearts. They were simple young men and all they wanted was to get away from their father and to get a good job somewhere far away. And that's just what they did. But when Shamus, my grandfather, reached an age where he too could have left, he didn't. He stayed behind to care for—and protect—his mother and his three youngest brothers.

One night his drunken father didn't come home. Grandpa Shamus never told me the details of what happened, and I've never wanted to imagine what could have occurred that night. But the result was that Shamus, his mother, and the three youngest boys were at last left in peace. However, their profligate father had left behind nothing but debts, and a house that was barely fit for habitation. The family was so poor that I don't know how they survived.

Grandpa Shamus said that to his mind, what was worse than the poverty, was that his entire family was the object of ridicule. His main enemy was his cousin, Angus McTern, who was to become the laird of the clan. As boys, they fought often and the clan always took Angus's side. When the clan's property was gambled away, Shamus said he rejoiced that Angus's future of power and wealth had been taken from him. But the clansmen still looked to young Angus to be their leader—and they still laughed in derision at the Fraziers. "Big enough to be an ox, but not the sense of one," he heard a man say when he was a boy.

My grandpa said he "got the man back," but he wouldn't tell me what he did.

It wasn't until a young English woman named Edilean Talbot came to live in the McTern castle that Shamus decided to make use of the Heartwishes Stone. As he held the Stone in his hand, he said that he wished for gold and a lot of it.

His mother, Mary, had seen that the Stone had a perverse way of making wishes come true, but also of making them go wrong. She'd had years of misery to think about her late husband's wish, and she didn't want that for her boys. She didn't know if she was enough of a Frazier to be granted a request, but she tried to counterbalance Shamus's unplanned wish. She took the Stone from him and said that she hoped he got the gold, but that she also wanted him to have a better life. By that, she meant for him to have love. That none of her sons had wished for love hurt her more than her husband's beatings had. None of her sons had ever seen True Love, had certainly never felt it, and she very much wanted them to have it.

Grandpa Shamus used to laugh when he told the rest of his story, how he'd come to America and ended up rescuing Angus

McTern from certain death. "It was a day for rejoicing," he said. I knew he meant that he celebrated at his cousin's humiliation.

I loved to hear of his courtship with Grandma Pru. He said she came to the old McTern castle looking for Edilean's uncle, and when Shamus saw her, he loved her from the first moment. "She was riding a horse big enough to pull a loaded wagon," he used to recall with eyes misted over with love. "And when she slid down, she was nearly as tall as me."

I'd heard Grandma Pru tell the same story, but she was more pragmatic. She said that the first time she saw Shamus Frazier, she wanted to throw him into the hay and have her way with him. "I was so very tired of girlish men!" Whenever I heard this story, I marveled that the two of them had found each other. She was the daughter of an earl, while he was little better than a stable lad. My grandmother was a large woman, not fat, but tall and big-boned. And even in youth, her face had not been pretty. "Beauty is in the eye of the beholder," she used to say, laughing, then slap her husband on the back so hard that, had he been a lesser man, he would have fallen.

By the time I was seven, my grandparents were very old, but Grandpa Shamus said he wasn't going to leave the earth until after his cousin Angus died. Angus's wife Edilean died in 1817, and after that, Angus didn't want to stay on earth. He died the following year. Grandpa Shamus used to say that he'd be filled with joy when Angus was gone—"my old enemy" as he called him—but he wasn't. After Angus died, Shamus deteriorated fast, and when Grandma Pru died, Grandpa Shamus lived only three more months. "Everyone is gone now," he told me as I held his hand as he lay in what turned out to be his death bed. "Enemies, friends, family, they're all gone now. I think I'll go and see them. I would like to play a trick or two on old Angus and see him get angry!" he said, laughing. He died three days later. Just went to sleep and never woke up again. My mother told me that he was smiling when they found him. My father, Colin, said that he was with Prudence so he must be very happy. "They weren't much without the other."

On the afternoon my grandfather died, I was the one who asked after the Heartwishes Stone, as he had always kept it in the box with the family Bible. My father had told me the story was just a myth, but then he'd never cared much for the old stories. He was a man who lived in the day, and his great passion was anything with wheels. His company built wagons and carriages that were the finest in the country. President Madison even ordered one from him. (My father laughed because he'd had to make the seats higher so that when people saw him they'd think the tiny man was taller.)

"May I have the Heartwishes Stone to remember Grandpa by?" I asked and he mumbled something that could have been yes. I had learned that if I asked my father something while he was under duress, he'd say yes just to get rid of me. On the other hand, my mother had a keen eye and ear, and she always knew what I was up to, so I didn't mention the Stone to her. It was my hope that my father would fail to mention it to my mother. I wasn't so fortunate as to achieve that goal. She saw that it was missing and knew that I had taken it. She took it from me, and it wasn't until I was an adult that I found the little lead case in the bottom of her bureau. (The lead kept its magic contained. Let it out and the Stone started blinking as it did its work.) The second time, I didn't ask permission of anyone but took the Stone, held it in my hand, and wished with all my might that Robert Allandale would love me.

I guess the wish wasn't from my heart because Robert still betrayed me. He found a woman whose father had died and left her with three houses. When my parents died, I was to inherit a tidy sum, but until then I was at the mercy of their generosity, and Robert knew that.

The legend about the Stone was that it granted only one request to each Frazier, and if the one about Robert had failed, that meant I was still owed a wish. With that in mind, I hid the Stone in a portmanteau I was taking to England. When my mother saw that the Stone was missing she knew I was the one who took it. My brother was as uninterested in it as my father was. May the Lord forgive me, but I swore to her that I had not removed it and didn't know who had. Since that was the day Robert was getting married, I figured the Lord might overlook my blatant lie.

I took that Heartwishes Stone to England with me, meaning to use it so that I would return with a man on my arm. But it was Winnie who needed the Heartwishes, not me.

She and the beautiful Julian fell deeply in love and wanted to marry. But his stepmother, that snobbish woman who hated all her husband's American relatives, couldn't bear the idea of Julian inheriting. She so very much wanted her fat, ugly son, Clive, to have everything.

I never told Winnie, but I saw Julian's stepmother watching them out the window. He and Winnie were laughing together. Even though they weren't touching or doing anything untoward, it was easy to tell that they were in love. I was the only one who knew that they were planning to elope the next day. Something about the way the woman looked at them frightened me. That night I took the Heartwishes Stone out of its lead case and wished with all my might that Julian and Winnie could be together forever.

I had no idea that when I made that wish, Julian was already dead.

The next day, when Winnie was told that Julian's body had been found, she was stoic. She didn't cry. Only those of us who loved her knew the pain that was inside her.

The tears were all shed by his stepmother. I never believed that Julian's fall from the roof was an accident. When his odious stepmother cried so hard she had to be helped into the church at the funeral, I sneered at her tears. I told Aunt Cay that I thought the woman had murdered Julian.

Aunt Cay said nothing to that but I think she agreed with me. We left England soon after that, and on the voyage home, Winnie found out that she was carrying Julian's child. That was when her tears came—tears of joy and happiness.

To me, Winnie's news was proof of the truth of the Heartwishes Stone. It had done its best to fulfill the wish, but I have always wondered if Julian would have lived if only I'd made my wish sooner.

I didn't tell Winnie of the wish, for she would have scoffed at it and told me how babies were made. Besides, I didn't want to take away from her happiness.

She wanted to run and tell Aunt Cay and Uncle Alex right away. As we ran through the ship to their cabin, I was afraid of the wrath of the older folks, but there was none. There were no lectures about the sin of fornication. In fact, they looked at each other with twinkling eyes, as though they knew about youthful passion.

Still, I worried about Winnie's parents' reaction. She agreed to let Uncle Alex talk to them first. Whatever he said worked because there was only happiness surrounding Winnie's news. Her parents arranged that the church records would say the boy, named Patrick Julian Aldredge, was born to her brother and his wife. Legitimacy would keep the child from being ridiculed.

Winnie used her inheritance from her grandparents to build a lovely little house out of town beside a lake, and there she raised her child. She was never officially certified as a doctor, but she learned enough from her father and grandfather that she had a thriving practice.

Young Patrick grew up to be as handsome as his father and became the town's doctor.

As for Winnie, she never got over her loss of the man she loved; she never married. Aunt Cay carved a little portrait of Julian and put it above the fireplace in the house that Winnie built for herself and Julian's son. Uncle Alex figured out an ingenious way to make a code to open the picture. Behind it we hid the Heartwishes Stone, and I hope its secret is never found out. As it turned out, I did not need any magical wishes to find a man who would love me and who I could love in return. My life has been good. However, I do not mean to be maudlin, but even after all these many years, I miss Winnie every day of my life.

Turn the page for a preview of Jude's newest novel,

Stranger in the Moonlight

From Pocket Books

Prologue

EDILEAN, VIRGINIA

1993

IN ALL OF her eight years, Kim had never been so bored. She didn't even know such boredom could exist. Her mother told her to go outside into the big garden around the old house, Edilean Manor, and play, but what was she to do by herself?

Two weeks ago her father had taken her brother off to some faraway state to go fishing. "Male bonding," her mother called it, then said she was *not* going to stay in their big house alone for four whole weeks. That night Kim had been awakened by the sound of her parents arguing. They didn't usually fight—not that she knew about—and the word *divorce* came to her mind. She was terrified of being without her parents.

But the next morning they were kissing and everything seemed to be fine. Her father kept talking about making up being the best, but her mother shushed him.

It was that afternoon when her mother told her that while her father and brother were away they were going to stay in an apartment at Edilean Manor. Kim didn't like that because she hated the old house. It was too big and it echoed with every footstep. Besides, every time she visited the place there was less furniture, and the emptiness made it seem even creepier.

Her father said that Mr. Bertrand, the old man who lived in the house, had sold the family furniture rather than get a job to support himself. "He'd sell the house if Miss Edi would let him."

Miss Edi was Mr. Bertrand's sister. She was older than he was, and even though she didn't live there, she owned the house. Kim had heard people say that she disliked her brother so much that she refused to live in Edilean.

Kim couldn't imagine hating Edilean, since every person she knew in the world lived there. Her dad was an Aldredge, from one of the seven families that founded the town. Kim knew that was something to be proud of. All she thought was that she was glad she wasn't from the family that had to live in big, scary Edilean Manor.

So now she and her mother had been living in the apartment for two whole weeks and she was horribly bored. She wanted to go back to her own house and her own room. When they were packing to go, her mother had said, "We're just going away for a little while and it's just around the corner, so you don't need to take that." "That" was pretty much anything Kim owned, like books, toys, her dolls, her many art kits. Her mother seemed to consider it all as "not necessary."

But at the end, Kim had grabbed the bicycle she'd received for her birthday and clamped her hands around the grips. She looked at her mother with her jaw set.

Her dad laughed. "Ellen," he said to his wife, "I've seen that look on your face a thousand times and I can assure that your daughter will *not* back down. I know from experience that you can yell, threaten, sweet talk, plead, beg, cry, but she won't give in."

Her mother's eyes were narrowed as she looked at her laughing husband.

He quit smiling. "Reede, how about you and I go . . . ?"

"Go where, Dad?" Reede asked. At seventeen, he was overwhelmed with importance at being allowed to go away with his dad. No women. Just the two of them.

"Wherever we can find to go," his dad mumbled.

Kim got to take her bike to Edilean Manor, and for three days she rode it nonstop, but now she wanted to do something else. Her cousin Sara came over one day but all she wanted to do was explore the ratty old house. Sara loved old buildings!

Mr. Bertrand had pulled a copy of *Alice's Adventures in Wonderland* out of a pile of books on the floor. Her mom said he'd sold the bookcase to Colonial Williamsburg. "Original eighteenth century and it had been in the family for over two hundred years," she'd muttered. "What a shame. Poor Miss Edi."

Kim spent days reading about Alice and her journey down the rabbit hole. She'd loved the book so much that she told her mother she wanted blonde hair and a blue dress with a white apron. Her mother said that if her father ever again went off for four weeks her next child just might be blonde. Mr. Bertrand said he'd like a hookah and to sit on a mushroom all day and say wise things.

The two adults had started laughing—they seemed to find each other very funny. In disgust Kim went outside to sit in the fork of her favorite old pear tree and read more about Alice. She reread her favorite passages again, then her mother called her in for what Mr. Bertrand called "afternoon tea." He was an odd old man, very soft-looking, and her father said that Mr. Bertrand could hatch an egg on the couch. "He never gets up."

Kim had seen that few of the men in town liked Mr. Bertrand, but all the women seemed to adore him. On some days as many as six women would show up with bottles of wine and casseroles and cakes, and they'd all laugh hilariously. When they saw Kim they'd say, "I should have brought—" They'd name their children. But then another woman would say how good it was to have some peace and quiet for a few hours.

The next time the women came they'd again "forget" to bring their children.

As Kim stood outside and heard the women howling with laughter, she didn't think they sounded very peaceful or quiet.

It was after she and her mother had been there for two long weeks that early one morning her mother seemed very excited about something, but Kim wasn't sure what it was. Something had happened during the night, some adult thing. All Kim was concerned with was that she couldn't find the copy of *Alice's Adventures in Wonderland* that Mr. Bertrand had lent her. She had *one* book, and now it was gone. She asked her mother what happened to it, as she knew she'd left it on the coffee table.

"Last night I took it to—" The sentence wasn't finished because the old phone on the wall rang and her mother ran to answer it, then immediately started laughing.

Annoyed, Kim went outside. It seemed that her life was getting worse.

She kicked at rocks, frowned at the empty flower beds, and headed toward her tree. She planned to climb up it, sit on her branch, and figure out what to do for the long, boring weeks until her dad came home and life could start again.

When she got close to her tree, what she saw stopped her dead in her tracks. There was a boy, younger than her brother but older than she was. He was wearing a clean shirt with a collar and dark trousers; he looked like he was about to go to Sunday school. Worse was that he was sitting in *her* tree reading *her* book.

He had dark hair that fell forward and he was so engrossed in her book that he didn't even look up when Kim kicked at a clod of dirt.

Who was he? she thought. And what right did he think he had to be in *her* tree?

She didn't know who or what, but she did know that she wanted this stranger to go away.

She picked up a clod and threw it at him as hard as she could. She was aiming for the top of his head but hit his shoulder. The lump crumbled into dirt and fell down onto *her* book.

He looked up at her, a bit startled at first, but then his face settled down and he stared at her in silence. He was a pretty boy, she thought. Not like her cousin Tristan, but this boy looked like a doll she'd seen in a catalogue, with pink skin and very dark eyes.

"That's *my* book," she yelled at him. "And it's *my* tree. You have no right to them." She grabbed another clod and threw it at him. It would have hit him in the face but he moved sideways and it missed.

Kim had had a lot of experience with older boys and she knew that they got you back. It didn't take much to set them off, then you were in for it. They'd chase you, catch you, and pin your arm behind your back or pull your hair until you begged for mercy.

When she saw the boy make a move as though he meant to get down, Kim took off running as fast as she could. Maybe there'd be enough time that she could reach what she knew was a great hiding place. She wedged her small body in between two piles of old bricks, crouched down, and waited for the boy to come after her.

After what seemed like an hour of waiting, he didn't show up, and her legs began to ache. Cautiously and quietly, she got out from the bricks and looked around. She fully expected him to leap out from behind a tree, yell "I got you!" then bombard her with dirt.

But nothing happened. The big garden was as still and quiet as always and there was no sign of the boy.

She ran behind a tree, waited and listened, but she

heard and saw nothing. She ran to another tree and waited. Nothing. It took her a long time before she got back to "her" tree, and what she saw astonished her.

Standing on the ground, just under her branch, was the boy. He was holding the book under his arm and seemed to be waiting.

Was this some new boy trap that she'd never seen before? she wondered. Is this what foreign boys—meaning ones not from Edilean—did to girls who threw dirt at them? If she walked up to him, would he clobber her?

As she watched him, she must have made a sound because he turned and looked at her.

Kim jumped behind a tree, ready to protect herself from whatever came flying, but nothing did. After a few moments she decided to stop being a scaredy-cat and stepped out into the open.

Slowly, the boy started walking toward her, and Kim got ready to run. She knew not to let boys who she'd thrown things at get too close. They prided themselves on the quickness of their throwing arms.

She held her breath when he got close enough that she knew she'd not be able to get away.

"I'm sorry I took your book," he said softly. "Mr. Bertrand lent it to me, so I didn't know it belonged to anyone else. And I didn't know about the tree being yours, either. I apologize."

She was so astonished she couldn't speak. Her mother said that males didn't know the meaning of the word *sorry*. But this one did. She took the book he was holding out to her and watched as he turned away and started back toward the house.

He was halfway there before she could move. "Wait!" she called out and was shocked when he stopped walking. None of her boy cousins *ever* obeyed her.

She walked up to him, the book firmly clutched against her chest. "Who are you?" she asked. If he'd said he was a visitor from another planet, she wouldn't have been surprised.

"Travis . . . Merritt," he said. "My mother and I arrived late last night. Who are you?"

"Kimberly Aldredge. My mother and I are staying in there"—she pointed—"while my father and brother go fishing in Montana."

He gave a nod, as though what she'd said was very important. "My mother and I are staying there." He pointed to the apartment on the other side of the big house. "My father is in Tokyo."

Kim had never heard of the place. "Do you live near here?"

"Not in this state, no."

She was staring at him and thinking that he was very much like a doll, as he didn't smile or even move very much.

"I like the book," he said. "I've never read anything like it before."

In her experience she didn't know boys read anything they didn't have to. Except her cousin Tris, but then he only read about sick people, so that didn't count. "What do you read?" she asked.

"Textbooks."

She waited for him to add to that list, but he just stood there in silence. "What do you read for fun?"

He gave a slight frown. "I rather like the science textbooks."

"Oh," she said.

He seemed to realize that he needed to say more. "My father says that my education is very important, and my tutor—"

"What's that?"

"The man who teaches me."

"Oh," she said again, but had no idea what he was talking about.

"I am homeschooled," he said. "I go to school inside my father's house."

"That doesn't sound like fun," Kim said.

For the first time, he gave a bit of a smile. "I can attest that it is no fun whatever."

Kim didn't know what *attest* meant, but she could guess. "I'm good at having fun," she said in her most adult voice. "Would you like me to show you how?"

"I'd like that very much," he said. "Where do we begin?"

She thought for a moment. "There's a big pile of dirt in the back. I'll show you how to ride my bike up it then race down. You can stick your hands and feet straight out. Come on!" she yelled and started running.

But a moment later she looked back and he wasn't there. She backtracked and he was standing just where she'd left him. "Are you afraid?" she asked tauntingly.

"I don't think so, but I've never ridden a bicycle before, and I think you're too young to teach me."

She didn't like being told she was "too young" to do anything. Now he *was* sounding like a boy. "Nobody teaches you how to ride a bike," she said, knowing she was lying. Her dad had spent days holding her bike while she learned to balance.

"All right," he said solemnly. "I'll try it."

The bike was too short for him and the first time he got on it, he fell off and landed on his face. He got up, spitting dirt out of his mouth, and Kim watched him. Was he one of those boys who'd go crying to his mother?

Instead, he wiped his mouth on his sleeve, then gave a grin that nearly split his face in half. "Huzzah!" he said and got back on the bike.

By lunchtime he was riding down the hill faster than Kim had ever dared, and he jerked the front wheel upward, as though he were going over a jump.

"How'd I do?" he asked Kim after his fastest slide down the dirt hill. He didn't look like the same boy she'd first seen. His shirt was torn at the shoulder, and he was filthy from head to toe. There was a bruise forming on his cheek where he'd nearly crashed into a tree, but he'd pulled to the left and only grazed it. Even his teeth were dirty.

Before Kim could answer, he looked over her head and stiffened into the boy she'd first seen. "Mother," he said.

Kim turned to see a small woman standing there. She was pretty in a motherly sort of way, but whereas Travis had pink in his cheeks, she had none. She was like a washed-out, older, female version of him.

Without saying a word, she walked to stand

between the two children and looked her son up and down.

Kim held her breath. If the woman told Kim's mom that she'd made Travis dirty, Kim would be punished.

"You taught him to ride a bike?" Mrs. Merritt asked her.

Travis stepped in front of Kim, as though to protect her. "Mother, she's just a little girl. I taught myself to ride. I'll go and wash." He took a step toward the house.

"No!" Mrs. Merritt said, and he looked back at her. She went to him and put her arms around him. "I've never seen you look better." She kissed his cheek then smiled as she wiped dirt off her lips. She turned to Kim. "You, young lady . . ." she began, but stopped. Bending, she hugged Kim. "You are a truly marvelous child. Thank you!"

Kim looked up at the woman in wonder.

"You kids go back to playing. How about if I bring a picnic lunch out here for you two? Do you like chocolate cake?"

"Yes," Kim said.

Mrs. Merritt took two steps toward the house before Kim called out, "He needs his own bike."

Mrs. Merritt looked back, and Kim swallowed. She'd never before given an adult an order. "He . . ." Kim said more quietly. "My bike is too small for him. His feet drag."

"What else does he need?" Mrs. Merritt asked.

"A baseball and bat," Travis said.

"And a pogo stick," Kim added. "And a—" She broke off because Mrs. Merritt held up her hand.

"I have limited resources, but I'll see what I can do." She went back to the house and a few minutes later she brought out sandwiches and lemonade. In the afternoon she returned with two big slices of freshly baked chocolate cake. By that time Travis had learned to do wheelies, and she watched him with a mixture of awe and terror. "Who would have thought that you're a natural athlete, Travis?" she said in wonder, then went back in the house.

In the early evening, Kim's uncle Benjamin, her cousin Ramsey's father, yelled, "Ho, ho, ho. Who ordered Christmas in July?"

"We did!" Kim yelled, and Travis followed her as she ran to her uncle's big SUV.

Uncle Ben wheeled a new shiny, blue bicycle out of the back. "I was told to give this to the dirtiest boy in Edilean." He looked at Travis. "I think that means you."

Travis grinned. He still had dirt on his teeth, and his hair was caked with it. "Is that for me?"

"It's from your mother," Uncle Ben said and nodded toward the front door.

Mrs. Merritt was standing on the step, and Kim wasn't sure but she looked like she was crying. But that made no sense. A bicycle made a person laugh, not cry.

Travis ran to his mother and threw his arms around her waist.

Kim stared at him in astonishment. No twelve year-old boy she knew would ever do something like that. It wasn't cool to hug your mother in front of other people.

"Nice kid," Uncle Ben said, and Kim turned back to him. "Don't tell your mom but I went over to your house and did a little cleaning. Any of this look familiar?" He pulled a box from the back of the car and tipped it down so Kim could see inside. Five of her favorite books were in there, her second best doll, an unopened kit for making jewelry, and in the bottom was her jump rope.

"Sorry, no pogo stick, but I got one of Rams's old bats and some balls."

"Oh, thank you, Uncle Ben!" she said, and followed Travis's example and hugged him.

"If I'd known I was going to get this, I would have bought you a pony."

Kim's eyes widened into saucers.

"Don't tell your mom I said that or she'll skin me."

Travis had left his mother and was looking at his new bike in silence.

"Think you can ride it?" Uncle Ben asked. "Or can you only handle a little girl's bike?"

"Benjamin!" Kim's mother said as she came out to see what was going on. Mr. Bertrand stayed inside. As far as anyone knew he never left the house. "Too lazy to turn a doorknob," Kim's father once said.

Travis gave Kim's uncle a very serious look, then took the bike from him and set off at a breakneck speed around the house. When they heard the unmistakable sound of a crash, Uncle Ben put his hand on Mrs. Merritt's arm to keep her from running to the boy.

They heard what sounded like another crash on the other side of the house, and at last Travis came back to them. He was dirtier, his shirt was torn more, and there was a streak of blood across his upper lip.

"Any problems?" Uncle Ben asked.

"None whatever," Travis said, looking the man straight in the eyes.

"That's my boy!" he said as he slapped Travis hard on the shoulder. He closed the lid of the SUV. "I've got to get back to work."

"What work do you do?" Travis asked in an adult-sounding voice.

"I'm a lawyer."

"Is it a good trade?"

Uncle Ben's eyes danced with merriment but he didn't laugh. "It pays the bills, and it has some good points and bad. You thinking of trying the legal profession?"

"I rather admire Thomas Jefferson."

"You've come to the right place for him," Uncle Ben said, grinning as he opened the car door. "Tell you what, Travis ol' man, you get out of law school, come see me."

"I will, sir, and thank you," Travis said. He sounded very adult, but the dirt on him, the twigs and the bruises, made what he was saying funny.

But Uncle Ben still didn't laugh. He looked at Mrs. Merritt. "Good kid. Congratulations."

Mrs. Merritt put her arm around her son's shoulders, but he twisted away from her. He didn't seem to want Uncle Ben to see him so attached to a woman.

They all watched Uncle Ben leave, then Kim's mom said, "You kids go play. We'll call you in time for dinner and afterward you can catch fireflies."

"Yes," Mrs. Merritt said. "Go play." She looked as though she'd been waiting for years to say that to her son. "Mr. Bertrand is going to teach me how to sew."

"Lucy," Kim's mom said, "I think I should tell you that Bertrand is using you for free labor. He wants his curtains repaired and—"

"I know," Lucy Merritt said, "but it's all right. I want to learn to do something creative, and sewing is as good as anything else. You don't think he'd sell me his machine, do you?"

"I think he'd sell you his feet, since he rarely uses them."

Lucy laughed.

"Come on," Kim's mom said, "and I'll show you how to thread the machine."

For two weeks, Kim lived in her idea of heaven. She and Travis were together from early until late.

He took to having fun as though he'd been born to it—which Kim's mom said he should have been.

While they played outside, the two women and Mr. Bertrand talked and sewed. Lucy Merritt used the old Bernina sewing machine to repair every curtain in the house.

"So he can get a better price when he sells them," Kim's mom muttered.

Lucy bought fabric and made new curtains for the bathrooms and the kitchen.

"You're paying him rent," Kim's mother said. "You shouldn't be paying for them too."

"It's all right. It's not as though I can save the money. Randall will take whatever I don't spend."

Mrs. Aldredge knew that Randall was Lucy's husband, but she didn't know any more than that. "I want to know what that means," she said, but Lucy said she'd told too much already.

At night the children reluctantly went to their respective apartments. Their mothers got them washed and fed and into bed. The next morning they were outside again. No matter how early Kim got up, Travis was always waiting for her at the back of the house.

One night Travis said, "I'll come back."

Kim didn't know what he meant.

"After I leave, I'll return."

She didn't want to reply to that because she didn't want to imagine him being gone. They climbed trees together, dug in the mud, rode their bikes; she tossed the ball, and Travis hit it across the garden. When Kim brought her second best doll out, she was nervous. Boys didn't like dolls. But Travis said he'd build a house for it and he did. It was made of leaves and sticks and inside was a bed that Kim covered with moss. While Travis made a roof to the house, she used her jewelry kit to make two necklaces with plastic beads. Travis smiled when she slipped one over his head, and he was wearing it the next morning.

When it got too hot to move, they stretched out on the cool ground in the shade and took turns reading *Alice* and the other books aloud to each other. Kim wasn't nearly as good a reader as he was, but he never complained. When she was stumped on a word, he helped her. He'd told her he was a good listener, and he was.

She knew that at twelve he was a lot older than she was, but he didn't seem to be. When it came to schooling, he seemed like an adult. He told her the entire life cycle for a tadpole and all about cocoons.

He explained why the moon was different shapes and what caused winter and summer.

But for all his knowledge, he'd never skimmed a rock across a pond. Never climbed a tree before he came to Edilean. He'd never even skinned his elbow.

So they taught each other. Though he was twelve and she only eight, there were times when she was his teacher—and she liked that.

Everything ended exactly two weeks after it began. As usual, as soon as it was light outside, sleepy-eyed, Kim ran out the back door, past the back of the big old house, to the wing where Travis and his mom were staying.

But that morning, when Travis wasn't already outside and waiting for her, she knew something was wrong. She started pounding on the door and yelling his name; she didn't care if she woke the whole house.

Her mother, in robe and slippers, came running out. "Kimberly! What are you shouting about?"

"Where is Travis?" she demanded as she fought back tears.

"Will you calm down? They probably just overslept."

"No! Something is wrong."

Her mother hesitated, then tried the knob. The door opened. There was no one inside, and no sign that anyone had been there.